D

D0839620

A FAIRY TALE OF NEW YORK

Books by J. P. Donleavy

The Ginger Man
A Singular Man
The Saddest Summer of Samuel S
The Beastly Beatitudes of Balthazar B
The Onion Eaters
A Fairy Tale of New York
The Destinies of Darcy Dancer, Gentleman
Schultz
Leila
Meet My Maker the Mad Molecule
The Unexpurgated Code: A Complete Manual
    of Survival & Manners
De Alfonce Tennis
J. P. Donleavy's Ireland
Are You Listening Rabbi Löw

A FAIRY TALE OF
NEW YORK

J. P. DONLEAVY

THE ATLANTIC MONTHLY PRESS
NEW YORK

First published in the United States of America by Delacorte Press in 1973
Published simultaneously in Canada
Printed in the United States of America

Library of Congress Cataloging-in-Publication Data
Donleavy, J. P. (James Patrick), 1926–
  A fairy tale of New York / J. P. Donleavy
  ISBN 0-87113-264-8 (pbk.)
  I. Title.
 [PS3507.O686F26   1989]   88-10325   823'.914—dc19

Atlantic Monthly Press
841 Broadway
New York, NY 10003

98 99 00 01 10 9 8 7 6 5 4 3 2

A FAIRY TALE OF
NEW YORK

1

Three o'clock in February. All the sky was blue and high. Banners and bunting and people bunched up between. Greetings and sadness.

Great black box up from the deep hold, swinging in the air high over the side of the ship. Some of the stevedores taking off their caps and hoods. With quiet whisperings, swiveling it softly on a trolley and pushing it into a shed.

Cornelius Christian standing under the letter C. The customs man comes over.

"I'm sorry sir about this. I know it isn't a time you want to be annoyed by a lot of questions but if you could just come with me over to the office I'll try to get this over as quickly as possible. It's just a formality."

Walking across the pier through the rumbling carts, perfumes, furs and tweeds, the clanging chains and into the little warm hut with typewriters pecking. Tall dark customs man, his fist with a pencil on a piece of paper.

"I understand this happened aboard ship."

"Yes."

"And you're an American and your wife was foreign."

"Yes."

"And you intend burial here."

"Yes."

"It's just that we've got to make sure of these things because it can save a lot of trouble later. Don't want to burden you with anything unnecessary. Do you have any children travelling."

"Just my wife and myself."

"I understand. And are all your other possessions your own property, all personal effects. No fine art, antiques. You're not importing anything."

"No."

"Just sign here. Won't be anything else and if you have any trouble at all don't hesitate to get in touch with me right away. Here's my name and I'll straighten out any difficulty. Just Steve Kelly, customs'll get me. Vine funeral home phoned here just a while ago. I told him everything was all right and he says you can go see them at their office, or phone any time this afternoon or tonight. You take it easy."

"Thanks very much."

Customs man giving Christian a pat on the back.

"And say, Mr Christian, see the stevedore, guy with the fur jacket. Just tell him Steve said you'd help me with my stuff. O k. Don't worry about anything."

"Thanks."

Out through the grinding winches, clicking high heels, the stacks of gay baggage and colored labels. The great tall side of ship. And coming out to it as it sat on the sea in Cork Harbour. A stiff cold vessel. All of us bundled up as the tender tugged us out on the choppy water. And left the pink houses on the shore twirling early morning turf smoke in the sky. Black rivets on the ship's side. And I climbed up behind her. On the stairway swaying over the water. And now through this jumble and people gathering each other in their arms. This stevedore with fur jacket, a hook tucked under his arm. Hard muscles across his jaw.

"Excuse me, Steve said you'd help me with my stuff."

"Oh yeah, sure. Sure thing. Got much."

"Three small trunks, two bags."

"O k. You just follow me all the way. I'll put the stuff down the escalator. Meet me the bottom of the stairs. You want a taxi."

"Please."

Under the roof of girders and signs. No tipping. Escalator rumbling down with trunks and crates. Crashing and crushing. The treatment they give things would break open her box. And

2

they shout, this way folks. Five bucks, Grand Central. Three fifty, Penn Station. The stevedore has scars on his face, keeps his hands on his hips.

"Mr. Christian, this guy will take you wherever you want to go. Stuff's on."

"Here."

"No no. I don't want any money. I don't take money for a favour. You'll do the same for somebody. That way it goes round the world."

"Thanks."

"Forget it."

Cornelius Christian opening the door into this gleaming cab. Horns honk everywhere. This driver with a green cap turns around.

"Where to, bud."

"I don't know. Have to think of somewhere."

"Look, I haven't got all day. I want to catch another boat coming in."

"Do you know where I can get a room."

"I'm no directory bud."

"Anything."

"Place is full of hotels."

"Do you know anywhere I can get a room."

"Boardinghouse for a guy like you. Just sort of dumps I know. This is some time to start looking. Everybody want me to find a room I'd be starving. As it is I make peanuts. O k. I know a place west side near the museum."

Taxi twisting away. With smiles and arms laden with coats others get into cabs. The trip is over. Some made friends. And we go up a hill to the roaring highway.

"It's none of my business but what's a guy like you doing coming all the way over here with nowhere to go. You don't sound like a guy got no friends, don't look it neither. O k. Takes all sorts of people to make a world. Keep telling my wife that, she doesn't believe me. Thinks everybody's like her. Across there long."

"Went to college."

"Good education over there. Don't you feel lonely."

"No, don't mind being alone."

3

"That right. Got a right to feel that way if you want. But look at this, how can you feel alone. Everything looking like it's going to explode. And I got a face looks like a monkey. Know why. Because I used to own a pet shop till a relative got the big idea to make a lot of money. So what happens, I lose the whole thing. Now I'm driving a hack. Kick in your teeth and every guy after a fast buck. What a life. Keep going, keep going till you can't stop."

Christian folding white gloved hands in his lap. Cars stream along the highway. The wail of a police car zooming by.

"Look at that, some guy murdered his mother for a dime. Guy like me got to drink milk all day, live like a baby. I tell you, it's a crime. Sweat our guts out. Something awful. God damn place jammed with foreigners. Think they'd stay in Europe instead of coming over here and crowding us out. You foreign."

"No."

"You could pass for foreign. It's o k with me mister if you're foreign. My mother came from Minsk."

Clouds come grey and east. Ice down there on the edge of the river. Smoky red weak sun.

Taxi turns down off the highway. Between the pillars holding up the street above. Serve beer in there. Bar stools and sawdust. Stevedores with hooks. They say keep your mouth shut and you won't get hurt. Safe in a crowd. Close in there by the elbows, next to the sleeves where all around me are just hands to shake and squeeze.

"O k mister here we are. Give me five bucks."

Red grey stone they call brownstone. An iron fence. Where the rich lived years ago. Tall steps up. First five dollars gone.

"Mister ring the bell downstairs and I'll take your bags, never get rich this way but you look lonely. Mrs Grotz'll take care of you. She's crazy, but who isn't."

Mrs Grotz, cross eyed, wrapped in a black coat and a collar of silver fox, standing in the door.

"What's your business mister."

"He's all right, Ma, just back from college over in Europe. Just ain't got no friends."

"Everyone ought to have friends."

4

"How do you know he wants them."

"Friendship means a lot, you crazy cab driver."

"My wife thinks I'm crazy too, but my kids think I'm god."

"Go home you crazy cab driver. Follow me mister, I got a nice room."

Carrying the bags behind this large bottom shifting up the stairs. In the onion smell. And scent of dust.

"Stairs for me is work mister. Got to do everything myself. Since my husband. He drop dead right in his underwear. Right while I was watching. Such a shock. Go to turn off the lamp and drop dead right on his face. I'm nervous and shaking like this every since. So all husbands drop dead sometime. You think they have manners and do it quiet in the hospital."

A room with red curtains high on the window. Double bed like one I saw in Virginia where once I was walking down a street and climbed in a train standing in the hot sun. Always wishing I could save the heat for the winter.

"Four fifty dollars a night or twenty dollars a week. Look what I supply, radio, shelves, gas stove, hot water. Don't play the radio loud."

"Could I let you know in a day or two how long I'll be staying."

"Give you till Friday and you got to make up your mind. You got a funny voice, you English. Learn to speak at college."

"Just a bit."

"Was that the accent you was born with."

"I don't know."

"Give me four dollars and fifty cents."

> And now
> You own
> The Brooklyn
> Bridge

5

2

New world. Opening up the suitcases on the bed. Turn on the oven. Out into the hall past another brown door. Everything in the dark. And cars go by in the street like boats and soft bubbles.

Find the switch for the light in this bathroom. Green towel crumpled on the floor. Lift the seat. All gentlemen are requested. When little you never lift the seat and mommy tells you lift the seat. Pick up the towel. Go back. This door has a name on it under the cellophane. And now the only thing I can do is wait and wait and wait. It's got to go away. She could never pack things and her bag's a mess. I told her she was sloppy, why don't you fold things up. And I've got to go down there. To a funeral parlor. Just wash my face. No one to be with her. And I was so full of dying myself. I hope I know how to get down there after all these years. How much is it going to cost. Just end up being buried among a lot of strangers.

Christian steps down into the street. Grey tweed on his back. White gloves on hands. Street full of shadows. And dark cars parked. And straight ahead the stale stiff fingers of trees. After so much ocean. And I don't know what to say to this man. He'll be in black or something. Do I have to give him a tip or cigar. He might think I'm not sorry enough and can't concentrate on the death.

Grey tall windows of the museum. Down these steps to the subway. Chewing gum everywhere. Turnstile reminds me of horses. Coin goes in so neatly. Click through. Could step right

6

under a train. Just let it roar right over me. What have you got to touch to get electrocuted. How would they know to take me and put me with Helen. It would have to be written down in my wallet. In case of death take me to the Vine funeral home and bury me with Helen. So slaughtered you could put me round her in the same casket. I just can't bear for you to be cold and you said last thing of all to put you in the ground. And you always wore a green shadow around your eyes. Came near me in your silk rustling dress, you sounded hollow inside. Listening with your eyes. And the first day at sea I didn't want to see you spend the two dollars for a deck chair. Now I'd let you have it. I'd let you have anything now. Helen, you could have got two deck chairs or three and I'd have said nothing. It wasn't the money, I didn't want you to get cold because you looked so ill you'd freeze up there and no one knew how sick you were. And I pulled on the towel. Pulled it right out of your hands when you said you'd spend the two dollars. It wasn't the money, I'd tear up two dollars here right on this platform. God, it was the money. I've lost you.

Head bowed. A white knuckle rubbing under an eye. A man steps near.

"Are you all right, buddy."

"Yes I'm all right. Just a lot of dust blown up in my eyes."

"O k, buddy, just wanted to make sure."

Roaring train in the tunnel. Sweeping into the station. Train with the tickling noise under the floor. Doors growl shut. Then up, out, crossing each avenue, when the lights turn red and the cars slide up and stop. And it's all so new around me and so old. When I was young and walked here I heard a car screech and hit a boy. Saw the white shirt on his shoulder. And I wondered if all the people would be gathering around and keep him warm and not like me running away.

Where the street slants down, further on, the elevated train, tall buildings and a river. Closer. There it is. Double curtained doors, two evergreens on either side. Push through. God, what a place for you. Soft carpeted hall, luxurious in here. Warm green light flowing up the walls. So soft everything. This isn't bad. This door's open. It gleams and I'll knock. Man's black shoes

7

and gartered black socks sticking out from a desk. They move and shine. His hand in front of me.

"Good evening, you're Mr Christian aren't you."

"Yes."

"I'm sorry that you've had to come. I'm Mr Vine, please sit down."

"Thank you."

"Will you smoke. Cigarette. Cigar."

"No thanks."

"Go ahead, make yourself comfortable. There are only a few little things here. Customs man who dealt with you telephoned after you left the pier. Very nice of him and I'll certainly do everything I can Mr Christian. Only these to sign."

"Thanks."

"I'm not just an ordinary man in this business. It means a great deal to me and if there is any special help I can give anyone I'm really glad to do it. So understand that."

"That's nice of you."

"We can only do our best Mr Christian. We try to understand sorrow. I've arranged burial at Greenlawn. Do you know New York."

"Yes, I was born here."

"Then you may know Greenlawn. One of the most beautiful cemeteries in the world and it's always a pleasure to visit. My wife's buried there as well and I know it's a place of great peace. We realise sorrow Mr Christian. I'll take care of all the immediate details for you and you can have a chat with them later on. All under my personal direction. Arranged as soon as you wish."

"Could it be arranged for tomorrow morning."

"Yes. Will it give mourners time. The notice will only be in tomorrow's Daily News, only give anybody couple of hours to get here."

"I'll be the only mourner."

"I see."

"No one knew we were coming to New York."

"I can put you in our small suite there across the hall."

"Just for a few minutes. I want to keep it very short."

"I understand. In the way of flowers."

8

"I'd like something simple. Perhaps a wreath with, my Helen."

"Of course. Something simple. I'll see to it myself. We try to make friends with sorrow Mr Christian. That way we come to know it. You'd like us to use glass. For permanence."

"That's all right."

"And where are you located."

"Near the Museum of Natural History."

"I'm pleased you're near there. There's much to reflect upon in that building. We'll send our car for you."

"Is that anything extra."

"Included Mr Christian. Shall I make it nine thirty, ten, whenever you wish."

"Nine thirty is fine."

"Mr Christian, would you like now to have a little drink before you go. Some Scotch."

"Well I would. Are you Irish, Mr Vine."

"My mother was. My father was German."

Mr Vine's little snap of the head and blink of the eyes, crossing his soft canary carpet. Puts a neat white hand under an illuminated picture. Sunlight filtering through mountain pines and brass name beneath says In The Winter Sun. Panels drawing apart. Shelves of bottles, glasses and the small white door of a refrigerator. He must drink like a fish. Pick him up like a corpse every night. I don't have the nerve to tell him I was raised in the Bronx.

"Soda, Mr Christian."

"Please."

"Now, the way you said that. Just one word. I can tell by your voice you're an educated man Mr Christian. I also like your name. I never had very much in the way of education. I was a wildcatter in Texas and then became the manager of an oil field. Wouldn't think of it to look at me, would you. I left school when I was nine years old. I've always wanted to be in this business but I was thirty before I got a chance to do a high school course. Did it in the navy, then went to mortician's school when I came out. It makes you feel closer to people. It's dignified. And art. When you see what you can do for someone who comes to you

9

helpless. To recreate them just as they were in life. Makes you able to soften things. You're a man I can talk to, a person who's got a proper mental attitude. I can always tell. There are some of them who make you sick. Only thing I don't like about the business are the phonies and I get my share of them. Here, have another, do you good."

"Thanks."

"Some people think I'm outspoken but I've given a lot of satisfaction and people put their whole families in my hands, even in a big city like this. I opened up another branch in the west fifties. But I like it best here where I began. My two little girls are growing up into big women now. You meet people from all walks of life. I'm a bit of a philosopher and I feel anything you've got to learn you'll learn just through what you have to do with people, in that way I never miss an education. It's a fact, I never graduated. It's especially sad when I bury those who did. But everything is how a person conducts themselves. That's how I know all about you, customs man said over the phone you were a real gentleman. Would you like now for me to show you the establishment. If you don't it's all right."

"I don't mind."

"You'd like to feel that she was somewhere where she's really at home. Come along, we're empty now, there's just two reposings on at my other branch although it's a busy time of the year."

Mr Vine rising. Gently bent forward. Flicks his head and bends one shoulder up to his ear. Frown around his eyes and hair sticks straight up. Holding door ajar. Smiling with his tilted face.

"I never want to have an establishment of mine get so big you lose the personal touch. It must be warm and intimate to make people feel at home. I call the other branch a home, bit of an expense to change here because parlor is in the neon sign. I feel parlor is a word that lets you down. Something poor people have. I like the word home. I don't gloom at people, I smile. Death is a reunion. A pause in the life of others. You understand me."

A low corridor. Mr Vine touches Mr Christian slowly through the soft lights, soft step by soft step.

"These are the various suites. These two have their own private rest rooms. Which has been of great success. I wouldn't say it to most people but certain functions get stimulated at the passing of a cherished one. You've noticed how I've used green light and how it glows from the walls, it's a special kind of glass that makes it do that. Only kind in New York. You don't mind me showing you around."

"No it's all right."

"In a few years I'm opening a branch out in the country. For some people the country signifies peace. You saw that picture, the forest, in the winter sun. Looking at that gave me the idea. It's not conducive to peace to come in off the street. And you hear that elevated train out there. Thinking of tearing it down. Won't be too soon for me. Shake the teeth out of your head. But I learned to accept it. And in here is our chapel. I thought I'd make it round just like the world and again green is my motif. And out here again there's the door to our work rooms. We call it the studio."

"It's all very nice."

"That makes me feel good. I'm pleased. And I hope you'll be satisfied you dealt with me. I always want people to feel that. You can trust me and know I've got reverence for my work. To love your work is happiness. It means I meet someone like you too. I'm never wrong about people. I know the real tears of death and they don't go down the cheeks. And this is my largest room, the first one I ever used. One or two personages been here. Mr Selk the manufacturer. I had that privilege. And we light a candle behind this green glass when someone is reposing. I think it gives, or rather, let me say, lends a sacredness to the occasion."

"Yes it does."

"You go home now. Put all bother out of your head. Get a good night's sleep. Remember it takes time. But time is a friend of ours. And I'm here, remember that, for any kind of request. Our car will be there in the morning. Good night, Mr Christian."

Mr Vine and Christian shook hands. Vine gave Christian a catalogue. Pushed open the door to the cold electric light of the street. A last smile, a wave.

The windy canyon of Park Avenue. Crossing a winter city. Cold heels on the pavement. Doormen rubbing hands, clicking feet, looking up, looking down the street. Beginning to snow. Like the first winter I got to Dublin. When the skies were grey for months. And I bought thick woollen blankets at the shop and they smelled like sheep.

Christian, hands plunged in pockets, takes a lonely subway west and north. Back by the shadows of the museum. And along by the stone mansions. Where I live tonight.

Music coming from the door with the name under the cellophane. Dim light in the hall, a smell of wax in the air. Dust in the nose. Door slamming. Voice yelling. Pipe down.

Must go in through this door and sleep. Pull aside the thick red curtain so tomorrow the light will wake me up. Snow streams down under the street lamp. Someone else's house is more your own if it's filled with strangers. Helen, I wouldn't have brought you to a room like this. Makes me feel I'm casting some poverty on you because this isn't the type of place you would ever be. Yours were bathrooms shining with gleaming rails and hot towels. All this plastic junk. Couldn't have been in the studio while Vine and I were talking. Couldn't talk like that. But that's the way we talked. Like pies peaches or eggs. Helen's not a pie peaches or eggs. She's mine. Taking her away. Gone already. Where is she nearest to me. Asleep on top of my brain. Came with me all over the ship when I couldn't stand them staring at me everywhere I went and whispering. Our table out in the center of the dining room. They were all thinking of the day when they had the gala occasion with the paper hats and balloons and Helen just sat there at the table and wept, pink handkerchief tucked up your sleeve and pearls like tiny drops from your face and none of them ever saw you again. They even came up to my cabin door after you were dead to listen to hear if I was crying. And the steward who said they wouldn't do your washing. He stuck his brown face in the door and closed it quietly when he saw me prostrate on the bunk. And he slammed the door in your face. Both of us utterly helpless, could do nothing could say nothing. I held the three dollars in my fist and watched his brown hand come up from his side and pull them out and leave quietly closing the door. The waiter who filled our plates with things we didn't want and came over the second day and said your wife don't eat no more and I said no. And lunchtime he came back saying he was sorry he didn't know, the wine waiter just told him and he got me a plate covered in smoked salmon. He kept as far away as he could until the last meal when hovering for his tip he asked me if I was a refugee. Then I went out, and from the ship's rail I looked at the strange flat shore with the fragile white fingers in the sky. In that cabin, Helen, where you left your soul and I've got to lie a night here between these sleepless sheets without you.

> Darkness
> In all my
> Grief

3

Sound of snow shovelling in the street. Ship's whistle from the river. Tingling and banging in the pipes along the wall. Outside the wind blows hard and shivers the window. Knocks on the door.

"Mr Christian there's a man for you down stairs."

"Please tell him I'm coming right away."

Christian looking into the street below. A man in dark coat, green shirt, black tie. No hat over his half bald head and grey wisps of hair. A black long car. Come for me. Can't keep him waiting. Can't stop them putting you in the ground under the snow.

Mrs Grotz at the door, hunched, breath steaming in the cold air, her hands rubbing. Watching Christian pass and meet the chauffeur halfway down the steps. A solemn soft voice and placing a black cap on his head.

"You Mr Christian. I'm from the Vine funeral home."

"Sorry to keep you waiting."

Grotz edging her slippered feet out into the snow. Straining ears to listen. Her mouth open, eyes wide.

"Hey what's the matter. Who's hurt. Some trouble. You from a funeral."

Christian stopping turning. Pulling gloves tighter on his hands. Looks up the steps at Mrs Grotz.

"It's my wife."

"What's a matter, you got a wife. Where's your wife. What's a matter your wife."

14

"She's dead."

"Mister. Oh mister."

The park ahead, little rolling hill in velvet snow. So white and christmas. Birds taking white baths. Ploughs pushing it up, conveyor belts pouring it into trucks. I've no black tie. But a green one will suit Mr Vine. People we pass look at this expensive car.

"You comfortable. Mr Christian."

"Yes thanks."

"They're shovelling salt. Then when the snow melts the guy's tires in front shoot it up on your windshield. Some problem. They know it's going to snow every year, you'd think they'd do something."

"Yes."

A morning sun shining in slits along the crosstown streets and in shadows across the park. These tall hotels. All so slender women walk in. Where the lights glow. And everybody's scared of everybody. And maybe Vine and his personal touch.

Green neon sign. Vine Funeral Parlor. Everybody calls it a home. Sanitation department truck stopped outside. Bedraggled men filling it with snow. Mr Vine waves his arm. Seems red in the face.

"Good morning, Mr Christian. Had to tell these men to get this garbage truck out of here. Come this way, Mr Christian."

Vine pushing open the door. A firm handshake, nodding his head and twitching. Shaking water out of his ears after swimming. Now he beckons the way.

"It's my favourite music I've chosen, Mr Christian. She's very beautiful. She's waiting for you. Our Miss Musk will take care of you. And just press the button when you want me. All right."

"Yes."

This young woman steps forth from the shadows. Can't look at her face. Just see her slender ankle and leg. And hear her friendly voice.

"I'm Elaine Musk, Mr Vine's assistant. May I take your coat."

"I think I'll keep it on. For a moment."

15

"The music hasn't begun yet. And if there's anything, just anything, I'm here to help."

"Thank you."

The room dark. Curtains drawn across the window to the street. And the green light flickering behind the glass. Casket gleaming and black. On a pedestal, the wreath illumined in green. My Helen written with the tiny white heads of lilies of the valley. A table with a Bible. Chairs along the wall for mourners. Even has my flowers lit up. He must rake in the money. I'm glad the casket's black. I'd die if it were green. Now go and kneel. So soft and I can't look at you. See just the tips of your knuckles. You don't have to shake Vine's hand, he almost broke mine. If you'd move. Encased in glass and you can't get up. Forgive me because I haven't got the courage to look at you. Because I'd see you dead forever. What happens to all the flesh and blood. No child. You leave nothing except the pain of missing you. And I didn't want the expense because a baby cost money. I wouldn't part with a penny. Only reason I had. I knew you were begging me and I'd always say let's wait. And we waited. Your casket's so smooth. Funny I put my hand along the bottom to see if it's stuck with chewing gum. Vine would never allow that. And although he must be half crazy he's given me comfort because I don't feel you're laughed at or joked over dead. Got to keep my head down or I'll look by accident. Thought I would cry and I can't. Helen, I wish we were different from everybody else. Scream for some sort of thing that makes us you and me. Neither of us nothing. And on the ship you said you wanted to lie down in the cabin. Those first Americans you met just tired you out. And I was so proud of bringing you back to my country. I wanted you to like them. And even after you'd gone, I didn't want anyone to come and touch me on the arm and back with a pat or two and say I'm sorry about it, about your wife, have courage or something, but I did want them I wanted someone to show something. Anything. But not a soul on that damn ship came near me except for money. And each second you get further away from me. Dig the hole with the straight sides and before it gets dark they've got you covered up. And all the times I wished you were dead. So I could be free. They were black thoughts of anger. But I thought them. Must get up. Look out the window.

16

Silently crossing the room. Parting the thick curtains to the late morning light of the street. And people hunching by in the cold. Over there Murray's Best For Bargains. Vine said press the button when you're ready. Does he take ordinary lipstick and put it on the lips. Or take it out of a pot they use on everyone. And all sorts of lips. And make them the kind that gleam and don't have cracks, and are red and now over ripe. Vine had a green handkerchief in his pocket. What has he got against the color green. Most of his life must be whispering, nodding, hand rubbing, and the five words, we'll take care of everything.

Christian turning from the window. Mr Vine leaning over the casket wiping the glass.

"Must be a little condensation on the inside Mr Christian. But I hate anything to mar such a lovely face. Woman's lips are one of the most beautiful parts of her body. I can always tell a woman who looks at a man's lips when he talks instead of his eyes. Are you all right."

"Yes. Do you think we could leave now."

"Yes, a few minutes. Our large reposing room is busy this morning. We never know in this business."

"Mr Vine I think maybe you're telling me too much about your business. I don't want to say anything but it's getting me down."

"Don't get sore. I forget sometimes. I try to make everyone feel at home and not treat the funeral business as something strange. People ought to know about it. My own funeral is already arranged. But don't get sore. When it happened to me and it was my wife, I found I wanted some sort of distraction and because I arranged the services myself it made me feel better. And I thought you wanted to take an interest."

"This isn't distraction."

"Take it easy son. You're not alone in this, remember that. If I shot my mouth off, I'm sorry. I don't want to do that with nobody. But getting sore isn't going to bring her back. Beauty is the only thing you can remember. Try to remember beauty. Come on, I like you, be a sport."

"My wife's dead."

"I know that."

"Well, what the hell do you mean, sport."

"If I understand you correctly Mr Christian, you'd rather I didn't conduct this any further. I can put you in the hands of an assistant if you prefer."

"All right, all right. I'm not the kind of person who wants to start trouble. Leave everything as it is. I'm just worried about money and what I'm going to do."

"Look. Listen to me. I want to tell you straight. I don't cut cash out of nobody. I don't conduct this business on those lines. You've got as long as you want and longer. Understand me. And if that isn't long enough I'll think of something. If you hadn't come here alone from another country I wouldn't take all this trouble but you seem to be a nice guy. I even thought you were a type for this profession and that's a compliment as far as I'm concerned. You're a gentleman. And when it's over, if you want to come back and see me, I'd like that. There's a place for you here, remember that. And if you make that decision, I'd be honored. Shall we close it now, Mr Christian. You're ready."

"All right."

"You can wait with the chauffeur."

"O k."

"We'll take care of you, Christian, remember this isn't death. All this is life."

Walking out of the hall. Through the curtained doors. Putting up coat collars. The chauffeur smoking a cigarette. One of his grey wisps of hair hangs and goes into his ear. Christian coughs. Chauffeur getting out to open the door. A flash of yellow socks with white stripes.

The car pulls across the road. The hearse draws up in front of the Vine Funeral Parlor. Three men step out, rubbing their green gloved hands, stamping their feet on the hard snow. Elevated train roaring by on its iron trestle at the end of the street. The garbage truck has taken away its pile of snow. Chauffeur blows a smoke ring. And he turns around.

"Would you like this blanket, Mr Christian. Put it round your legs in case you get cold. Always a few degrees colder when you get out of the city."

"Thanks."

"They are coming out now, Mr Christian."

Mr Vine standing aside, holding back a door. Coffin on four shoulders. Like an elephant, four black legs. Vine twitches his head, bends his ear to his shoulder and rubs. Goes in again. Comes out in a black overcoat, papers in his hand, hatless, eyes bright. Crossing the street. Stepping gingerly with his gleaming black shoes over the ridges of snow. Leaning in the window to the chauffeur.

"To expedite the journey, Charles, we'll take the West Side Drive. Go up Park and crosstown on Fifty Seventh. You all right, Mr Christian."

"Yes."

Vine pausing, a car sweeps by. He looks upon the rest of the world as something he will bury. His gravel voiced military manoeuvres. I guess we're going. No use fighting over it. He's only trying to be nice. First time anyone ever offered me a job.

Hearse pulling out. Vine signaling with his hand. And we follow. To the end of the street. Another elevated train. Wake Helen up. Window full of refrigerators there. Say they're giving them away for nothing, almost. Just step inside for bargains beyond belief. I feel like there's nothing around me in the world. Highway on the curve of the earth. Everybody knows why I'm in this car and Helen in hers.

The two black vehicles swiftly moving across Fifty Seventh Street. Past the opera house on the corner. People huddled up under the marquee waiting for the bus. The sky opens up where the city ends and the Hudson flows by. Up the ramp and flowing out into the stream of cars on the smooth white highway. Towering cold bridge over the Harlem River. Farther and the red tiled roofs of houses behind the leafless trees. Along here the rich live down to the water's edge.

Road curves up through the second woods. Ran through them playing as a kid. When deer stood frozen still. To escape an enemy eye. And chipmunks auburn striped sped up and down branches. This cobble stone road once had trolley tracks. Tell no one anything. You don't want the world knowing about your life. Or this lake we leave behind in the valley, a swamp and golf course. Great chains hang from post to post. Tall iron gates. Monuments inside with stained glass windows. Some with spires.

Take you in here and lay you down. This cold day. Knuckles frozen. Breasts still. Where no love can taste. Tickle or tender.

Man in soft grey uniform salutes. Mr Vine steps out across the snow. Up the steps into a grey stone building. Thin veins of ivy. Vine's coming to speak.

"There'll be a few minutes delay. Just a formality. Charles, just pull the car up in front there and wait for us."

Chauffeur turning, ice crackling under the wheels.

"It's nothing, Mr Christian. Just identification. They have to check everybody who's buried."

Coffin on the four shoulders disappearing under the canopy and into the squat building tucked into the side of the hill. Be looking at her again. They give us no privacy. They'd shout back at me if I object. If you own a bird and it's flown away you run out to tell the whole world. And they say to you to shut up, you're disturbing the peace.

They come out. Shift and slide it in. Engines purr and we move. All these winding roads and trees. People under the stones. So white and white. Branches frozen silver. Paths criss-crossing everywhere. Tombs on the hills. Heads in sorrow. Can't believe I worked here once cutting grass. Lightning in a sky in summer. A bronze woman melted and cold on a door. Cowled face with a hand on her cheek. Hold away the world from the rich bones inside. A white marble man and woman stand up out of their rock. Look out over a sea. Where ships die. And men slip below the cold water. And where are you nearest.

No trees here. Four men stand by the tent. They've brushed away the snow. Fake grass over the mound of earth. Clarance Vine comes back to this car.

"Mr Christian. I thought since you've got no religious preference I might read something. And I've just told Charles to give a few dollars to the grave diggers if that's all right, it's the average tip."

"Yes."

"We'll go then."

Gently sloping hill. Snow lies for miles. Fades below the stiff dark trees. High grey sky. Know young girls you love. Take cigarettes from lips and kiss. A dance band plays. Grow up

20

loving memories. Die leaving none. Except the Christmas Eves. When the whole year stops. These Polish hands who shovel on the dirt. They lick their lips on pay day and sit at poker tonight and drink wine. Downtown in the city. Where they take away a wife who clings to railings along the sidewalk and she screams and they lock her up. Can't see her anymore because she's crazy. Love you as much as love can be. Cooking and washing. Mending and waiting. Each thread of body till it breaks.

"If you'll just stand there, Mr Christian, I'll read these few words I've got here."

Cornelius Christian next to Clarance Vine. Who holds out his little paper. Nods his head to the diggers. Straps stiffening under the coffin. Mist in the air from his voice.

"We are gathered here as brothers and we pray for another soul. The birds, trees and flowers are life and they are around us to give birth in spring. This interment is life and for us the living, a beauty to ennoble our lives, to give us a kiss to caress us in our living pain. We gather to see the soil give one of us peace, to all love and remember her forever. We now give her to her God. O k boys."

> Milky life
> Alive
> Lowered in
> The brown

4

Mornings to wake up cold. Shivering breeze blowing in the thin crack of open window. Lie looking at the ceiling with rosettes and plaster leaves. Clattering garbage pails and covers down in the street. The sanitation men come collecting. And times through the day an ocean liner's whistle throbs and trembles.

New world. Soot lies smearing the soles of my feet. Baby cockroaches sneak back again behind the basin. Everything a green in the bathroom. Tattered shower curtain with vines and jungle leaves. Specks of pink soap. Long strands of blond hair. Whole city tightens around you. Till you go out and get three doughnuts from a sweet smelling little bakery. And a newspaper off the stand down the street. Bring it back each morning to read. The stabbings and stompings. Percolate coffee in an old battered pot. Sit here so outstandingly unknown. Drink a cup to make me crap.

Eleven thirty this a.m. Christian passes out the dark hall. Push open the cut glass and mahogany doors and down the steps of this dusty house into the street. Dressed in the best I have. Counting each day the dollars left. Forty seven kept in a box on the mantel while I sleep. Watch and feel each dime go slipping out through the fingers. Taken by a gladder hand. Pumped into a counting turnstile. Or a slot where a window opens and you reach in for a rye bread ham and lettuce sandwich.

Catching a bus by a white stone building. Tell you all the history of New York inside. The faded pages of little green books with the names of people. Blacksmiths, bakers and candlestick makers of a hundred years ago. When the park out there was heaps of boulders and mud. Now mommies wheel their little children to push them on the swings. All carefully cuddled up against the cold. Vine said on the phone he'd be glad to see me.

The bus stops at the corners. Across the street a low roof nestled in the trees, a place called Tavern on the Green. People climb on. The click click of the turnstile. Money drops down. Then spouts out like a milk churn. Eyes look once then fade away. Button has just popped off my coat. Never find it between all these legs. I swear to christ. I'm coming apart. Have to hold my elbow over the straggly thread. Vine will say good to see you. And o boy it's really going to be swell to be seen. Gathering spiritual assets together. Clutch tight as they drip away through the fingers. Run from the fears. First thing I did when I walked out again in the world after the funeral. Was get my shoes shined.

The bus roaring past a statue of a man on a pedestal. Say he first discovered the place. Put him up there made of metal. With horns blasting and traffic pouring round him day and night. Get ready to get off. A man with a grey cap gets on. Smiling between big fat cheeks stubbled with beard. He gaily salutes the passengers as he comes along the aisle. And sits sad and silent when no one salutes or smiles back. His eyes light up as I give him a nod. The friendly kind they give each other at the institution.

Walk east crosstown. Wind biting and raising whorls of grit and paper scraps. See the sky blown blue somewhere far out over Flushing. As a little boy I thought it was some strange big toilet bowl. Where giants took their craps.

Dark between these buildings. Cabs go bouncing over bumps. Thick iron manhole cover clanks and rocks under the passing wheels. And little clouds of steam puff out. A button off my coat. That's all you need in this town to show you're going down. And for friends to look fast for other faces.

Bronze plaque now below where the neon sign used to be. And the thunderous letters of Vine. Above the smaller words of Funeral Home. He must be going up. High over the tiny letters of Incorporated. Where he can swing from his trapeze into his heap of dollars.

Christian pushing through the gleaming glass doors. The reddish yellow carpet. Under the potted palm tree, a black urn filled with white sand to extinguish cigarettes. Knock on Vine's door, the main motif of which is contemporary splendor. Green light looked warm last week now looks cold.

"Come in. Ah Mr Christian. Good to see you. Here let me take your coat. Sit down. It's cold out."

"Cold and windy."

"Well now Mr Christian you're settling in."

"I think so."

"I'm glad. Takes time. You're young. Events finally erase the most painful part of sorrow. If they didn't this town would be so many weeping cripples. But you'd like to discuss your position wouldn't you."

"Yes."

Vine in his chair swivels. Light catches the side of his face. He tilts his round head. Shakes out the cuffs of his shirt so white and stiff. Diamonds sparkle there. Short hair standing up with little flecks of grey. All of him tucked neatly in his leather seat, eyes glistening. Finger pushing at a pair of black leather gloves on his desk. The world sinks down a little. On the carpet where you come out of the dirty street and walk softly.

"May I ask you just one question Christian. I'm going to put it to you man to man. There's a place for you here. And I mean that. The salary's not bad. It would be a beginning. And there'd be a future. I can tell you that. Will you come to work for me."

Christian bowing his head. As eyes stare out of control at the ceiling. Get them back to sea level. Saliva flows into the mouth. Swallow it all down and try to keep my shoulders from twitching.

"Mr Vine I don't know what I'm going to do yet. When you said first you were glad to see me the words I nearly said were boy it's really swell to be seen. I've hardly even spoken to another person since the funeral."

"Well I'm glad I'm seeing you then Mr Christian."

24

"Mr Vine I don't know what I owe you. But I've only got forty six dollars and ninety two cents to my name. I can't even pay the bill they charged me for freight and storage and packing my wife on the ship. You've got me at your mercy."

"Now wait a minute, Mr Christian. Now you just wait a minute there boy. I haven't got you at my mercy. And I don't like that remark."

"Well maybe you haven't. But I need mercy."

"You may need it but I haven't got you at my mercy. Don't you ever think that. I'm offering you an opportunity to assume a role in a hallowed vocation. I know the normal everyday person does not gravitate towards this calling. But I'll tell you something. I'm a good judge of men. And I recognize in you Christian the imaginative capacity to pursue this mission in life. I'm convinced you could be outstanding."

"You mean going back in there and handling dead bodies. People I don't even know."

"If you wanted to acquaint yourself with that sacred craft I'd be glad. But I'd like you to be a front of house man. With maybe the occasional assist in the studios."

"The occasional assist. Holy cow, Mr Vine."

"It may surprise you Mr Christian but it is that part of my work in which I take the greatest pride not to mention as I wouldn't do to most people, pleasure. I would not insist if you found it a source of disquiet. The real nature of your duties here would be to tend to the grief of the bereaved. To dispense the small kindly formalities and understanding so necessary when a family convenes at the abyss of death. I know you've got the sincerity. I know you've got the culture and the elegance of demeanor. It's all in you Christian."

"How much do I owe you. Mr Vine."

"That is not a question you need to ask."

"But how much do I owe."

"Four hundred and eighty six dollars and forty two cents. Including tax."

"O boy."

"Mr Christian that is not a problem. And you don't have to take it like that."

25

"How do you want me to take it. That plus one hundred and eighty six dollars I owe the shipping line is nearly seven hundred dollars. How can I ever pay."

"Now listen to me Mr Christian. I've told you once before and I'll tell you again. I don't cut cash out of no one. This is one business where most people pay their bills. Call it superstition but people don't like to owe on the death of someone near and dear. And if they were near and not so dear they're even gladder to pay for their elimination. So I'm not hurting with a cash shortage and I'm not asking you to pay up. You've got time. Plenty."

"How long."

"Six months. More if you need it. Free of interest."

"Eighty six dollars a month."

"Eight one Christian, eighty one dollars and seven cents."

"Any day someone is going to track me down from the shipping line."

"There is no problem about an advance on salary."

"I'd be socially ostracised."

"I would be less than candid if I did not admit people don't trip over rugs making a rush to shake hands to get to know you. And many friendships are cut adrift. But you'd be surprised at some of the deeper relationships you can make in this profession. It was how I met my wife. Searching for a shade of lipstick at a drugstore counter. That's a fact. I was an apprenticing mortician. She asked me what color hair and eyes I was trying to match. I had just picked up a box of bicarbonate of soda she dropped. She responded by pointing out the shade. It was one I would have picked myself. We walked outside together. She had the bluest eyes and the whitest skin. I told her what the lipstick was for. She was a little shy but then she understood. We went right back into the drugstore and had two raspberry sodas. I still remember the sound of our feet together on that porch. She had the kind of ankles you'd find on an angel. Seven months later we married. I feel just as close to her in death."

"Mr. Vine."

"Call me Clarance, spelt with an a. My step parents called me Tobias but I was named Clarance at birth. Just excuse me I've forgotten to tell Miss Musk I've changed a musical selection.

26

Miss Musk, in suite four, the Ricardo family I think needed something faster in tempo but I think it's time now before closing the casket to slow it down. O k. Thank you. There's an instance Mr Christian of the delicate decisions which constantly must be made. I feel that you would ably carry out such responsibilities.''

"Mr Vine I wouldn't know what tune to call for someone's funeral.''

"Please, call me Clarance. I'd like that if you would.''

"Until I pay my bill I'd just feel better calling you Mr Vine.''

"All right if that's the way you feel.''

Vine's eyes glittering in the soft yellow lamp light. His finger pushes the switch of the intercom up and down. The throb of faint solemn melodies. Neat tiny knot of his black tie tucked tightly up to the stiff collar. Red strong neck which he turns and twists. I'd be out in front of his establishment. Skipping and clapping hands in the cold. Encouraging in the customers. This way folks. To Mr Vine. Knows sorrow like the back of his hand. A reduction if there's two of you. His shade of mouth paint will suit you better than the one you're using now. Your husband won't be able to keep his lips off you in the coffin. This way folks. What's happened to Vine has happened to me except I didn't embalm my wife or meet her in a drugstore. His tiny feet. He looks so much bigger than he is. A man who has armies or ships. And wins battles. While he watches the lips of women. What does he do these days for orgasms.

"Mr Christian you're miles away.''

"Just admiring your green curtain.''

"I never let the light of day in here. That way I let my own mind roam. Being a Texan it's natural to me. That's a beautiful word isn't it. Texan.''

"Yes.''

"There are a lot of beautiful things. Early this morning I was out trying to stop those sons of bitches trying to park in my loading zone. Three young girls passed by. They go to a select private school up the block. Young gracious girls. They were laughing about something. And it was beautiful to watch. They weren't aware of their grace. They come from good homes on the upper east side and ride downtown on the elevated train. And

27

right in its shadows lie broken men. Men who might have once been just like those girls' fathers. With high salaries and big responsibilities. Now their salaries are gone. I buried one of them. He used to panhandle on the corner. Sometimes I take the train myself. I'd give him a quarter. A year before he was a company vice president down on Wall Street. But deep down in the back of his eyes you could see that he was from Michigan, just a poor lost kid in the big city. His wife and kids still live in a nice apartment with rustic type architecture in Forest Hills, Queens. Do you know not one of them would come to his funeral. They said they could prove if they had to that they didn't know who he was. It's that kind of human frailty that sickens you. But I haven't yet lost my faith in human nature. You meet people like them. And you meet people like you. Of quality. Which I define just by calling you a gentleman."

"How much would I be paid."

"Mr Christian you're surprising. O k the remuneration. Seventy five a week. Plus the clearing of your debt after six months. You'd be working under Fritz till you get the hang of things. He's sick with pneumonia now. But Mr Hardwicke at my west side branch would always be available for advice when I wasn't around. He's my top man. Meanwhile you'd be co host here with Miss Musk. Once in a while you'd take a doctor or nurse out for a drink. They can be helpful in this business. At nine o'clock we call muster out there in the hall. Start the ball rolling."

"You mean stiffs."

Vine thrusting out a lower lip. Lifting his chin. Waiting as Christian waits. And taking a deep breath. Which he sighs out slowly.

"I do not like that statement. And I hope it's the last time I will hear it. It's a word we don't use here. I know sometimes people have to be cynical. It relieves their fear. They often talk about us with smart remarks. But just as some other people love and respect what they do for a living so do I. But let's forget that. When my upper east side branch opens, that's when your opportunity will come. That branch will be endowed with the ultimate in funeral service in this city. No solemnity which can add grace or reverence to the carriage of death will be wanting."

Behind Vine's head a glass cabinet of leather gold embossed volumes. MODERN MORTUARY SCIENCE, ANATOMY AND POST MORTEM SANITATION, ORGANIC CHEMISTRY, CHAMPION TEXTBOOK ON EMBALMING and ANATOMY FOR EMBALMERS. Vine leans back. A pencil tightly gripped in his fingers. A smile on his lips.

"Now you're going to be too hot in that suit Mr Christian. I keep the thermometer at seventy eight point five on the button during the winter months. Sorrow demands a perfect temperature. I mean that. One thing I'm a stickler about. The other is I always like to be on the ball. You get over there to Brooks Brothers, corner of Madison and Forty Fourth. Tell them up on the third floor I sent you. They'll know what to do. It will go on my account. You know Christian, I'm really glad you made this decision. And I hope you'll never have cause to regret it."

Vine standing. Turning to his library cabinet. Taking down the volume Modern Mortuary Science. Blowing off some imaginary dust and handing it to Christian. As he leads him by the elbow to the door.

"Come, meet Miss Musk."

Crossing the canary carpet along the softly lit hall. Here's where I'll be tomorrow morning. With the numb lingering pain I'm getting right up the arse. Feels now I've been here all my life. Two men in black overcoats and hats and a sleek willowy blond woman in furs passing by. Vine nods gently. His lips say words one can't hear. Must be the understanding whisper. The dark doorways and curtained doors to the green glowing suites. Miss Musk in a dark brown dress. Stands up from behind her desk. In a tiny office. A tall green filing cabinet with two silver trophies on top. Fluted pillars holding up a drum majorette.

"Miss Musk, Mr Christian is coming to work for us."

"I'm so glad."

"He has the makings."

"I'm sure he has. I can't say how glad I am."

Handshakes. Christian bowing his head to the light haired Miss Musk. Has long fragile fingers. And limp moist hand. A gold bracelet falls down on her wrist as she takes back her arm. And a blue vein bulges across her knuckle. Face all tanned. Says goodbye with a smile of team spirit. Her teeth gleam. Her breasts blossom in their brown.

29

Vine guiding Christian by the arm. Past the chapel's open gothic arched door. Four candles burning inside the blue glassed golden topped tabernacle on the altar. Another color getting a chance. Two figures kneeling in the round domed interior. Looked like little children. Bent heads and hunched tiny shoulders. My heart pounding. As we go in this direction. To where there's that door.

"Just through here now, Cornelius, you don't mind if I call you Cornelius."

"No."

The narrow hall. The temperature drops. A fire department notice on the wall. Red handled axe held by steel clips. Behind a glass door a big brass nozzle on a canvas hose wrapped around a brass wheel. What could ever burn in this chill. Door swinging open. Can't tear my eyes away. No where else to look but the ceiling with two big square sky lights. A cold grey falls upon two white coated and masked figures. Each bent over a colder body. Heads of deceased tilted up on tables of stainless steel. Two more covered in green sheets. Trolleys of tubes, rolls of cotton wool and bottles. The smell of air. Sinks into the lungs. Will never come out again. Makes the toes curl. How do I get out of here. The indignity when they get you stretched out like that. Pulling a needle and thread out of a nostril. Squeezing bulbfuls of fluid into your arm. That you can't raise to sock him on the jaw. Stop it.

Vine suddenly turning and reaching out as Christian sways and plunges forward. Great heaving sigh from his lips. Two morticians rushing round their tables. One catching him under the back another by the feet. Vine holding him by the head and shoulders. Three undertakers lever him onto an embalming table. Pull loose his tie. Open up his shirt. Another button pops off. Rolls on the red tiled floor. And stops. Two little vacant holes in the pearl for eyes or thread. Sew it back on please.

Before the fatal
Rigor
And the final
Mortis
Sets in

5

Snow white this Monday morning. Began falling in the night. Traffic sounds faint on the avenue the end of the street. Wake up with icicles on the window sill. Already an hour late for my first day of work. Not an ounce of heat coming up in this building.

Christian putting on his dark tweed suit. Little wetting of the hair. A discreet pee into the basin. Steams up urinish upon the nostrils. Flakes still falling outside. Man in plaid lumber jacket, leather cap and black furry ear muffs shovelling snow. A police dog tied to the iron railing. Go out to face death now. Day after day.

Muffled sound of the garbage men approaching. Radio says temperature twenty two degrees. Shuttered window opens across the street. A girl I watched Sunday night undressing. In a red kimono. Takes in a container of milk. Saw her get down to her underwear and when she finished brushing her hair the lights went off. Nobody gives a good god damn they're interrupting your show.

Christian making his way along the shadowy hall to the bathroom. To face this color again. Like a wave of seasickness. In a green sea of grief. Reeking of formalin. Still feel faint. Everytime I think of that chill day. After Vine gave me a tumbler of brandy from a barrel in the embalming room. I hurried away up the street. Another limp handshake clinging to my palm from Miss Musk. Took the subway south. And stood waiting for the ferry. On the uttermost tip of town. Desperate to see sky and breathe air. Of which there is neither in this crapper. I spent

31

that Friday afternoon three times cruising back and forth across the harbour. Devoured two bags of peanuts packed in Suffolk, Virginia. Forking out my future salary. Ate two hot dogs slathered in mustard and sauerkraut and downed with two rootbeers. Which are roaring through me now. Was hoping to say to Mr Vine I'm really glad to be part of your operation. And nearly ended up undertaken. As the masked faces looked down. I looked up and fainted again. Now no damn toilet paper. Use my only clean handkerchief. Dried my wind watered eyes with it on the last trip of the ferry when the sun set. Little dots and glimmers of light in the tall buildings ahead. Passengers opening the sliding doors to stand on deck. Cold air pouring into the cabin. The flat bottomed vessel pushed across the waves. Carrying on the rows of wooden benches all the faces. To the most unpleasant ones I flashed the title of the mortuary manual. Those who understood the words turned their heads away in a god damn hurry. To watch an ocean liner sailing by. Decks lit up. Tiny dark figures standing under the life boats. Fluttering pennants strung from funnel to funnel. And sadly watching the passing great silhouette, smoke floating a darker darkness in the sky. There came a tapping on my shoulder. And a face. Smiling. Waving his grey cap. The man with the fat cheeks on the bus. To whom I gave the friendly nod of the institution. Strange pleased grunts coming from his lips. As I shook his hand thoroughly. And now someone is pounding on this crapper door.

Christian opening up. The sallow moist cross eyed visage of Mrs Grotz. Her grey kinky hair greyer and kinkier. Face contorted. Keeps her big boned knuckled hand pressing her daisy flowered dress closed. Or they may be petunias. Of the deadly nightshade family. If I dared to look closer. As I better not do. As she looks about to erupt.

"I got something to talk to you."

"Yes."

"What do you think you do in my house."

"What do you mean."

"You mortician. I see book. Are you mortician."

"No."

"Why you have book."

"I don't think that's any of your business."

"You want I should lose all the tenants out of my building I work hard in. I should know with that voice you got. And the funeral car. You give me bullshit your wife die. I think you pervert with women's clothes."

"I beg your pardon."

"You think you come in here and live like that you crazy."

Christian pushing out of bathroom. Past the heaving boobs of Mrs Grotz. Who carries hidden in the folds of her dress a lead pipe. Just about two feet long. Sticking out. What a friendly god damn country. Just get the hell out of this hall. And into my room. Never leave a door open again. She'll see the bed erupted asunder. Caused by a dream last night. That Clarance Vine had opened his new mortuary on the upper level of Grand Central Station. Folk were wheeling in their deceased. From the Mississippi and Boston. Trains loaded with cadavers. From Bronxville, Crestwood and Tuckahoe. Teams of morticians in football uniforms pounding down the Forty Second Street ramp. Vine with a megaphone blasting out commands from the Vanderbilt Avenue balcony. Directing the bodies laid out in vast rows as he watched through his binoculars. Organ music throbbing under the immense vaulted blue ceiling. And I was there. Trying to look the last word in fashion. With my dark brown trilby hat. The throngs of newspaper toting commuters stood still, silent, and scared shitless. I was glad to see Vine. Went to him. Nudged him with a friendly nudge from behind. Said in my best American, how's it going Clarance. He said hey how you doing kid, good to see you, everything's going fine, real fine, if you feel like embalming grab yourself a cadaver.

Christian turning to close his bedroom door. Mrs Grotz sticking her foot in it as she pushes it open. And Christian lunges it shut. Thump. A leaden object dropping. Christian slipping on the chain latch. Grotz's fists beating on the mahogany panels. Welcome to West Idiot Street.

"What do you do in my house. I don't want no wise guy like you. You hear me. Get out before I call the cops. You dirty bum."

A crash against the door. Screws flying from the latch. With

33

another shoulder shoving. The growl of a dog. Door slowly yielding open again. The plaid arm of the man down shovelling in the street. Christian with a rather amazing collegiate heave assisted by a foot against the wall, crashing the door shut again. A throatful gasp out of Mrs Grotz, her high heeled shoe caught bent and crushed. Too bad it was footless. Just about had enough insociability. Ask that fucker in the plaid jacket when he got castrated and what else has he got going for him. As I hear the sound of a siren coming down the street.

"Pervert. You wait my other nephew Broken Legs Vinnie fix you."

Faint smell of garlic breath. Pity that marvelous bulbous herb has to taint some mouths. Give the poisonous words a flavour. With this kind of population embalming is the juice of justice. The siren subsiding. Car doors slamming outside. The police. Be charged with female impersonation while in possession of a mortician's manual. Sound of feet pounding up the stairs. Voices outside the door.

"Arrest him. Him voodoo. In there pervert."

"Take it easy lady. What's going on. Open up."

"Women's clothes he's wearing."

"All right lady. Is he armed."

"How do I know. But I got hemorrhoids since he moved in."

"Did you see a gun or a knife."

"I see dirty pictures of dead peoples he's got. Without no clothes. You can see the balls."

"O k lady we know what kind of enchantment. Open up in there. For the last time."

Christian pulling back the door. Four heads waiting in the shadows. Dog growling and snarling. Two blue caps and uniforms. No one gives a hoot I'm a recent widower. A gun pointing at me. Get shot before I have a chance to scream I'm wracked with refinement. Raise my hands. My fly is open. An additional felony of wang wagging. While human balls lie unbouncing on an illustrated page. Sewing mouths closed in Vine's studio is going to be a relief.

"O k buddy."

"That's him. There the clothes. In the suitcase. I told you. Tell by his voice he wear dresses."

"Lady give us a chance. O k put your hands down. What have you got to say buddy."

"Those are my wife's clothes."

"Where's your wife."

"Dead."

"He butcher her."

"Will you shut up lady. Now what do you mean buddy, dead."

"Dead, just what I said."

"Come on fella don't get smart."

"I'm not. She's dead. Her funeral was over a week ago. Those are her clothes."

"All right. Now the dirty pictures. Where are they."

"There I suppose."

"You suppose."

"Well it's a manual for morticians."

"What are you a funeral undertaker."

"Yes I am. I pursue that hallowed vocation."

"No kidding. What are you living in a place like this for. All the undertakers we know live on Park Avenue."

"Arrest him."

"For the last time shut up lady or we'll arrest you. This guy has got a perfectly normal story. For this precinct anyway. Can you prove this. Your name Cornelius Christian on this tag."

"Yes."

"Hey who called us anyway. O k it doesn't matter. Now everybody pipe down and stop pushing. Lady you got a telephone."

"Yeah you pay to use it."

"O k buddy who do I check your story with."

"Vine funeral home."

"Is that right. You mean Clarance. Vine."

"Yes. And I'm late for work."

"Hey well you're working with him. Used to be my beat. Sure I know Clarance. Real nice guy. He's so successful he's opening up his third branch on the east side over there. Goes right down five floors into the foundations. Going to be really something. Well what do you know. O k lady this show's over."

"He legitimate."

"That's right."

"Well he's undertaking."

"That's right lady."

"He should live with other undertakers. Not in a house with normals."

"Nothing to do with us lady."

"Cocksucker could have disease he catch off the bodies."

"Now lady why don't you have some manners. Calm down before you get yourself into trouble. Call the commissioner of health if you're worried. This is how murders happen. Be glad he's not a snake charmer with a bunch of cobras under the bed. And why don't get someone to put salt on the ice on your steps."

"My nephew here Angelo's doing it."

"Hey whose lead pipe is this."

The contingent departing. Foot shaped puddles of water from the melted snow on the floor. Christian putting on his grey tweed overcoat and grabbing his manual. Quickly down the stairs. Past the sneering greasy face of Mrs Grotz peering from her door. Nice to know what makes people dislike you. To call you a cocksucker. And there's Angelo the brother of Broken Legs Vinnie. Four glaring brown eyes, two belong to his dog as he looks up from his shovel. Policemen in their squad car. One gives a wave. Other writes in a notebook. He's winding down his window. Have to find a taxi I'm so late.

"Hey, Mr Christian, come on, get in. We'll give you a lift. We're going your way."

Leaping across the drift of snow in the gutter. Christian getting in the back of the squad car. In the static coming over the radio a voice announcing. Go to the intersection of Fifth and Fiftieth. Man on sixteenth floor threatening to jump into Fifth Avenue, calling all cars.

Siren blaring. Squad car skidding away. Streaking across the snowy winding road through the park. In the Hunter's Gate and out the Miner's Gate and down Fifth Avenue. Lady bundled in furs turns to look as her poodle in mink lifts a leg to pee. Good to be regarded with a glance or two as one goes ploughing by. Without a siren it's hard to get noticed. This jumper could be a prospective customer. Who may have to be cleaned off the street.

Unless he's on the sixteenth floor of a doll's house. Might get embedded in the roof of a car. Or land on five pedestrians. Be six for Vine. Fire engine. Flags waving. Just in front.

"Well Mr Christian. This guy jumps there could be plenty of custard around. How's this for service. Tell Clarance Dick was asking for him. You ought to change your address."

Crosstown east. There's the dark green awning out. Covered in a mantel of snow. Buses splashing grey masses of frozen slush. Vine's pickup truck busy at the loading entrance. Street empty. Save for a solitary trudging head down shielding a big brown envelope. Commerce continues. Snow on the elevated train roaring past down the street. Enter here. Warm and comforting. Snow melting inside my shoe.

"Where've you been Christian. You're late."

"I'm sorry Mr Vine. My landlady tried to throw me out because she thought I was a mortician. Professional prejudice. The police came. One of them knew you. Dick."

Vine a dark visage planted the center of his canary carpet. A pearl pin in his tie. His thumbs rubbing up and down on his curled index fingers. He's ready to bark my head off, fire me, and hand me my wife's funeral bill. As I stand here soaking up the warmth thoroughly delighted. For the first time to have a job. In this new land of hair and perhaps prick raising opportunity.

"O k. Don't let it happen again. I'm sorry if I seem angry but we're short handed. Fritz now has double pneumonia. And my short wave says there's someone ready to jump down on Fifth and Fiftieth. If the snow stays and gets any deeper they'll be a lot more. They go out the windows like pop corn off a red hot pan. Happens everytime there's a blizzard."

"I do apologise Mr Vine. It won't happen again."

"O k then, on the ball now. Two reposings, Miss Musk is taking care of suite two the Brennan family. I need your sense of protocol in suite four. The Sourpusses. It's nothing to worry about. Cortege be ready to move in half an hour. To Greenlawn. Interment in a mausoleum. Think you can handle it."

"I think so."

"Charlie the driver will know what to do at the cemetery. Now take off your overcoat. Wipe your shoes, comb your hair. Just go

37

in quietly. On the right inside the door is the temperature control, if it's o k make believe you're adjusting it anyway. Gives people a feeling things are being looked after. Mrs Sourpuss, you can't miss her, the blond, introduce yourself as my assistant. The deceased was a wholesaler in ladies garments in a big way. Just keep an eye on things. No one's getting their feet wet with the tears. I'll see to the flowers. You ride with Charlie and the casket.''

A blond in black. Saw her passing in the hall the other day. Sitting reading a fashion magazine open across her lap. Two gentlemen standing each at a corner of the room. And this one near me inside the door looking me up and down. An older woman kneeling at the coffin, head bent. The deceased in a blue business suit. Saw him on the slab when I fainted. Looks twenty years younger now. Wearing eyeglasses and good lord an old Etonian tie. Stand here. Check the thermostat. Excuse me sir. Whoops. A degree too low. And the green light is just a shade too bright. Music sounds like a slowed down Polish polka. Just another step forward. The wife must have been half his age. Carrying a lot of gold embellishments on both her wrists. And an acorn sized diamond on her finger. Am I allowed to sit. Better not. Wow what legs she's got. Black gleaming stockings in the emerald light. Introduce myself.

''Excuse me. I'm a Mr Christian, Mr Vine's assistant. Is everything all right. Is there anything I can do.''

''Well. Yes. Would you mind getting me a pack of Kools.''

''I beg your pardon.''

''Kools.''

''What's that.''

''Cigarettes.''

''O. Of course.''

''Just put them on the bill.''

Christian trotting down the street. In a previous pair of footsteps. Past a grimy statue of a cigar store Indian shading his eyes as he looks out under the trellises and girders criss-crossed darkly against the still falling snow. Shout Kools to the man over the crashing rumble of an elevated train and he hands across a pack. Says mentholated. With a free book of matches. In

38

Europe they make you pay. Man thinks I'm nuts running around without a coat. At the moment I'm feeling good. With this snow cleansed air and a fresh change of people. Some with fantastic legs. Gives one a hope. That I could be good if not stunning at this job. Even show Vine a thing or two about pomp and ritzy circumstance if I had the right choice of socially elite people. Have my own band of Viennese musicians. And maybe two guys with spears and armour standing guard at the entrance. With a funeral parlor eight floors down into the foundations. And only an hour ago I was nearly a pervert. And a cocksucking mortician spreading pestilence.

"Madam."

"Thank you. Aren't you a very sweet young man. Thank you so much."

"Glad to be of any service madam."

"I'm Mrs Sourpuss. I suppose you read all about it in the newspapers."

"I'm sorry I don't think I have."

"It was quite awful. You're not a New Yorker are you."

"No, not at the moment."

"I didn't think so. You sound English."

"Thank you."

"What on earth is a nice young man like you doing working in a place like this."

"Well, madam, it is as you might say, my calling."

"You got called. To this."

"Yes. It's my vocation. I'm hoping to work myself up. Perhaps even one day having a place of my own."

"What a marvelously unglamorous ambition."

"I want to help people. My profession gives one an opportunity to do that."

"You sound just like Mr Vine."

"I'm very flattered to hear that."

"Don't you get sick of this."

"Madam giving comfort to the bereaved, to those left behind sorrowing is a fulfillment of my own peace of mind."

"Hey are you kidding me. But you do have a beautiful accent. Have a cigarette."

"No. I don't, thank you. Do allow me please."

Christian taking Mrs Sourpuss's lighter from her one tightly black gloved hand. Down upon which the gold bracelets cascade. Her jaw line stern and strong. Skin blond and smooth. Eyes a greeny light blue. Get a little closer. To her perfume. Eyes more blue than green. And as I came in this morning. I was waiting for a whiff of formalin. If I'd had breakfast I might have vomited. Right on Vine's canary carpet. This lighter heavy. Must be solid gold. There's a blaze of shit hailing at you out of the heavens. And especially from your rented bedroom ceiling. Then suddenly one's standing with an erection punching one under the chin. With a vision of a mourner's thighs. Making you deaf around the ears.

"Tell me Mr Christian. My you do have beautiful delicate hands. Will you be coming to the cemetery."

"Yes I am."

"I'd appreciate it, if possible, if you could ride with me in my car. I'd like to have someone to talk to."

"I'll ask Mr Vine. I'm sure it will be all right. We'd like to be of any assistance we can."

In the emerald night club darkness Christian's eyebrows rose. Shyly retreating. Stopping under a ceiling light of the lobby to take a good look at my hands. Yes. They are rather splendid. If I don't wait and think of something to make my engorged perpendicularity go down Clarance will think I'm trying to put it up the bereaved. And he's right. A great life. This disposal of the dead. The only thing that can stop me now is failure.

Or
If death
Gets out
Of style

40

6

Madam's car was grey. With tiny little round windows in the rear sides. Like the portholes of a ship. A long antenna sticking from a snowy roof. Dark gleaming fur rug inside. Had a last look at Mr Sourpuss. Whose composure and bald pate was immense. Rouge on his chubby cheeks. Must have made a lot of money. Lips sealed. Otherwise I'd ask him how.

Along Fifty Seventh Street Mrs Sourpuss hummed the slow Polish polka. Turning her head to stare back at some fashion house windows. When our eyes met she smiled. The guy who was standing by the thermostat stood looking up and down the street while the other two watched me getting into the limozine. And Mrs Sourpuss's gum chewing chauffeur growled something inaudibly unpleasant as he slammed my door.

Traffic crawling through the deepening snow. Abandoned cars little mounds of white. The sky dark with clouds. Red funnelled ocean liner being nudged by tugs around the tip of a pier. Across the black cold water of the Hudson the undulating roller coaster of the amusement park atop the sheer stone cliffs. Went over there once after an annual June school boat ride. Was my city then. Belongs now to Vine. He just stared at me when I announced. That Mrs Sourpuss requested I accompany her. I stood waiting. Vine sat. Sheets of architectural drawings all over his desk. Held down at one corner by a small black book which in red said Social Register New York. Now he's found out I'm not listed, he might say what the hell do you mean trying to get familiar with the mourners. But he looked back down to his

41

papers. O k Christian. And said he'd just heard on the radio that this is a real blizzard we're having, make sure Charlie's put chains on all the cars. And Charlie's eyes opened pleasantly wide when I walked up to him. And he said Mr Christian what are you doing here. I said I'm working. And he said holy christ.

Mrs Sourpuss smoked Kool after Kool. I lit them for her with her lighter. She blew the smoke out from under a big wide brimmed black hat. Leaning forward to tap her ash in a tray pulled out from the walnut ornamented back of the driver's seat. She spoke to the chauffeur through a microphone like a little tea strainer. His name was Glen. He gave me dirty looks through his rear view mirror and once during a prolonged sneer crashed us into the back of the hearse. Charlie got out shaking his fist and shouting.

"For crying out loud can't you see me in front, you numbskull, you could have killed the deceased or something."

Mrs Sourpuss put her hand over her mouth as she laughed. And turned to me looking right down into my fur covered lap. Where I was most rapidly rotating my thumbs.

"Are you interested in sports, Mr Christian."

"Sometimes I put on the gloves. I boxed."

"Really."

"I'm pretty able to take care of myself."

"But it would be terrible if something happened to your hands. Do you like good books and music."

"Yes I do."

"I do too. Really good books. I really love books."

"I like books."

"I knew you did. It's written all over you."

Crossing the bridge high up over the water where the East River flows in and out of the Hudson. Leaving the island of Manhattan. Arrive on the mainland of the Bronx. Mrs Sourpuss took off her hat and put her head back. Opened her mouth and rolled her tongue around in each cheek. Tapped ash from her cigarette and took a long drag. Up there in front of us, her husband. In a white satin lined casket covered in wreaths and flowers. One's own sorrow all dried away. Think it will never go. Till it's gone.

"What's your name I can't keep calling you Mr Christian."

"Cornelius."

"You must have had an old fashioned mother and father to give you a name like that."

"They were immigrants and left me an orphan."

"Hey that's sad."

Cars keep away from a funeral on the highway. Folk rushing for home in the blizzard. Perched on the rocky knolls those houses where people live who look safe from life. Behind their cozy window panes. In rambling rooms. Refrigerators full with ice cream, olives, pimento cheese. Sliced bologna and roast beef all ready to lay thickly between the mayonnaise slathered rye bread. Sit on a big sofa in the sprawling living room. Sink your teeth in all that eating and wash it down with soda pop. A big fire blazing. Dozens of radiators tingling hot all over the house.

"Where are we now. Cornelius. How far is it."

"Not far madam."

"Do me a favor and cut out that madam. Makes me feel old."

"Sorry."

"My name is Fanny. Where are we."

"This is the Bronx."

"Doesn't look like the Bronx."

"It's the Bronx. It has woods, deer, fish, muskrats, possum, owls, snakes."

"I didn't know it was this kind of burg. When are they going to civilize it. Hey that hurt your feelings what I said."

"O no."

"It did."

"I was raised in the Bronx."

"No kidding. There. There are more woods. Just like you said."

"The cemetery has a lake with ducks."

"No kidding."

The cortege climbing the winding hill through the woods. Grey limozine without chains, skidding on the ice. Another two cars behind. White clouds of exhaust rising from the back of the hearse. Where I waited with Helen we wait for green on the stop lights. In my own romantic Bronx. I was a new little boy all the way from Brooklyn moved on the street. Made a friend called Billy whose mother just died. He asked me over. To try out his

43

boxing gloves he got for Christmas. His father watched us from a ring side seat on the cellar stairs. I thought he would be too sad to fight and instead he beat the living shit out of me.

"What's that Cornelius."

"The last stop of the elevated train."

"That's a bar, where it says Wickies."

"Yes."

Mrs Sourpuss took a new crisp ten dollar bill from a black shiny purse. Her eyebrows raised, she lifted her microphone and told Glen to stop. The hearse went on crossing the wide avenue, followed by the two cars behind. A man in a grey uniform directing them to halt inside the gates.

"Would you be a real marvelous darling Cornelius and get me a bottle of whiskey."

"Certainly of course. Any particular kind."

"Canadian."

Stepping out under this haunted structure. The many times I climbed up and down from this train. Like a house on stilts full of windows. The end of the line or the beginning if you're heading downtown. Bartender with sleeves rolled up. Travellers hunched over drinks at the circular bar. Jukebox playing jingle bells, a sleigh ride through the snow. A customer saying that's what you're going to need in another hour if this keeps up.

Outside snow getting heavier. Telephone wires bending along the lonely avenue north. Across the street the black high iron railings. And beyond, the rooftops of the great marble monuments. Some granite and grey. Spruce trees and winterish maples, oak and beech. All the death out there covered up. Cold white and lonely. Mrs Sourpuss pulling open a cabinet.

"Have some Cornelius, it's going to be damn cold."

"Thank you, no. Not while I'm on duty."

"You call this duty."

"No."

"Well then let's have a few shots."

"I think I better not."

"Be a pussy foot. Don't expect me to sit here gushing tears."

"I suppose some mourners are sadder than others."

"Don't give me that. Plenty are glad. Unless it's a kid or something."

44

"Here's your change."

"You keep that, it's yours."

"I'm sorry but I just couldn't accept such a thing."

"You know in just a minute I'm going to pin a medal on you. You're just so god damn nice. Take it."

"Well thank you very much."

"Don't mention it. I married it. Well here's seeing you."

Fanny drinking back a mouth full of whiskey, adam's apple going up and down as she swallows. Can't wait till I see her black stockinged legs again. Vine never mentioned tips. As part of what looks like my fantastic emoluments. To use an old fashioned term. Throw it to Vine to increase his word power. Took Fanny two sentences and a gargantuan gratuity to relieve me of a life time of self respect. Nearly seven dollars richer. Just for being her errand boy. Enough to buy hot dogs and root beer on plenty of ferry trips and still have change for a pizza.

"Cornelius, you're strong aren't you. Don't let anybody touch me."

Now wants to know if I'm a Samson. Glen smirking again up front. Think he'd learned his lesson. Be driving us next in the door of the Sourpuss mausoleum. Knocking the liquids out of the deceased. Send the attendants running for their lives. And give me a chance to stop somewhere quiet and count my money.

"I was married to a football player, Cornelius. He could hold me up over his head in the palm of his hand. But he couldn't make a dime. Cried like a baby when I left him. He kind of got sick in the mental department. Tried to kill me when I wouldn't come back. If he's waiting, Cornelius sock him, will you."

A winding road up and down these vistas. Past a statue of a little boy with his knickered legs crossed sitting on a bench. Holds a red carnation in his hand. I was dressed like that when I lost my first fight. They left me back a grade for being dumb. And I thought I could beat the second toughest kid in the class. He had books under his sweater where I hurt my fists. Knocked me into a hedge and I started to cry. Now Mrs Sourpuss wants me to unleash a haymaker on the iron jaw of some huge gorp.

"Tell you the truth Mrs Sourpuss. I'm athletic. But this guy your first husband."

"My second husband."

"Well your second. He sounds pretty big. Do you really think he'll be waiting. I mean we like to give complete service where possible. But I could need some help."

"I've got three private detectives with me. But I don't want any shooting."

"Shooting. Mrs Sourpuss. This is a solemn ceremony. There are cemetery regulations. I'd be fired if there's shooting. Shoving and pushing, that happens at lots of funerals. But Mr Vine absolutely would not want gun fire."

Went that way with Helen. The economically priced graves. Row after row. And this way to where teeth may be socked like dice all over the tomb. If bullets haven't shattered everybody's bicuspids first. All round here, edifices rear in their snowy elegance. Right behind any one could be Mrs Sourpuss's second husband. His telescopic high powered rifle aimed. The rest of his football team coming charging out with tomahawks. Not much has changed on this old Indian hunting ground.

Ahead eight men in green uniforms. A canopy leading up an incline of path. A mausoleum dome held by columns and arched windows of stained glass. Cedar trees by the entrance. Cortege stopped. Whoops. Another two cars added to the funeral. Clarance I know would want me to use my own judgement. Prostrate myself on the floor of this vehicle. After the massacre is over take the survivors to the hospital. And Charlie can take the dead to Vine.

"Mrs Sourpuss I don't want to appear as if I'm ungallant but before we get out. Do you see your second husband anywhere. In that car. There's someone sitting in it. For your own safety we ought be sure before you get out."

"Willie has a glass jaw. Just sock him. You scared Cornelius."

"No I'm not. I'm a little rusty. I mean I should speak to an official of the cemetery. If there's some kind of unfortunate incident that could mar the dignity of the occasion. They don't let things like that happen here."

Charlie pulling and twisting the door handle of the hearse. Which sneer faced Glen jammed closed. If Vine were here he'd be climbing screaming up the walls of a mausoleum. Charlie now prizing with a spanner. And has just landed backwards on his

46

arse in the snow. Putting a deep frown on that cemetery official's face. This could be my first and last funeral. Three of them pulling now. Whoops. Another down. Cemetery official scowling. Four tugging. Budging. A squeal. It's open. The whole door bent. Fanny squeezing my hand. I'll be stepping out of this car prick first.

"Boy Cornelius. What a bunch of rubes."

Attendants taking the flowers laden down their outstretched arms. Six more in their green capes drawing out the casket. Neatly heft it on their shoulders. Charlie stands watching ashen faced, his grey wisps of hair catching snowflakes. On that little green post it says Paradise Avenue. Instead of way up Shit's Creek. Fanny patting on her makeup. Snaps a gold case shut. A little fragrant powder up my nose. Here we go now. Vanity first. Before violence.

"Please tell me if you see him Mrs Sourpuss."

"Who."

"Willie."

"Don't worry you can't miss him he's six foot eight."

Mrs Sourpuss in high heeled black rubber galoshes. Christian shivering. Pause under the awning just like the one that goes into Vine's. Left my coat back at the office. Smell her perfume stronger out here in the fresh air. Her black legs against the white. Everyone waiting. A strange group getting out of the two other cars. Four women in black head dresses and long black veils. Three dark swarthy men, one in flowing robes. Three detectives, two at the top of the steps and the other across the road.

"Who are those people in black Mrs Sourpuss."

"Peasants. My husband's relatives. I'm just letting them have their own little jamboree. Because that's all they're getting. Bunch of immigrants. They should go back to Bulgaria."

Take her furry elbow. Winds blow through my tweed. Along with a feel of her right tit. Cool down my perpendicular. Stands every time she stands. Steps swept clean. A moment to extend her a little amiability. Before any conduct unbecoming explodes.

"You look very pretty Mrs Sourpuss."

"I'll bet you say that to all the mourners."

Cold musty interior. Smell of cement and plaster. Nearly

answered Mrs Sourpuss. That she was the first mourner I'd ever met. She stands rigid and close to me. As the group gathers around. Tall bearded man in black robes has a little altar. Female angels kneel with wreaths up on the stained glass windows. Under that one it says Pax Vobiscum. All I know is I better try rejoin the athletic club where I first learned my fisticuffs and get in shape fast. Tragedy comes just like you're staring at a watch at exactly the moment it stops. That's when the bell rings with a good punch in the head and the round begins. Come out fighting. All low blows are especially allowed. So nobody's balls hang in peace. Mine presently dangle in awe. From a very stiff gibbosity. Standing in honor of Fanny.

Flakes still falling from darkened skies. Snow plow clearing the cemetery roads. Mr Sourpuss in his water tight lead lined case lifted up to rest behind a great pink slab of marble. While the immigrants mumbled prayers. And as we were returning down the steps. A tap came on my arm from behind. My right hand curled into a fist. Best to cut this big Willie bugger to pieces across the midsection. I was astonished at my bravery. But it was Charlie asking me in his soft sad voice was I coming in the hearse. I said yes. Mrs Sourpuss said no. And tugged me frozen stiff back into her car. She squeezed her fingertips on my knee.

"You poor boy you. Here let me rub your hands."

And poor old Charlie. Carries enough grief in his brown eyes to start a bank of sorrow. He was handing out the gratuities as we pulled away. Cruising along these undulating roads. With a bed and fireplace one of these mausoleums would make a good place to live. With gates locked for the night be able to go out and stroll in the evening peace. In snow shoes. Amidst the beauty. Safe from landladies. Iceskate on this frozen lake. Just avoid the hole in the center where the ducks and geese are standing around. A little stone bridge. A blue jay squawking flying up to a tree branch. There beyond a plot of small headstones and through the fence, the red fronted fire station. Looks warm and cozy inside. And down along this avenue among these older graves I worked a high school summer cutting grass. Thought I was a barber clipping green hair sprouting up from all the dead.

"Mrs Sourpuss if you stop right here I can catch the train."

"Aren't you going to stay with me."

"Well I don't know where you're going. Mr Vine might have something I ought to be doing downtown."

"With the stiffs."

"We don't use that word."

"We. Who's we."

"Well Mr Vine. And I too perhaps. We prefer to use the word deceased outside the studio and inside the word body."

"And I too perhaps. The way you say that. I just love your accent. And I too perhaps. Have a shot of whiskey Cornelius, I'm just kidding you. You have just about the cutest and most innocent face I've ever seen in my life."

"I'm not so innocent."

"Come on have a shot. There's just one left. Don't you ever relax and enjoy yourself. You're so dead serious. You've got to have some fun sometimes in life."

"Well I've had a lot of trouble."

"Everybody's had for pete's sake. Everybody's got trouble. Look at me. I just packed away my husband. You don't fight it. You go with it. O k Glen pull over."

Stopping on this bridge. Underneath go trains and flow cars and the Bronx River. Mrs Sourpuss clinking the whiskey bottle on the glass rim, pouring in the last drop. Son of a bitch Glen must have drunk the rest. Reached back here through his sliding window and took a few slugs. And just gave me one more dirty look. As we wait. Parked across from the station. Out through the porthole it says New York Central. Southbound. Down there the swaying rooftop of a train approaching. Roaring towards Connecticut. Taking fathers back to their little families. Complaining about the best of everything. That money can buy. I've come back across an ocean to this blank wall of people. Afraid to look out of their eyes. Or let a spark of feeling escape from their frozen faces. Terrified a finger will point and say, you, you're guilty. Of thinking. That this whole god damn setup is full of shit.

"You've got no coat, Cornelius. You could maybe freeze to death."

"There's a waiting room."

"Gee it's a blizzard."

"The trains are running."

49

"But look over there on the hill, a nice cozy looking inn. Come on. I'm dying for a chicken sandwich. You can phone Mr Vine from there. Did you have lunch."

"No."

"Well come on. There must be a union of funeral employees. Could close Vine right up, not giving you a lunch hour."

"All right."

"Glen, let us out over there at that Rendezvous Inn. Get yourself something to eat and wait in the parking lot."

Inside the warm tinkling interior, a circular bar. One at each gate of the cemetery. The bereaved can pour out and drown their sorrows. Organ music. Sprinkling of customers. Brass rail for feet. Two windows look out on the falling snow. From a side door more patrons pile in. Bridesmaids in pink and a dark haired familiar faced girl in a white wedding dress. Head towards the dining room and dance floor in the back. Where I follow Mrs Sourpuss in her high heeled galoshes. Through the soft colored lights flashing across the darkness. Round faced waiter leans over to take an empty glass and clean the ash tray. This late winter afternoon. My first day's labor in the new world. A blond black widow right across the tablecloth. Ordering two club chicken sandwiches, a bottle of beer, whiskey and soda. Waiter nods.

"All righty folks."

Mrs Sourpuss standing. Putting her two hands flat under her breasts and pressing the clinging cloth down across her belly. Takes a lung full of air. Puts out her chest. Raises her eyebrows. Picks up her purse. And with a fluttering of lashes smiles down at me.

"Excuse me Cornelius while I powder my nose."

On the table a black leather book. The gilt edged pages closed with a tiny gold heart shaped lock. Next to it, folded newspaper pages. Mrs Sourpuss carried them in from the car. Take a peek in this faint light at the newsprint. A headline. Wild Dogs Attack Man In Bronx. And another. Doc Plunges To Death. And at the top of the obituary column.

Harry Z. Sourpuss, 67, a Bulgarian immigrant whose sewing patents revolutionized the garment manufacturing industry here, died of an apparent heart attack on Thursday. He was a penniless itinerant knife sharpener before establishing a national merchandizing empire which made him a millionaire. He constructed the Sourpuss building, a skyscraper midtown whose roof is a replica of the Nevski Cathedral in Sofia. Mr Sourpuss was also a noted fund raiser and contributor to many Bulgarian causes. Funeral services will be held at the Vine Funeral Parlor Monday at 11 a.m. And the remains removed to Greenlawn. He is survived by his widow, the former Fanny Jackson, and two brothers, Sheldon and Izaak.

Christian opening up another folded newspaper page. The Wall Street Journal. A headline across three columns. Founder of Sourpuss Corporation Sued By Wife In Boardroom Battle. Holy christ, fold this back up again. Everybody's got trouble. Even the rich. With her lips so soft and motherly. How could she sue. With those wise congenial eyes. Hair swept back from her broad face and under her powder a freckled skin. She must carry a black rage that comes out with tiger's claws. Until she gets what she wants. And smiles again.

Waiter setting down sandwiches and drinks. Christian slipping him the five dollar bill from his gratuity. Enough to buy some underwear. Five new pairs of socks. The crotch of my drawers rotted out. Hole in the toe and heel of my present hosiery. Shuffled around the funeral parlor this morning so my trouser cuff did not reveal that little tiny rising sun of flesh. That tells the world of further hidden tatters.

"Get out of here, and leave me alone. I'm with someone."

Christian looking up. A giant with blond hair pecking out from a blue and gold skull cap. A big grey overcoat with melting snow on the shoulders. Standing behind Mrs Sourpuss who only reaches his shoulder.

"Who are you with. Him. Who are you buster."

"I'm with Mrs Sourpuss."

"Well what do you say I sock you one then. Because I don't like you being with her."

Christian standing slowly, pushing his chair back. Lifting his arms out from his sides. Amazing how fast the heart begins to pound. And the shoulders hunch. To give an immediate if not lasting appearance of an ape in the shadows. Willie who can hold an ass aloft in the palm. Wears the same fashionable sneer as Glen. A smile now coming across his lips. The weak give the strong a marvelous appetite. To beat the living shit out of them.

"Buster you some kind of jujitsu artist or something going to throw me around the place."

"No. But if you don't leave this lady alone. I'm going to break you in two."

"Heh heh heh. Well you just step forward now there and let's just see you break me in two."

"Please Cornelius let me call the manager. O god no."

Christian stepping out round the table. Walking up to Willie. Whose smile got bigger as Christian's hands reached out for his overcoat lapels. Willie putting out his own big mitts. Cornelius suddenly grabbing Willie's fingers and with a swift twist spinning them upside down and bending them back up under his wrists as he rose on his toes with a gasp of agony.

"Now you big lout are you going to leave this lady alone."

"Why you little, hey watch it you're breaking my fingers."

"Shut up."

"Boy if I get loose of you I'll kill you."

"I said shut up. One more word out of you you gorp and I'll snap your wrists like dandelions. Get down on your knees."

"I can't, it's going to bust my fingers."

"Get down, down."

"I'm going, I'm going, for christ's sake you're breaking them, you've broke them."

"Now put your head back. Right back."

"What are you going to do to me, for christ's sakes what did I do to you."

"You entered my presence without permission."

"What are you a jujitsu artist or something."

"I'm just brave and strong. Next time I'll snap your neck, tie your ankles around it in a bow and give you to the sanitation department as a present."

"O k you've got me."

"When I let you go put your hands together and pray. If you get up, I'll break you in two."

Christian releasing Willie's fingers. His hands falling limp at the wrists and trembling. Willie staring down. Then up at Christian glaring back from his wide footed ape style stance. A crowd of onlookers packed in the door. Someone said my fee is ten dollars, is a doctor needed. Glen peeking in over a shoulder and taking a cigar out of his mouth. Manager pushing through.

"Hey what's going on here. Break it up."

Christian moving a silent Mrs Sourpuss away by the elbow. Back between a squeeze of wedding guests. Into the circular bar by the hat check where the waiter took Fanny's coat. Out the side entrance past a cigarette vending machine. Fanny clonked in a coin to buy a pack. In the freezing fresh air I took a ferocious hidden pee on a defenceless piece of shrubbery. And crossed the snowy parking lot. Fanny tugging me into her folds of fur. Glen trotting behind.

"Was that Willie Mrs Sourpuss, was that Willie."

"Yes it was Willie."

"Boy I never thought I'd see the day. You want to come this way, Mr Christian. The snow's been trampled. I'll get that door open for you."

Mrs Sourpuss bending down headfirst into the grey portholed limozine. I had the unholy desire to shove my hand right up through whatever folds of flimsy fancy cloth there might be adorning under her mink. And there arrived take a tasty handful of her vibrant arse. With Glen holding open the door. I step in. Past his audible words, yes sir Mr Christian, yes sir. And that's when you think.

> Happiness
> Is
> A big cat
> With a mouse
> On a square mile
> Of linoleum

7

Standing on the deep maroon pile of Fanny Sourpuss's carpet. Where she lives twelve floors up, the phone constantly ringing, on the east side of town. I hold a tall glass of scotch poured over dancing ice cubes and splashed with bubbling soda. This sprawling apartment of marble tables and icons. Looks down on the grey wind swept slate roof of an embassy, its flag flying in snow and darkness.

Friendly Glen shovelling sticks of chewing gum between his jaws, drove us downtown under the elevated train. Along the cobbled trolley tracked avenue called White Plains. Past drifts piling high against darkened store fronts and up steps and over porches. Cars stalled and buried lining empty white wasteland streets. The big limozine skidded and slid crossing a trestle bridge into Manhattan. Lights of barges on the river and edges of ice along the shore. Mrs Sourpuss's hand came searching for mine under the furry rug. And as we pulled up outside a frozen marquee halfway down the canyon of Park Avenue she said you must come in for a hot drink. A grey uniformed Irish doorman in knee boots led us across the black and white tiled lobby to the elevator.

"By the powerful strengths of himself on high, weren't you lucky to get back safe from your husband's funeral."

"Yes. This is my nephew Mr Peabody."

A pigeon crouches sheltering, fluttering its wings in the snow on the window sill. Just to feel the warm softness here. Stare out at the blizzard. And other yellow lighted windows. The city stopped. I could not desert the bereaved. Lost as we were in the blizzard. Believe me Mr Vine, it was somewhere in the god forsaken Bronx, east of Eastchester. West of Hart's Island. Where prisoners bury the amputated arms and legs and the unclaimed dead. And Clarence I sincerely thought of all the money you were losing.

"How about some cold cuts Cornelius. I got some potato salad. Don't be shy. Make yourself at home."

Christian sitting at the black grand piano. Playing a sad melody. Up and down the smoothest of ivory keys. Staring at a white fluffy ceramic dog. Fanny sweeping in and out in a long green dress with legs. Heard her raised voice speaking to someone and then a door slammed. She came back carrying a platter. Placed it on the coffee table in front of a sofa. Stacks of rye bread, white little tub full of cubes of butter. Bowls of olives, swiss and pimento cheese, potato chips and plates of liverwurst, bologna and salami.

"Come on. Dig in Cornelius. What are you waiting for."

She stands eyes lurking under longer lashes. Notches tighten a chain of silver buckles around her waist. Golden slippers and a black satin bow tying her hair behind her head. She knelt. Stared up at me. Blazing away with her blond skilled beauty. As I bit a bologna and swiss cheese sandwich. Cemented together with mustard. Chewed down with a cascade of olives.

"You hungry boy. You don't mind if I just sit here and watch you."

"No."

"Have you always been fearless."

"Yes."

"How did you get that way."

"I don't know."

"I don't think I've ever met anyone like you before. Just watching you play the piano. So beautifully. So effortlessly. You've got something more than just nerve. I can't understand what you're doing in the funeral business. With your kind of class there are hundreds of better slots for you. Let me ask my lawyer."

"Mrs Sourpuss."

"So formal."

"I am when I talk about my business. Being an undertaker is performing a guardianship. Both for those living and dead. Bringing one closer to people. It's dignified. Might even say it achieves the quality of art. Death also brings a renewing pause in the life of others."

"I'll go along with that."

"It also allows me to meet someone like you. And Mrs Sourpuss believe me when I say, I know the real tears of death and they don't go down the cheeks."

"Christ almighty. Sitting here like this. With an undertaker. Don't get me wrong, I've got nothing against your business. But it really takes the cake. My phone is off the hook. Because every guy I ever knew is ringing me. Want to rush right over. So I can put my head on their shoulders. And there I am. Harry threw his seven. And I'm with the man who buries him."

"I merely assisted. And I hope I'm not imposing."

"Who's imposing. You protected me. A big guy like Willie, that'll humiliate him for the rest of his life. All he had. Just being able to stand up and say I'll kill ya. With his bare hands."

Mrs Sourpuss stabbing an olive. Licking it with the tip of her tongue. Then wrapping her lips around the green and sucking it into her mouth. To chew and wash it down with whiskey and soda. She sits over on her side propped by a hand. The fat oval diamond on her finger glinting blue and flashing white. Raises her foot and kicks the sole of mine with her slipper. Lamp light fanning up on the wall. The gilt framed gold red and blue of icons. Holding up crosses. Heads of saints. Photographs and drawings of the Nevski Cathedral. And my crotch is rotted out of my underwear.

"This is a very pleasant apartment."

"Harry owns an interest in the building. Which according to my lawyer is my interest now. I knocked down a lot of walls his first wife had up. Her taste was for the birds. What lousy taste she had. I got in these two queers. They danced around flinging up the fabrics. Put in those blue and white tiles around the fireplace. I think it looks kind of cute. Those green glass balls

56

hanging there used to hold up real fishing nets. They call it seaport elegant. They said fabric was going on walls these days. These days. Who knows what days. A month later they were telling me spring was coming and nobody who was somebody would want to get caught with the winter walls. So I went along with them. Knocked all the plaster off down to the brick. That lasted the summer. Till it was the New England drift wood look in the autumn. I finally said take every god damn thing off the walls, plaster them and paint them orange.''

"It's very nice.''

"Help yourself to some more whiskey, Cornelius.''

"Thank you. Will you.''

"Yes. Fill her up. I guess I could say I have what most girls want. Anyway I always knew I was made for fancy living. I sure didn't want my mother's life. Ironing in the cellar. Upstairs putting our best table cloth over the table for Sunday dinner. Bored me crazy. Since the age of five I was always trying to escape. I was married and divorced at sixteen. Married again at seventeen. Holding out in a little hole in the wall while Willie was getting his nose broken trying to make a living playing football. We never went out. He wouldn't let me make friends or anybody see me. Then at exactly three boring o'clock one afternoon. I was sitting reading a magazine. I remember everything on that table. A box of fig newtons. A glass of milk. I read if you eat beets you pee pink. This was the biggest thing I had to look forward to. So I had two beets I was trying to peel. And a box of cookies I had just ate. Then I turned this page. There were these bunch of rubes with a god damn motor boat on a tropical island that one guy owned. With his own golf course and seaplane. And these babes drinking mint juleps on the beach. I said fuck this shit I'm getting out of here and going there. In one big god damn hurry. I did. And here I am all my grey hairs later and boy do I like it. At least I'm going to from now on. Soon as I get over all these damn worries. You just don't know when you're safe. Like today. The detectives leave. Willie shows up. They cost a hundred dollars a day. But it's cheap compared to Harry keeping a dozen sluts in about a dozen very expensive hotel suites in about eight states. Right this minute they're all checking out. I called each one personally. With the happy news. That it was the last stop on the gravy train. All get off. Because now I'm the only one getting on. And boy. Let me tell you. But for christ's sake what am I telling you. What would a mere infant like you know. But I guess you do know. The way you're just sitting there listening. Wish I was an orphan like you."

Mrs Sourpuss getting up. Changing the record on her player. Which says spelled out in elegant letters, Stromberg Carlson. Mandolins throbbing. She puts up her arms, wiggling her hips across the floor. Staring at Christian with his mouth in the middle of his latest sandwich. As she put out her left hand she pulled in her right and the left came out like a snake again. Hard to know what to do with a mouthful. Go on chewing. In tune with the music.

"Tell me something Cornelius. I don't know that much about you. You're not by any chance married."

"No."

"Little late anyway to be calling your wife. Who wants to wait on the end of a phone. Live your own life. That's what it's all about. You look for ways to kill an afternoon. Ice skating in Rockefeller Center when every time you look up you know half the people looking down are detectives. Checking on the dolls. Pirouetting on the ice. Cornelius you want to dance."

Christian chewing through a nice garliky bit of salami. The skin of which is wrapped strangling around a couple of my molars. Each window shade with its little knitted ring hanging on a string to put a finger in and pull down. Far away from the west side of town. Across a park by now a mountainous wintry waste of snow. Over here they have money. Flows out of some secret vault down deep somewhere in the bowels of these giant structures. So they can live in the soft of the big. In the ripe of their flesh. If they let you sit down in their glamour you never want to leave. Shy till you get there like starting a new term at school. Autumn. A little boy come with the smell of fresh squeaking books, sniffing the sweetness breaking between the pages. All the empty lines. You'll fill with a newly sharpened pencil. Last year's books thrown away. Another chance. And maybe they won't leave me back again for being dumb.

"Ouch. Whoops. Cornelius. It's all right but I've got an ingrown toe nail on that foot. You can step on the other one if you want."

"Sorry I'm not so good at dancing."

"You're doing fine."

Feel her green hips moving, the bones turning in there. Flesh and cartilage alive under my hand. In this orange inferno. Disappeared out of the world. Where no one knew I was anyway. Warmly tucked up in here. Arms around me. Her breath smelling of apples. Her throat of perfume. Long lashes make her eyes look bigger. All those guys on the telephone. Might be heading over here on their sleighs, balls jingling. Barge in and find me. Up to my neck in bologna, down to my arse in olives. And popping fly buttons. Off my flag pole.

"Cornelius you've got a little bit of everything."

"I beg your pardon."

"You know, make some nice girl a nice husband. You have such etiquette. I took an elocution course. But I think I sound better the way I am which is the way I get whatever I do, especially if I have a few drinks. Do I scare you."

"No."

"Come on, don't tell me all mourners are like me. Dancing after her husband's funeral."

"Well it's not the usual behavior of the bereaved."

"I always knew I was different from the first time I could remember. My parents' neighbors on the street. All they ever thought was what hot shit they were. They were them and I was me. And me. I really knew I was hot shit. I just figured I belonged up there and everybody should know it. But ouch. That's a corn. Hey why don't you say something. You say yes, you say no, you say I'm sorry. But you don't really say anything. Hey you didn't by any chance, I mean I don't want to sound gruesome, but did you embalm Harry. Maybe you shouldn't tell me."

"I'm a front of house man."

"That sounds like you sell tickets to a movie or something."

"I didn't embalm your husband."

"O well I guess it's, you know, you feel somebody's hands did something, and you think what the hell those hands did that and

59

maybe, well I'm ticklish and there are other things you don't want hands to do if they've done something else. Let's have a drink. I mean let's have a party. I want to see some action. For christ's sake let's wreck this joint.''

Mrs Sourpuss picking up an oval piece of glass etched with a swan. Throwing it across the room hitting the wall above the record player and crashing down on the record.

''Come on Cornelius, don't just stand there. For christ's sake can't you see me trying to wreck the joint. Let's wreck it.''

''Mrs Sourpuss, these things are valuable.''

''Sure I sold my ass for them. You're damn right they're valuable. Don't you think my ass is valuable. It's the most valuable god damn ass in New York. My ass is worth millions. Millions.''

''I perfectly agree.''

''You perfectly agree. Now isn't that nice. You've said something. Well I'm glad you do. But now Cornelius I'm going to tell you something, what good is it having an ass worth millions if I've already got millions. The whole point of having an ass worth millions is to sell it for millions. I sold mine for millions. And I've got millions. But I've still got my ass. I guess I could sell it for more millions. That's the answer. More millions. Now come on. Let's wreck this joint. I've been wanting to get these god damn icons out of here for ages. Take that. And that. Right in the eyes I got that son of a bitch bishop. Who the hell does he think he's blessing. Come on. Poke the eyes out of this bastard too.''

''Mrs Sourpuss I would very much like to help you wreck your property. But.''

''Well come on then.''

''If Mr Vine heard that I went home with the bereaved and tore her apartment apart, smashing paintings, wrecking the place, well I don't think he'd like it.''

''If he doesn't like it, I'll buy him out.''

''Mr Vine's a pretty big operation.''

''Not for me he isn't. I could buy him out just like that. Hey what are you trying to do, ruin the party. Where's all that gism you had flipping Willie to his knees.''

60

"I'm tough when it's required Mrs Sourpuss but painfully shy otherwise."

"O k you be painfully shy now while I'm just going to break this fucking god damn French piece of imported eighteenth century gilt shit bureau or something that Harry's first pot bellied sag tit wife paid seventeen thousand dollars for with its crummy inlaid flowers. Just watch me. With this other god damn swan. Now. Carumph."

The glass swan smashing down in the middle of the table. A book, vase and salt cellar bouncing off to the floor. Could be my life time wages. As she stands there wide eyed with joy.

"Well what do you know, it's strong. Try again."

"I think I should be going, Mrs Sourpuss."

"You're not going to leave me."

"I think I better start going home."

"Don't leave me. Don't do that. Please."

"I have to be at work and with the snow I'll have to get up early."

"I don't have anybody. Nobody. I'm just so god damn unhappy. I just never got what I wanted. Before I got too old. O jesus I'm crying. Am I crying. I guess I'm emotional. I didn't want it to get like this. Only up till a month ago I thought I was dying. And every god damn friend I had hoped like hell I was. I swear when I knew that, I swore I wouldn't god damn well die to please them. O jesus I'm crying. Don't leave me. I beg of you, Cornelius don't leave me. I'll do anything if you don't leave me."

"I won't leave."

"Just come here. Come on. The second you walked up to me in the funeral parlor I wanted you. Jesus you said is there anything I can do. I could have anybody. Anybody I want. Are you glad I want you."

"Well yes. I'm glad you feel that way, Mrs Sourpuss."

"Don't you do that don't you do it. Stop. Don't you ever call me Mrs Sourpuss again. I'm Fanny Jackson. Queen of the fucking may. Don't ever ever ever call me Mrs Sourpuss again. Ever."

"All right."

"Kiss me. Kiss me for christ's sake."

Mrs Sourpuss standing up on her sandalled toes. Ingrown with a nail, pained with a corn. Putting arms up around the neck of Christian. Widow and widower. Entwined. Squeaking and buzz from the record player. Her lips a parting soft big peach. Go deep down. Sinking. Little fissures. All the people wait. In the silence of the snow. Till it melts. Then they'll gather up their little pieces of paper and their envelopes. And come out again. Spend their late mornings and afternoons wandering from crapper to water cooler. Across the thousands and thousands of floors. Built up from the ground where I was born. In this city where I walked my frozen way to school. Stood mild and big eyed thinking you could reach out and touch the world and they wouldn't mind. And kids shoved me out of their games. And once. Just once. A man was kind to me. When I walked on small legs with a troubled fearful soul. Dressed the first time in beauty. With my hair combed, face washed wearing a little sailor suit. Standing on a broken piece of sidewalk. This tall man towering came up to me, smiled down and patted me gently and kindly on the head. And a whole new world began. Where I've looked for that smile ever since. Mrs Sourpuss I know what you mean. The heart spills out its diamonds. They lay awhile. Till other greeds come. To take them away. When the years make you hard. And you must pull them back. Tears dry. The precious moments keep. Safe stepping stones through soul poisoned faces. All my forty nine dollars wouldn't buy me a ride on a flea making a landing on your million dollar arse. But dead it could go to Vine. He'd get a feel without charge. Bargains galore. Here. Come this way. Where arses are dead.

"O god Cornelius I like your mouth. You're a baby. My poor baby. I've never had one and you're the kind I've always wanted. You really are. Talk. Go on. Talk. Say Fanny."

"I don't know what to say."

"Fanny, Fanny, god damn it call me Fanny, just once please."

"Fanny."

"Now did that hurt."

"No."

"Sorry about my tears, they dripped all the way down to my chin. Weren't the real tears of death. But of being horny as hell. Christ almighty I need a screw. Your boss Vine lays on everything a mourner needs. That's why you can't go. Because I'll put in a complaint. If you don't take your cock out. Right now."

Fanny hanging herself like a cloth on Christian's chest, her mouth open, teeth glowing and arms languishing. Stepped out of her sandals. A bell clanging. A fire engine down below in the street. She must have been a package guys paid ransoms to unwrap. Cover by cover. Filling her vault with gold.

"Come on you big strong mortician, undertake me."

By
The
Living
Cheeks

8

The morning bright blue with sky. Cold strong wind. Blowing and whistling outside the windows. Fanny's head back on a pillow, her hand stretched out upwards towards the ceiling. Her mouth open wide, snores sucked back in her throat and up her nose. Faintest darkness at the roots of her blond hair.

Fear and chill. A slit of window blows a breeze over a radiator clanking and tingling with heat. Nose and mouth dry. Clarance will be standing on the canary carpet. Like an admiral on the bridge of his ship. Where I swab the decks. Court martialled for being late on watch. Sneak out of here while she's still asleep. Her foot sticking out of the covers. We tore loose last night. Get to work before I'm out of a job.

Christian in a marble pink bathroom pulling on trousers over dangling shirt tails. Flushed my underwear drawers down Mrs Sourpuss's lavatory. They got stuck and the whole bowl filled up. Flooding all over the floor. Which is still wet. Reached in up to my shoulder to push the god damn rag down. Woke up through the night. In this room of mirrors. Once in a cold sweat. Heard the busy tone beeping on her phone under the bed. She said I'd like to keep you around lover boy. Make it worth your while. You've got such a marvelous twitching cock. Which was still in her while I fell asleep. And woke. As she lay there in my dream as a cold cadaver. A Vine assistant handing me a lubricant from the big shelf of chemicals. Said use this Mr Christian, we find it helps. And her teeth were dry and tongue was dead. Hanging out the side of her mouth. A pair of cold arms clanking round my

64

neck. Till more noise of fire engines passed. Then she turned into Helen. And I lay clutching myself.

Close each door quietly. Tip toe along this hall. Hear someone down at the other end. In there the orange living room. She battered around. Nip out into this lobby. Table mirror and vase of plastic flowers. Little white pearl button to push. Hear the elevator coming. What makes one want to run away so fast. From the horror of life. Back to the business of death. Which I may catch from cold on the way.

"Good morning to you now Mr Peabody. The city has never had the likes of such a snow storm. Did you see the fire last night. Just around the corner. Two alarms raging it was. Two people trapped seven firemen injured. You're not going out in the likes of that."

"Yes."

"You won't get two blocks. Without boots and an overcoat."

"I like the fresh air."

"You must be then an enthusiast."

Christian leaping from track to track made along the snowy sidewalks. Running outright along the cleared stretches. And leaping the drifts at street corners. Heading downtown in a hurry. Past all the peeing dogs held by doormen out of rich Park Avenue entrances. Forty five minutes late. Both shoelaces undone. Hands too stiff and cold to tie them. Let Vine do the talking. Get him on the subject of his life which he loves to hear. My shoes will be sopping wet. My prick and balls frosted. And miserable countenance frozen.

Vine standing legs astride dead center of the lobby. His favourite spot. Arms folded behind his back. One eye squinting. His lips twisting his mouth back and forth. As I come at speed through the swing front double doors, pushing both open at once.

"Where the hell have you been. Look at the time."

"Mr Vine. I guess it's the blizzard. I'm just not used to them."

"That's no reason to be running around like that. Get into my office. Before anyone sees you."

Vine's hair standing up straighter than usual. Miss Musk looking out her office door. Tried to give her a little wave. To get a little friendship back. But my arm is paralysed with cold. Paper

65

cup and carton of hot coffee on Vine's desk. The rolls of architects' drawings on the floor.

"O k you weren't on the ball yesterday and you're not on the god damn ball today. What the hell do you think this is here, some kind of rodeo. Why didn't you get back yesterday."

"The bereaved, Mr Vine, was in terror. She was frightened of her life."

"She was fine when she left here. She was even reading a god damn magazine."

"Well things got worse at the cemetery."

"Charlie said everything went according to plan and you went off with Mrs Sourpuss."

"She asked me to. She was distressed."

"Christian when the corpse is interred and you leave the gate of the cemetery your duty to the bereaved is over. And what the hell do you mean coming in here with your shoelaces undone, no overcoat, and god damn it, now two buttons missing. I take umbrage."

"All right Mr Vine, I don't blame you, take some umbrage."

"You don't blame me. Take umbrage. You bet I'll take umbrage. The way you've come crashing in here this morning in that state. Could lose me a generation of customers. Why didn't you get back here last night. I told you in a blizzard the suicides get high, didn't you know that."

"Yes."

"Well what the hell were you doing then."

"Please don't shout Mr Vine. I know I'm late. I know I'm a little dishevelled. I know you've got a lot of suicides on your hands. But I'm just a victim too."

"Now cut that out. What do you take me for. Get on the ball. What do you want to do, end up pushing a hot dog stand. Plenty of room right at the end of this block if you want to be down and out in the gutter. But it breaks my heart to see someone like you go to waste. I gave you a chance here. Put you out front with a bit of responsibility. And what the hell do you do."

"Mr Vine, please, don't relieve me of my duties."

"Give me one reason why not."

"I saved the life of the bereaved. From an attacker."

"Charlie never said a thing about an attacker."

"It happened after."

"What do you mean after."

"After the cemetery. There was a confrontation."

"How. You were in her car."

"Well there just was, I mean I guess he could have attacked out in the snow. But he attacked inside."

"The car."

"No."

"Where."

"A building."

"Now cut out the bilge Christian, I want the facts and I want them now. Or I dispense with your services."

"O christ Mr Vine, I was in some kind of a roadhouse I guess."

"A roadhouse."

"Mr Vine, please, your saying the word like that makes me nervous. Well maybe it wasn't a roadhouse. The architecture was very late Georgian."

"In two seconds Christian I'm going to call up Mrs Sourpuss."

"Please, that's not necessary. I'll give you every fact. When the husband jumped us."

"The husband, Christian, if you remember at all, was in his casket."

"It was her second husband, the one before this dead one."

"You mean the deceased."

"Yes, well Mrs Sourpuss was getting in a terrible state over the death."

"Hogwash."

"I mean it Mr Vine it really hit her in the haggis. She begged me to get her a bottle of whiskey. She had a few drinks. I assisted her going up the steps. I preserved her dignity. You can ask Charlie. There was no tripping or anything like that. But she said whatever you do don't leave me alone. Mr Vine as you know I'm new at this. I wanted to do my best. I thought I was to use my own judgement."

"Not to end up in a roadhouse you weren't. Mr Sourpuss was a multimillionaire. Newspaper reporters might have been there.

Could ruin me. A member of my staff in a roadhouse with the next of kin of the deceased. God damn ruin me.''

''Don't get upset Mr. Vine.''

''Upset. Standing out there waiting for you. Sending a car last night to where you live and your landlady spitting in the driver's face. At the mention of your name. Don't get upset.''

''O k, all right. Fire me. I'll pay for Helen's funeral somehow. I'll shovel snow. But I'll tell you one thing, Mr Vine, you'll get every single penny I owe you. I ran all the way here. Coatless through the freezing cold just to get to work as soon as I could.''

''Sit down Christian, sit down. Now listen to me. I've got to rely on people. I'll lean over backwards to give you a break. Because you're one of the most quality people I've ever met. But look at the way you're dressed this morning. You've let me down. Twice.''

Somber glistening eyes of Vine. See the world out beyond. His kingdom. Stands in his vestibule waiting. One by one they become his citizens. Into his hands commit their flesh. Each anointed by his sadness. Each by green and candle light laid softly in satin. His loneliness invites you. Come. Take your rest.

''Cornelius I go home at night. Sit at my kitchen table. It's cracked and chipped, made of porcelain. A container of milk sits there. And a piece of crumb cake. Sometimes my daughter comes in from doing her homework. I think over the day's happenings. She might stand next to my shoulder. Feel her hair on my cheek. Just like her mother's used to be. When she cooked, and I came up to kiss her, a smudge of flour on her nose. That woman was all of my life. The tears of her death run dripping inside me every day. She made pie crusts on that table. And just to have my hand there touching where I knew hers had been. I loved that woman I loved her.''

Vine's eyes brimming with tears. He turns his bent head away. Leans over the edge of his desk. His fingers spread. Each gleaming nail with its moon tip of white. Soft cloth of his suit stretched across his back. Whine and whirr of a snow plow passing in the street. A strain of music.

''I'm sorry Christian. It just gets me that's all. I don't know what to do with you. If I ask you any more questions I know the answers are going to get worse. I'd like us to be friends. Not only because we've both lost our dearest one and we have a bond in that but because I see a vision of greatness in you. This business I've got to run. It's my life. Up at six every morning. I drive by each premises. Just to see if there's been a fire or something. I'm not finished till late at night. And then see that bag, my lunch is in that. Sandwiches I make before I go to bed. I earned my first pennies when I buried a friend's pet bird. Charged him seven cents. Even offered him a choice of cigar or shoe box. He picked the cheaper shoe box. I painted it black and dyed cotton wool with some of my mother's bluing. It's the only thing I ever wanted to do."

"Mr Vine could I trouble you for a little coffee."

"Sure you can. There's plenty. And we'll send out if you need more."

"Thank you. Thank you very much."

"You're welcome Christian."

Vine picking up the ringing phone. Cushioning it to his ear with his shoulder. Holding a pad on his desk with one hand and writing with the other. The little quiet murmurs of his voice. And Miss Musk at the door. Same brown dress, her hair swept up on the back of her head. Giving me a weak sour smile. Nobody likes me much this morning. Lose this job and ask Mrs Sourpuss for a loan. She stuck her tongue nearly down my throat. Friendlier than a bank would be.

Vine replacing phone. Writes another few words on his pad. Miss Musk leaning forward, her hand caught around the door jamb. Her ears are small. The muscles flex in her calves. She stands in her patent leather high heels and walks pigeon toed. As a kid I thought it was the very latest way to run. Till I fell on my face.

"Mr Vine sorry to interrupt you and Mr Christian but the west side branch is sold out."

"You mean fully reserved Miss Musk."

"Yes I guess I do mean that. They want to know if we can take two more, with no facial problems, starting seven this evening."

"Christian are you free tonight."

"Yes sir, I am. Absolutely."

"O k take them Miss Musk. The Mario funeral will leave at two thirty. It could be bad out in South Queens. I'll have to get over to the west side myself."

"Very good Mr Vine. I'll catch a bite to eat around five or if Mr Christian would prefer I could bring something in for both of us."

"That o k with you Christian. There won't be time for lunch."

"Yes sir."

"Miss Musk take Cornelius, see what you can do about his shoes. Those pants could be pressed too."

"Certainly Mr Vine. Would you come this way, Mr Christian."

"And Cornelius. Stay on the ball."

"Yes sir, Mr Vine."

Christian following Miss Musk as she beckons him out. Downing the coffee. Following her past her office. And the chapel. Woman stands in the entrance handkerchief to her face. Eyes and nose red. Black veil over her black hair. Man behind her with his hand on her shoulder. Gang of children in the chapel seats. Three nuns kneeling in the last pew. Two more mourning faces pass by, eyes fearful and staring. We go this way. That door again to the cadavers. And the fire fighting equipment. How do I say to Miss Musk don't take me back in there. But we go to a different door.

"This way Mr Christian, you've been here before."

"No."

"Are you all right."

"Yes. I'm fine."

"This is the store room where supplies are kept. The laying out room is attached to the embalming room through a corridor there. Mr Vine likes to keep this door locked at all times. Mourners walk out with anything that isn't chained down. They unscrewed all the imported antique crystal door knobs we had. Do you have any preference in the fabric of your socks."

"Wool if possible."

"We have silk too if that might be your preference."

"No, wool's swell."

70

Miss Musk's dress rising on the backs of her muscular legs as she bends over a large drawer. Pulled out from under a shelf with compartments across the wall. Two open caskets stand on trestles, one lined in purple the other in crimson. Shoes, shirts, suits. Whole place like a naval store room. If there's silk around ask Miss Musk for a pair of undershorts. What a time to get another hard on. Unrestrained by an undergarment. She's bound to see it.

"These should fit. What size shoe are you."

"O nine. But I'm a double A in width."

Miss Musk holding a dark pair of shoes. Rather pointed in the toes. With a sprinkling of those natty little holes. The kind guys wear on the executive ladder to step on the fingers below. Just bend over slightly. Must never point. An organ. Or she might take it like an insult. When I only mean it as a joy.

"Sit down Mr Christian."

"Sure."

"Take off your shoes. And give me your coat. See if I can match the buttons."

Christian taking off his shoes. Musk looking for buttons. Put the socks away back in my pocket. Where they make a nice cold wet impression on the thigh. If you get up one strange female. The organ wants to get up another. Globes of her arse. Mouth watering rotundities. Hear hammers banging. And something being sawn. Vine has turned undertaking into heavy industry.

"How do the shoes fit."

"Fine."

"Here. The buttons aren't exact but you can't really notice."

"Take off your pants."

"I beg your pardon."

"Don't you want them pressed."

"I think they're all right."

"Mr Vine likes everyone to have a sharp crease."

"But this is tweed. Bagginess is de rigueur."

"I don't know what this rigor is but Mr Vine still likes a crease. It'll only take me a minute."

"Miss Musk all I've got is my shirt tails. I was in such a rush this morning to get to work I forgot a lower undergarment."

71

"I don't mind. I'm open minded. As naturally you'd expect I would be."

Christian stands unbuttoning his trousers. Miss Musk turning away. Clearing her throat as she pushed back drawers and stacked back shoes. Cornelius's shirt tail draped over his projecting organ. As Miss Musk reaches for the trousers held out to her. Stares me right in the eye. Her skin has peach fuzz. My stiff and naked prick has none.

"Miss Musk I want to thank you very much for doing all this."

"You're welcome."

"I guess you really enjoy your work."

"Yes I do. It's so interesting. And such a privilege to work for such a great man like Mr Vine."

Miss Musk unfolding an ironing board from the wall. Plugs an electric cord into the two little socket holes. Lays and smoothes out a trouser leg. Takes off her gold bracelet. Sprinkles water on a cloth from a bottle.

"What did you do before you became an undertakeress."

"I tried to be a model. But I guess I wasn't good looking enough. They said I had the figure but not the face. Then I went back to graduate from high school."

"I think you're very good looking."

"Well thank you."

"Are you athletic."

"Yes very. My best subjects were civics and physical education. I was head of the cheer leading squad and then drum majorette. I won the Bronx twirling championship and the trophy awarded annually by Mr Vine."

"Really."

"And he offered me a job. I've never regretted it. All the important people you meet. In suite three, the deceased was killed by his wife hitting him with a plank. It was all over the papers she only weighed ninety eight pounds and her husband was two hundred. Wonderful how she did it. And in suite two next to the chapel it's the boy who was murdered by this gang. He was from a good family and home. The gang just stabbed him to death. All over the face and body. Twenty two stab wounds. Mr Vine prepared him. I'll show you, he looks marvelous. You just couldn't tell where the knife went in. Just let your pants dry a minute.''

Miss Musk hanging Christian's trousers over a casket trestle. Slips her bracelet back on. Turns to face me. I sit my shirt tail poked up. Just like her nose. Her shoulders slightly heaving. As she walks past and locks the other door behind us.

''I wouldn't like any one to walk in Mr Christian while you're like that. So easy for someone to get the wrong idea. If they came in. With all the going and coming today we've got.''

''Miss Musk can I ask you a question.''

''O sure.''

''I hope you won't be offended.''

''O I won't be offended.''

''Would you hug me.''

''What are you asking. I mean I'm not offended but I don't know whether I could answer a question like that.''

''You mean no, you won't hug me.''

''It's during working hours. And it's kind of fresh. Besides I hardly even know you.''

''It would help you get to know me.''

''Well I don't get sexually excited at the drop of a hat.''

''I was only asking for a friendly touching gesture.''

''You're a fast operator. How do you know I do that kind of thing.''

''What thing.''

''Hugging.''

''Do you.''

''Well I think that's my business.''

''Just an endearment, a dalliance while my trousers are drying.''

''I don't think you should get so familiar, undressed like that Mr Christian. I know sometimes girls are forward but I'm not that kind of girl, even though I'm very broad minded. But I'm not offended.''

''Then don't stand so far away.''

''Well I've got to, lordy sakes. I have responsibilities.''

''I admire your fingers. They're so delicately tapered. The soft

73

peach fuzz. You have on your arms and your face haven't you. Please, may I. Just rub it. Please.''

"Just ordinary little hairs that's all."

"Please. Come closer."

"You haven't even dated me."

"I'd like to. Come on. Just a touch."

"I'm engaged to be married."

"Is he an undertaker."

"No he's a salesman. And maybe I think you've got your nerve. You didn't seem like that kind of person at all."

"Miss Musk, I'm an orphan. And just a pampering enfolding caress, sinless and pure often rids me of the awful glooms I sometimes feel."

"Well gee I'm sorry you're an orphan but everybody feels that way once in a while, lordy sakes. People just don't get right away what they want. I'm just surprised. I wouldn't expect that from you being cultured the way you are and coming back from Europe. Such a lousy trick too, to pull on your wife. She was one of the most beautiful deceased we've ever had. Sorry. But that's how I feel. Here maybe you should get your pants back on."

"This city is against me."

"No it's not at all. Not if you give of your best. And please don't feel I don't appreciate what you've said to me. I would like it if we got to know each other better. Mr Vine said you were very smart. And that you would go a long way and get right up to the top."

"And jump off."

"That's cynical."

"What's your first name, Miss Musk."

"Elaine. My friends call me Peaches."

"Ah Peaches would that you give me a chuck under the chin at least."

"Can we have an understanding. I would like you to get over your wife's death first. And then."

"And then."

"Well then. I don't know. But lordy the time. I've got to get back to work.''

Trousers creased I watched streams of school children enter

Vine's Funeral Parlor. Miss Musk organising them in relays throughout the afternoon. The little attention buzzers ringing. Folk standing in the lobby smoking cigarettes. A squeak in the rest room door as it opened and closed. Miss Musk found me a can and I oiled the hinges. She smiled at me. Made my pecker go up again. Then two little boys approached.

"Mister are you the undertaker."

"Yes."

"Well we brought our own plant here and we wanted to put it by the casket of our friend who died in there but they wouldn't let us. Could you put it somewhere for us. Everywhere they got all those roses. Guess our plant doesn't look so hot. But we don't have any money for flowers."

"O k kids. Follow me."

Christian entering the suite. Dead boy with his hands folded one across the other. Entwined with rosary beads. Faintest pink marks on his face. Where the knife went in. The white casket top open under a bower of fern. Red vigil lights burning. A pillow of flowers. A small blond head and wavy hair. Christian taking the plant from its wrapping and placing it center of the green draped altar.

"There you are kids."

"Thanks a lot mister. He was our best friend. We don't hold no grudge against the killers. Now that he's dead. What good would it do. But we want the police to catch them. And give them their just desserts."

Darkness falling. Vine leaving his office. Carrying away his rolls of drawings. Miss Musk holding open the front swing doors for him. I checked the temperatures and ushered people to their suites. Took coats and hung them in the little cloak room. Couple of people gave me a quarter. Read the newspaper on a long visit to the crapper. Where I thought the thoughts of all my dreams. When I would come to this new world. And skim over the highways singing, arms out in a cross in the sun. A land sprinkled with money. Cry out for joy stuffing it in my pockets. And climb into the sky rich and strong. Instead of sitting here. Leaky arsed forlorn. Staring down on the black and white tiles. In this steel grey walled cubicle. So hoping Miss Musk would get down on her

75

knees and take it in the mouth. But everybody wants to blow their own horn instead of yours. No matter how much your melody is laughter sweet.

Passing cars crackling the ice as people dwindled away out into the cold night. Taking their sadnesses home to sleep. Sat starving till ten o'clock when Miss Musk came back with food. In a big brown paper bag. I waited tilted back on a chair against the wall. Folded hands in my lap. Licking my lips as she took out the neat white little packages. Set them down in their wax paper wrapping. Rolls with slabs of virginia ham and caraway seeds. A container of hot coffee and cinnamon buns. Two pickles and cardboard trays of potato salad.

"I hope it's o k what I got. Well what a day. So cold out. It's zero. There shouldn't be any more mourners this late. I've locked the front. Now how do you like that, there's the emergency bell. I'll go. Help yourself."

Something strange. Makes you get up. Just as you enjoy a mouthful and it gets lumped in your throat as it squeezes down. Just take a look. Two policemen entering. Politely taking off their caps, standing asking something. Miss Musk points this way. Move my balls to the left side of my trouser leg. I need to pee. All three turning to look at me. What in god's name have I done now. Besides make a carnal suggestion of hugging. Just beginning to feel at home here. Genuinely liking the hushed whispers, the odd little wail. The sorrow, the peace and quiet. The blue uniforms approach.

"You're Cornelius Christian."

"Yes."

"We're police officers. Don't do anything foolish now and put your hands up."

"I beg your pardon."

"We're arresting you under suspicion of murder. Frisk him Joe."

Christian slowly raising his arms. Miss Musk open mouthed backing away. Officer behind Christian patting him up and down. And over the pockets. From one of which he pulls my still wet lump of socks. A mourner coming out of a suite, her bent head straightens and her handkerchief drops from her face.

Takes only a casual incident to knock sorrow for a loop. When you become a prisoner. Other people become free. And look at you.

> And
> Murmur
> Golly
> Winikins

9

Squad car siren roaring through the icy streets. Pulls up outside
a red brick police station. On the west side of town. Up the stone
steps between the twin globes of light. Inside desks and shirt
sleeved policemen. And through a very brown door. The bars of
cells.

Christian sitting on a plank. With a blanket and a pillow.
Across from a man lying his hands folded behind his head
quietly murmuring mother fucker and staring at the ceiling. Joe,
a policeman pounding a type writer, shook his head and offered
me a cigarette as I sat by his desk answering questions. Said
what does a presentable decent looking guy like you want to go
and shoot someone for.

And just before midnight. On my second day of work. In
prison accused of murder. Said my fingerprints were all over the
joint. I said what joint. You know fella what joint. An elegant
guy like you killing people with such a cheap gun. Sit with the
nightmare storming through one's head. Mrs Sourpuss's soft
pliant body riddled with bullets. Doorman saw me coming and
leaving. She looked alive and snoring when I left. They ask why
did you do it. And I wish I were Mr Peabody instead of me.

A loud voice outside coming along the corridor. Familiar
drawling quiet words of power. Keys opening up the cell. Mr
Vine stepping in.

Cornelius standing. At absolute attention, hands straight
down at my sides. Clarance Vine with a black satin collared

overcoat. A white silk scarf flowing from his neck. Black gloves folded in his hands, his cheeks red and eyes watering.

"Christian. When are you going to get on the ball."

"I'm innocent."

"Take it easy."

"I didn't kill Mrs Sourpuss I swear it. She was asleep when I left."

"What do you mean, Mrs Sourpuss she was asleep."

"She was. There wasn't a thing wrong with her."

"Now wait a minute Christian, let's get this straight."

"I only know her foot was sticking out from under the covers."

"I see. Sticking out. From under the covers. Well that's nice. And where were you."

"I was standing right there. I mean I went to the bathroom to get dressed so I wouldn't wake her up."

"I see. A true bedroom gentleman. Well that's very interesting Christian."

"I heard someone at the end of this long hall as I was leaving. It could have been Willie looking for revenge."

"Well I hope I'll get my revenge for being woke up after I just got to sleep. I don't know Willie but lucky for you I know the captain of this precinct. Otherwise you'd be spending the night here."

"They're going to let me go."

"That's what the sergeant says."

"Why, have they found the killer."

"They caught him twenty minutes ago in Brooklyn."

"Wow thank god. Who did it."

"Her nephew. They're still getting the confession. And by the way Christian, the victim was a Mrs Grotz."

Wednesday morning and for every morning of that week I was nineteen minutes early for work. Would have been twenty but I spent a minute's silence rejoicing outside Mrs Grotz's door. This town might yet be fit for the pure of spirit. Clarance Vine took me to a diner after my arrest and bought me two hot chocolates and two pieces of lemon meringue pie. Also gave me a little lecture on loose living and electrocution. And as I left the taxi he said Christian maybe they should have booked you on another charge. Lady killer.

Lay in bed that night hands cupped upon my organs of regeneration. Thinking of the electric chair. Which Vine said is not nice to watch nor smell in use. But no shortage of folk on the train to Sing Sing who slip in for the show. Photographs of previous clients up on the wall. Some of them nice looking guys. Just like you would have been Christian if you'd got the hot seat. They slam in the volts. A nice and generous serving at first. Supposed to blot you out instantly. Then five hundred volts every half minute for two minutes afterwards. To get rid of your twitches. If that doesn't work they cut you up in an autopsy to see why. One guy walked away alive twice. Hadn't drunk enough water recently to conduct the electricity. Which heats up the spinal canal. And your heart's hot when they cut it out. Also nice and soft at first but it then shrinks, the blood goes dark and the heart gets hard. Not nice if people still have feelings after death.

Miss Musk clapped her hands silently upon my return. Rising on her toes in a navy blue dress. Said lordy sakes Mr Vine wouldn't believe me when I said you'd been arrested. And she brought me the daintiest of delicacies for our little snacks we shared on her desk. As well as her pictures in the newspaper when she was twirling champ. In boots and thighs and a flimsy satin skirt. Said she liked my tailoring I got from Brooks Brothers. Where the gentleman haberdasher remarked confidentially that I was one of those rare customers whose body was just made for their suits.

And Saturday afternoon. I sat alone after four times counting my week's pay. Browsing through the Social Register. Not even one Christian mentioned amid all the awesome privileged names. Among which I would love to be deeply embedded. Born in Brooklyn, raised in the Bronx and elevated to a listing. With an address of a yacht anchored off the Bahamas. And a string of clubs designated after my name. The morning mailman wobble kneed with a bag full of invitations. To play real tennis and dine later with the titans of industry. Warmly smiled upon by their loose living face lifted ice skating wives.

And the phone rang. Said please may I speak to Mr Christian.

I said speaking. She said I just thought I'd call you, it's Fanny here, how have you been.

"I was in prison for murder."

"Already."

"I didn't do it."

"Well come over here and see me why don't you Monday about eight."

Sunday washing all my socks, shirts and underwear, hanging them drying on a string strung across the cold room. The tenants of the house shouting out their doors. Complaining of no heat. And Monday I had a full day. First in the crimson lined casket and then in the purple. Vine shouting everytime I smiled, to be dead serious Christian or it ruins the picture. Amazingly comfortable lying head back on a soft pillow. Miss Musk powdering my face and pressing my hair in position with her fingers. The photographer behind his box and under his black cloth, squeezing his little bulb saying steady now, here we go, that's it.

Vine paid me an extra ten dollars for posing. Said I really had the knack when it came to looking like a corpse. I said thanks a bunch. And Miss Musk helped me dismount and gave me a reassuring squeeze of the hand. Her boy friend took her to Radio Center Music Hall and night club dancing afterwards. I stood sneaking a look out between Vine's curtain as her swain opened the car door for her. Can tell by the roadster he drives and the kind of natty hat he wears that he can't take punches in the belly. Which I'd like to give him free of charge.

And on a former afternoon. Taking a breather from a rich Italian mother whose fat son was killed in a car crash. And who after seated convulsions of sobbing would rush to rain kisses down upon him in his casket, smearing the cosmetic work all over his face. Miss Musk finally took her to the private rest room. While I read the afternoon newspaper in her office. And thought of Fanny's gem like belly button. Foot up on a chair, elbow on my knee and chin cupped in the palm of my hand. Took a feel of the tiny silver tits on Miss Musk's drum majorette trophy engraved with Donated by the Vine Funeral Parlor. And foot steps came in. And I said how are you doing, Peaches, how about that hug. In the lengthening silence I looked up.

"O I'm sorry Mr Vine, I thought it was Miss Musk."

"Christian, you do make it tough for me at times. You know that."

"Yes Mr Vine."

"And with the door open here and you standing there like you were at the race track."

"Sorry."

Vine also said with the air warmer and the snow melting, pneumonia and the flu would be getting them these days. And water dripped down the brownstone steps of Grotz's. Who had a whole gang of distant relatives sizing up the premises. I looked out the door right over the head of the hunched backed lawyer who came collecting the rent. And one long eared swarthy lout suggested I give him my key so he could look around my room at his leisure. I quietly said out a crack in the door in my cultured accent. Get the hell out of here. Before I come out there. And hand you sliced to the seagulls. After I blast your god damn head off. And shove a fire hydrant up your arse. And turn it on. So you get a jumbo enema.

Monday was the bluest day above. A balmy air rolling down the street. Felt it on the back of my ears as I headed for the park. To trot and walk to work. Save bus fare. And get into shape to carry out the threats I make. For the sake of instant justice. Went by the lake. Tossed a couple of stones at the ducks. Cantered up a rocky hill and across the open space they call The Green. Which is white with grass and brown with mud and never green. Walked down the back steps of the zoo past the bears. The seals through the water crashing up and down and churning back and forth. The camel peeing. The zebra with a hard on. And kids' colored balloons caught up in the trees. As I headed out onto Fifth Avenue. Jauntily strolling. Nearly said a cheerful how do to people. A sure sign you're out on an airing from the institution. And as a matron took umbrage at my passing gaiety. I whispered. What kind of soulless additives are you using to preserve you, madam.

Christian loping down past Fifty Sixth and Seventh Streets. Traffic thick. Gleaming richery exploding out of the ground. Curtained glass and radiant jewels. Placed softly ready for females. Who ease out of their limozines. Choose diamonds in the mornings. And sit under the face packs in the afternoons. Men with hairy wrists fussing a lock of blond dyed hair into a curl against Florida tanned skin. Massive windowed monuments ascending into the sky. Where pale pigeons unleash trifling indignities splattering on balconies and window sills. The glamour clean within. Where someday in glory I'll hide myself away a mystery with all my riches. With room to fart and sneeze in peace.

Miss Musk wearing clinging pink this morning. A well known publicity agent in the theatre industry reposing. With my best possible face and demeanor I waited at the door of the suite. Any second I could be discovered. And instead of imprisoned, cast in a movie. A role of swashbuckling ball clanging romance. With a huge salary dumped on me weekly with a wheel barrow. And a very chesty nipple conspicuous Miss Musk waltzed back and forth on the canary carpet. Arse wagging like a flag in a hurricane. Flying from the pole I had which·made me have to sit down. But no one came to see the deceased with his kinky grey hair except a rabbi in robes and an ancient thin wife hobbling with a cane and helped by the janitor of their building. But the bier was stacked with wreaths. From Jimmy and the band. From Tally on tour. From Zeke The Human Zeppelin. From Perth Amboy.

I helped Miss Musk prepare the casket. With a bower of lilies of the valley. At seven p.m. we were alone with this show biz departed. And his sunken eye sockets. And large round nose. Miss Musk kneeling, still trying to be discovered, making a list of names she thought might be famous. I put my hand on her shoulder. She turned, looked up and smiled. Teeth sparkling for stardom. And I don't know what made me do it. Except my enfeebled sense of humour. To anoint Miss Musk for fame. And reach and take the hand of the deceased with one big diamond ring on a finger. Lift it stiffly over, put it where mine was. On Miss Musk's back. Silently tip toe away. Leave them together. To make publicity.

Christian taking a paper cup from the glass cylinder. Pressing a foot on the pedal of the brand new water cooler recessed with terra cotta tiles in the lobby wall. Just as Clarance Vine enters, his coat open, a small black briefcase in his hand.

"How's it going Cornelius. Did the O'Shawnessy reposing get

a crowd. He was prominently connected with the dramatic arts.''

"No Mr Vine."

"Gee that'll be tough on the wife. She said he had a lot of friends. Boy I'm tired Cornelius. Sons of bitches are threatening a strike. And nearly every employee of this city is up there on the building site with his hand out. Feel like giving them beads they gave for this place in the first place.''

A long blood curdling scream coming from the O'Shawnessy suite. Vine's eyebrows converge. Like two battleships in collision at sea. And the hairs go up on the back of my neck. And a bowel or two trembles.

"What the hell is that Christian.''

"I don't know.''

Vine dropping his briefcase on the hall table. Christian following him along the corridor and into the green darkness of the Isidore O'Shawnessy suite. Miss Musk on her back on the floor. Absolutely spread eagled. Her mouth open. Pink dress half way up her muscular thighs. Stockings pinched and pulled tight with a bright red garter belt. The deceased's arm hanging out over the side of the casket. Fingers dipping into the tips of the lilies of the valley.

> Fuming up
> Their fragrance
> When all
> We need
> Is smelling
> Salts

10

With a snap decision in an emotional atmosphere, Cornelius Christian departed the Vine Funeral Parlor in a hurry. Skidaddling crosstown. Popping up out of the shadows to take a nervous pee in an hotel. Through bronze revolving doors bowered with curved panels of gleaming glass. Four East Fifty Fifth Street. One big grey block of stone piled on another.

"The male retiring room is down the stairs and just along and to your right, sir."

There's a chap as what has an idea as how to address a seemly gentleman. At low moments the best I can do is make believe I'm a tenderfoot executive. And when someone stands aside to point the way. O merciful god what a splendid relief. I don't have to slug them. Practiced sitting behind Miss Musk's desk. Build myself an empire of bargain priced self service funeral parlors. With attached crematoriums generating electricity. Volts and amps of grief. Juice from burning hearts. And Charlie came in, said Cornelius, you look good sitting there.

Cross over and turn right up Fifth Avenue. Past this brown stone church. Faint organ music inside. Wrote to reinstate myself at the Game Club. As each day now I get richer. Dollar by dollar. Be able to show those posturing international celebrities a thing or two who think they're such hot shit hanging around that hotel lobby.

Fifty Seventh Street and Fifth. The bull's eye of wealth in this town. Makes me so nervous I need to take another pee. Wait for the red light to change. Look down into a refuse basket. A book thrown away. How To Make Profitable Judgements In A Time of Continuing Economic Stress. Instead of, I guess, Bewildered Decisions In Times of Mercantile Terror.

"O what a sweet little sight. Sir can I take your little daughter's picture."

Man with a camera stopping another man with a small girl. As she stands with a flowered umbrella and raincoat. Just as it begins to rain. All delighted with smiles as the flash bulb pops. And people turn to look. A tiny moment like that. And the world knows you're there. Sallying forth. Suddenly noticed. A second's pleasant recognition. To coax you through hours of gloom.

Christian walking round the splashing lamp lit fountain under the branches of the cottonball trees. Step between rows of purring limozines. Go up these crimson carpeted steps by people descending to opening car doors. Drenched in finery. Their money more beautiful than beauty. And Vine said to me, Christian do you know what's eating this city. Besides envy and graft. The cockroach.

In the small mirrored men's room. Unleashed another pee. Down into the gurgling porcelain. Tipped the man a dime. Who turned a faucet to fill a basin and laid out a little towel for me. And some god damn son of a bitch came in and gave him a quarter. For doing nothing. Except maybe counting the drops he was shaking off his prick. Which all added up, made him a big shot. One of those chaps so dressed and so postured that to bring his conceit to its fullest fulfillment only required a resounding slap across his meaty long sideburned jowls. Quake some humility into him.

Christian striding by this elegant enclosure where musicians play. In behind the palms. Beyond the marble pillars. A clutch of loud mouthed women waiting to get inside. Sun scalded skin gaudy with gold and diamonds. And ripe for thieves. To descend and grab the gems from their puffy polished bodies. Enter this other lobby. Past the counter of newspapers, books, candy, magazines and chewing gum. Doors of elevators opening and closing. Telephone ringing on the manager's desk. Dressed just the way Clarance dresses. And saying yes with an understanding face. As someone touches me. O so gently on a shoulder. Just as I put the dead hand on Miss Musk. And I turn to see this face. Radiant beneath straw colored hair.

"Pardon me but you aren't Cornelius Christian. O you are. I just couldn't believe it was you. You remember me. Charlotte Graves. I followed you all the way from Fifty Seventh Street where the man took the picture of the little girl. I only got up just enough nerve to ask you."

"I'm glad you did."

"You look so fine. And gosh distinguished. I'm so thrilled to see you. It must be something like five or gosh seven years. When did you get back."

"Last month."

"Your accent. I think it's beautiful. What are you doing. Are you staying."

"I have a job."

"It must be something important."

"I'm an executive ostiary."

"I don't know what that is but it really sounds something."

"It's not too bad."

"O gosh. I'm just still nothing. Didn't even go to college. It's so good to see you. You're even married now I hear."

"My wife died."

"O gosh I'm sorry."

"I'm all over it now. I'd like to see you sometime. Where do you live."

"I still live in the Bronx. Same old place. I was walking from Lexington Avenue window shopping. I was just on my way to meet a girl friend. We're going to a show."

"Can I call you."

"I'd love you to. I better go. I'm late and I've got the tickets. Gosh I'm glad I got up my nerve. Even waited till you came out of the men's room. I just kept thinking it couldn't be. Then I thought it is, it is. You've got so mature looking. Anyway that's enough flattery. My number is still in the telephone book. Goodbye. Please call me."

Go east now and north. After nearly lying to the first girl who ever loved me. Cut through the tip of the park. Where the evening marauders are lurking. Swiftly to get you in headlocks or at knifepoint across the throat. If they don't smash you first to the ground from behind. Look back. The lights glow where I met her in the lobby. The big buildings fight away the little buildings. They grow up high and put out their towering chests of windows and say down at the little dirty roofs below. Get the hell out of here. Before my shadows snuff you out. And a sign posted to this tree.

Diabetic dog lost needs medication. Desperate. Please phone Butterfield 8297. Answers to the name of Julia.

Up Park Avenue. Where that pinnacled building stands down at the end of the canyon. Till a taller one comes one day to tell it to go away. Charlotte Graves. All her smiles she gave me years ago. As I thrilled her coming to her house for a date. Because no boy had ever asked her out before. And I had three girl friends already. All pure in the sight of god. At whom I had not yet shaken my fist.

Another two blocks. Blue uniformed doorman in that entrance. Digging a tooth pick in his mouth. The street number out front on the awnings. Rain thuds down. Turn left on the cement pavement. Into this panelled lobby. Mr Kelly. Sits in front of the great marble fireplace. Gazing out on the blacks and whites of the marble floor. Dreaming on his throne.

"Ah good evening Mr Peabody. It's showing signs of spring. A heavy rain the like of that washes the winter away. Won't be long now till we're scalding fried eggs on every street corner. It's up to your aunt is it."

"I beg your pardon."

"Your aunt, Mrs Sourpuss. That's where you're going. Wouldn't that be the truth now if you were telling me no lies."

A leather chair and small desk in an alcove. Looks like where a manager sits. Kelly pulling open the elevator doors. His red moon face and balding head. Walks with a little stoop. Tilts his head to view me sideways as he pushes the expanding steel door closed.

"Funny thing. Was a murder just over the street there. The night after the fire. Hadn't your aunt Mrs Sourpuss left just a few hours before. Out to the airport for Florida. And didn't this detective come in wanting to know had I seen any suspicious characters. Unsuspicious ones would be more like it. Three bullets in his head while he was shaving. And didn't the coroner say your man cut himself as he fell with the razor. You wouldn't know when you were safe in this city not even on your own bathroom floor and that's a fact."

Mrs Sourpuss. Smiling in a white long flowing gown. Stepping back as she opened the door. A white cowl up around her bronzed face. Smoky long lashed eyes beckoning me in. A new array of jewelry on each arm. Clanking as she takes my grey tweed coat. Pushing it on a hanger between other coats in a large closet crammed with furs. The former orange inferno now white. Icons gone. Replaced by drawings of birds. Yachting magazine on the coffee table. And a glass bowl full of the one eyed oily seeds of caviar.

"I'm mad at the moment Cornelius for anything white. And I've got this crazy urge for champagne. Have some."

From a bucket at the side of the chair Mrs Sourpuss takes a dripping bottle, a towel neatly around its neck. Filling two glasses.

"Well how's business."

"Fine."

"Did you get a customer from across the street."

"I don't think so."

"Right on the same floor as this. He was murdered. I think his wife, she has a penthouse kennel on the roof for her eight white poodles, had him rubbed out. He wasn't cold in the grave before I see her with a boyfriend sitting around drinking out of beer cans in their underwear. I have such high powered binoculars, I could count the hairs on this guy's chest. Might even be there tonight. Well how are you."

"Fine."

"And how's Vine."

"Mr Vine is fine."

"I just paid his bill. I had my detectives check him out it was so high. You know what their report was. I can't believe it. Scrupulously honest. He must be sick. Or nuts. But not that nuts. Guess you know he has a controlling interest in a demolition and exterminating company."

"No."

"Well he has. And nobody's got anything on him. Your Mr
Vine is beyond reproach."

"Well I think that's true."

"Well I think it's a lot of shit. I think he must be in on
something."

"I don't think Mr Vine deserves that remark."

"Are you kidding. He gets the rats and bedbugs and cockroaches out of a building. Then he gets the people. Then he can
knock the whole thing down. And start all over again. He's even
a widower. That guy's not taking any chances. Well how are you.
How are those beautiful white delicate hands. You like this
carpeting I got specially to match them. You haven't even given
me a hug or a kiss. I nearly got bitten by a giant rattle snake on
the golf course in Florida. You might never have seen me again.
Wouldn't that have made you feel a little bit sad. Go ahead,
drink your champagne. I'm fishing for compliments. But you
know I've got a bone to pick with you. That was your first day
working for Vine. Boy I could have killed you. Did I believe the
load of shit you gave me."

"I beg your pardon."

"O I beg your pardon. The stuck up way you say that. Speak
English for christ's sake. Where did you get that accent."

"I have always spoken as I do now."

"Bullshit. You know what I think you are. I think you're a
phony."

An ashen faced Christian rising to his feet. Fists clenched,
teeth locked. Air stilled in his lungs. Let people sidle up close.
Let them peek in to see your all loving unblemished soul. And
they scratch hatred on it. Their hallmark of being alive. In this
skyscraper paradise.

"Hey what are you doing, Cornelius."

"I'm leaving."

"For what. For what I just said."

"Yes."

"Wow, no kidding."

"Goodbye."

"Hey come on I'm kidding. Wow. Are you sensitive."

"You're god damn right I'm sensitive. Nobody talks to me
like that."

90

"Well all right nobody talks to you like that. You want me to apologise. I will. You're like a firecracker."

"You're god damn right I am. I'm not one of your little rat scared shits scurrying around this town. I stand. I fight."

"All right all right, you stand, you fight. I believe you. I'm the last person you have to prove that to. Sit down. Please. I just felt I'd been taken for a little ride. I've got feelings. Someone says they're a professional undertaker. You believe them. Then you put yourself in their hands. And boy did I put myself in your hands."

"I am. I'm an undertaker. I gave you professional attention. Even though I was just a beginner."

"You're a beginner. Wow. With that beautiful sad face of yours, wait till you get going. Come on. Please. Sit down. I'm sorry. But you can't stand and fight over everything. Sometimes you've got to go the way of least resistance. Everybody does. And that's not so dumb neither. Come on. Hello there. Get rid of that gloom. You're such a damn good looking kid."

"Don't call me kid."

"Whoops. Sorry Mr Christian. I mean can I turn on some music. You know I've made strong men cry. Who thought they could push me around. Men with a lot lot more going for them than you. Not glorified doormen."

Christian turning away. His knee catching the white soft sofa cushion and knocking it to the floor. Picks it up and fires it across the piano. Mrs Sourpuss lowering the cover of the record player. A grin slowly souring on her face. A deep trembling throb of a cello. Christian out in the hall opening the closet door. Inside a light goes on. Over all these fur coats of fox, sable, mink, beaver, leopard, and maybe even chipmunk and polar bear. Pull mine out. Woven from sheep on the outer Hebrides. A long voyage back. To where a salty sea wind cleansed and curled this fibre. Bellowing down across the mountain side heathers. An energy sweet. Trembling the threads of life. Gossamer. Which wrapped you in fragile peace.

"Now wait a minute Cornelius. I like and respect you. Let's patch this up."

"Patch what up."

"Why are we fighting. I could do a lot for you. You're in a

crappy funeral parlor. With all those ghouls. Let's really shape you into something.''

"Who do you think you're talking to. Nobody shapes me into anything."

"All right, all right. Nobody shapes you into anything. But what's wrong with being a vice president or something. You name it."

"Nobody buys me. And Mr Vine is not a ghoul."

"Hey look. Let's have some caviar. Just you. Just me. And some champagne. The way they live in Europe. I got it all ready for you. As a surprise. High brow music. Lemons. Toast in a napkin. Even went all the way over to the west side to buy some special butter. Then we get into this awful argument. Come on. Take off your coat. You're just a really independent guy. So I'll go along with it. I just don't know how to handle it. Yet. O k now. I'm learning. Here. Come on. Look."

Mrs Sourpuss lowering to her knees and stretching forward face down on the floor. White gown aflow on the round golden hued oriental carpet. Slowly twisting her head to look upwards. At Christian. Through her parting locks of blond hair.

"Walk on me. I mean it. Go ahead."

Cornelius staring down at the prostrate form. A priestess ready to be consecrated. To cook, scrub, screw and adore. The prick that rises now above. While she'll get cuffs across the jaw. Be good practice balancing on her cheeks. For the long tightrope walk ahead. Across my modest income.

"Hey jesus christ. Your shoes hurt. You're heavy."

Christian stepping down from the ice skating strengthened arse of Mrs Sourpuss. Had a foot on each solid globe. As her hands come behind her to grab me by the ankles.

"I didn't mean kill me. I just meant walk all over me. Lightly. One foot at a time. Maybe with your shoes off. And your coat."

Christian taking off his shoes. Once a dead man's. Still walking in life. And in that cold wintry mausoleum, as multimillionaire Sourpuss was lifted into his niche I thought I heard her say, there goes that old grey fart. She tugged my arm and shivered. How sad she couldn't be sad. Make her even gladder now she's got all his money. And a pair of feet to walk on her.

"That's better. That's nice too. Master. Sweet boy. Now every time I open my big mouth I'm your slave. I really mean it. I'll show you. I really will."

Sounds drift up from the street. Honking horns. Squeals of tires. Sirens wailing along the avenues. Drone of an airplane. Can hardly hear a cello or anyone tip toeing up behind me. As I follow Mrs Sourpuss hunched over her folded hands. Back into this alabaster clarity. To the sofa. Ease me down on a pillow. She kneels at my feet. Pulls off each sock. My heels cupped in her palms.

"Whew your feet. Sorry. No your feet are terrific. Just beautiful. Long thin and delicate like your hands. Just sponge on a little champagne. Make them taste better. I'm going to eat you."

Mrs Sourpuss wrapped her lips softly around each smallest toe. The bigger ones tickle. Sucking them gently. Now licking up round my ankles. Her hands reaching to undo my belt. Close my eyes on the glare of her sparkling diamonds. Zipping down my fly. Pulling off my trousers. The crotch of this underwear intact. Sporty coloured in fact. With candy stripes. She might be able to taste. As she lowers them down. I get out of my jacket. She says, no master. Let me. Me slave. Me giveum you muchum comforts. You no move. Me squaw. And me going eat you, yum yum. You come for me at slave market. Me black too. Maybe even Polish. A lousy rotten slave. Me do what big strong wonderful chief wantum. Me eatum.

Cello throbbing. I bought a piece of fabric remnant, chocolate with yellow and red chevrons. Looked like an Indian decoration for a wigwam and hung it on the wall. Above the whorls of dust in every cranny round my floor. And near midnight listening to the radio. As a symphony faded. A soft voice murmured something about the cares and sorrows that infest the day, shall fold their tents like the Arabs and silently steal away. And perhaps their shadows go as death goes. Gathering wives loved. Gentle hearts stopped beating by bitter ones. I had a spouse. To build a life with. In the same bed through debts and worried nights. Shoulder to shoulder. Till hers battered, caved in. Left standing alone. Outside that ship's doctor's cabin. Great vessel throbbing its whistle in a mid ocean fog. The white hardness of your bony breast where I knocked. Hoping you'd let me in. To shout my blue skyed promises inside you. Come to my country I said. To the cranberries and pumpkins and fourth of July parades. Come even to the barren shores where I used to run a mile on the hard sandy soil. Across a wasteland near a little creek. Incarcerated in the navy. I was an amphibian. Off to the beaches. Sailing at break of day. To get the shit blown out of you by some armour piercing shell instead of a luscious mouth. Silver in Mrs Sourpuss's hair. Licks my knees and along my thighs. And sucks. Like a cook on our ship. A Virginian gentleman who hunted to the hounds and charcoal broiled our stolen slabs of steak. Who baked fluffy golden delicious biscuits and in the evening handed around his photographic scrapbook of undraped bodies connected to other nude bodies in an avalanche of orifice ways. The whole crew got an appetising hard on. Which cook would eat without salt one after another on his knees in the galley. According to rank. While furious bets were laid. On how many cocks the cook could gorge. Including those gulped in a second helping. The boatswain's mate counting, said the final record was twenty three or flatteringly two and a quarter fathoms of phallas. It was a happy ship. Nicely perched on the waves. Until the score keeping monstrous pricked boatswain's mate with two years of sea duty, a purple heart, one bronze and one silver star, ruptured a blood vessel in the cook's throat. And poor cook unable to take more pricks in the mouth tried to put his own down into the arse hole of some unappreciative bible toting machinist's mate who lay in the bunk below. Cook navigating through a silk embroidered aperture in his canvas hammock. The whole crew begging the machinist preacher to let the cook have his simple lubricated delight. Keep the good food coming. And the ship's drive shaft churning. While cook's throat was healing. Like Mrs Sourpuss's hand. Touches gently squeezing. Tip toe on the harp strings strung across my brain. The music it makes wakes up a balmy sunny day. At sea. Boatswain whistles blowing and anchors aweigh. My naval rank so low. I promoted myself. To admiral. With bright teeth and seafaring skin stretched tight by the salt and sun. My rigging taut like tiny little lines creeping out from Mrs Sourpuss's eyes. Sucking she sucks. On my each ovoid jewel.

Her mouth now stretched round. Lips sealed tight halfway down my pole. To see me looking as she looks up. Out of twin friendly greeny blue eyed pools. Dip a finger in. And taste. Molasses sweet. Soft as song. That the Annapolis Glee Club used to sing. Bringing tears to my eyes. They must still be humming somewhere. In their white and blue. And maybe all blown. By visiting debutant mouths. Each as they were. Princesses perched on pedestals. Whose mothers would convulse with sobs. That their daughters would do such a thing. For a midshipman. Who chants.

> When you find
> A friend
> Who is good and true
> Fuck him
> Before
> He fucks
> You

11

Four pink capped bottles of champagne. Poured down with toast, lemon and caviar. While between bouts Fanny Sourpuss crawled bare arsed on the white long haired rug to her Park Avenue windows to watch with her big binoculars the bare arsed show the murderess and her boy friend were giving across the street. Through their half pulled down shade.

Christian gesticulating undraped on the coffee table. To the tempo of a French organ clock hooting the time with tuneful pipes from its gilt and gold cabinet topped by two horned goats ridden by cherubs. Tell god with prick shaking grief to be good and merciful to my own romantic Bronx. Bless all who live and die there. North across fourteen bridges and three tunnels. Under the flat tarred roofs. In the buildings zig zag with iron staired fire escapes. Stacked on the hills, brick hives of grey and brown. Packed with ginneys, micks, kikes and coons.

So friendly in bed with another human. Until Fanny with stiff nipples ashake on her breasts woke sweating and gasping. Said she had a nightmare that she was losing her hair. Turned on the light. Holding her arm up across her brow. Dark stubbles in her arm pit. And rolling over. A large mole in the middle of her back. She spoke out into the side of the pillow. Said she had five abortions. During three years she lived on the road. Taking planes when she couldn't take trains. Up and down the east coast like a yo yo. Winning at gin rummy in the club cars and for prices sky high fucking a whole gamut of guys. Every stinker she loved threw her around like an empty box of breakfast cereal.

96

Till one day in the middle of her misery taking a cold shower she wised up. And stood on the steps of the fanciest hotel in Palm Beach. The sea breeze blowing her white thin skirt against her freshly tanned legs, hair floating back over her shoulders. And a rich old son of a bitch came cruising up the curving entrance drive in his brand new saffron yellow open car. The moment he saw her he crashed into the back of a big black limozine. Smashing his cigar all over his face. She smiled at him. And that was Mister Sourpuss.

"I had his fly and wallet open in no time. And his lawyers divorcing his first wife. That twisted minded bitch had her talons sunk right into his assets and boy did she start to claw. Tried to get me arrested. Poured sugar in my gasoline tank. Painted hooker in big red letters across the back of my white sports car. Smeared dog shit all over my apartment. I bit the lobe right off her left ear and socked her one when she was pulling my hair in the lobby of the Waldorf Astoria. That cunt wouldn't let go. She's still suing me. Cornelius I get just so god damn miserable sometimes. Did you know that they thought they would have to cut off my tits. I told you that didn't I. Inside me is a mother. And I've got such beautiful tits. Don't you think."

Fanny sat up in bed, breasts pouring forth swollen pink tipped and white. Freckles sprinkled in between. Two little rolls of fat around her belly. Asked her if she was still a slave. She said cut it out, I've got a headache.

My own skull next morning throbbed and my knees trembled. Waking in the darkened mirrored room. Looked out the window. Air shafts and chimney pipes rising up bolted to sunless sooty walls. Grimy panes of other windows. And way down far below a cat meowed. Went stumbling nude looking for the phone. And headed dry mouthed searching for grapefruit juice instead. To moisten my tongue so it could move again. Thought I saw Glen's profile reflected in a mirror taking a bottle from a closet. As I turned down the long hallway. Lurching through a swing door at the end. To find a fat armed dark complexioned lady sitting at the kitchen table with a cup of coffee, a magazine open and half a cinnamon bun just bitten in her mouth. She knocked over her coffee as she got up and retreated. Arm raised to ward me off as if I were a dog ready to jump and bite. Her vast breasts heaving under her blue white collared uniform, her finger pointing at my private particulars as she shouted. You don't none come any nearer, you don't you.

Under a canopy of pink towel, I dialed from the living room. Champagne bottles and pillows and torn pages of the yachting magazine strewn on the floor. Everything lies in peace the night before and then jumps at you in the morning. A quarter past twelve. Spoke to Fritz. Who didn't believe I was mortally ill. Throbbing, shaking and pained in head and limbs. A doctor in attendance. A thermometer up my rear. Stethoscope on one of my balls. To see if it might explode. Said my medical adviser thought I'd be all right tomorrow. Fritz said it sounds to me as if you're all right today. I let a minute tick by of utter devastating silence. Take plenty of time to swallow the insult. Digest it under a freezing cold shower. And time now to go.

Dressed with my ovoid jewels and spirit all shrunk up. An Ethiopian appearing gentleman took me down in the elevator said Mr Kelly had this shift off. Saw Glen sitting reading a newspaper parked out front in the grey limozine. I ducked and turned west around the corner, crossing Madison and Fifth. Down grey steps in front of the ivy covered administration building in the zoo. Along a winding path under a stone bridge. Scrawls scratched on the arch. Julie sucks. Martha takes it in the ear. And Fanny Sourpuss eats me. Said she had no niche or purpose in the world. All she had was what everybody else wants. Money.

And sun melting the mud that Tuesday early afternoon. I took in lungfulls of air. Breathing out the alcohol. Walking so small with the distant windowed mountains all around pointing in the sky. Climb up there and be rich. Undo the shoelaces of all these grey blunt arsed guys. Sitting behind their desks on every rung of the ladder making decisions to kick me off. Faded winter weeds grow out of the crevices of these grey bulging boulder rocks. Down there under flying flags they ice skate. Up on the top of that hill they play checkers and chess. And I hear the sounds of a merry go round. The air mild. Children shout and play.

Cornelius Christian jauntily bounced up the steps of the Game Club. A brass sign says strictly private. Walk in as if I own the place. And right away the green uniformed man asks me if I'm a member. Yes. I'm a comical caucasian Christian. Of the human race.

Through here I used to pass so long ago. Sauntering over the marble floors to check my coat. The kindly greeting gentlemen behind the counter. With all their hangers and hooks and little tags for bags. The green leather chairs where the Mrs Sourpusses sit. Perfumed legs crossed under furs. Waiting for their steam bathed husbands. To lay the world worshipping in front of them tonight.

"This way sir next elevator."

Man with white gloves points me past the gleaming brass doors. Lights buzzing and binging. Five please. All so welcoming and courteous. Just a growl now and again you'd hardly notice. Before me a grill, a cage, a man in there. Put my wallet and change in this brown envelope. Press down the iron handle. Pinch it together. Like Fanny's pair of thighs. Pinch. When I'm between. And they're apart.

Along the shadowy rows of named and numbered lockers. Attendant says here this is a nice one. Close to the main aisle. In his deep voice he sells me sneakers, jock strap, shorts and shirts. Shot with a purple arrow, the emblem of the club. Undress between these dark green lockers. As I did all those years ago. Looking out the window over the tree tops. The cars snaking on the curving drives through the park. And night when lights sprinkled across the whole grey vista. To put the heavens down below. With the stabbings and stompings. You watch from windows safe and warm.

The sounds of sport. Down a long corridor. Clashing fencing blades. Feet pounding as they run. Knees crackling as they bend. Go in through this door. On the walls are pictures of fighters with muscles, others with smiles but all standing ready to punch. Athletes come in. Where others fear to tread. Due to fists. And a blond haired man sits at a desk. Bent over the afternoon newspaper. Slowly turns to look up. Frown on the face. Puts the newspaper down. And hollers.

"Well what do you know. Now if it isn't Cornelius Christian. Where you've been all these years."

"Over in Europe."

"No kidding. Well what do you know about that. Well it's good to see you champ. Hey you look good. Well what do you know. Europe. Have they wised up yet over there."

"I think so."

"That's good. They keep unloading these backward people on us. Well what a surprise. Must be three or four years."

"Seven."

"Well what do you know about that. Seven years. We still got the admiral around. And all the sea captains. The judges. The mayors. The actors. The industrialists. I'm still trying to sell them my antiques. Bunch of cheapskates. Won't buy my Sheraton and Chippendale. They don't understand them big words. The best genuine furniture ever made in my back room in the Bronx. But Cornelius champ, you look real good. Don't hurt to keep in shape. With the crime in this town. It's crazy. Even a decent criminal isn't safe. They're murdering right in the subway now. Lucky if you get home alive at night. In the day time too. Say what are you doing Cornelius, you got a job."

"Yes."

"What at."

"Guess you'd call me a host."

"A host. You handing out free beer. Send me an invitation."

"Certainly."

"Cornelius champ you know it's nice to see you."

In this green floored room. As an admiral and a judge step in. Punching bags thundering. Bells and sirens of fire engines passing by down the street. My heart warmed. By the first man glad to see me. With his twinkling blue eyes. His happy round pot belly. Takes away the loneliness. Plants hope. Right where I was on my knees fervently praying. Dear world hear my tiny voice. Just let me say bleep. Before you tell me to shut up.

"Hey Admiral, now you remember Cornelius Christian."

"No."

"What. You don't remember Cornelius Christian. The Bronx Bomber, middleweight champ. With the best left hook and right cross in the business."

"No. I don't. But he needs a shave."

"What do you mean shave."

"What's he growing a beard for."

"Hey Admiral he's not doing nothing. We're shaving every day."

"I don't care, beard stubbles like that are an insult to women."

"What have you got to say to that Cornelius, beards are an insult to women. Maybe the judge here should put out a warrant for your arrest. But maybe they like hair in Europe. And American women don't like hair. What have you got to say to that Cornelius."

"American women are a commodity."

"What. Wait a minute, cut out them big words Cornelius. You mean buy and sell them. Like cattle. To make a profit."

"Yes."

"Well what do you know. I better go home and count my daughters."

O'Rourke standing his hands on his hips. A plaid cloth bathrobe hanging down past his knees. A towel unwrapping from around his throat. He gets into the ring with the Admiral. As I tip toe out. And the punches slam to midsections and sail past noses. The sweet smell of sweat and fluffy warm towels. The best of underwear. No dirt under any fingernail in this building. Kept a fart bottled up all last night. So Fanny wouldn't get the stink. And she blasted me with one instead. Must think I'm a giraffe. Who savor the pee of one another. Her limbs still cling. Feel them round me as I go down these grey stairs. She said women always hated her. And she hates women. And shook her head at the window. Putting down the binoculars saying I can't focus my eyes. Just as the scene was getting hot across the street. She asked me what's happening now. And I told her a long string of dirty lies.

Through these black swing doors. Smell of more towels and rubbing alcohol. Little alleys of panelled booths to dress in. Each with their own little shoe horn. Big face of the weighing machine. Where I stand and the pointer stops at one hundred and sixty four. Glass of blue water filled with combs. Jar of petroleum jelly. Basins and mirrors. Walls and floors of tiles. Water splashing in the big blue green expanse of swimming pool. Naked men and others wrapped in towels. Fanny said she saw her first pair of balls on her father and even though he was so sweet they disgusted her. And then she said but I like your balls. They glisten when I squeeze them tight. And Cornelius why don't you give me a surprise. Something precious. That makes me feel loved. Think of something. Something really wonderful. That I can look forward to. Because jesus christ they're trying to get me, and Cornelius I have nobody I can trust. You don't want me for my money, do you. You know what I mean. You know what I'm saying. I need to have somebody with me. It's like you only walk where there's a crowd. Because people alone are meat for sharks.

Christian wrapped in a towel. Entering this vast arched room with its green twinkling bathing pool. Look behind over a shoulder up at the time. Just past three o'clock. Gentlemen recline wrapped in sheets under the palm fronds. Reading, talking, smoking and asleep. Names paged over the public address. Manicured hands reach to pick up phones. To date dames and do deals all over the city. To bluff and call bluffs. To step on toes. And to play the role which stars in a profit.

A little black dial on the wall reads one hundred and forty degrees. Push the brass and glass door open. Enter a cavern filled with steam. Like the Isle of Man. When lights light along the coast. And desolate fog horns tremble across the mist. Sit on a wooden bench now and hear voices in the vapours. Yeah the weight was down ten pounds, and I go to Florida and come back and I'm up seventeen, what can you do, I got to eat, you'd think they'd discover something and take the nourishment out of food so you didn't have to starve.

Christian making a pillow of a towel, to lie back down in the hot mist. Stare up from this bench at the white ceiling. Warmth and peace. The muscles soften. The beads of sweat bubble. Steam goes down into the lungs. Arrived in this city. Carrying as I was explosive hope. All turned to grief. Then the grey hard walls of struggle rise. And all your sorrows get shooed away. Stacked up like skyscrapers in the heart. And anyone can come. And they do. To push them toppling and shattering. Debris strewn all over your soul. And the pushers get their teeth capped, noses

102

shortened and ears shaped. To look good. So they can walk smiling past your doorman into your life. Saw a sign don't miss an opportunity to work in the midtown area. Another slander of Brooklyn and my Bronx. Whose citizens crawl up out of the subway trains. Sell shirts, shoes and soap to the endless daily supply of big shots. Sporting bulging college rings on their fingers and who look like they zoom to Scarsdale and Connecticut smashing back cocktails in club cars rocking on the rails. And out to Hicksville beyond Queens. And in here tan club members pick out their seats on the benches. Holding paper cups of ice water and paper cups of beer. More steam comes hissing out. Got to get up on my feet and howl victory. Standing on a mountainous bushel of dollars. All I need for my niche and purpose in life. Having as I already do such a storehouse of marvelous other qualities. Perhaps only lacking Fanny's star twinkling ass hole. The little wrinkles like rays of heavenly lights. To be watched as the world goes dark. When fear comes. And mothers run away with their children. As they do. When they see the friendly apes screwing. In any monkey house of any zoo. Red pricks up. Heading into the bright red bottoms. Another voice through the steam saying he would like to acquire some artificial aging, since success had come to him so young.

Christian after a shower and a swim taking a reclining seat. Swaddled in towels and sheets at the edge of the pool. Swimmers cruising back and forth. Flipping like fish at the turns. Boiling up the water. Guys stop to tap other guys on the knee and talk. Hey John how are you. Good to see you. How you doing. And everyone is doing fine. Just fine. And a voice sounds next to me.

"Excuse me, but are you busy."

"No."

"You don't mind if I talk to you. O don't worry, you can turn me off anytime. I'm a buyer for a department store. What's your name. I mean you don't mind me talking to you. Do you. You can turn me off anytime. I can tell you're very athletic. Do you mind if I ask your name. I don't mean any harm."

"I think perhaps I'd rather just remain private if you don't mind."

"O I don't mind. But there's no harm in just knowing a person's name. Just a first name. I mean why don't you just tell me. You can turn me off anytime."

"Could I possibly turn you off now."

"O sure. I don't mind. Some people think they're better than others. The way you speak for instance. And if they think that that's their affair. I mean you could tell me what you do."

"I'm a mortician. I cut incisions, remold faces and pump embalming juice into people."

"Well it was nice seeing you. And having this little talk. You sure never can tell where you're going to meet folk not in your own walk of life."

Gentleman rising and leaving. A figure reclining on the next steamer chair, head wrapped in towels, a little hole for the nose to breathe. A hand it seems I've seen before lifting the white folds of cotton slowly away. And hear a voice sooner than I see the face. A sound I've got to know quite well. For its fair minded generous understanding qualities. Upon which I call now with all my heart.

"You know Cornelius. You've got me beat. What the hell are you doing here."

"Mr Vine I can explain everything."

> Even why
> The moon
> Sometimes
> Changes shape
> The way
> It does

12

All that week that followed. Of temperatures and breezes mild. Every single morning down my side street standing just before the steps up to another brownstone stood my fat cheeked institutional friend from the bus and ferry. Smiling up at my window as I took in my container of milk. And opening his coat. He uncovered a large red white and blue sign.

GOODNESS IS A BUTTERCUP

Tuesday I gave him a wave. In his grey cap and grey long scarf wrapped around his neck. And he stepped backwards up a brownstone entrance. With a broad grin, opening one side of his coat. Revealing a word and then with open mouthed laughter uncovering the other side. Just as the girl I watch undress came down apprehensively out of her house. To see me saluting this friendly chaps motto.

NEVER WHATSOEVER

My confrontation with Mr Vine that morning was bowel moving. After telling me rapid fire at the poolside to get a shave and my ass pronto back to the funeral parlor. And to stay there till every last mourner was gone. And be back nine o'clock sharp next morning. I stood there on the carpet in front of his desk. Trying to do everything right. Even tempted to say never whatsoever. But instead nervously saluted. And he said at ease Christian. I put legs astride and folded my hands behind my back. Be bewilderingly military if not naval. And in the preliminary silence I blurted out.

"For god's sake Mr Vine I know I deserve to be really."

"Really what."

"Well I guess really yelled at."

"You think all I should do is yell at you."

"Maybe I deserve worse. I've got no excuses for yesterday. I don't know why I took off from work."

"Well I do. You were screwing Mrs Sourpuss all night."

"Gee Mr Vine no I wasn't. That's an awful accusation. Especially as I was going back and forth on the Staten Island ferry till about midnight. Even had my mortician's manual with me. I was studying. I got a chill, felt lousy next morning."

"You felt lousy. You're going to feel lousier. Because I know where you were. Because that blond broad Mrs Sourpuss has been trying to check up on me. And that means I have to check up on her. And I can tell you this. I don't like it. Do you hear me. I don't like it."

"O k Mr Vine, you've got me dead to rights. But I'll tell you something. I was thoroughly shocked. When she told me she was doing a thing like that. I really was shocked."

"What the hell is the matter with you Christian. Don't you know when you're well off. Is it really asking too much for you just to come to work."

"No Mr Vine."

"Why do you have to make me get angry with you. I heard what you said, to that guy in the swimming pool. That's not the kind of talk befits someone working for me. God damn it I don't know why I do it. But I'm going to give you just one. And I mean one. Last chance. If you put a foot wrong. There won't be any more little chats like this."

"Thank you Mr Vine. Thank you. Really thank you."

"Don't thank me. Just get suite number one ready. I want every inch of it double checked out. The special floral arrangements. The glass enclosed displays. Lighting, rest room, everything. We've got the first reposing of a double casket New York has ever seen."

"Really."

"Yes. A double deceased. A Mr and Mrs Jenkins. She's Esme on the floral display and her husband is Putsie. If you had been on the ball you would have seen the picture on the whole front page of the Daily News. Big elm tree fell on their house in Astoria."

"Gee whiz that's terrible."

"I got a tip off. Went straight out. Right by the Consolidated Edison Gas Plant. Where Mr Jenkins worked. Just a lucky stroke of luck and being on the ball. Her daughter liked my idea. They were a devoted couple. Lived happily in the area thirty years. Tragic the way the tree they loved growing right outside their nice little house crushed them both in bed."

"I can't think of nature doing anything more horrible Mr Vine. Must have squashed them something awful."

"Right across the lumbar and thorax. Just a little bit of facial damage. We rebuilt the pleural cavity. You could have learned something Christian. But I don't know. That kind of calamity makes you wonder. Even what you cherish most can kill you. But the majority of homicides in this town are acts of genuine justice. Ninety nine percent of the time it's what people get for being rude. That's what causes the killings Christian. Discourtesy. And maybe I ought to tell you something. Just a few days after your wife's funeral. I happened to see you. Coming out of Saks Fifth Avenue. Helping a big fat colored woman out the door with her packages. And then you held it open. And one person after another came through. Not one of them gave you even a nod of thanks. And still you stood there. Too polite to let the door slam in anyone's face. I didn't want to impose otherwise I would have gone over and shook your hand."

"I don't think I remember that Mr Vine. Are you sure it was me."

"It was you. My memory for faces alive or dead is just about infallible. And talking about faces. Those coffin pictures we took of you are really producing results. A funeral director from Rochester said he's never seen such classic dignity in both casket and deceased. We've had a fifty percent increase in orders since our ad was printed."

"Well I'm really glad about that Mr Vine."

"I keep telling you Christian, you could have an honorable future with me here."

Vine's twitch of neck and shoulders. His stiff sparkling clean shirtcuffs. Pearl stick pin in his black silk tie sprinkled with the purple little arrows of the Game Club. He's just had a haircut. Puts his arms out on the desk. Folds his hands and crosses his manicured fingers one over the other. Leans forward. His voice solemn and soft.

"Christian I come in here in the morning like this. To the silence and peace. The music and reverie. To the people and their sorrow. Surrounds you. Like having your own death comfort you every day you live. Mourners' hearts opening up to their grief. As that body lies there. Its life gone. Chewed out of it sometimes by a greedy wife. My pleasure is to bring back to the ravaged face some of its childish innocence, some of its dreams, some of its promise. Erase the crevices of worry. The aging around the eyes. I see them sometimes as little children. And I've wept more than once. Sadness is a private garden. With high stone walls. And I would never leave it."

"I understand Mr Vine."

"I don't think you do Christian. I just wish you did. And that one day you would whole heartedly embrace this vocation."

"Guess you'd like me to work out back in the studio."

"Yes I would Christian."

"Well I wouldn't mind a shot at it. If I could be left completely alone. To do my own deceased."

"I'll give you that chance."

"O k Mr Vine."

"By the way Christian I didn't know you were a member of the Game Club."

"I got an athletic membership for boxing. When I was at prep school."

"You can box."

"Yes sir."

"Well I wouldn't mind sparring with you sometime Christian. I used to do a bit in the navy."

"Anytime sir."

"Provided, and I don't want to be a spoilsport, that it's not on my time I'm paying for. You're a guy of many talents Christian. All I'm asking of you. And it's little enough. Is just stay on the ball. Can you do that.''

''Yes sir. I can. I know I can.''

''Good.''

On Wednesday the double deceased slammed to eternity by the big elm tree were buried. Fritz with his black hair parted down the middle giving me orders like he was afraid one day I might get his job. Shook when he coughed, his lungs rumbling. A real advertisement for a funeral. Didn't give any comfort to the bereaved as he stood hacking and heaving over a fender of a limozine. And before we shipped out to Astoria I came creeping to steal some of Miss Musk's paper hankies out of her office. She caught me red handed. Standing right behind my elbow in her brown dress. Her peach skin turned red as a red tomato. Her eyebrows recently plucked to give her face an Egyptian motif. A string of imitation pearls around her neck. In my fist a wad of tissues and in her's a pencil upon which she pulled. Made my front tail fatten. But her voice thinned it down again.

''That was a dirty rotten trick you did.''

''What are you talking about Miss Musk.''

''You know what about. I'm no snitcher but boy if you stand there denying it and stealing my tissues I'll go straight to Mr Vine. And you know what that will mean.''

''All right. I did it.''

''Why. That's all I ask. Why.''

''I don't know. A good luck gesture from a show biz departed. His hand was just right there. I thought it would amuse you.''

''You call that funny. That's your idea is it.''

''Well things are gloomy around here Miss Musk.''

''When I told my boy friend. He was so mad he said he would come around and sock you one.''

''Miss Musk, you better warn your boy friend that I can really fight.''

''He entered the golden gloves.''

''I don't care what he entered. I'll give him a departure. Right through the wall.''

''Boy you talk tough don't you.''

"That's right, when necessary I do."

"Well doing a thing like that, that you did, gives me the impression that you must just not like me. And you could have asked permission to take my tissues."

"That's not true, Miss Musk, I like you. And I'm sorry, I just didn't think you'd mind if I took a tissue or two."

"Guess you thought my dress was too tight that day."

"O no. You have a most exciting figure."

"Do you really think so."

"Yes."

"O k, just so long as we understand each other. And I want you to swear right now you won't ever try anything like that again."

"I swear."

The double deceased funeral surrounded by photographers taking pictures. When we finally closed the big coffin, visiting undertakers were scrutinizing the special air and water tight join down the middle of the twin casket lid. Cameras were whirring and. lights beaming. Clarance handing out drinks in his office, smiling and pleased with compliments of his fellow undertakers. Even Miss Musk grabbed me by the arm and said isn't it exciting. Her fingers stayed a moment. Looking into each other's eyes. She said Mr Vine is going right to the top. And both of us could go with him and all those horrible old building codes, fire and health regulations and zoning laws they hound him with are not going to stop us.

On that triumphant Wednesday a particularly testicular Christian leaned towards Miss Musk. Putting his hands down on her desk and reaching to give her a peck on the nose. She closed her eyes and lifted up her lips. Just as Fritz came in growling. And promptly sent me back to the jammed suite of Esme and Putsie Jenkins. Whose daughter was trying to sign a contract for her life's story. Amid flash bulbs popping. And nosey mourners from other suites. The smell got pretty unpalatable. Vine with his head shyly tilted at the publicity. Finally raised his hands and said that's enough.

At three o'clock we were all ready to go. Shaking hands with visiting morticians. A reporter even asked me my name. We were a happy little go ahead team. I kept drinking ice water. And nervously taking frequent pees. And suddenly found Clarance standing right beside me. Both of us pissing. Said if only more husbands and wives could throw a seven at the same time. Could make use like they do on towels and bathrobes of the words his and hers.

At three o five, motorcycle cops were revving their engines outside. The line of limozines went all the way down and around the corner under the elevated train. Even the janitor of the warehouse across the street brought out his chair to sit and watch. And there standing alone against the massive red brick depository wall. Waiting for me to come out. Fat Cheeks. Flashing open his coat with his usual grin. And a brand new sign.

VOUCHSAFE AND BEHOOVE WHOREMONGERS

A setting sun sending shadows east. The long motorcade crossing the Queensboro Bridge. Down past dingy roofed factories. Cigar of land sitting in the East River. They call Welfare Island. In that building there you drive in with a truck and an elevator takes you down to the island. A community of hospitals. Institutions charitable and corrective. A home for the recreation of indigents. For the aged and blind and chronic diseased. For the nervous ill. And those fatally dying. And once it was a pleasant peaceful pasture for pigs.

Vine said he never had a funeral like it. A message of sympathy from the mayor. Five motorcycle cops leading the way, sirens blaring, clearing traffic ahead. Vine in personal command. Riding with the local police captain of Astoria. Charlie and I in the flower car. Signs to Maspeth, Flatbush and Ozone Park. Charlie full of information said there was a whole Chinese farm on the North Shore growing Chinese vegetables. And heading past the gas works. Men lined the streets. Hats and caps in hands. Planes on the skyline taking off the runway of the nearby airport. Riker's Island out there on the grey East River. Charlie said three quarters of it was made from subway excavations. And I remember when I was a little boy. When I must have looked across all these lands. Sent away from Brooklyn by my uncle. Holding my smaller brother by the hand. To live high up in the back of a house. With a foster mother and father and a little foster sister and another brother. And I kept wetting the bed. And the woman screamed at me in the morning. All my comfort that summer was to lean out at night on my Bronx window sill. And waiting for the first fireworks to shoot up bursting in the sky. From the World's Fair. A sphere and a pylon like a cock and balls. An erection in Flushing Meadow Park. Imagined it so green with milk and honey and all the people of the world walked around with white angels landing on their arms and sticking lollypops of any flavour they wanted right in their mouths. Cried every night to sleep because my little brother kept asking why our mother and father would never come. He kept begging me please please big brother bring them back to me. I had to leave the window to hold his hand. And sometimes on dark stormy lightning afternoons he would kneel on his knees and with tears pouring down his cheeks begged god just for his mommie if he didn't want to give his daddy back.

During the interment hailstones fell. A frown on Vine's face as they bounced off the big coffin. Drone of cars along Astoria Boulevard. Barren landscape of headstones. Patches of grey dead grass. A single mausoleum on a rise of hill. Die slowly so I can see where my own life is going to end. Drop suddenly in your tracks and no telling where they might shove you.

In the studio that evening I clipped a clothes line pin on my nose. And George gave me my first lesson in embalming. Powdered hands in tight rubber gloves. Told me to be beware of cuts. And stood in my goggles and fresh laundered white gown. Over a twenty three year old girl. Dead of double pneumonia. With thick black hair and shrivelled up nipples on her flat chest. Her pubic hairs recently shaved from an operation. Climb up and lie between her knees nobbly and cold. Throw one last screw into her before burial. And maybe get the clap. Or a spark of life out of her eyes icy blue like the color on a bird. I lifted her bony shoulders as George slipped under a wooden block and tenderly placed her arms. No crevices of worry in her face as we made an incision just above the collar bone. The dark flesh of the carotid artery against the white side of her windpipe. The black night above on the skylight. And the light aflood on the alabaster corpse. Must have gone tip toeing out of this life. From a hospital bed. With a gold ring on her finger. Says Mount Saint Ursula.

That night walked crosstown on Fifty Seventh Street and turned left up the tiny hill into the automat. For the two dollar bill I gave the woman in the little booth she swept into the hollow of her marble counter a fistful of nickels dimes and quarters. Took deep breaths of air along the big shadowy darknesses of Fifth Avenue to bring back my appetite. Went back and forth examining the thicknesses of meat between the bread sitting in these glass tabernacles. Dreamt all my young life of moments like this. When I could shove in the nickels and open up all the doors on all the doughnuts and pies I wanted. And show my little brother that I was magic.

Cornelius Christian sat in the window with a ham and lettuce sandwich. A cold glass of milk clutched in his hand and a piece of blueberry pie on a tan thick plate. Talcum powder white under my fingernails. After my longest day. And that girl's life running all over my mind. Once was a smile on her face. Carried books to school. Swigged a bottle of soda pop. Bought groceries for her mother. And handling her body is like handling meat. Cutting fat off a steak. For ten dollars a week extra pay. I shivered piercing the roof of her nose. Right between the eyes. George showing me how to drain the cranial cavity. Sit now at this table, faces alive I see dead passing on the street. And they all look in. Who can I ever marry again. Where can I ever live. Or soft green garden ever find. Out of this waste land of signs and blaring voices telling you to buy. Scrape up the tiny sweet berries of my pie. Touch my lips to milk. Comes down the little faucet when you place your glass and pop in your nickels. Lick away the couple of salty tears that reach my mouth. God don't let me die. Alone unknown. Swept up from the streets. Strangled by my dreams. Unclaimed on a slab in Bellevue morgue. Practice for students to embalm. Or dissected at a medical school. Wake up with them using your veins as rubber bands. Or piled on the barge tugged along the East River. Stacked with hundreds of others. Through Hell Gate and out across Long Island Sound. With all the loose legs and hands and amputated arms. Prisoners

113

dig your grave. And on a granite cross. They put. He Calleth His Children By Name. And I've got to shout. For god's sake I'm Cornelius Christian. Never whatsoever the widower.

Man sitting across the table hurriedly lifting his plutocrat plate of mash potato, sliced carrots, sausage and gravy. Retreating away as other customers look. And Cornelius's fist pounds the table. Utensils clatter. Man rushes back to retrieve his grey converted pork pie fedora. Worn by guys who think they're going places. Hold tight because I'm cracking up. With no night to sleep in. Throwing tiny fists at a looming big grey bleak city. Never stops long enough for you to catch up. Every highway droning round the clock. Wait for me. And no one hears. Run down Broadway through the pedestrians panhandling for one hello. Any smile from any face. A howdido. Whoa. Gently now. Else the horse runs wild forever. Once it takes you galloping. Where my uncle sent my little brother and me one summer. Scared shitless with our blood pumping all the way to Mount Kisco. On the big thundering train.

Beads of sweat on Christian's brow. Puts his head in a hand. People stop to look back just before they go out the revolving doors. Catch their eye and they skidaddle fast. Comfort me. And they glimmer back with their own fear.

An old gent shuffling to sit down at Christian's table. Slowly places his saucer and cup of coffee. And another plate with a piece of coconut cake frosted and white on top and pineapple in the middle. Looked it over before I bought my blueberry pie. He takes away his tray and reaches for the sugar. The table rocks. And he looks up at me.

"How do you like that. They make a bomb. They send rockets like crazy all over the sky. And here, you'd think maybe they could make the table sit still."

Christian stopping to look in the window at all the gleaming pianos across the street. And walk the rest of the way home. To just a cockroach cavity in a wall. Old gent at the table said three times a week he came on foot from Astoria. Didn't know the Jenkins but read about their tragedy in the paper. Just minded his own business living retired alone in his own life. Was a traffic shunter in the railroad yards. And played chess in summer in the park. But only with men he valued as gentlemen.

"Just like I think you are sir."

Christian from a new pay telephone in the hall phoned Fanny night after night and no one was ever home. Only soul to visit or knock on my door was the hunchback collecting rent. Even Fat Cheeks was missing for a week. And then showed up one morning waking everybody on the street. Perambulating by under my window blowing a bugle and pushing a black baby carriage flying the six cornered blue star on the white and blue striped Israeli flag. Bleary eyed I was up half the night perusing the Champion Textbook On Embalming cover to cover. Sat exhausted in the morning on my bed, head in hands with worry. Dressed in despair. Robbed of a nickel change buying the paper. My confidence slowly draining away. The rest of my life sticking tubes into the dead. And then one morning as I came back to the studio from a pee. George pointed.

"There you are Cornelius, compliments of Mr Vine. Your very own first deceased."

A grey bushy haired man of sixty five. Owner of two cut price shirt stores. His threadbare shoulders. Sad to see. Face hollow cheeked and gouged deep with lines. And with hands gloved just as I was about to proceed, Fanny phoned. Said she'd been to Utah. I said I'm sorry but I'm very busy. And before I could say I'm desperate to see you. To hold any warm quivering body, my face and cheeks rolling pressed in breasts. To smell sweat instead of the heavy gloating reek of death. To hear a voice come out of a mouth. Instead of a gasp of putrid gas. Before I could say anything. There was a click and silence on the other end of the phone.

George said the deceased had a low moisture content. Keep down the percentage of the formaldehyde and not to let him dry too much. Got the contours of the face back injecting cream at the corners of the mouth and eyelids. With a nice generous squirt to raise his sunken globes of eyes. Youth came back into his cheeks as they fattened. Massaged and molded them to give him a look of puzzled amusement. Which is how anybody might look if they could see themselves dead. As I've done for the last few days. And George pursed his lips. Tilted his head just like Vine. And stood back.

"Yes. Yes. Color a bit strong. The composure a trifle too

spirited. But not bad Cornelius. Little over filling in the cheeks. Just a little. But not bad for a first try.''

Miss Musk helped me with the suite. Said she missed my amusing remarks now as I was out in the studio. And together that night we went to the laying out room. Told me how she admired my work. Between our bouts of screwing. And the rings of her boy friend on the emergency bell. The deceased's name was Herbert. His wife's Harriet. No double dead. Because boy was she alive. Arriving first with six women members of her bridge club. All wearing fur capes and wraps around their shoulders. Black tight dresses and pinned white roses. I bowed deeply. Said good afternoon madams. One to each. Followed by a click of heel. Led them to my specially arranged crescent of seats. Corsets crackling, mouths chattering, jewelled hands stroking their patent leather black bags. Pressed the switch for the music. Thought Herbert might like a movement in andante. Just add that bit of light footed elegance. And the whole bereavement launched now with a nuance Clarance would be proud of.

Christian in a far corner cutting a dead leaf from a potted palm that Vine had just installed in every suite. Holding the brown dried frond. Miss Musk's silhouette in the doorway. As fast as the world's tentacles get you down. You squirm and cut and slash away. To rise unhanded with a brand new anger. And the old gent in the automat slipped me a badly needed compliment. To light me a candle of cheer. Lifted my head to breathe again. All through a wet dream screwing Fanny till morning. Trees budding green. The tall city tilting towards spring. Got to have a picnic on some lake edge or grassy mound of land. And what's that. A gasp. Prolonged and rising in pitch. To a scieam. Of immense protest.

Christian crossing the soft dark green carpet. To the middle of this arena. Pink satin lined casket set in a bower of fern. Two red vigil lights both ends of the bier. Harriet a silver belt tightly buckled around her bulging belly. Spinning around to her girl friends and back again pointing to Herbert. And then to Christian. That tender hearted, do gooding Cornelius.

''Hey what the hell happened. What is this. That's not my Herbie. What did you do to him.''

"I beg your pardon Madam."

"You made him into a playboy. Looking like that."

"Madam, is there something wrong."

"Wrong, you ask me is there something wrong. What the hell did you do to him. Fix him up looking like a whore. He should look dead. Dead and old like he was."

"Madam his preparation was deluxe."

"Deluxe. What deluxe. You call making him a fat clown face. Deluxe. I call it a crime."

"Please Madam. Please. Lower your voice. We have other mourners."

"You have other mourners. You think I have another Herbie."

"Just take a seat Madam."

"Sit. While I'm hysterical with what I'm seeing. I should sit. I should sue you. When I don't recognize my own husband. Come in off the street to a complete stranger. You ask me to sit."

"Very well, certainly stand, if you wish Madam."

"Sonia, you saw Herbie when he died. You saw what he looked like. You see what he looks like now. Look at that. I'll tell you something mister."

"Mr Christian."

"What are you trying to be funny."

"No Madam that's my name."

"You deserve it. While my lawyer changes it fast to bankrupt."

"Madam please. Certainly there's something we can do."

"What are you going to do. Tell me. Take the stuffing out of his face. Make him look old, when you already disfigure him making him look young. Margie, you can see too."

"Please Madam. I beg of you."

"You beg of me. Is that what you can offer me. Begging. I don't want his body. I'm not burying that. You keep it."

"O god, please Madam. I'm responsible."

"You."

"Yes."

Christian standing hands clenched at his sides. Lips compressed. Shuddering and atremble. Harriet pointing her arm

117

again. Wrap falling off her shoulders. Christian picking it up. Her arm knocking it away.

"You did it to him. To my Herbie. You did that."

"I was trying to do my best."

"Your best huh. My husband you paint up like a five and dime doll. What did you do to his skin. It was normal before. A nice insult to an old widow. Margie witness every word out of his mouth."

"There could be some kind of refund."

"Refund. Margie hear that. This fella says I get a refund. What are you running here, bargains for damaged merchandise."

"Yes. We are. And I'll pump you full of formaldehyde and sell you as a bloody monster if you don't shut your ass you god damn fucking bitch."

"What. What. What did you say. To a widow. In front of her dead husband you hear what he says."

Christian storming from this dark suite. Past Miss Musk, nearly her whole hand clamped between her teeth. To go out again for the last time across this canary carpet. With your every ounce of energy. Do a good job. Sweat and slave. Shampoo and comb every hair. Polish each fingernail. Even use one of my own plaid bow ties. The whole god damn thing makes you want to cry. The hours of work. The hope and promise. That people would come in. Full of sorrow. Have their hearts quickened by an earlier memory of a man's life ravaged face. Touched for a last moment with a glow of youth. A final pirouette in the silence of peace. A spark of blessedness.

In
This
Cantankerous
City

118

13

Christian striding rapidly west, coat tails flying. Over the honky tonk avenue of Lexington, the wide boulevard of Park and the elegant emporiums of Madison. To walk up one side and down the other of a people flooded pale grey Fifth Avenue. East chilling wind bursting out of the crosstown streets. Blown over Brooklyn. Through the bars of all the institutions. Where the imprisoned troubled eyes stare.

Pass by the doors where Vine said he saw me. Polite and patient. Now a man stands clanking a tin cup. A seeing eye dog sitting before him on a carpet. Street lamps hang, two big tears above signs. No parking no commercial traffic. When it's all a long flowing stream of folk up for sale. Charlie said I want one of these golf driving ranges when I retire, that's where the money is. A dollar for a pail of balls. Just rake it in. Free pail to guys who hit the bull's eye, they stay there swatting all day trying. Said there was room for everybody to make a dollar. Even selling blood as well as hair.

Four thirty on the clock inside that plate glass window. Where blue uniformed girls smilingly make people passengers on airplanes. Vine soon will be calling on his usual evening inspection tour. When my goose shall be cooked. And served gorging to every member of Harriet's bridge club. I know I'm a good embalmer. Just too forward looking for backward people without the cultural criteria to appreciate my creative up to date expertise. In through this window up high I see gold embellished

119

ceilings. Behind that massive stone and shadowy shuttered windows I could stand shaving late to rush down or uptown for a date. Born to life pedigreed and rich. A daily new jade pot to piss in. And all I can do is keep walking. Moving all the time. Hoping for a master stroke of solace somewhere.

Christian cruising past the crimson carpeted steps of this monumental hotel. And by a subway entrance you never see anyone come up or go down. Stand waiting for the traffic lights. Where they've just put out shrubs and stretched a striped cafe awning for gay sidewalk customers smoking big cigars. See a woman there with a hairdo. Would look good in my repertoire of styles for female deceased. And have a husband roar in complaining. You stretched out my wife like she was in a beauty contest. You bet sir. She's a winner. In a dead heat. Ha ha. You fuckpig you.

Christian face down into his hands. Rubbing temples over the eyes. Wait for the green light to say go. Ankle deep in slander. Struggle ahead into my life across the street. A delicatessen and an apothecary tucked in the bottom of that tall tan hotel. On the edge of the waiting pedestrians a dark haired girl. Smiles at me. Gust of breeze blows open her white rain coat and see her flowered dress. A blue umbrella in her white gloved hand. Whiff of her perfume out of the traffic fumes as she passes. Heard her whisper a faint hello. Stop up on the curb. To turn and look. As she stops. And turns and looks. With another smile.

Christian standing. She could be gone. If I don't make a move. Someone to talk to. A brain and soul still alive. For wrestling in love and happy in heaps of dreams. To make her eyes pour faith on me. For my nobility. She snatched right out of the crowd. Spend my saved fortnight's rent and maybe even take her to dine. In one of those bars with cozy booths. Where they slather gravy on big slabs of roast beef on rye. And wash it down with a golden cascade of beer.

Her name was Carlotta. With soft shiny winey lips. I said can I buy you a drink. She walked in front of me down three steps and through swing doors into a dark bar. Fingering the blue and red beads around her throat. Waitress said what do you want. I said she wants a rye and I want a ginger ale.

"You can't just have ginger ale."

"Why not."

"Because you can't. You've got to have a shot of something."
Christian had a ginger ale and Carlotta had two shots of rye.
Big blobs of bright red on her nails. She poured her shots over
the ice and crossed her legs.

"What do you do if you don't mind me asking mister."

"I'm an airline pilot."

"You really."

"Yes. Just flew in from Europe."

"I thought you had a funny kind of voice. You want to get me
some cigarettes."

Cigarette girl waltzing by with her tray. Takes a pack and
unwraps the cellophane. Christian hands over a dollar. To get
thanks and no change. Control myself. Don't boil over into
another rage. Once you let anything out of your hand in this
town it's gone. Even the olive skinned beauty of this tiny big
brown eyed girl. Unless I dig in my pocket and spend. And just
this week I've nearly paid half of what I owe for Helen.

"Must be exciting that kind of life flying all over."

"Yes. What do you do."

"What do you mean."

"Well I don't know, where do you come from."

"I don't know whether I should answer questions."

"Why not."

"Buy me another drink first."

Christian buying another drink. Carlotta pouring them down.
A little bird behind the bar keeps dipping its beak. Stay brave
and sober in a crisis. And go insane with worry.

"I come from upstate. Geneva. That's on the finger lake. But
it's none of your business where I come from."

"Where are you going then."

"Back to the room. I haven't got all day. It's twenty dollars
for an hour. For ten dollars I'll suck you off."

Big shadows gather in the darkness. A wide gentleman approaching the table. After Christian cried out in some anguish.
Turning to rage as the waitress slapped down the check. And
stood over him waiting for twelve dollars. Free of charge I get

121

out of one fiasco and get robbed to get into another. Look for love and lose your money. Safer to stand up slowly. As this bouncer glowers. Rotating his steam shovel shoulders. Sticking out his chin. Curling down his lower lip. To show me he's tough.

"Hey what are you a wise guy or something."

"No I'm just a quiet citizen."

"You don't come in here making trouble buddy. Because you get smart, we get rough. Now you pay that check and get the hell out of here before I bust your head."

Christian's eyes flashing over this figure. See if there's a bulge of gun. Lucky I look like a pushover. Folk feel they need only lightly shove and it saves them bullets. The shadows of customers bent over drinks. Mirrors behind the stacks of bottles. Bar stools for swinging and ash trays for throwing. Neon green and red lights bouncing round the darknesses. Holy mary mother of god I'm praying to you for old time's sake. Because a foster mother made me be a catholic once. Please don't let me slip into another abyss. And Vine's right, rudeness results in all the murders in this town. Hear Carlotta's voice.

"Son of a bitch says he's an airline pilot and all he is is a cheap skate."

"O k wise guy flyer, you heard what I said. Pay. And get wings. And move."

"No."

"Look I'm going to tell you once more. Pay. And move."

"And I'm going to tell you. Touch me and I'll bat your brains out through the back of your skull."

"Hey what are you kidding sonny boy."

The wide gentleman calling over his shoulder to a shirt sleeved barman rushing down the bar. Christian feinting with a left and stepping back. The wide gentleman steps forward. With one hand reaching like a great claw the other tightened in a fist. Waitress spilling her drinks as she raises her tray like a shield. Customers turning. A jukebox with a voice crooning. Peanuts crushing underfoot. Last seen in a bowl on the table. O to be back puncturing with my trusty trocar in one's happy embalming room. As this wide gent whistles a fist by my nose. And bang into Carlotta as she stands up. And slumps down again with a groan. The waitress screams.

122

"Tony Tony her eye is rolling on the floor."

Tony looking down. Just long enough for Christian to make him look up. With a right hook arcing with slow motion strangeness from Christian's crouching kneecaps. Landing under Tony's jaw. Turning his neck lifting him two footed off the floor. Sending him crashing backwards his head slamming the curvature of the oak bar and sinking arms outstretched to rest in peace, one hand in a spittoon the other palm upwards over a brass rail. The low whistle of jesus christ through the teeth of the bartender as he stops in his tracks. And slowly steps back raising his hands. At an approaching Christian. Fists hanging loosely at the hips from the end of each half cocked arm.

"Don't hit me mister, starting from right now I'm on your side believe me. I'm just trying to keep the place civilized."

Waitress staring at the floor, her clutched hands held up to her cheeks. A voice yelling at the bar, get a doctor, keep the eye warm, they can put it back in. And at the end of an outstretched arm a wavering finger pointing at Christian.

"That's the guy who did it. Knocked her eye out."

Bartender, natty garters on each sleeve, gaining courage. Raising his own finger to take umbrage in the pursuit of justice. Only stepping back two paces in the pursuit of safety. As he raises his hands shielding too high and too late from a lunging Christian whose right fist silently sailed in a wide low curve to land with a gurgling thud under his heart. A lightning left crashing on his right lung. Matches, cigarettes and pencils scattering from his shirt breast pocket. Bartender pitching forward, hanging suspended over a blizzard of rights and lefts to crumple flat faced in his oozing vomit.

Two customers jumping over the bar. Another rushing for the back room latrine. A drunken one standing down from his stool. Hat back on his perspiring head. Mouth pursed and brow frowning as he wags his finger at the oncoming exit seeking Cornelius. A bleary eyed face colliding with a back handed swat from Christian. A hat sent flying. As Cornelius takes a crotch loosening leap up the steps past a last ring side customer trying to reach out and pat my back as I pass.

"That a boy champ. Haven't seen slamming talent like that since Sugar Ray."

Christian turning right, taking advantage of a little hill and running. Weaving down the shadowy street. No need to make it easy for bullets if there are any. And if not can always use the extra exercise. Past these clip joint maws of horror. Little temples of avarice. None greater than mine tonight. You fuckers. Because jesus christ before I'm finished I'm going to join the pacifists. Stroll if necessary lily livered under my placard of peace. Screaming stop all ball crushing, eye bowling, arse puncturing, violence and war. Because. To be sure Cornelius that constant Christian himself is quite pleased to escape any such blood bubbling debacles.

Slipped in the back entrance of the Game Club which is nicely situated in the shadows. A marble tablet in the gentleman's convenience says don't remove this like you've done everything else or you'll get your head broken. Stood in a crapper to recover a little breath and nonchalance. Present storm over. Comb hair in the mirror. Pat a bit of soap and water gently on the face. Stride out and down the marble hall. A wary eye for Vine. Cross the lobby. Earned a holiday. From the malapert and insolent. From all shabby inglorious rascality. From all bumptious bullying. And if you're lonesome strategising. To move honorably upwards. Into precious profit, luscious gain. And private peace. Have your ruses ready.

Wavy grey haired bartender. Comes with lilting brogue and twinkling eye. To enquire ever so pleasantly of my frail requirement. In this low ceilinged softly lit room. Horses and hounds thunder by leaps and bounds on a mural over the bottles behind the bar. Beer I want. Please. In a tall cool glass. Take it golden and foaming to an oak table by the window. Sign my name and number. On a pink little paper.

At a long table. Two white hatted chefs stand presiding. Over a baron of beef. A great side of ham. Sharpening knives. Cutting steaming slices. Laid so neatly out on your bread. Pick up your pickle and dig a little potato salad. Free of charge. To those who never hunger. Replace energy. Sit looking through this polished window at the lights changing. In this cathedral of a city. Where the skyscraper organ pipes trumpet. The tragedy and pain. Skin deep under the foolish alive forever smiles. All along Fifth Avenue. And I go and sit high up on the wind swept stone. To play the harp of great cables strung sweeping the gothic arches of Brooklyn Bridge. Trembling a music solemn and sad. For all those down deep and listening in their street walking sorrow. If the clatter, blast, clang and boom ever quiets. Hear me play. Melodious in the lull. Cornelius that Bronx and Brooklyn Christian. Orphaned by parents and wife. Fingernails strumming the singing cables. My hands Fanny Sourpuss said were so beautiful. When they're not tightening in these two knuckle hard justice givers. And now months ago. Seagulls were squawking over the water front. Tug boats nudging the great ship. When I came back to my land on a winter tide. All the waiting faces looking up. And even with my sorrow I thought they wanted me. Possessed of my little bag of beauty I had to bring. To awaken eyes just as I did those of Charlotte Graves. Who loved me first. When I was a little boy. And as she had said, you look so fine and gosh distinguished. I hoped that they would say grand, how splendidly you've changed. How lovely to have you back. And find them changed. And unlovely. Killing time in fear. Traitorous to any courageous voice.

Waiter bringing Christian beer after beer. Till it was time to stand up. Murmuring one's most recent code. Do unto others as they would so treacherously delight to do unto you. George told me as I washed our instruments, of all the undetected murder that came to rest on the slabs. Not for rudeness but for lust, greed and even glee. And Clarance Vine said. Death alone is our domain. And we comfort. And we die and let die.

Christian quaffing a last beer at the bar. Room crowded now with pin striped sportsmen and a laughing group of light footed badminton players. At the tables a sprinkling of graduates from the personal defence class. Trained to brave the sidewalk distance from doorway to limozine. Hop skip and jump before the addicts and muggers get you. And if they do. Flip the attacker on his skull and rub out his teeth with your toe. And for me. If only I could find one person to amaze. Without having to knock his god damn head off. Just go back down these beige marble steps. Face the portrait of an epeeist up on the wall. A tranquil vision of selfpossessed dignity. To encourage one onwards. Out through these bronze revolving doors. Towards a cool body. I can rapture upon.

Walking west under the floodlit canopies. Fat short men following tall slender women in and out. Playground of all the Sourpusses. Paying mints for part interest in a piece of ass. Patted and steered past scrambling doormen. Planted in seats of dining rooms. Like a cherry in the middle of a pie. That everyone wants a slice of. Now head north up Fifth Avenue. More canopies. Into the stacked palaces of the rich. Turn east. Between the shadows of the grey stone town houses. And come to an empty space in the sky. A high board fence around a massive excavation. Little grilled in platform where you can look down and down. Mounds of exploded rock. Strewn mesh blankets of steel. A lonesome steam shovel. Scaffolding down five stories into murky ear splitting darkness. Red hatted carpenters hammering. Under floodlights. Men bending wire and cutting steel. Huge crane rearing from a truck up into the sky. And a black sign. In the center of which are four large gold letters.

VINE

At another street corner Christian stopping. A blaring stream of cars in a traffic jam. Long black limozine pausing and purring. A grey gentleman sitting four feet away. Deep in his upholstery. Legs crossed with black silk socked ankles. Shirt cuffs closed with golden links. His pale hand offering to his lips an iced martini. Which makes what's left of my own threadbare world crumble. Look up for solace at Fanny Sourpuss's windows. One dimly lit, flanked by pillars, a gabled cornice above. Shade half down. Said she could set me up. Make me a vice president of a corporation. Give me chauffeurs and them plenty of cars to drive. And then I'd sit back. Hardly seen nestled in all the steam. I'd make. Because I'd be. Such hot shit.

Mr Kelly on duty. Said hi Mr Peabody. And as we ascended said long time, no see. Stepping out in the little lobby. Pushing the pearl buzzer and waiting. Mr Kelly before sliding his doors closed says your aunt is in. Since late afternoon. Chauffeur brought her back with stacks of packages from shopping. And Christian again pushing the buzzer. And knocking. Silence inside. Then a creak. On the other side of the door. Stand here unwanted. By everyone. All rushing to new faces. Past the old they already know. And find so handy to step on. I dread to stop to think. What a god forsaken unpleasant struggle life has been.

Christian beating a fist against the white panelling. And shouting. Open up in there Fanny I know you're home. And then her face. Peeking out between the elegant antique chain latches. Looking me up and down.

"You're drunk."

"You're damn right I am."

"And I'm busy. Goodbye."

Door closing. Latches clicking. Another anguished incurable moment stamped on my passport. To all whom it may concern. Prevent the bearer from free ass. Deny all lawful aid and grant any hindrance. Even molest if possible. Two knuckles rapidly swelling on my fist. Fanny is in there. Explode her with lust. As a kid I played the most dirty filthy disgusting games. Down cellars. Up alleys and prostrate in vacant lots. Little girls to whom I wagged my prick asking me do you want to see what I have. Always said yes. Out of chivalry.

Cornelius standing back. Aiming. Mid point in the panelling. Many's the deeply moving memory I've lost in distress. Comfort my left wrist with my right hand. Put the least used shoulder through first. Closed the door in my face. After inviting me into all her tempting nooks. Tasting to her delight my ovoid canapes. Washed down with brimming thimble fulls of the juice of generations. I don't squeeze lightly.

Cornelius sailing across the little lobby. By the plastic flowers. Under the white ceiling. The door swings open and Fanny Sourpuss in a gold silk dressing gown stands back. As I go flying in. Right across the hall. Whistling past the door to the living room. Slow enough just to catch a glimpse of Glen in his underpants dragging trousers as he hot foots it towards the kitchen.

"I'll get him. I'll get him."

"You leave him alone Cornelius. You're drunk."

"You're god damn right I'm drunk and I'll kill that Glen."

"I'm calling the police."

"Don't move."

"Now wait a minute Cornelius, what makes you think you have any right to come barging into my apartment like this uninvited."

"I have a right."

"You have like hell."

"I have. And I'm going to get that Glen. Running around here without his clothes. It's a disgrace."

"Ha ha you should talk."

"What was he doing."

"Just what you do when you come here."

"You cheap bitch."

"O boy. Wow. That's just terrific. I'm a cheap bitch. For your information I'm an expensive bitch. And to you I'm priceless. That's how you get me so cheap. What happened to your hand."

"None of your business."

"O boy. I telephone you and you answer like I was something the cat dragged in. Now you come running round here like you own me."

"You've been away."

"I was skiing. Don't look at me that way. As if that wasn't all I was doing. Because it sure wasn't. I can have all the guys I want. Anytime I want. And I do. They have a name for me. I'm a nymphomaniac."

Christian slowly bowing his head. Loosening his fists as he stands. Fanny watching. Two big tears plopping from his eyes. Go smashing down and bouncing right off the tip of my toes. Where they sink into the carpet.

"O jesus christ Cornelius. What the hell are you doing. O jesus. What awful thing are you doing to me. You're the most unpredictable son of a bitch I've ever come across. I can't say anything now to unsay what I said. You just make me angry. So damn angry. Please. Does it mean anything. If I say I'm sorry. What do you expect me to say. We all can't be like you. I'm not sure I want to be either. O dear. Please. Will you let me do something. Can I put my arms around you. Please. Just let me do that. I want to so much. And to hold you. Because god I think you need me."

You
Tiny
Little
Man

128

14

Lying the night next to a body who owns some of the fortune one treads with footsteps on the pavements of this city. Awake to a hammering on pipes. Fanny in tight blue jeans brought me breakfast. The tray laden beneath her naked breasts. Said she had to go to a board meeting. And dressed as I cowered in bed with a hangover quaffing glass after glass of grapefruit juice out of a giant can. Bravely followed by a plateful of long thin strips of bacon, toasted corn muffins, grape jelly and coffee. I crapped dropping it from the stars like an angel. And showered singing in perfumed lathers.

Her worried eyes when Fanny came back at one o'clock. Stood in the doorway in a brown neat suit throwing off her black cape. And veins bluer under her skin. I sat listening to a vesper in the white room, thinking of Europe. And as an ebony black maid came vacuuming Fanny said let's get the hell out of here, it's such a beautiful day.

We lay on the grey beach. Long rolling waves pounding the sand. Seagulls dipping beaks in the foam. Fanny said she hadn't been in a subway for years. And didn't want to go. I said all right don't and walked away up the block. Eyes blazing she ran after me. Slammed a charley horse with her hard little fist into my arm. My shoulder slumped with a molar loosening pain. And laughing we went down into the dark roaring interborough rapid transit. Could see her anxious watchful eyes. Darting over the endless people. Fat women bundled in their coats. Old men zipped up in jackets, white socks in crumpled shoes, staring out from their dreams. A rabbi in black holding the hand of a wide eyed little boy. Picture of Miss Subways. Wears the same smile Miss Musk wears. When she knows I'm staring through her dress at her body beautiful. The sun out. Crossing the islands of Jamaica Bay. The dirt and grime of the train windows. Shacks on the flatland marshes and muddy inlets. Smoke from garbage dumps. And at the last stop, across strange pavements, we headed for the ocean. Down the block between grey empty houses. Walking the boardwalk she held my arm tugging and hugging. Balmy breezes blowing back her hair. Clutched me lying on the sand. Planes landing and taking off from the airport. On the horizon ships. The sun warm. Sea scented air. The ocean crashing its waves. Fanny holding hands, said Cornelius.

"Must be the ass hole of the world out here but this is the loveliest day I've had for years. No matter whatever else happens, I'll always be glad I knew you."

Lying on the sand till darkness. Her hand gently playing with my friendly front tail. Which made me bark and bite her throat. Howling with sweetest agony. As she moved her blond head down and rolled her lips and tongue in a long lullaby on my flute. My hands up under her cape. Warmed by her juicy overflowing breasts. Out here in the greying darkness along this shore. Under signs which say frozen custard, gift shop, pizza playland and cigars at city prices. As a little boy I feared sharks out there under water. Which tore a boy's white skin into red bloody pieces. Pull down Fanny's drawers. He died with people screaming and running up out of the waves. Pulsing fresh oils between her legs. Soft comfy and warm. Dear god please let me win. Give this apprentice mortician out of a job a chance. Remember the favours I did now. Distributing justice in my youthful backyards to all those lousy neighborhood hypocrites. Who shouted and shook fists at me when I was just a fun loving defenceless kid. Smashed tomatoes on summer screens to spray Friday night bridge players with a measle like decoration. Planned forays with another midnight friend. People with meanness on their faces who were dirty lousy rats sentenced to suffer. Here on earth. Especially on Saturday nights. When wearing three pairs of socks we dug each plant shrub and bush and exchanged the whole god damn lot with the garden next door. Miller's roses growing on Sunday morning in the Duffy's garden. Now Duffy's dahlias blooming their colors along the Miller's borders. As Sunday morning they looked up twice frowning over the edges of their newspapers. Not knowing who the fuck to shake a fist at. Two of them property owners in shirt sleeves, pillars of the community standing hands on hips viewing the situation. As I strolled by their picket fence to church. Later after much shouting and brooding suspicion they both sued each other. Me the mastermind at midnight work. Fanny trying to squeeze every last drop out of my balls. Pick one off like a plum with a snap of her fingers. Blast my white eager gush into her. As she groans up her steps of pleasure. Dark wind blowing above our heads. A chill rising with the tide. An ocean liner's lights ablaze heading for Europe. Sun pink glint of a plane's wings sweeping over the water, changing pitch of the engines as they go in to land. First time I ever got drunk was out here. Came with a gang of other boys. All the way from the Bronx. Days swimming on the beach and nights groaning with sunburn. On the porch of a bar on One Hundred and Third Street met a black haired dark eyed beauty of a girl. From east side downtown Manhattan. And a policeman later found me reeling along the boardwalk and said it was a disgrace, a kid drunk at his age.

Fanny and I stopped in a corner drug store. With a black and gold glass sign which said Pharmacy. Sat across a plastic topped yellow table. Man in his white coat and brown mustache served us two hot chocolates with a double dose of cream on top. Two cookies each on the side of our saucers. Called us madam and sir in his broken accent and bowed as he handed out two long polished spoons and placed between us a jar of colored straws. Brought a napkin dispenser and said there you are folks, enjoy. Fanny smiling and reaching out her hand over mine with all her diamonds glittering, all her smooth slender wrist loaded with gold. Way out here in lonely Far Rockaway.

Through that unemployed week. I lay in bed each morning. Breakfasting from a silver tray engraved with a large stag. Reading the nice clear print of the Wall Street Journal. The

131

thunderous precious ingots shovelled back and forth. The vast mergers. The silent monster profits. Some of them delivered right to Fanny's door. While I was drinking creamy coffee, slapping bologna and salami slices between butter slathered golden toasted Jewish rye bread. Chewing it down with gusto. And at twelve as I descended, Mr Kelly saying hi Mr Peabody and gave me the day's barometric pressure. Following which, without a trace of innocence, he frequently farted.

Went to the shoe shine store and sat up on one of their thrones. Little bald headed man with his wizened skin on hands and arms. Would stand back each morning to survey the leather. Quickly laying out his selected pots of creams when inspiration seized. To send me with another rare hue walking the streets in my footwear gleaming. My nose and ears following the scent of smoke or sound of sirens. Zooming round the corners. And once thought the end of the world had come. Eleven squad cars convening down the streets. To surround a little grey old man mumbling a Baltic tongue and pushing a baby carriage with his homemade pretzel toaster. They took down his long name and wheeled his dainty smoking contraption up into a truck and roared away. As he stood watching tears in his eyes. And a man next to me saying.

"Look at that. Look what they do. They could go and arrest a dozen big gangsters robbing this city blind and instead they come and take away this little guy's living."

And as four o'clock approached I walked on to the Game Club. Sparred a fistic and verbal round or two with O'Rourke. Getting daily less terrified of seeing Vine. Till one afternoon lying on my back on a bench in the steam. Gestating on all the god damn flood of money flowing through this country's secret conduits that I haven't got a license to fish in. And an attendant came in and said Mr Christian there's a very important letter waiting for you out at the front desk. I thought the committee for membership had convened to take a vote of confidence to throw me out. For moral meanderings and tricky Far Rockaway turpitudes. Seen windswept and blown on a beach. Socking it into the said Fanny Sourpuss.

The long white envelope was passed over the marble counter.

132

In this evening's lobby sprinkled with elderly yachting gentlemen. Went to a green leather chair behind a pillar. To tear it open and read. Scrawled in a tiny neat hand.

My dear Cornelius,

I quite understand your hesitancy in not showing your face around the old branch. I know that in the past there have been a few uncommendable slip ups but although you don't deserve any medals for discretion, your last delinquency wasn't all your fault. I consider myself as much to blame as anybody. I have tried without success to get in touch with you at your address and hope this finds you. I want you to come and see me. I'll be at my west side branch every day from ten a.m. till one p.m. Do that for me.

Yours most sincerely,
Clarance Vine

P.S. I hereby cancel your remaining debt to me of $243.21.

C.V.

Woke one night. During a dream that Vine was running an airborne burial service. With a hearse plane, flower plane and planes carrying the mourners to an airport surrounded by a cemetery. Fanny's bedside lamp on. She lay face up, her head cushioned by the billowy pillow. Could just see over the edges of mine. Her eyes staring at the ceiling out of their pools of moisture overflowing down her cheeks. Reach for her arm to ask what was the matter. And I didn't. For fear I'd touch something untouchable deep in her secret pool of sorrow. A look on her face. That something was running away she couldn't catch. Yesterday I saw people who knew her, waving as they left the oak panelled room where Fanny and I met for a drink after I waltzed down from the club. They kept smilingly shaking their arms and she looked straight through them.

Took Fanny on a trip north out of Grand Central Station. Clutching each other in the tiny little world abuilding we made out of our lives. Said why don't we just go and get on any train. After I have a pee. Went up steps into the great pissoir. Chose one of the marble latrines. Where three gents were standing wild eyed side by side, feverishly pulling their stiff white pricks. Told

Fanny on the train. When I'd recovered from my shock. Said she wished she could see. Her dream was to be fucked in her three throats, top bottom and back, by three pricks while holding two more, one in each hand. Gave her a religious feeling she was being crucified. And made me wretched with jealousy all the way to Mount Kisco. Walked around town. Then cross country. Relieved I never saw four guys. But everyone staring as they sped past on the road. Showed her the white clapboard house where my little brother and I had been sent in the summers. The lake we swam in and belted poor bulging eyed bull frogs over the head with canoe paddles as they sat grunting peacefully in the water. Always watch out where you sit sunning.

On the way back to town police stopped to arrest us as vagrants. Fanny flashed sixteen one hundred dollar bills. And they arrested us as crooks. Three phone calls later locating Fanny's lawyer they apologised and let us go, said someone heard my accent and was suspicious I was a spy.

The big train thundering back towards the city, it began to rain. Saw a face I knew from the Bronx as a boy. Just clipped our tickets as if he'd never seen me before. An only child to whom his parents gave everything. Even his false teeth to replace those I knocked out in a fight. Watched him go down the aisle and back into the past, in his blue conductor's uniform. His mother and father pampering him as a princeling. The world later on casually slamming him in the balls.

Fanny bought me a pair of rat skin gloves. And she knelt nights in an array of jewels and gowns by the side of her round tiny dining room table. As I tore into rare thick steaks and defenceless mounds of creamed spinach. Running lower and lower in cash. Getting higher and higher up Fanny. Our bodies clapping together on the bed. In sweaty crescendoes. Through musical interludes over the radio. My own naked recitals I gave at the piano. Fanny blowing me through a slow movement to an incredible tune my fingers played. Soft or hard it seemed my cock was hardly ever out of her mouth. Unless it was in her somewhere else. And the sudden midnight arrest we watched of the murderess across the street. Who shot her lover seven times down the spine. Red lights flashing, blue uniforms disappearing into the building. Ambulances and squad cars taking everybody away. And before we went to sleep, the murderess was free on bail. Returning triumphantly in her giant chauffeured limozine.

Now this morning Fanny tightening my tie said my poor little baby wear your gloves and let Glen take you over to Vine, I insist. Please Cornelius, it will make you feel so much better getting out of a chauffeured car. And I walked. Flashing my shoeshine. Gloriously stubborn to the last. Approaching this elaborate yellowed brick emporium. Five stories high. Bay trees in big barrels at the entrance. Brown carpeted lobby. Not a sign of green anywhere. Man with a pince nez and waxed twirled mustache asks can I help you.

"Yes, I've come to see Mr Vine."

"He's busy right now. Your name please."

"Cornelius Christian."

"O. In that case, Mr Christian I think Mr Vine would like to know you're here. I've heard a lot about you. Nice to meet you. My name is Nathaniel Hardwicke. Excuse me please, won't you. Please, do be seated. And here, have something to read if you like."

Wow. That guy could bury you with both hands tied behind his back. Striped trousers and cutaway coat. Almost joins his hands in prayer as he speaks. Soft calming words. Calling you hither. Makes you feel apologetic for being alive.

Mr Hardwicke bowing Christian into an elevator. Up two floors. Past a nodding smiling girl with, my god, another of Vine's drum majorette trophies on her desk. Turn right down a corridor lined with photographs of celebrity funerals. Into an ante room full of evergreens. A heavy panelled door marked private. Which Nathaniel opens. Into a large room. Clarance seated behind a massive mahogany crescent desk. Immaculate and dark suited as always. Facing out from a corner flanked by two windows. Three gentlemen with big cigars, seated before him. One a baby faced enormity swelling out of his chair. One shadowily familiar with a bandaged jaw and head, gravel voiced in sun glasses and three feet wide. Another hawk nosed and four feet wide.

"Excuse me gentlemen, I hope you won't mind, but I'd like to introduce my associate, you won't object if he sits in."

"No we don't mind. Sure sit him in. Like we said, it's nice to see such a classy staffed operation as you've got, Mr Vine. That's why we come to you. With the kind of all around consultancy we could offer. Like you need a bundle. We got a bundle."

"I'm fully financed gentlemen."

"O k, you know, we understand that too, so you're fully financed. But what operation doesn't need more customers. We can push business your way, isn't that right Zeke."

"Sure Tony, a trickle or an avalanche whatever Mr Vine wants."

"Now Zeke here, he covers a lot of areas. The big hotels for instance. Some of them got maybe a dead guest a week. Out of ten or fifteen hotels you got a steady supply of a dozen corpses. Maybe minus a few who don't have money. We're selective."

"Gentlemen I'm not short of deceased."

"O k, o k, it was only if you was short. Now maybe you don't have the best sanitation service. We got good rates for taking your garbage away. With reverence. Isn't that right Zeke."

"That's right. Removal with reverence. We got good rates."

"I've got a fine garbage collector already."

"So all right. We still think you could be benefiting from our service. You know. I mean look at that place you're opening up. I mean let me tell you something Mr Vine, we think you're a pretty successful guy. I mean Zeke here, he's done calculations. With a successful guy we feel we got something to offer. That nothing interrupts him. Extra fire protection for instance. I mean take this place. Gee what a fire could do to this. This ain't no new building."

"I'm insured gentlemen."

"We know you're insured, isn't that right Carmine."

"That's right."

"But Mr Vine, sir, what we was thinking was would you be compensated for the loss in momentum of your operation. That's what worries us. You know."

"It doesn't worry me gentlemen."

"Excuse me Mr Vine, can I ask you just one question."

"Please do."

"Look at us. There's Zeke there. Some people think he's ugly, call him Two Ton. But he's got a nice house out in Flatbush.

136

He's got neighbors he's proud of. He's got a son already studying to be a lawyer and a daughter who goes to a good school. Just like your two daughters.''

"What do you mean like my two daughters.''

"Nothing, nothing believe me. You know, today there's crime everywhere. It's just like we was all pillars of the community and should stick together. Now take Carmine, he's a credit to his neighborhood. Sure his good friends call him the Slim Wop. They enjoy kidding. But they like him, a good family man from Hoboken. We don't want to give any offense Mr Vine. You know. That's all I was saying. I just wanted to ask you, do you think as businessmen we would waste your time and our time if we didn't feel deep down sincerely that we could assist you, help you. Render you down to earth honest to god service. Like the sudden need you funeral guys talk about. That you don't know hits you till it's knocking on your doorstep. And here we are. Ready to help. A loan, sure. A big loan, all the better. A fantastic loan. Well as I say, we're there. Isn't that right Zeke.''

"That's right.''

"Hey now what about your assistant.''

"My associate.''

"Sorry that's what I meant associate. What's your name again young man. Hey you know I'd swear I knew you from somewhere.''

"I'm Mr Peabody.''

Tony taking the cigar out of his mouth, putting his hand up to his bandaged jaw. Tilting his wide head with its pair of tiny sunken ears. Brushing a lump of ash off his monstrous knee.

"It's funny I really think I know your face. Anyway that name sounds like you was somebody, ha ha Mr Peabody. But no kidding. Maybe you can see what we drive at. You play baseball.''

"No I don't.''

"Maybe you play football.''

"No I'm against violent sport.''

"You must play pinochle.''

"Sorry, no.''

"I guess guys like you and Mr Vine are really too busy. But

137

sports is what has made this country great. Well we don't want to take up your time. Except Mr Vine we want you to know that sometimes we know certain things. Like when a big funeral's going to happen. When I say big. I mean big. Maybe twenty thousand dollars worth. Now what kind of an operation wants in their sane mind to brush off business like that. To kick such an opportunity in the face. In six months we could line up five like that. Am I right Zeke."

"Right."

"And our commission would be hardly nothing. Like five percent. Real low. Of your gross operation. And everything's protected. I mean we heard right away, about this woman suing who says you made a whore out of her husband. That's horrible. What kind of operation wants that kind of publicity. Which is avoided when we explain to her lawyer the back breaking inconvenience he's going to find in his way. Satisfaction guaranteed service that nobody bothers you. Isn't that gospel Zeke."

"That's gospel."

Clarence Vine quietly smiling. Tony removing and wiping sun glasses. Zeke protruding in his chair. Huge bull neck bursting out of a white starched collar. Gold chain across his light brown waistcoat. Upon him all things bulge. Knees elbows and eyes. Chair creaks and squeaks as he moves. Carmine shining his fingernails back and forth on his blue jacket. Spreads out his fingers in the window light and blows lightly on each nail one by one. Turning to look every minute or so behind his head at a photograph of Vine shaking hands with the mayor of New York.

"Well Mr Vine. Mr Peabody. I thank you for your valuable time. I only naturally hope that our endeavours here today will put our service working for you making those extra meaningful dollars. Take the wife to Florida for the weekend. And I know the nicest place. You just go in and say Big Tony sent you. On a free scholarship."

"Mr Peabody and myself are widowers."

"O hey I'm sorry to hear that, that's too bad. Well maybe two healthy distinguished looking men like yourselves. Well what girl wouldn't be proud to stand next to you in any lobby you want to mention along Miami Beach."

"Thank you for all you've said Mr—"

"North. Tony North."

"Mr North."

"And Mr East and Mr West. Easy to remember just like we do business. In all directions."

"Well thank you for coming gentlemen."

"Our pleasure believe us. And goodbye Mr Peabody it was real nice you could sit in. Still think I've seen you somewhere. Hey you wasn't by any chance ever flying airplanes like an airline pilot or something."

"No. I can hardly ride a bicycle."

Blue suited Tony standing, adjusting his sun glasses. As chocolate suited Zeke rises. And with him the whole chair, four legs sticking out from his arse. Tony and Slim Wop reaching out to grab. Tugging at the antique's legs and arms. Vine rapidly coming from around his desk. All three pulling. As Two Ton Zeke holds the edge of Vine's desk. One leg snaps. Tony crashing backwards. Breaking the glass in Vine's photograph with the mayor.

"O gee whiz I'm sorry to break everything Mr Vine. Hey Zeke what the hell's the matter with you. Couldn't you see you shouldn't sit in that chair."

"What do you want me to do stand everywhere I go."

"No I just want you to look before you sit."

"Gee Mr Vine we'll fix that picture and send you two new chairs tomorrow."

"Well that chair happens to be Louis Quatorze."

"Loui. We know a Loui makes furniture right down the avenue here. Don't worry, a chair exactly like that. We'll have it tomorrow, at the latest."

"Hey come on Tony. Don't stand talking about two new chairs. Get this old one off me."

Zeke's ass wedged. Thighs straining at the sides of his trousers. A tug. As he shouts don't kill me. The chair yanked off. Floor trembling. Clarance Vine wiping his brow with a dark green silk hanky. And these gentlemen of the compass picking up their cigars from the ash tray, plunging them back in their mouths as they wave at the door goodbye.

"Nice meeting you mister. Your name just slipped my mind, had a nice clean sound to it."

"Mr Peabody."

"O yeah, Peabody. You sure are familiar from somewhere. And sorry about the busting up, Mr Vine."

Clarance standing over his gilt embellished chair. Bending to look at the broken back and one leg wrenched off. Shaking his head back and forth.

"Well Cornelius, or should I call you Mr Peabody. You just saw what is sometimes described as muscle. Flexing in one of my chairs. Sit down. I'm glad you've come around like this."

"Those men trying to blackmail you Mr Vine."

"If I let them. Yes. If I don't. No. I can tell you one thing though. Guys are trying to get into this business like it was some kind of sawdust sausage factory. Nobody gives a good god damn about the dead anymore."

"Mr Vine, I really am sorry for what's happened. Is Mrs Silver really suing."

"Here's the letter from her lawyer. But don't worry about it. That's my problem."

Christian leaning forward. Sunlight flashing on the white sheet that rattles in his hand. A spear of pain flaring up one's bowel. Clang of bells and sirens as a fire apparatus roars by down in the street.

Dear Sir,

We communicate with you on behalf of our client Mrs Silver, concerning the extensively damaging outrage (hereinafter referred to as The Outrage) regarding her late husband Herbert's funeral arrangements, who, as numerous people know held an honorable position in the business community of this city for many years.

The Outrage upon our client occasioned grievous ego injuries and an outbreak of warts over her entire body. We are holding your firm accountable as well as your employee Cornelius Christian who prepared the remains.

Further concerning The Outrage, my client has complained bitterly regarding the cavalier manner in which she

140

was treated in her interview with you with a view to rectifying the matter to the satisfaction of all concerned. We fail to understand your refusal to discipline your employee and to require him to apologize to Mrs Silver. The menacing comment, "I'll pump you full of formaldehyde," was a direct threat to do grievous bodily harm to my client, to maim, spiritually grieve, and abusively imperil her life. The malicious slandering of the words, "sell you as a bloody monster," and other words too offensive to mention has rendered my client to total incapacitation since, and her disfigurement by warts has forced her to withdraw from the outside world.

What the hell, yes, I use the word hell, kind of mental scourge do you think innocent people should be subjected to these days when laying to rest their loved ones. We are sure you would prefer that the matter not be litigated with the attendant publicity. And in such event, my client, to compensate for her acute and prolonged suffering, would consider the matter closed upon payment of adequate damages.

Yours,
Wartberg & Blitz

"It was all my fault Mr Vine. O my god. The last thing I wanted to do was to hurt your business."

"I know that Cornelius, I know that. But it could have happened to anybody. You put your heart and soul into doing the best you could. George told me that. And you got a snarl in your face for thanks. There are no hard feelings here."

Vine's eyes. They go through you. Seeing every layer both living and dead. Knows every thought you think. Both funny and sad, serious or glad.

"And by the way Cornelius, if you don't mind telling me. How the hell do I shift that guy with the sandwichboard outside the east side branch. Says he's a friend of yours waiting for you. Has a god damn new sign every day. O k, I understand. You'd like me to leave him alone."

"I guess so Mr Vine."

"Sure. Somehow there's not much left of the soft and loving.

Like the shape of an ear. The ear of a beautiful woman. That you know is going to melt away. I wish you luck Cornelius. I have a feeling your name is going to be on our lips someday. And I hope I can say then without being presumptuous, that we were friends. I don't know Christian. But that's what's most precious to me.''

In all
The dark dooms
Where courage
Must live
If life
Is not
To die

15

Cornelius Christian strolling away up the street from Vine's west side branch. Staring into the sunshine pouring upon this wide long teaming avenue. Trucks cars and buses at the traffic lights. Stand with folk collecting to cross the road. Easy to look good in such a sea of ugly people.

Christian pausing on the sidewalk. Big smiling picture of a man sitting chained to an egg. Inside the window of a bank. Above which the flag of this country flies red white and blue with stars and stripes. Over the passing heads decorated with faces. In which Vine said he could read a whole life. During the secondary flacidity when the rigor mortis passes off. And just up here is an automat. Have some milk and apple pie while I worry. About how I find another job.

A tanned dirty hand placed on Christian's arm. A ragged pedestrian, his coat clutched closed at his throat. Soup stained silk blue tie hanging out, white streaks of lightning down it. Shoes bent and broken. Dark red gums holding yellow teeth as he speaks.

"Buddy can you spare a dime."

"Sorry, no."

"Just a dime. Hey come on, give me a break."

"I need it for myself."

"Well at least you're honest. But I really need a dime."

"What for."

"For a cup of coffee."

"Sorry."

"Buddy it's just a little charity, make you feel a better person."

"I feel good enough already."

"Buddy believe me if I had something to give you I'd give it to you."

"All right. You can give me your life's story."

"What for."

"Because I'm paying for it."

"Who said I was selling."

"Do you want a dime or don't you."

"I want two dimes for my life story."

"O k, two dimes."

"Buddy, what do you want my life's story for."

"What do you want two dimes for."

"So I can get a cup of coffee and a roll."

"Well I want your life's story because it will make my hair stand on end."

"What are you fella, some kind of pervert. Anyway for that I charge a dollar."

"I'll give you two quarters."

"What, fifty cents for my whole life story. It could be worth a fortune."

"O k, goodbye."

"Hey wait a minute mister what about a quarter and I'll tell you where I was born."

"No I want the whole story."

"It could take me nearly an hour to tell it."

"I'll wait."

"It's too public to stand here while I tell it."

"O k. Let's go into the automat. I'll buy you a cup of coffee."

"Hey mister I go in and have a cup of coffee with you I could be missing making dimes from guys who don't want to know my whole life's story, be reasonable will you. I mean what's to pay for my time and overheads."

"Take a risk."

"Buddy in my life every risk is like wearing a noose round the neck while you jump the Grand Canyon. I mean what's with you. What do you want with my life story."

"I don't know yet. I'm taking a risk."

"Fella why don't you take an option. Be a sport. Just give me a dime. Meet you here tomorrow same time."

Christian looking into these eyes. Only need a token bit of touching up. Easy to flesh out his cheeks. Hair shampooed and combed, a close shave and he'd look good in his coffin. Hire mourners. Maybe a cockroach would come running out of him. Like the one George said once scampered along the edge of the antique embalming table and sent Vine into a rage, smashing bottles on the marble slab as he missed the scurrying bug, drenching himself in embalming fluid.

"Hey look, see what's happening. While I'm talking to you. Look at all the handouts I might be missing. People walking by who could be giving me maybe quarters. And here I'm stuck making no money talking with you. Good way to go broke."

"You mean you're not broke."

"Hey now buddy wait a minute. Why should I tell you a stranger my finances."

"Why not."

"Gee whiz fella, already two dozen possibilities I've seen walk by. Hey look, for christ's sake. Forget I ever asked you. Why don't I give you a dime, and you go your way and I go mine, how about that."

"O k."

"Jesus christ, it's crazy, what the hell kind of a world would it be if every guy was like you. Here. Take it."

"Thanks."

"O boy fella, don't thank me, thank you."

Christian slipping the thin coin into his dark tweed waist coat pocket. Passing a vegetable shop, green peppers, bulging red and yellow tomatoes, purple egg plants and fruits stacked out on the pavement. Buy myself an apple. With one nickel. Make a phone call with another.

Christian entering this drugstore. Glass cabinets jammed from floor to ceiling. Smells of soap, pastes and powders in all their glossy wrappings. Mustached man in his white jacket. Smiling behind his glasses. Happy at his little counter where he mixes the cures. From his storehouse of knowledge. Come in looking yellow and he gives you a blue pill and you go out green. Helps you soak up the sunshine. Now tells a woman examining a toothbrush that last year dentists said brush up and down and now this year they say brush back and forth so maybe it's better to brush in a circle till they make up their minds.

Christian in the telephone booth passing a finger up and down the names. Write the number on the back of a Vine business card. Pop in the coin, hear it go clink and bing down into the black box. Bell ringing far out over the tenement cliffs of the Bronx to where on the northern borders of the city it's wooded and green again. At the other end of all the miles of wire. Hello. Hello.

"May I please speak to Miss Graves. Charlotte Graves."

"Speaking."

"This is Cornelius Christian."

"O hi, how wonderful to hear from you. You know, really amazing only a minute ago I was thinking of you. Of my first date I ever had. It was with you."

"Could I take you out. Again. Tonight."

"Gee, I'd really love to but I'm sorry I've got to go to a party."

"O."

"But wait, why don't you come."

"I'd be imposing."

"O no. You wouldn't be. Please. Come. I can bring someone if I like."

"O k."

"Why don't you call for me. It's on the way. You remember where I live."

"Fine. What time."

"Eight."

"Gee I'm really looking forward to seeing you Cornelius, gosh so good to hear from you, just out of the blue like this."

"Well fine. Tonight then."

"Yes."

"Goodbye."

"Goodbye."

Walk now a street. Empty houred. Till eight o'clock. Fill it with Fanny. She'll be waiting. For me to come back. To lie

146

twinging a little in fear. As I did when she said again about all
the pricks up her throats at once. That she wanted all the guys to
blow their tops together. And in her own hysteric rapture she
would supremely shudder. The white soft liquids pouring over
her hands. Gently up and down into her throats. That strange
sad tired look brooding over her elegant face. Two darkened
eyes afloat on her placid sperm silkened skin.

Cornelius Christian crossing the street into Central Park.
Look down and see all the bottle tops embedded in the asphalt.
Pair of fat grey squirrels running up a tree chased by a dog.
This whole massive country. One vast incitement to the appetite.
One monstrous insult to the delicate spirit. Go up to every
seemly lady on a bench. And ask. Awfully politely. May I make
use of your service entrance madam. Deliver you a catastrophic
fuck. From your local supplier.

Saunter up the winding path to the top of this stone hill.
Hands folded behind back. Sun warm on my face. Silent men
cluttered around the concrete chess tables. Fingers tapping, lips
pursing over the death and slaughter drenched chess boards.
And sitting there ready to checkmate a sour opponent, the man
who valued me as a gentleman as I sat in the automat. Enveloped
in my doom. In a sea of silent suffering. One little word of
comfort saves you drowning.

Down beyond another little rocky hillside, mothers fathers and
kids on the merry go round. Boys and girls lifted on the wooden
ponies. Big platform turning to the trumpeting music. Few
sneaky parents trying to get a ride too. Stand here, out of the
funeral business forever. Done enough to Vine already without
asking him to take me back on the job. Walk here homesick. With
a hard on. For the soft carpets upon which sadness treads. The
cool skinned mounds of Miss Musk's arse floating by two
cheeked. Where in there between them I had so hornily deeply
planted my pole. With nothing else to say after orgasm. Except
let's do this again real soon.

Four o'clock by the bronze glockenspiel in the zoo. Musky
smells and random roars of the big cats. Keeper looking so god
damn confident in his faded dark green uniform, leaning against
the wall. Finished hosing away all the shit. After the tiger's

147

meat dinner. The clock tower bell chiming its tune for an audience of balloon toting kids. Stand with them alive in peace. Till some new fucker comes gliding out of the shadows to tell you he's got some oral rapture for sale for five bucks. And as you rush that much poorer to consummate he trips you up, cuts your trousers off with a razor and lifts your wallet. Dear god. Got to fight. Claw my way up through all the grey brains and heads, shrunken cocks and shrivelled balls, flat asses and hanging bellies. Who say no to me. That you can't run wild across the plateau. Where the dollars swarm like autumn leaves. Deep under foot. And falling everywhere.

Christian in the blue balmy splendor of this afternoon strolling eastwards. Stepping into a marble townhouse filled with paintings. Natty gentleman with a watch chain sporting the recent hot shit look. This picture gallery where folk come sniffing the profit lurking in the contours and colors. Drawn by innocent bastards looking for beauty. Sold to rich cunts craving esteem. Make a murmur in my best accent.

"Shit."

"I beg your pardon sir."

"I said shit."

"I thought that's what you said, sir."

"Yes that's right, that's what I said."

"Might I ask are you referring to any particular piece sir. If you are, perhaps I might be of help. You see I quite agree with you. With one or two exceptions."

This smiling chap steps forward on the marble. In a nicely tapered brown suit. To conduct Christian throughout the gallery. As if I had a platinum pot to piss in. Must think I'm in Who's Who. Or exdirectory in the monstrous volume of who aint. Opens mirrored doors into private enclosures. Treasures calmly leaning against tapestried walls. Awaiting my nod. A frisson of recognition. Gee what a swell painting.

Back on the street. New hope out of elegance. Man of a private female means. Socked in on Park Avenue. With the pale limbed Fanny Sourpuss. Calm eyed mother and daughter pass. Means a husband and father somewhere sweating. Heads of people wave along in swathes of sunshine rippling like fields of flowers. If you don't look too close. And see the vampire faces.

There it is. Vine's edifice goes up. Floor after floor. Six red hatted men. Stand round a long sixteen wheeled truck. In yellow tough shoes. They hold guide ropes in gloved hands. A huge tank hoisted. Clarance will use it to hold his formaldehyde. Down deep he'll be shaving the dead in barber chairs. As if life didn't matter at all. It doesn't. Once you blast your head off. And find out. Or wait awhile. Alive. And maybe someone will give you a smile. Shoot him dead instead. To keep the dying up. And the courtesy down.

Christian threading through the pedestrians. Who stop to look up. None of you realize I know Vine. Personally. And when God taps you on the shoulder. I'm ready. To christen his new building. Embalm a body right out up on that girder. Tubes hanging down like seaweed. And balance puncturing my trocar. What about you madam. Repose that arse. Face down, two cheeks up. Nude deceased. Revolutionize the industry.

Window of a delicatessen store. Caviars and cheese. Delights Fanny put out for my devouring. First hours I've had of utter peace in this new world. To watch a man with a dog going by. A canine breed I knew in childhood. Who jumped on my dog and bit him while he was still a puppy. And the dirty rotten owner laughed.

Christian stepping in a doorway. To peruse this man in his lightweight grey flannel toting his curly blue dog on a fancy braided leather lead. Waiting to cross the street. A woman sits just starting her car. Which roars suddenly into life and motion. Smashing another parked in front and bouncing backwards, engine racing, crashing into another behind. Step deeper into my doorway. Like any good New Yorker. Man with blue curly dog shaking his fist at her. Shouting abuse in the window. Driver already out of her mind with panic. As she begs silently for help. Man with his dog, his hand raised shouting, rushing to stand in front of the car she smashed, just as she tears forward again with screaming tires smoking on the asphalt and gives it another slam. Sending the light green empty vehicle rolling over the grey suited man. With his blue dog, both prostrate in their separate puddles of blood. After this automotive rampage. Fire engines come, ambulance and police. A group of strong citizens lifting off the car. Doctor shaking his head over the man and dog dead.

Caught in the jaws of a random justice. In a few more months Clarance could handle them both. Right across the street. In a coffin for master and pet.

Suddenly gloomy afternoon. To go slamming punching bags in the athletic smells of the Game Club. The Admiral popping farts as he practiced his corkscrew left hook that paralyses. After a shower in ivory suds took a glass of beer. Walked east. Through the furred and gold plated men and women. Descended into the Lexington Avenue subway. The rush hour crush of tired silent faces. Breathing all over each other. Someone's hands trying to open my fly. Easing fingers in under the foreskin. All the way to the Bronx, didn't know who to punch. For borrowing my privates without permission.

The last stop overlooking the golf course and the woods. Went down the shadowy iron steps and waited in the line of people for the bus. A face. Pair of blue eyes. A girl who sat in front of me at school. Loved her. For two solid months. Tempted myself thinking I could have her as a girl friend anytime I wanted. And all we ever did was smile. Now she stands nine years away.

Christian pulling the cord to stop the bus. On the next corner a big gas station and bar. Horseshoe courts and shuffleboards beyond the trees. Fourth of July parades ended there. Took my little brother and bought him ice cream. Along this parkway. By the houses where I had friends. Grew up here in all my dreadful innocence. Tiny soul so beautiful, so full of fear. Stared down at by big mean faces. And you never forget. The courageous boys bigger than me. Who told bullies who kept me out of stickball and hockey games, that they would punch them in the eye. Gave me all the hope I had. Shipped back and forth between the foster homes. Waiting for a hand to snatch us away. With my sobbing little brother. To brand new cold hearts and strange bed springs. To people who want you to call them uncle and aunt. Because they think you're something the cat dragged in.

These same slate sidewalks. Scratched with marks hoboes made. In the cement on this street corner, my best friend's name is scrawled. All that's left of him. Since a Christmas in a hard frosty month. They said on the telephone he was dead. I went over to church and sat downstairs in the back in the singing and incense. I thought of summer and the maple leaves. And how they grow to make tunnels of the streets. And if you die you go away up somewhere in the sky where the airplanes are and it's white and blue. And it's red and gold. They had to bring him back from Florida and all the sunny months. Where the big bugs bang the windows and the golf courses have spongy grass. Loading him in the train on the lonely night north, wrapped in a flag. Over his cold blond smile. Same blue pavements then over the stone hard ground. And kids' marble holes worn shallow. As children here we were catholics come together. And altar boys trying to touch god. Stealing apples and cherries Saturday. Sunday adoring the holy ghost. Sat out nights on rivers, skating on lakes in the moon. And each summer getting black in the sun and chasing through the waves. He was on the train crossing Virginia through Emporia on that flat sea level land. Over Maryland and the dark green hills. And then Newark where beyond the swamps are the thin white sparkling things sticking in the night and how you go in that endless tunnel, the river crushing your ears and come out rumbling by the long platforms to a stop. Where they slid him down and wheeled him to a truck with a soldier standing by. The lights sad and the flag bright. Someone there to meet him. To take him north again to the Bronx. In the last month of the war. So many years ago. The woods where we trapped, shot squirrel and caught snakes by the tail. Tied a big swing high in the oak that I never dared try. Everything green then in a fat sun. Each girl friend was forever in talks through the night on some fence. When we washed ears and polished face, hair and shoes until they were health. And we went places where we said hi there, isn't it swell we all met like this. A game played with hearts and fingertips. And he had moved away during the war to where there were no trees and lives of people on top of lives and more beside more, in hallways holding grey tiles, footsteps of strangers and silence. On the hard sad day. I drove down the avenue under the roaring elevator train. And parked in a side street of gloom and grey. Asked the man at the door and he said softly the Lieutenant is reposing in suite seven to your right along the corridor. His name up on a little black sign with moveable white letters that slide on for the next and the next. I shook hands and nodded with these other friends. Some smiled beneath their crinkled eyes and say it's good to have you here. I knelt at the casket to pray. Always the holiest hearts are dead. Yet he had punched me in the mouth when I had braces on my teeth and crushed my model airplane. And I had loved his sister. He was under glass where I didn't want to look. Next morning mass and casket and people stepping out into the dreary cold. And a long line of black cars went north again to the cemetery they called the gate of heaven. I was the last car filled with his girl friends and sniffles. Off the highway and up the mountain road past a hot dog stand, a few last gold leaves wagging on the trees and white islands of snow spaced through the woods. The little green tent and fake rolls of grass they spread over the dirt. The diggers behind the gravestones putting on caps and jackets, a great heavy row of European hands hanging from the smooth covert cloth. Soldiers lined up and let go a sudden crack in the sky and the bugle with its death sounds down the valley and coming back again from the hills around. I stood behind some people and never saw him going down. His girl friends cried and one screamed and was held away and she knelt, her nylon knees sinking in the mud, and we all began to pray and say things to ourselves.

Like
I promise
I promise

16

Up three brick steps. A summer screen door. Warped through the winter. Darkness in there behind the venetian blinds. Ring the bell on the house of Charlotte Graves. Lean to look in the window. See a memory of red walls and a black coffin. Screen door opens out and the glass and curtained mahogany door opens in. To her large smile.

"Gee come in. You're early. I'm just half ready. Should I take your gloves."

"Sure."

"Gee they're nice."

"French rat skin, the leather is exceedingly smooth and soft."

Living room with its blue carpet and brown sofa chairs. As it was all those years ago. When mothers said you come through here like it was a train station. Graduation picture of Charlotte standing among all the other white gowned girls. On the brink of marriage. Or near the downhill years of spinster doom.

"Gee let me look at you. You seemed to have lived. That sounds crazy to say I know. But I just haven't lived. Can I get you a beer."

"Please."

"Sure. Certainly. I'm so excited I don't know where to rush. Just washed my hair. And it's dried all wrong. Rinsed it in the wrong brand of ale. Hey Mom Cornelius Christian's here."

Shiver at the sound of one's shouted name. That I'm here. Where I knew all these streets and houses. And the summer at

153

eight o'clock each morning. Running down the sidewalk in pointed shoes with no laces. To cut my grass in the cemetery. Saving money. To date a rich girl I'd met. To climb up and be with her in her dazzling world. Far from my own, orphaned and poor. I was as good as anybody else. But I had no proof.

"Well hi you there Cornelius. Well what a sight. You haven't changed one bit."

"Thank you."

"Maybe that accent is a change. Charlotte's been getting me to wash and iron everything she owns. Think the girl never had a date before."

Mrs Graves's smiling kindly eyes. Made you want to be seen. Always wished she was my mother. What sorrow hit her. Made her hair go grey. She always welcomed me. Into the comfort of her friendly beauty. Everywhere else I stood in people's hallways. Waiting. But she invited me in. Gave me a glass of root beer and cookies on a plate.

Horn beeping outside the house. Charlotte leading Christian. Introducing him. This is Cornelius Christian, Freda and Joan. That's Stan, that's Marty. As they sat hands draped over the backs of seats of this low blue purring streamlined automobile.

Softly groaning power and wheels squealing round corners. These easy carefree voices. Sons and daughters of lovely mommies and distinguished daddies. Talk about where everybody went to college. Majoring in gladness. And I look across the upturned nose of this girl's face and out the window at the light on the passing grass. Of another world. Delivering newspapers. Up and down these streets. When I thought I was going to be a millionaire. With moroccan bound books for looks everywhere. Every afternoon loaded down. Folding papers with a slight of hand and flicking them on the grey porches. And even in an open window for a laugh. Which I thought I needed.

Christian squeezed between these soft hips. This night in springtime. The musk of Charlotte. Deep and sweet. What you loved were all the dreams. A sound. The brand new world of snow on spruce. The light from a winter window when you held her hand. Carry it all to sleep at night. In confidential whispers. That a slate roofed gabled house amid the trees would be yours

154

one day. And there's the grocery store where I fished a seven up from the floating lumps of ice and said hi to the rival newspaper boy. Along this frontier road picked berries, grapes and went stealing peaches. Friday I collected and most said come back tomorrow and I objected but turned my sad face away and mumbled it was only fifteen cents. You'd think it was a crime every time I rang a doorbell and even those with chimes and added up the weeks they owed. In there they sat warm and reading, with smells of steak and pizza pie. Stood dancing with my cold toes, lips chapped with frost. And thought I might die. But in the sun on these quiet roads under the trees near the river. The green grass, the cliffs and hills and bridges bent over the trains. Cool summer halls to click heels and spin down the stairs on my educated wrist. And now we pass that street. The big brick house with the side entrance. Where the lady opened the door a crack on pay day in her black bathing suit. Scared the shit out of me as she asked me in. Four o'clock in the wild silence of that afternoon. To stand in the hallway as she closed the door and went through her purse. She was wet and dripping. Said you don't have to go right away, I'll give you some cherry juice. She grabbed me by the arm and held me there, staring in my eyes, licking her lips. Kept saying she was forty years old. I kept saying you owe me thirty cents for two weeks papers. She gave me half a dollar. I took the big coin with the cracked bell on the back and fished out some change. She opened up my fly and pulled out my prick. Which pumped lotion all over her floor. And she said you dirty little boy, mess my carpet up, get the hell out of here. Once they get their own way folk are so god damned unfair.

This shadowy road we roll along. These bland breezy unsuffering voices. New little white boxes built between the bigger older houses. And that one there. With the great grey porch. Italian girl in my class. She was big. Of heart and bust. Said didn't I feel lousy being an orphan. And if I came to her house when her parents were out she would give me jello and ice cream. Never went because I never could be sure who liked me. Made so many mistakes. Walking into snarls. And instead went alone along the streets. With my Bronx Home News. Ringing bells, knocking on doors. To say pay me please. And the heads with after lunch eyes came out too beaten to refuse. In my little book I marked them paid and with some quiet charm of mine I tried to make them feel it was not the end of the world. But some heartless called me liar and lingerer. Napping under trees, banging on doors and a whistler in halls. I whispered something about freedom and they shouted don't come back no more and slammed the door. I walked away young tears melting with despair. They'd all be sorry when they found me Christmas Eve shoeless and starved, dead in the snow. And one dawn on Sunday in black winter. I wrote across the newspaper's front page. How does it feel to cheat a child. Monday creeping through the streets. The raging faces watching from windows everywhere. And a man on a porch shaking a fist which he said would break my head. And fearful and forceful I told him to drop dead. And ran.

Charlotte Graves reaching to touch Christian's rat gloved hand. And smile. As the swaying car glides up round these curving roads. And turns in a drive. Beyond the clipped shrubs and lawns, a house with gables over its tall mullioned windows. Spruce trees blue and sprinkled yellow with light. An entrance like a castle. Slamming car doors. Loud hellos inside. Follow Charlotte on her slender legs. Over the soft carpet. Till someone stops her on the arm. And I go down these steps into this large sunken room. A great stone fireplace. And a tall dark haired chap in a yellow button downed collared shirt.

"Hi don't think I know you."

"Cornelius Christian."

"I'm Stan Mott, good to see you. That's my mother with the gold hair, that's my father with the grey. Help yourself."

"I beg your pardon."

"To a beer or whatever you want to drink. By the way I think you're pretty funny."

"Thank you."

Christian backing up to a space of clear wall. Next to the marble mantelpiece of the fireplace. A picture of a ship with bulging sails on a blue green raging sea. Up steps through an arch, a massive dining room. Table covered with silver urns.

Charlotte had the biggest tits of any girl friend I ever had. Waited through three dates at the movies and three pineapple sodas before I reached and felt them. Then felt like a dirty rat.

Stan's grey headed father in his shirtsleeves, cuffs rolled up to the elbow. Toasting a bun on a long fork at the fire. Tweezes up a steaming frankfurter out of a simmering bowl.

"Here, you want some mustard on it."

"Yes please. Thank you."

"Who are you, son."

"Haven't got that old yet but my name's Cornelius Christian."

"That so. Well I'm old enough to be Stan's pa. Pretty good crack you made there. Always like to keep up with Stan's friends, never get the chance. Like to see the young people more often. Get to thinking old fashioned if you don't meet the young people. Hey there you are Charlotte."

"Hi Mr Mott."

"Don't Mr Mott me. Just telling this young man here I don't get a chance to keep up with you kids. Well you're looking prettier everyday. Just like your mother. Nearly married this girl's mother. She was the most beautiful girl in her time. Turned me down she did."

Gathering swelling. Music pounding. More glad faces entering. The overflow of promise. Girls demurely waiting with the lock and key of love. Calling out their familiar notions. Eyes flashing for fashion. Ankles astride in their goatskin shoes. And much other footwear. As Mr Mott enthralls his little audience of two.

"When you start forgetting when you last saw a pretty face then you're getting old."

"You just try to make me feel good Mr Mott. Cornelius here is an old friend. He's just come back from living in Europe."

"That so. Don't get to Europe much these days. But those European women. They sure are something. Gosh Paris. London. Those women. I don't know what they've got. But boy they got it. You know what I'm talking about Cornelius."

"I think so sir."

"Mr Mott Cornelius was married and his wife died."

"O I'm really sorry to hear that. I've got another bun toasted,

157

have another hot dog. And how you spending your time these days Charlotte. Did you ski this year."

"I'm working Mr Mott. You talk as if I were a lady of leisure. I work forty nine weeks out of the year."

"Well I work fifty two. My doctor keeps telling me, slow down Jim, slow down, can't last like that. So I'm slowing down. Cutting those eighteen hour days. Right down to sixteen. Got to do what the doc says. Coming up to see us at the lakes this year Charlotte."

"I hope so Mr Mott."

"That a girl. Bring your friend here. I try to get away for a few days up there. Last year when I began to see that little old red spot. Went away soon as I got up there but soon as I get back. Whooeee, there she is, that damn little red dot. Keeps right there, there it is just over the corner of the fireplace. Soon as I try to look at it to see what it is, it takes off right across my vision. There it goes. On the other side of the room now. Keeps moving away and I can't track it down. But by golly it comes right back and does it all over again. None of the docs seem to know what it is and I've been to every top notcher on the east coast."

"That's pretty awful Mr Mott I mean maybe it's over work. Or something like that."

"Got to go on making those sparkplugs Charlotte. But that's what the docs say. Went to one of these guys tells me he's got special treatment, you lie down and hum. Puts a mask over my face. I say look you know what you're doing I hope. So I hum into the mask and colored lights play across my eyes. And bells start to ring. Thought I was in heaven. Only I knew it was earth when I got the bill. But come on you kids, don't stand there listening to an old fogey like me. Enjoy yourselves, I'm here to serve. You two are my special customers for tonight so come back for more."

The shy profile of Charlotte Graves. Leans out of her long flowing hair. She stands a moment with hands folded and staring down. A neighborhood girl. Pure and serene. While I smoked cigarettes and spoke sinful philosophy down deep in the sewers. Walked to school, the icy wind on my legs. Saw my foster mother with her dirty blond curly locks and rolls of blond fat up on top of my foster father in their bedroom. As I was going by the open crack of their door. My breath came out of me so fast, had to cover my mouth as I stared in. So eager to look I didn't know what to look at. Said in all the dirty books I read that it was how a baby was made. They had a little son I beat the shit out of once. Because he made my little brother cry. And the foster parents had me in the kitchen. I stood while they sat. Told me I would go to jail. My uncle came from Rockaway on a Saturday afternoon. They all sat looking out on the little back garden. My uncle had big strong hands and took a folder from his shabby grey coat and wrote them a check.

"You know Cornelius. Gosh I don't know why I'm saying it, but I sort of feel proud of you. Mr Mott told you so much about himself. Just as if you were an old friend."

"Mr Mott in his palace of new rich vulgarity could buy and sell me."

"Gosh Cornelius, someone might hear you, come on, why do you say a thing like that. I'm surprised at you. Take me to dance."

Charlotte tugging Christian by the hand. Lustre on her straw golden hair. Along a hall. Of this great rambling interior. Had a boyhood friend whose house had a laundry chute. From the bathroom to the basement. Was the world's first marvel I ever knew. Down these stairs. To a long room. Polished pine floors waxed for dancing. A great juke box with its fan of rotating colors. Photographs of baseball and football players across the walls. And one of Mr Mott on a golf course under a palm tree. Couples swaying, dipping and spinning as they dance. And stop. At a great loud crack and blue flash of electricity. The lights out. A female scream. A little nervous laughter. Silence. And voices in the dark.

"Something's happened to the music."

"Something's happened to the house."

"Christ's sake let's get out of here."

A glimmer of light coming down the stairs. And more as matches ignite. Mr Mott's fearless enquiry. What's happened. Chap in his saddle shoes and white fluffy sweat socks. Turns to his snub nosed girl friend with bright blond bangs.

"Gee the way Mr Mott's moving in. Takes the situation right

over. Sizes it up. I mean holy cow that guy is fact finding all the time. You can tell an important person anywhere by his quick decision making.''

Mr Mott flashing his light over the juke box. Lowering to his knees he looks behind the musical monster. The light goes on again. Just as the rear end of Mr Mott sails out in the air landing in the middle of the floor. Flat on his back groaning. Chap in saddle shoes standing his ground.

''Will you look at that. Which way is the bomb shelter. The electricity crawled right up the wall as if it was alive. I saw it.''

Figures around Mr Mott. The back of whose hand slowly reaches to rub his forehead. A stampede of kids fighting to get out up the stairs. Screams and punches. And more pounding on the doors of the elevator.

''It's getting unhealthy down here.''

''Don't panic.''

''Don't panic he says up there. Come down here and say that why don't you.''

The lights back on. Stan by his father prostrate on the floor. As the figures return and slowly percolate again around the floor. Folk crowding round Mr Mott. Stan holding out an arm.

''Everybody back, everybody back, he's all right. Gee Dad, what happened.''

''I'm all right, help me up. Get me some brandy. The good brandy out of the safe. What the hell's the matter with that damn juke box. Get it out of here before it kills someone. All right folks, I'm all right. Just a close shave. Just one of those occasions when your emergency capability gets tested. I think I passed.''

''You bet you did Mr Mott.''

''Whole life flashes before you. Times you were fishing and swimming and having a kibitz with the gang. You kids should know about these things.''

''Mr Mott I guess it must have been something like up at the front. Shell blast.''

''You said it Terry boy. That's why when it comes your kid's turn to get into the holocaust, that might come again any time,

160

you want to know this type of experience. I have a tape recording of the sounds of war. Want you kids to hear sometime. If I had more time I'd listen to it a lot. If you kids will excuse me. I'm all right. But I'm going to get up to bed. Something must be wrong, I can't see my red spot anywhere.''

Mr Mott helped to the sliding door in the wall. Turning waving goodnight. Door slides open. With a buzz click and a clack. Mr Mott gone. Upwards. In his elevator.

Terry boy rubbing his hands. Stan opening a can of beer.

''Come on everybody don't let Dad's little accident stop the fun.''

''He's a pretty brave guy Stan. The way he took that.''

''Yeah Terry I guess so.''

''Had his wits about him all the time. The way he put everybody at their ease.''

''Yeah the way they were rushing away up the stairs.''

''Well Stan there could have been real panic down here.''

''Well there wasn't.''

''I'll give you that Stan, I'll give you that. But you got to admit it was your dad's cool head. Wish I had a dad like that.''

''Yeah Terry, yeah, I know.''

''Well anyway Stan it was an impressive sizing up of the situation at hand.''

''Size this up.''

Stan swivelling round, his eyes searching the faces of the room.

''Who said that.''

It was
Me
You bunch
Of
Rubes

17

At dawn's early light. Corner of Fifth and Fifty Seventh Street. Cornelius Christian seated on the twin brass outlets of a fire hydrant sticking from this stone wall where it says Manufacturing Trust Building. A solitary stroller a block away. Sanitation department truck, grey lumphing insect vehicle squirting water and spinning a big brush along the gutter. The traffic lights change. Green yellow and red. And a breeze blows my dreams abandoned down the street.

Charlotte said I was drunk and disrespectful. To people who were only trying to be nice. Made remarks that I was an undertaker. Embalming their dads. Tired broken work horses silenced after screaming wild in their nightmares. Begetting the little sons who grew up as gods. As honest and brave as dad was crooked and coward.

Charlotte had tears in her eyes. As I left her on her steps.

"O Cornelius you don't mean the things you say. The country is not like that at all."

I leaned to kiss her. Lips touching lightly. And I ran off roaring. The nation needs a king. Vaulted a fence and trotted casually through a mile of undergrowth and shrubbery. Stopped a cár on the cobble stoned avenue which cut through the woods. Said I fell from a plane. Parachute caught in a tree. And I fell into a thicket. Guy kept wobbling the steering wheel he was so excited with my story. Said I could sell it to the movies. If I deepened the plot a little. He'd like to be the agent. Till I told

162

him I abhorred greed and crass opportunism. And he said he wasn't heading at that moment in my direction.

Climbed up the steps of the elevator train. Looming over the tavern just closing where I got Fanny her whiskey. Met another drunk lurching out of the last car. Mumbled and pointed. Said, going right up over there now. Asked him where was there and when was now. He grumbled that there was over there and now was right now. And sure enough. All the white head stones and mausoleums rear on the landscape where my Helen lies buried. He's the only wanderer at large tonight who knows what he's doing. And back at the party Terry boy told me that Stan was going to have to get married. Because a girl said to him as he was on top of her. Go on you can come off in me. She got pregnant. And got a lawyer. While Stan's pa went berserk. And sent the girl to Paris for an abortion and a tour of all the fashion houses. She came back three months later better dressed, bigger in the stomach and got two lawyers. And now she wanted to go to Venice. And all I ever wanted out of life as a little boy was for someone to take me to the rodeo.

Sit here worn and tattered. Across from the big display windows of diamonds and necklaces. Where at comfortable times of the morning the likes of Fanny ambles out from her bath bubbles. Patted with powders, dabbed with perfumes and waltzing past the slit eyed detectives inside the door to buy an emerald before lunch. The only other passenger on the downtown train asked if I needed medical treatment. Mental I said. And as he made for the door I soothed him. Said I was fine, just finished a cross country midnight celebrity race. For charity. My chauffeur broke his leg running behind me with my glucose. In the swaying train I wrote a shaky autograph. He stared at it, said I never heard of you mister but I'll cherish this anyway.

Christian with a lock of hair in his hand. Tugging it down over the left eye. This lone man now approaching. Stops, looks. He must see it written all over me. That I want someone to take me to the rodeo. Walks a step. Stops and looks back again.

"Why you god damn bum, you."

Christian looks up. You'd think with not another soul on Fifth Avenue that this passing cunt would feel some brotherly love.

163

For the sadness of me. A job hunting ex embalmer. Staring friendless across this asphalt carpeted canyon. Watching three sparrows flutter on the edge of that litter basket. But no. He twists his nose in a sneer and curls lips in a snarl. One's just too tired to start teaching this nation a lesson. In outdoor early morning manners.

"What are you a god damn homosexual. Bums like you making a blot on this good district. I saw you sitting there for two blocks."

Chap getting braver as he moves farther away. Say something choice out of my insane cauldron of anger and he'll damn sure run. Be too much effort to catch. Always like to bark big. Gives folk a sporting chance to get out of the way of my carnivorous bite. Hang my head down in guilt. Increase his courage. Get the innocent fucker to sidle up for another abusive onslaught. And I'll give him some togetherness he'll never forget.

Christian pressing his brow upon his crossed wrists. Man stops again, looks back and turns. Slowly approaching the beaten looking Christian. Stands now only ten feet away. Come closer you grossly unpleasant vulgarian. So I can seize you in one blissful pounce. Give a little groan. An aroma of dereliction. He steps nearer to savour.

"God damn disgrace, sitting next to an expensive building like that, dressed like that, you god damn bum."

Christian springing. Two footed, two handed. Grabbing this social umpire of Fifth Avenue. Who gasps as good old sinewy Cornelius whips his arm up behind his back, bending him forward face downwards at the sidewalk. Always like to use the leverage grips. Gives the victim an opportunity to see some sense. Before you break his ass.

"What are you going to mug me. Don't kill me."

"You unpardonable wretch. How dare you accost me while I'm taking the air and a much needed reverie on this handsome boulevard."

"O jeez you're hurting. My back's under a doctor's care. What are you an actor sonny."

"I am an orphaned prince."

"What kind of talk is that."

"Now before I kick your human rights right out of you, what do you do for a living."

"Gee you sound political I'm just a cab driver, I swear to christ kid. That's all I am. Just a cab driver. I don't do nothing to nobody."

"You abused my privacy here just now."

"No kidding I didn't do nothing. I didn't know you were private. I'm begging for my life. You must be an actor kid. You must be. Just take my money, I only got thirteen dollars, take it all. But I'm begging for my life."

"What makes you think you'll be lucky enough only to be killed."

"O jeez, I thought you was just an innocent bum, no kidding. I never thought you was a mugger."

"You mean sir."

"Yes sir, I mean sir."

"You said I was a homosexual."

"O no that was only before I knew you was a mugger. Sir."

"When did you last pledge allegiance to your country."

"Gee sir I don't want to get into a whole lot of politics and things. Just let me go. I'm a victim of heart trouble."

"Now you reprehensible repulsive cunt, let me teach you some manners. Not to open up your big stupid mouth to a gentleman taking his ease."

"No no no like a clam. I really mean it. And you're no mugger."

"So I'm a homosexual."

"No no no. That was just something came into my mind that got out before I knew what I was saying."

"Well in fact I am a homosexual, you wretch."

"Gee that's wonderful fella, no kidding I really mean it. More people should be homosexual. I think my son in law is homosexual and I tolerate it for my daughter's sake. I got two nice grandchildren but all I hear out of my daughter and her husband is gimmie gimmie gimmie."

"Are you a kind hearted fucker."

"O jeez christ please don't say anything like that to me, why don't you let me go, I promise I'll never squeal I was mugged.

I'm on duty in half an hour. They'll wonder what happened if I don't get to the garage on time."

"Repeat after me."

"Anything you want fella."

"I am an unconscionable, wretched fuckpig."

"I can't say that big first word. Can't I just say I'm a wretched shit."

"No."

"O fella have mercy I'm begging you. What have you got a knife or something."

"I'm going to de ball you."

"I'm begging you. I mean the way you sound, like you was a college professor, like I can't believe the words you're saying."

"I'll repeat them. I'm going to de ball you. Down on your knees, keep your hands up behind your back. If you move I'll put this knife right through your spinal column. Until your head doesn't know what your legs are doing when they start running to save your life. One move and you're dead instead of merely de balled. So another like you doesn't inhabit this earth again. I'm going to make it a swell place. Just for swell folks."

"O god fella, god had better have mercy on your soul for doing this to me."

"Shut up. One more word, one more movement and I rip this blade through the back of your neck. Now look forward, right at the building. Don't move your eyes."

Christian tip toeing backwards. And nimbly up Fifth Avenue. The odd car passing slows down to peek at the disciplining and then roars away with a smell of burning tires. Man still kneeling. Trembling in his terror. And now a blood curdling cry and scream of no no as he pitches forward on his hands and turns to look up behind into this dawning sky over Fifth Avenue. Out of which a flashing blade might come.

Christian, knees pumping, eyes watering in the wind. Speeding north and around the corner of this big toy shop. Teddy bears and trains in the window. All the lousy Christmases I had. Every toy busted by the time I wound it up. Foster parents always gave their own kids the kind of toys that took all day to break.

Turning in under this familiar canopy. The big heavy iron grilled glass door unlocked. Push it open. Dark complexioned chap on duty, feet splayed asleep. Rubs his eyes and jumps awake out of the big chair in the lobby. Sucked in his breath when he saw me. Wears one yellow and one blue sock. Makes you cross eyed seeing if they match.

"Hey how did you get in, is this a hold up."

"No, don't be nervous. Mrs Sourpuss please."

"Well I'm nervous. People are getting robbed while they're kneeling in church praying. Is Mrs Sourpuss expecting you. This time of morning."

"Yes."

"I better ring."

"Like hell you will."

"I'm only doing my job, I could get fired."

"You could get killed."

"Hey what's with you mister."

"Mister Peabody."

"You're Mr Peabody, that Kelly talks about."

"Yes."

"That's different why didn't you say so. You took that big guy. The football player used to be married to Mrs Sourpuss. Glen told Kelly. I mean man, he's twice your size. They said you had him down begging mercy like a baby. Hey no kidding, you don't look tough, could you do a thing like that."

"Maybe."

"Could I try it with you. I mean you're not that big."

"Grab me. Anywhere you want. Any grip."

"Sure. O k. Now wait. Here I'm going to try a head lock on you. O k."

Operator buttoning his uniform. Putting his arm up around Christian's neck from behind, tightening across Cornelius's throat.

"Now Mr Peabody. Go ahead. Get out of that. Ha ha. Not so easy is it."

Elevator operator swinging, feet up into the air. And crashing down on his arse the center of the black and white tiled lobby. Slowly sitting up and resting back on his hands. Nobody believes you. If you want walk the earth in peace. You've just got to bust asses. All the way.

Operator limping to the elevator. Said gee that was some flip as he deposited Christian on Fanny's floor. Stand here in the vestibule. When I first heard that word. Thought that's what women had. And they asked you in. After you were married to them and graduated from school. Where I had my friends Pitt and Meager when we played tag and ringaleevio. I beat Meager up. Because he was so big. Gave him a bloody nose. Teacher told me to confess it. Meager used to talk to me a lot. Pitt agreed when Meager said that although I didn't show it, I was smart. I was made Scrooge in the Christmas play when Meager sulked and said he didn't want to act. The girl I loved was the angel. Pitt made me mad when he gave her a feel when the lights were out. She had fairy wings and a wand. During rehearsal I sat at the back with the angel beside me. She said move over and let me sit too. And sat there hoping everyone would notice she was beside me. Before that she always wanted me to go away. She wore white high shoes that were clean every day. And when I looked over her shoulder in class to see how she could write, she told me to stop copying. She had brown eyes and auburn hair. When I stared at her she said don't look at me and mind your own business. And once with other girls in our class she was skipping rope and I stopped to watch and she said if you don't stop watching us we'll quit. Only when I got to be a star of the school play was she ever nice to me. And nobody's cast me in a leading role since.

Door opening. Fanny in her long voluminous lingerie. Blue gauzy folds sweep round her as she turns her back. Christian following her along the hall into the white room. Table lamp with china cherubs and leaves switched on. Get an expression ready on my face. To answer her low growling voice nearly whispering.

"Where the hell have you been you son of a bitch."

"Out."

"What happened to you."

"Nothing."

"You're in shreds. I waited all god damn afternoon. They said at Vine's office you left there at noon."

"I went for a long walk."

"A walk. What for."

"Can't I have some privacy."

"Privacy. You mean to come waltzing in here looking like that five thirty in the morning. Get the hell out of here if you want some privacy."

"O k."

Christian rising. Taking the dignified steps back into the hall. Past a little map on the wall I've never noticed before. Of an island. Put my hand up on this pearl button. Push for the last time. Feel eyes behind me. To hell with her. This is it. For good. Out into the discourteous world. Just when I need silken sheets, froths of pillow, my head sunk in soft breasts and entwined about me the languorous arms. That ferry grapefruit juice, strips of bacon and golden toasted breads.

"All right. Come back. I don't want you to go."

Christian marching back. Followed by Fanny closing the door. Sit and pick up this fashion magazine. To put something foolish on my mind fast. Fanny stands and takes a deep breath, hands on hips and a frown on her face.

"For christ's sake. Don't you know what it is to worry about someone, to wonder where they are, if something has happened to them or something. Can't you understand. What kind of misery that can be. Where were you."

"I got lost on Staten Island."

"Don't hand me that shit."

"I'll go."

"Boy one of these times I'm going to let you go and not ask you back. I could kill you. You were probably screwing some little cheap cunt. Like that Miss Musk throwing her ass all around that funeral parlor."

Fanny sinking with a sigh in her big fat white sofa. Christian slowly turning the magazine pictures of lavish jewelled and gowned women. A loose old photograph in between the pages. Faded brown and cracked at the edges. Man standing on a stoop. A bell in his hand, a wheel in a wooden frame slung over his back. Big ears sticking from the woven cap on his head. Christian holding out the picture.

"Who's this."

"My husband. He sharpened people's knives door to door. He started out as nothing."

"You're sorry he's dead now."

"Maybe."

"I see."

"He had the good manners to tell me if he was going to be away all night."

"Screwing dolls in a dozen different hotels."

"He earned it pretty boy."

"Don't call me pretty boy."

"Pretty boy."

"Don't call me pretty boy."

"I could kill you."

"Lot of people in this town been trying to do that."

Christian opening his black smooth wallet. Removing two photos. One full length, the other close up. Of Cornelius reposed angelic in a Vine coffin. Standing and crossing to Fanny to hold them down in front of her face.

"Here. Here I am. Dead."

A flash of agony across Fanny's eyes as she looks and slaps them out of Christian's hand.

"Get them god damn pictures out of here."

Cornelius picking them up. Putting them back in his wallet. Turning and walking to the wall. To view this bird hanging by its feet upside down with its blue, grey and black plumage. Says Crown Prince Rudolph's bird of paradise.

"O god Cornelius, I didn't mean to do that I'm sorry, they just scare me those pictures. Lately I don't know, my head is tired all the time. In this lousy dump alone. I just wanted you to take me with you. You're so young. I'm so damn unhappy. Marry an old guy with a lot of money. Then he'd die. And I'd be rich. That's what I used to think."

"And you did and you're rich."

"I'm rich."

"What's the matter then."

"You. You show up here for what you can get and then you'll beat it. Will you marry me."

"What."

"Is that what you say. What."

Fanny Sourpuss, her hands tightening diamond glittering fingers. Digging into the upholstery of her chair. She stares out across the early morning at Cornelius Christian. Three shots ring out. Down in the street. And a fourth. As she jumps to her feet, fists clenched and shaking.

"What was that Cornelius."

"Gunfire."

"It's so early."

"Early gunfire."

"Was it down in the street."

"Yes down in the street."

Fanny crossing the carpet, her negligee swirling. Hair on her shoulders. Marriage a prison. Where you do what she tells you. For the money she married.

"O god, three guys are laid out. Three guys."

Fanny pressing close to Christian as they kneeled and watched. Turning to kiss him on the cheek. Her fingers picking an embedded pine needle from his coat. As the sirens converge from all the distant empty streets. A breeze fluttering the curtain of the open window. Eleven green and white squad cars. Red lights flashing. Fanny's doorman rubbing where I flipped him on his ass and talking to the blue uniforms. Three tousled heads in pajamas sticking out of embassy windows. One looks up. Give him a wave. And he doesn't think I'm funny or friendly.

In the dawn light ambulances took the prostrate away. Fanny's brooding eyes watching me undress for bed. Still hear faint sirens. After this long day. Of this sulky fidgety city. Where strangers sleep awake the other side of all the walls. And die dead and vanished quick. Out of minds and memories. Leave not a spook. Pulled the building down where our mother died. And my little brother and I stood and whispered. That she was in the sight of god. She coughed through the nights. My uncle from Rockaway kissed her in her coffin. Tears running down his face. They pulled him away sobbing and his arms clutched around himself. She had ringlets of blond curls. So thin and her veins big and blue. Fanny's hands folded on the sheet pulled up over her breasts. Soon as she sees my prick her lips begin to move. Quiver to think she lies there my mother. Without my father who was a grey dark shadow. Hung his hat and coat on the back of the door. Saw him a last time when he came with a bottle of whiskey where our mother lived freezing with a stove in the middle of the room. She dried wash above the chimney that stuck out a hole in the window. That looked out on a wall you could touch. Drink was in my father's blood my uncle said, and I heard him tell my mother, I love you Nan. He took my brother and me and bought us black new suits with short pants and black shiny ties. I stood on the grey stoop of the undertakers. Around the corner from the outdoor jewelry market. Wanted everyone to see how nice and dressed up I was. Only an old pig tailed Chinaman noticed. And he gave me a strange lump of candy. Fanny trembles as I come near. Closes her eyes. Put a hand upon her hair. Marry and be rich. Stay free and be poor. Money was always something nobody had. Till my uncle sent us where he said there was fresh air and woods to play. Meager got to be my friend when his mother died. He taught me to have nerve. Against the whole bad world. Where everything was lies. I told him how I pushed a nickel into one of these machines where you had a little derrick to pick up a harmonica and all I got was a chocolate malted ball. We played hooky together in a broken building. His father was away, an engineer on the telephone poles. And after school Meager made his own spaghetti. And washed his own plate when he was finished. He said praying to god was a waste of time. That nuns put candles up themselves. And priests pulled their pricks. That's why they had such big white handkerchiefs. He said everybody at school thought I was dumb but he knew I was smart. We smoked cigarettes in under the eaves of a deserted factory. Meager folded his feet and said that he wasn't going to be ordered around by anybody. That teachers wouldn't do it. Or policemen. Or any other god damn person there was. He combed his hair straight back and parted it in the middle. Said I was small but the toughest fighter he ever knew. That my fists came out so fast you couldn't see them. He told me about screwing girls. You throw them down on the ground in the weeds. That's what they were

172

for and they should clean the house, wash the dishes and let you sit in a big comfortable chair doing nothing. Also they should keep their mouths shut till you wanted them to say something. But what they did was look for rich boys to marry so they could do nothing. Except hang around the house with cups of coffee. And his father hired an ex nurse to clean. Meager made a hole from the attic down into the bathroom. Saturday we watched her floating face up in the tub. When the water wet the hair down between her legs. Meager said that's the slit where you stick it in. Later we visited guys with sisters and Meager would make holes in their attics to peek through. And everybody sat around jerking off. In attics all over the neighborhoods. It was raining sperm. Till someone's mother started taking a bath. And there was a fight. The kid said I'm not going to let you look at my mother. Meager held him choking in a head lock. They wrestled around till plaster fell out of the ceiling on the mother down in the tub. Outside we ran for three miles. And hid in the woods. The kid's father went cruising by looking in his car. Meager said he liked the mother because she had such big ones. And that we were lucky not to have mothers. Because what if we wanted to screw them and then had babies who became our brothers. The hollow cheeks of Fanny's face as she sucks. Little girls used to wipe their mouths off after kissing me. Because I wasn't so hot looking. But Meager said I would make out swell in the dark at the gang bang we would have for graduation. You wouldn't know whose leg or nipple you had in your mouth. And in the dictionary they called it perversion. Fanny reaches out. Her expensive grip. To take my balls in the palm of her jewelled hand. Take this woman to be your lawful wedded wife. Who has her hair done every day. And bought a building which had the first double elevators in New York. Who sells a whole street of tenements. And has seven plants throbbing out textiles. To have and to hold. While she gets richer. And I get a worn cock. Till death do you part. And your prick falls off in heaven. Where wealth is useless in the utter happiness. When on earth it can save you from so much hell. Fuck me Fanny groans. On hot high school summers she used to lie naked on her bed. Wondering what the rich were doing. Said she had the windows open. Could hear old Mr Pribble whispering trying to beg a screw out of his wife, twelve feet away between the houses. Cornelius when I was a little girl that old scrawny fart put his hand up my dress. I wanted anyone to love me. Tried to kill myself. Cut my wrists. If only I had met you thirteen years ago. Before I ruined myself. Because I thought there would never be anything better. And if there wasn't I didn't want to live. Felt I was just standing in an empty train station. After all the people and the trains were gone.

Christian nuzzling his head and kissing his lips into the neck of Fanny Sourpuss. Holds part of me up inside her. So softly enwrapped. Her world dying as mine lives. Legs are the last of a woman to go down the byways of age. Cornelius listen to me. With money you can pay the price of anything you want. A face lift or love. Sleep till ten in the morning or two in the afternoon. You know that out there stacked up in the vault are stocks shares and bonds paying dividends. And you always own a gun to shoot yourself if they don't. I've got all these god damn lawyers. Don't know who's worse, them or the blackmailing relatives, who before I was rich hollered I was a hooker. Now they want me to buy them grain silos and finance operations on their ass holes. I need you Cornelius. A girl doesn't want to be alone in this world.

> Where
> The greedy
> Are waiting
> And grinning

18

The leaves a deepening green in the sunshine on the tree outside Christian's window. Fluttering in breezes till the end of June. The Danes celebrating Constitution Day, the Swedes giving a folk and festival dance in the park. And a nice bunch of kids dancing along the curb snapping radio aerials off the cars.

Fanny threw me out of her apartment for the fifth time. And I stayed away penniless reading a tome on job opportunity. The hunchback in his high politely pitched voice called through the door that he respected me as a gentleman and would I please pay the rent. And the pair of rude debt collectors sent by the steam ship company said we'll break this fucking door down.

Christian breakfasting in the automats pouring out unemptied coffee cups. Stealing folks' baked beans when they went looking for ketchup. Till finally getting credit from the Irish grocer round the corner by increasing the thickness of a brogue every day. With selected newspapers from the better garbage pails one sat reading in my window. Lots of action as that swell crew of youngsters dumped garbage on steps and threw bricks through the janitor's fanlight who came out shaking his fist. And once my institutional friend came by wearing white shorts sneakers and a baseball cap. With a new sign.

DOWN WITH DUST

A balmy morning a man stopped me on the steps just as I was trying to belch and sneeze at the same time. Thought by the way

175

he wanted to make sure it was me that he was from some contest, dozens of which I'd entered. And I promptly got handed a subpoena. To appear in court, ten o'clock of a Tuesday.

Christian with a last clean shirt and unholed socks went for a swim at the Game Club. Scrubbing the dirt off his heels with a big soft brush and pine scented soap. Members waddling by with their walrus rolls of fat. Could go without eating for weeks. Just as I lay in my increasing skin and bones, wrapped in three sheets, my name was paged for the telephone.

"Cornelius."

"Yes."

"This is Charlotte Graves. I hope I haven't disturbed you. How are you."

"Destitute."

"O what's wrong."

"I need a job."

"Why don't you go and see Mr Mott."

Christian dressed, hair combed leaping three steps at a time down into the subway. Thundering trains beating against the brain. A black gentleman sitting across. His shoulders going up and down, his fists banging on his knees as he chants man I'm gonna go, I'm gonna go, just set me alight. I'm gonna explode, I'm gonna blow the place up, I'm gonna knock the place down. Don't nobody stop me because I'm gonna go.

Christian going. Up dark steps and along a shadowy narrow street. Standing outside this towering beige colored building. Look up at clouds passing overhead and feel the world is falling over. Chiselled in the stone above the battery of bronze doors, the huge word Mott surmounted by an eagle. The pink marble lobby. A directory on the wall and the hot shit faces scurrying by with their briefcases.

Christian zooming up on the elevator. Stepping off on a wide brown carpeted floor. Paintings of countryside, rolling hills and hedgerows. Horses leaping fences. Just approach the reception desk. In all this gleaming polished tranquility.

"May I help you, sir."

"O I'm just sort of making a call."

"Whom do you wish to see."

"Well I guess I only know one person."

"I'm afraid I'll have to know whom you wish to see."

"I mean it doesn't matter, I was just passing and I thought I'd stop in."

"I'm sorry unless you tell me what your business is and which department or person you wish to be referred to I can't help you."

"Well I'd like to see Mr Mott."

"Mr Mott."

"Yes Mr Mott."

"Do you know who Mr Mott is."

"Yes. He's the owner or something. I'd like to see him."

"That's impossible."

"Why."

"Do you have a prior appointment."

"No."

"Then it's quite impossible."

"I'm a friend."

"Excuse me but there are people waiting behind you."

"This is a democracy."

"Would you mind, there are people waiting."

"I demand that you contact Mr Mott and tell him Cornelius Christian is calling."

Christian bending forward, hands on desk. Perspiration on brow. Bubbles there the instant the world decides yet again to cramp my style. This bitch sitting between me and survival. Tapping her god damn pencil on her pad. Smiling that smirk.

"Unless you have an appointment, I'm afraid."

"You'd better be afraid because madam Mr Mott would much prefer to be merely bothered by your enquiry for five seconds than have five squads of police roaring up through this building looking for me after I administer a suitable chastisement to you and send this line standing behind me running for their lives. Unless by god this instant you get in touch with Mr Mott and tell him Cornelius Christian is calling."

Receptionist with her blood red fingernails. Picking up the telephone. Raising her eyebrows and sniffing down her nose.

"There's a gentleman here, Cornelius Christian would like to

177

see Mr Mott. No he hasn't. But he insists. Yes. He really does."

Receptionist holding her hand over phone. Looking up at Christian. As more folk get off the elevator.

"What is the nature of your urgency."

"I'm offering myself."

"He's offering himself."

Grumbling guy trying to push the sharp point of a package into my back. Jesus what a town. No one will even give you two indifferent minutes out of their lives to save twenty five million desperate ones in your own. As this girl's jaw drops. And she looks up.

"Mr Christian, I'm sorry. You should have told me who you were. You can go in right away. Just see the secretary the last office on the left down the hall."

"Thank you."

This creature with a blouse of green and a grey flannel dress. Leading me along the hall. Across another reception room. Past flowers. Through a little panelled lobby and a door she pushes open. Feels good to be accidentally somebody for a minute.

Huge room and window. Looking out and down over the city. Water towers on all the flat tarred roofs. That statue of a woman holding aloft a torch over the grey green harbour of New York. Two flat ferries pass, one to and one fro. And this blue suited man with his whitening hair neatly combed back, holding out his hand.

"Well if it isn't my boy Christian, isn't it."

"Yes Mr Mott, it is."

"A party of my son's wasn't it."

"Yes sir."

"Well, sit down, nice to see you. Have a smoke, my boy. Good cigar. Just bought it yesterday, I mean bought the company. I like to use my new products right away."

"Thank you."

"Well what can we do for you."

"Mr Mott I'd like to make money."

"That's the smartest thing I've heard anybody say for a long time. Well now. How do you feel we can help. Got something to offer us."

"Myself."

178

"Well now, another pretty straightforward answer. I like that. Connotes purpose. It's Cornelius Christian isn't it."

"Yes."

"Well now, I'll call you Cornelius. Well Cornelius, so you'd like to make money. Want you to look out and down there. Wall Street and the harbour of New York. Like you could wipe your feet in it. What put us way up here."

"Well I guess the elevator."

"Boy, I'm talking on a different level."

"O."

"Ingenuity. It's a word we use around here. Say it."

"Ingenuity."

"That's better boy. I remember you. Came along with that wonderful girl Charlotte. Just back from Europe weren't you. You had a bit of sadness with your wife. Which I was sorry about. Juke box short circuited. It was like war for a minute. Remember a couple of comments you made caught my ear. Yeah."

"Yes I was at the short circuit."

"Look tell you what. Bit rushed just now, excuse me a second."

Mr Mott bending forward, his hand pressing down a lever. A left hand tapping ash from his cigar.

"Miss Peep, get me personnel, Mr How. Go ahead Cornelius, help yourself to the view. Ah. Hello Howard. Got a young man here, friend of my boy's. He wants to make money. Want you to talk to him and show him around. Thinks we can use him. Cornelius you free right now."

"Yes."

"All right Howard, you take care of that. Kids, Howard, o k. Long time no see. Fine. Well life will get less noisy as you get older Howard and the kids grow up. Great. Fine. Yes. That's great. O k. Howard. Bye. Well Cornelius, our Mr How will take care of you. See what we can do. Maybe we can have a chat again. I like to talk to the young kids coming along. Now what's that word."

"What word."

"That word. That we use around here."

"O. Ingenuity."

"Attaboy Christian. O k."

"Hope that spot's a little better. You know the red dot you had in front of your eyes, that keeps flying across your horizon."

"You got some memory boy. Yes you have. And memory makes money. Remember that utterance. Words are wonderful. Remember that too."

"It's been extremely good of you Mr Mott."

"Anything anytime for the young people. Keep in touch. Find Mr How five floors down."

"Thanks again Mr Mott."

Christian with a slow swaggering step proceeding along this corridor. Opening the mouth wide to fit in the end of this cigar. Blow a blast of smoke at the receptionist's desk. And one last puff out the elevator doors. As I plunge five floors to blue carpeting and narrower halls. Past a room, a sea of desks. Everybody empty faced.

Christian entering this pale green walled office. Another window looks out and down. Red and black funnels of an ocean liner slowly passing. Flags flying above the white black and monstrous decks. Someone sets sail. Out of this cauldron of woe. And this man sits smiling behind his desk and horn rimmed spectacles. Secretary closing the door behind.

"Mr Christian I presume."

"Yes."

"I'm Howard How."

"Hello. I'm thinking of moving to the Bronx."

Christian lifting a hand to his lips. Smoke pouring out between the fingers.

"You're what."

"O sorry, Mr How. Guess I'm nervous. I've just strangely had something on my mind about the Bronx. Once it was meadow land, I've been reading an old guide book."

"O."

"Yes, ha ha. Was thinking maybe some parts might still be meadow land."

"We manufacture spark plugs, Mr. Christian."

"Of course, of course. I don't dispute that for a minute."

"And there are no meadows left in the Bronx."

"I would never dispute that either."

"What do you dispute Mr Christian."

"I don't dispute anything. Nothing at all. O there are some things I don't like, all right. But I don't dispute anything. It's just that there must have been real Indians once canoeing around the bay out there."

"Well let's get back to the twentieth century now."

"Sure."

"And you're interested in our using you."

"I'd like it if you could."

"Point is Mr Christian, just what can we use you for. I note you smoke cigars and have a rather English tone to your voice. Didn't by any chance pick that up in the Bronx."

"As a matter of fact I learned it out of a book. And Mr Mott gave me the cigar."

"O now look, I'm not trying to hurt your feelings. For what it's worth you might as well know Mr Mott likes to have an English quality about the place. You've noticed the rural scenes of England in the halls. We know how to appreciate that kind of atmosphere here."

"Yes, nice and green. I mean, you know, rustic. I like it."

"Glad. We feel it's a nice contrast to the product. Well, aesthetically we've made progress together. Arrived at a nice base to use as a springboard. Now what Mr Christian are you exactly interested in doing. What are your qualifications, your degrees."

"Well as a matter of fact, Mr How."

"Good. The facts. That's what we want, Christian, the facts."

Christian pulling out a handkerchief from a side pocket. Might be able to muffle the words a little through the fabric. And hide my expression behind my smoke.

"Mr How I just missed, I guess, by only a few subjects of course, getting my degree. At the time I had a lot of things on my mind. You see I've always been deeply interested in human nature and I guess I got distracted."

"Sorry Mr Christian, but I understand you don't have a degree."

"Well. Except of misery I guess. But I almost made it. Gee don't write that down."

181

"Don't be alarmed Christian, these notes I'm making are just a few facts. Note you got alacrity with words."

"But I almost made it, I really did."

"Easy boy. Easy. We make spark plugs. You want to make money. Right. You know I can see you really do, don't you."

"Yes."

"I'm glad your desire is sincere."

"Thanks."

"We have progressed. You're a friend of Mr Mott's son I venture to conclude. Mr Mott's a friendly but very busy man and this affair more or less, you understand me, rests in my hands if we're going to find you a slot. Do you have any preference as regards production or management."

"Well I'd like to manage, if that can be arranged."

"Just give that pitcher of water a push in my direction will you. Want some water."

"Thanks a lot."

Christian taking his glass. Holding it up to the light.

"You got a far away look in your eye Christian."

"Well you see this water's got a history."

"O."

"You'll think I'm crazy Mr How."

"I'm prepared to wait until conclusions are conclusive. Let's hear the water's history."

"Well the water has got to come from the Catskills."

"That is fairly common knowledge."

"From the Ashokan Reservoir."

"Maybe that fact is not common."

"I read in a geography book as a kid what they had to do. Am I boring you."

"O no. I'm fascinated."

"Well I know it's ridiculous but I just can't forget what it took to make this reservoir. Fifteen thousand acres. Seven villages sunk. Thirty two cemeteries with two thousand eight hundred bodies they had to dig up."

How hesitating with his glass. Distant airplane crossing the sky. Somewhere over Hoboken. Above the grey swamplands, rubbish dumps, mire and slime. Put up my wigwam out there among the waving catkins. Live my final starving moments with the lonely ducks and seagulls.

"Boy you're just full of facts."

"I guess we might be drinking somebody's soul."

How pushing his glass away. Wipes a drop of water down his tie.

"Yeah."

"Mr How I'm glad I've had this drink. Thanks."

"Don't mention it. But I think we better reconstruct the relationship here. You're still looking for a job."

"O yes."

"O k. We want men with ideas. Ideas more than anything. I may mention along this line that we prefer these ideas to be of a red blooded nature as opposed to weird. Can you type."

"Well. My uncle gave me one of those little typewriters when I was a kid but I don't expect that would qualify me as a typist at the moment, but it's something I could pick up. I pick up most things rather easily."

"Like your degree for instance."

"Look Mr How. I'm after a job. I don't want to misrepresent myself or give a false impression, but as I said I'm interested in human nature."

"You said that."

"I don't have a degree. O k. Maybe I was too distracted by human nature in college. I got disappointed in human nature as well and gave it up because I found it too much like my own."

"Wow Christian you're some candidate."

"But I wasn't stupid you know."

"Look, Mr Christian. You don't mind if we don't bother seeing things today. I mean you'll understand that until we know what you can do there isn't really much point in my showing you our set up at the moment. I know Mr Mott's one of the friendliest men you could ever want to meet and I know he wants to help you but it is rather a question in the end, can you help us. Right."

"Guess so."

"You're a very presentable person and of course well spoken and by the way I like the way you tie your knots, that's a nice tie, always be sure of a man in this business if he wears a knitted tie. Just want both to face the facts. And that conservative suit too. Just the facts, Christian. Just the facts."

"O k."

"Got an opening for a courier representative. Dispatch and deliver various important papers. Expenses, taxi and all the rest. Good starting slot."

"Holy cow I'm heading for the age of thirty. You mean I deliver papers. Like a messenger boy."

"Not in so many words Mr Christian. Not in so many words. It's of the nature of a confidential dispatch agent and you would of course hold the title of executive courier."

"What are the friends that I once knew that I might meet, going to say. They'd be overjoyed. Never stop laughing. I went to college you know."

"A lot, an awful lot of people go to college, Mr Christian. Mr Mott never went to college and he controls a business extending to twenty nine states. We just added Texas yesterday."

"Well I've had a job before."

"I'm keeping an open mind. I'm perfectly reasonable you know, Mr Christian. What sort of work did you do. You see I'm not here to bring about a stalemate with applicants. I'm here to hire the right man for the right job. O k. Now what exactly are you experienced in."

"Does it matter."

"That's up to you. I'm only trying to help. Just testing your qualifications. Want to know the sort of work you're best suited for. Where your interests truly lie. We're an outfit you know, where, when it's expedient, we take off our jackets, you understand me and roll up our sleeves. And being a courier executive would allow your capabilities to rise to the surface. You see what I mean."

"To be frank, I've been, well, I'm experienced."

"O k. But frank with the facts, Christian. How were you used."

"They used me, I guess as a sort of representative, as you might say. A specialist in human relations. As I've said I could count myself as a former student of human nature."

"Yes I know you've said that three times now. You were in public relations then."

"Well yes sort of I guess. I wasn't too clear at the time because I had a lot of things on my mind."

"What firm was this."

"As a matter of fact."

"That's right, the facts Christian."

"It was a man called Vine. I guess incorporated."

"How's that boy."

"Vine."

"What's his product. Briefly."

"Death."

"How's that boy."

"Death."

"What."

"What I'm telling you, death. One word."

"You mean he rubbed people out."

"No he buried them."

"You mean an undertaker."

"Since we're down to one word, yes, an undertaker. Mr Vine said I excelled in that professional capacity."

"Well you know, god help me Christian, I honestly don't know what to make of you. Here's an ashtray for your cigar. Get that chair over there and sit down. It's not been in my experience previous to this to consider anybody in the light or forgive me, darkness of these circumstances. How long did you undertake."

"I undertook for, well, not long. I'm begging for a chance to prove myself Mr How. Just one chance."

"Easy. Take it easy. Just got to think. What an interview. I am deeply involved in this disorientation. Just let me ask you one question will you. Wait, excuse me a second. Miss Kelly, would you please play over to me the background music we've chosen for Friday's conference for our Chicago representatives."

The light efficient female voice, yes Mr How. The strains of soft violins. The saddened considerate face of How leaning forward.

185

"Cornelius. Now look, tell me, were you looking for this undertaking job. Don't have to answer that if you don't want."

"Someone close to me died."

"Sorry to hear that. By the way, you like this music."

"It's nice."

"Soothes, doesn't it. Guess it's been one of the most successful innovations Mr Mott introduced into business practice, almost like the invention of the wheel. But come on Cornelius cheer up. Only thing is we got a problem here. Your job in the funeral parlor business is not going to cut much ice with Mr Mott, in fact the mere mention of it will throw a distinct chill into him. But I'll tell you something before we go any further. You know, I like you, I think you're o k."

"Thanks."

"Most of the people sent along to me with pull with Mr Mott aren't worth their weight in paper, strictly between us, you understand. You strike me as a guy with imagination. I'm going to give you a chance. If I assign you to our idea department do you suppose you could get some ideas. It'd be a trial, you understand."

"Ideas about what."

"Come on Cornelius, what am I letting myself in for. Quick. Ideas. We make spark plugs. Mr Mott loves the use of words. Think of something quick."

"My mind's a blank at the moment."

How reaching forward in this emergency to press down a switch on his desk intercom.

"Miss Kelly give us something faster, for a fast idea session of approximately forty five seconds starting ten seconds from now."

Miss Kelly's routine voice. Coming she says ten seconds from now. Feel like I've got to come too. With my prick on a guillotine. An orgasm in eight seconds or else they lop it off.

"Gee Mr How I'm worried. My whole sex life, sorry I mean my life, depends upon what I might say."

"Wouldn't put it quite like that. Think. One sentence. One idea, a rhyme, anything, don't care what it is, so long as it underlines an inescapable fact."

"But all my facts have escaped."

"Go go boy."

"I can't go anywhere Mr How, I swear it. The facts have escaped."

"Go after them boy, listen to that music, I know you can do it. Think of something to do with a spark plug. Think of the money. Money boy. Think of the money."

"I am. Wait. If you've got a heart, you've got a spark that could be a heart by Mott."

"O boy o boy kiddo. Did you do it."

"Mr How when you said money, those words just came pouring into my mind."

"Don't be ashamed of that boy. Tell Miss Kelly. Miss Kelly, good, it did the trick, neat selection, make a note of it."

"Yes Mr How."

"And make a note, we've got a new man for our idea department starting right away."

"Yes indeed Mr How."

"Hey boy. Hey there."

Christian slumped in peaceful misery. How holding his glad hand out across the desk.

"You're in boy."

"Mean I'm hired."

"Of course."

"Just like that."

"Just like that."

"Well isn't it too quick. Isn't there something more. Can't I fill something out. I just don't feel it's me."

"Cornelius I think you've got what it takes. Yes. If you've got a heart, you've got a spark that could be a heart by Mott. Here, gee, have another drink of water. Yes. Ingenuity."

"Makes industry."

"Miss Kelly, can you hear what's happening in here."

"Yes I can Mr How it's wonderful."

"Well get it down."

"Got it Mr How."

"Flash those two things to Mr Mott. He's got to hear about

187

this right away. Ingenuity makes industry. A follow up to Mr Mott's favourite word.''

''But Mr How this is awful, I mean I feel overrated. Just a few words.''

How leaning back in his swivel chair. Raising his grey sleeved arm to slowly bring down a pointed finger at this applicant suffering the misery of his modesty.

''We find a guy, Cornelius with words like that coming out of his head, we buy that head.''

''Mr How I think I'd rather be a messenger boy.''

''Miss Kelly I want you to shout back just what you think of Christian's word formations.''

''They're really impressive.''

''Now boy, hear that.''

''But Mr How I'll tell you the truth, no maybe I better not. But I don't know a thing about spark plugs or industry. Except that there's money in it somewhere.''

''Isn't that enough boy. Money is the moment of truth. Don't sadden my life Cornelius. I want you to run with the ball. I mean how do I know sitting here that you're not some kind of god damn genius or something.''

''I'm only just a reasonably normal person.''

''You're not normal boy. I know it.''

''I beg your pardon.''

''O wait. Hold it. Whoa. Let's again reconstruct this relationship here. Miss Kelly would you see that Cornelius and myself are left undisturbed for a few minutes and stop all calls.''

''Certainly Mr How, anything for background music.''

''Not for the moment thanks.''

How standing. Shaking his brown curly head back and forth as he comes out from behind his desk. Paces to the window. The wind hums. Christian standing, loosening limbs. Throwing a left and right hook behind How's back. A white excursion boat heading up the river. As How turns to raise a pointing finger at Christian.

''Cornelius I'm going to give it to you straight. Do you like to win.''

''I guess so.''

''Answer me yes or no.''

"I guess yes."

"I'm going to risk my life. You know why. Because I like you. When you first came in here I just thought you were another snooty sophisticate out of the ivy leaves. But you know, you've got a real quality in you. Which goes deeper than a shirt and tie."

"My job in the funeral parlor I suppose. But it was the only job I could get when I first got back from Europe."

"That's what I want to talk about. It's Europe. That's the thing's given you this quality too. A sort of thing that's real. Breeding. But look. I've got absolute faith in you. You could dazzle this industry."

"Mr How thanks but I think you're making a mistake. I'm not like that at all. That's just the way I appear. Some of the things I really think and believe would revolt you. I'm almost a criminal type."

"What a remark. You're just full of ideas boy. Why you're not more of a criminal than I am. I mean we're alike. But look. I'm maybe ten years older than you. Got wife, kids, nice home out on Long Island. The real things. Sure I've got some gripes. But I'll tell you something. See those binoculars. Want you to look out there. You see any barges going past the Statue of Liberty. Got it. Now a little to the left."

"Yes."

"See those barges."

"I think so."

"That's refuse. Happens every day, all day. Come down the Hudson and out of the East River, filled with stuff that's no more use. They dump it. Christian it's made an awful impression on me. See, dumped. Maybe not in a river, but you know what I mean."

Christian wandering around the side of How's desk. Tests the swivel quality of the chair with a little push of the finger. The seat turns. Christian plops down and splays out feet.

"Mr How I've lost my ambition."

"Boy, don't ever say a thing like that. Not good for you to say and it's not good for me to hear. And I've heard an earful."

Stiff crease down How's trousers. A thin blue line in the grey. Gold buckle on the side of his shoe. As he stands center carpet.

189

Just where I was standing when I came in. To face facts. More foolish than fiction. To get big insights. To give moments of lucidity. During which we could start shooting each other.

"Cornelius I want you to call me Howard. And as a personal favor I'm asking you right now to take this job. I know everything's going to click. Do it for me. You know, I've got to laugh, here I am begging you to work for us and ten minutes ago I was wondering how I was politely going to discourage you."

"Dump."

"Well yeah, but no."

Slight drooping of flesh on How's face. Doggish injured eyes. As Miss Kelly's voice comes over the ether.

"Excuse me for interrupting Mr How but Mr Mott wants you to come up to his private reception room right away."

"Thanks Miss Kelly. There you are boy. What did I tell you. Now I'm asking you right now, please. Just let your personality come out as it's done with me. Just be yourself. Only don't give any hint of your past employment. Mr Mott's toleration for the suppression of facts is nil but to me, it's worth the risk. Just go in with the trace of a smile, that's all I'm asking. But don't look like that."

"I'm o k Mr How. My memory's just working."

"That's o k boy, which of us doesn't have a sadness once in awhile. But let's radiate the creative confidence. Anyway just say that thing once more."

"You mean about industry."

"Please. With conviction."

"I think I've got something better. Ingenuity made Mott, Mott makes industry."

"Cornelius, just what I said remember. How do I know I'm not sitting here with a genius."

> With the
> Very latest
> In popular
> Brains

19

How leading the way from the elevator. His natty heels clicking along the corridor. Christian in step behind. Into this great white domed amphitheatre. Voices echoing against the circular walls. Light flooding from corners and up through the frosted glass floor. In front of a massive white curtain Mr Mott seated on a gilt throne facing two spidery black chairs. Feel a big cavity between my two front teeth. As Mott's voice erupts.

"Howard you saw what I didn't see, at first sight that is."

"It was nothing Steve. Miss Kelly selected the background music."

"Sit over there Christian. Well let's hear all these nice things."

"Steve he's got something even better, didn't want to flash it."

"Give us a flash now Christian."

"Ingenuity made Mott, Mott makes industry."

"Very happy. Very happy indeed. Let's have that once more with lung. Lots of lung."

"Ingenuity made Mott, Mott makes industry."

"Not bad. It's good. Youth refreshes. Of course you don't expect to be paid much for that."

"No Mr Mott but I think it's good."

"O it's good. Youth refreshes. Well you're not kidding us son I can see that."

How leaning forward from his chair. Mott rocking his black

gleaming shoes in the fluffy white rug at his feet. How tugging out a measure of shirt cuff, elbows on knees.

"He's not Steve."

"No Howard, he's not kidding us. Now at the risk of sounding too full of myself, which I do not want to sound. On the other hand I'd like to sketch in my general attitude. Towards the way I personally tackle things. Don't get the idea that I think of myself as a king or anything. But I like to acquire the evidences of man's creative impulse from the outside of my own orbit. But sadly, not many are blessed with the creative impulse but of course there's the repulsive creative impulse too. We won't go into that. But brains are the cheapest thing money can buy. Even so, we need them once in awhile, and if there are bright brains at the right price, I buy. And I don't care what kind of head you got the brains in. Don't get nervous, your head's all right Christian. But a head, black, white, square, ten feet high or like a ping pong ball is all right so long as it works. But don't let me sound like a king. So I think you have a future, Christian. Now what about the past."

"Steve I've been through his past with him."

"Once more fast won't hurt, Howard."

"Thought we could get around to it later. Past's fine."

"I'm interested. At the party back there that night Christian, you had a lot of pretty pertinent things to say with maybe a few impertinent. What has a smart kid like you been working at."

"Steve."

"Howard will you give the boy a chance."

"Steve do you think with the pressure of time, that we should discuss this now."

"It has always been my habit Howard, to discuss things now. Because after now might be the hereafter. You get me. Christian's been out of college a while."

"But Christian here is a peculiar case."

"Why."

"I think his creative qualities are rare."

"That so."

"Well you heard him yourself Steve, a natural alacrity with words."

"Howard I'm going to press the button for the curtains."

"Yes Steve."

"I don't usually show people this. But I want you Howard to look out there. You see any barges going past the Statue of Liberty. Know what they are."

"I think I do Steve."

"Well it's a private little object lesson of mine."

"I understand completely Steve."

"Here today Howard and gone tomorrow."

"I completely understand Steve."

"So now that nobody is misunderstood let's hear about your past career, Christian. Not that I'm buying your past, just the future. Nevertheless past gives indication of future."

"Mr Mott I was employed as a star receptionist for Vine Incorporated. A funeral parlor."

"Howard."

"Yes Steve."

"Howard I'm talking to you."

"I know Steve."

"What about this."

"Mr Mott I was expelled from school for lying and cheating. Didn't get my degree from college. And since I've been performing a job in which I conducted the arrangements for those finding their final resting place. And nothing unseemly, except maybe once, ever marred the proceedings."

"Steve, it was in the nature of human relations. Of which Christian here is a serious student."

"I've got my own eyes and ears Howard. There are all kinds of relations. All kinds of students too. But let me utter three things. Life is for the living. A dime is a dime. And last and the most, a dollar is a dollar. I am not being vulgar mentioning money. I change my shirt three times a day. Like people they get soiled. I also yesterday was on a plane from Washington when the steward asks me was I any relation to the Motts who had a mausoleum at Throggs Neck, when I said yes he tells me his father takes care of it. This is the curiosity of life. But young Christian here tells me he's a liar and a cheat, degreeless and can smoothly conduct people to their final resting place. Run the Mott empire like a morgue. Now just what exactly do you take me for. Why weren't the facts laid bare in the first instance."

"Don't let facts fool you Steve."

"Don't you be too hasty Howard."

"I feel most recent facts take precedence over previous."

"I am of the opinion Howard, not wanting to be a king about it, that past facts forecast future facts."

"You're wrong Steve."

"Come again Howard."

"You're not exactly right in judging personalities."

Christian standing. Let the mouth gape somewhat ajar, make it easy for the titans to see I'm alarmed by their communication gap. Into which I have dropped one galling gaff after another.

"I think I'd better go."

Mott raising his emperor's arm.

"Stay Christian, we'll have this out."

"But Mr Mott I didn't think I'd be coming between two people. Breaking up a friendship."

Mott's small chuckle. Howard's faint smile. And Christian's wide eyed enquiring innocence.

"I know this is a business empire but aren't you two people friends."

"You have a habit Christian of asking a lot of direct questions."

"Well Mr Mott in the fact finding maybe I ought to find some that's all."

"Please Steve, Christian just wants to communicate. He really wants to contribute."

"O k Christian before you communicate and contribute, sit down. You don't sound like a liar and a cheat. I just would like to know what the score is on you. I don't want to be rude or hurt your feelings. But you know underneath this gentle innocent exterior of yours you seem to throw your weight about. In fact I distinctly feel I'm being pushed. That little remark about friendship and coming between two people. Yeah. And that night at my son's party. You remember my spot. And I remember something said about my house. A palace of vulgarity. Don't look innocent. And don't think I planned this either, getting you up here with Mr How to give you a working over. I was impressed but don't think you can push us all over."

"Steve I've never met such a candid fellow as Christian."

"Howard you think a fellow is candid because he tells you to your face that he is a liar and a cheat. And sweated away in a funeral parlor guiding people to their final resting places. And with a little background music he starts to spout beautiful utterances. Howard, don't be so naive. Christian here could dazzle you all night with slogans each one better than the last."

"Wouldn't it be sad then, Steve, to ignore this talent."

"It just so happens I'm acquainted with Christian's background. And by the way Christian, just want you to know, that Charlotte, she's one great kid. Don't you ever sell that girl short. If you do you'll have me and my son Stan to reckon with."

"I thought Christian was an unknown quantity to you Steve."

"Not when he sees my girl Charlotte. I've had Christian checked out. I loved that girl's mother. Charlotte's like my own daughter. And I want to know anytime she's in with the wrong kind of crowd."

"I think Mr Mott I ought to be going."

"Aren't you going to abuse us a little before you leave, Christian. Call us vulgar stuffed shirts."

"What makes you think you're in a position to say that, Mr Mott. Because you think there is nothing I can do about it."

"Don't threaten me."

"I'm not threatening you."

"Hey Steve, please. Let me in on this."

"And I suppose Christian you thought that if you used a frontal assault, just walking in on us here we'd think we were blessed. That we'd be afraid to go into this little background. But what happened between yourself and your wife is your own business. Only you haven't paid the shipping company yet. But that's your affair."

"Thanks."

"But what you do Christian where I'm personally concerned."

"Steve, Steve, isn't there a sunny side to this situation. Christian didn't tell me he was married."

195

"He's not."

"How does a wife come into it."

"She's out of it. For keeps."

"You mean she threw a seven."

"That's how Christian here got into the undertaking trade."

"Steve I hope I'm not disrespectful. This is way over my head."

How taking off and wiping his glasses. Christian turning to contribute a communication.

"I think Mr Mott wants to avoid unnecessary contacts with ghouls and charlatans, Mr How."

"That's enough Christian. You're already up in court subpoenaed for being a wise guy."

"Mr Mott I came here genuinely looking for a job to make money."

"And thought that I didn't have the guts to tell you to your face that I know the whole score on you. You know Howard, Christian happens to be pretty tough."

"O boy Steve you're way ahead of me."

"He's knocked people's teeth down their throats. Even won a few titles in the ring."

"Steve I mean what harm is the manly art."

"Plenty when he thinks he can sock his way out of trouble wherever he goes."

"Preposterous rot, Mr Mott."

"Don't go all British with me, boy."

"Don't call me boy."

"Steve, Steve. Can't we galvanize this into a new situation from which it might be possible to evolve a solution. What about that. I think, despite the terrible things that have been said here, that underneath it all we're good hearted people. That there is still something that could be considered constructive determined from."

"Determined to be a solve it all, are you How. Make Christian sweet for us to digest with your hired honey."

"Nobody has ever talked to me like that before, not in the three and a half years I've been working here."

"All right, all right, Howard, this is an emotional moment."

196

Christian in this alabaster glowing light. Slowly rising to his feet. Brush from one's person the crumbs cast of twit, niggle, gleek and fleer. Ought to mump and jump like that subway nigger on the boil. Cut a swath through this white trash. But for the sake of How, twinkle a little. With the bland. Gets you a little further till you really have to fight.

"Meanwhile I've been insulted but thank you Mr Mott for speaking the truth."

Howard How elevating a tiny torch of understanding. A finger pointing at the domed, voice echoing ceiling.

"Now there's something we can start with. If the truth was spoken, well don't we feel the better for it. Hasn't the air been cleared. Maybe. Just a little. Isn't it just a case where personal history has intruded needlessly, personal lives dragged in and personalities giving vent to feelings that have just become too emotional for words."

"I have never laid a hand on my wife when she was deceased Mr Mott."

"Stop being candid and embarrassing."

"It's only right that you should know. My wife's death was a blow and I might have drifted into a peculiar area of sorrow following it."

"Steve I was really proud of the impression Cornelius made on me. And I know the things you've said were tempered by some fact that could just as easily be fiction."

"Why weren't the facts laid bare, that's all, Howard. Naturally what can you expect if you attempt to obscure the facts. A funeral parlor can knock the hell out of real estate values."

"I'm sorry Steve."

"Well maybe Howard I was a little sudden myself. Sorry to drag in your personal background like that, Christian."

"Maybe Mr Mott I said some things I shouldn't have said."

"Well, even as board chairman, I guess I know I did."

"Steve, we all did."

Christian taking backward steps from this royal industrial presence. Flicking ash from the cigar held behind his back.

"Well I guess I better be going."

Mott's glinting eyes. Silk black socks. Just like Vine's. As he shoots from the hip. Towards the slender Christian. A voice opening up the future.

"There's a place here for you Christian."

How joining his hands beneath a glad smile.

"Construction from confusion."

Christian half way towards the sliding doors. Out on this slippery floor of glass. Taking a step into commerce. As Mott clears his throat for an utterance.

"We can use you Christian."

How shaking his raised squeezed tight fist.

"Steve, I'm glad you said that."

"Howard, I'm glad I was king enough to say it."

> And
> For all our royalty's
> Sakes
> That's saying
> Something

20

Christian passing through a flock of fluttering pigeons and mounting the wide grey steps up between the monstrous pillars of this hall of justice. Where everyone needs a face wash. Wearing all the dirty looks they do.

This sunny day. With no reason at all why the world should go on. Except that I've squirted an astringent under the arm pits and up between the legs for masculine freshness. To make me smell good in court. After two sweaty weeks in the employ of the Mott empire. Scribbling words which made me laugh and How cry. Who'd come into my little cubby hole with his plaintive complaint. Gee whizz Cornelius, come on, cut out the kidding, my five year old daughter could do better than this.

Taking an elevator upwards with gents carrying briefcases. The locust swarm of lawyers ready to descend on any green dollars clutched in the hands of plaintiffs or defendants. Coming down on the subway heard a man say to another that he lived next to a neighbor for twenty five years and didn't know him and the man said, well I'm living next to my neighbor forty two years and don't know him. And last night at midnight a female across the street sat for an hour with the cheeks of her ass stuck out of her window. Just getting aquainted. With her neighbors.

Clarance Vine in all his gleaming impeccabilities, black shining shoes and a black homburg hat in his hand. Twisting his neck in his stiff collar and twitching his shoulder. Leaning against the green wall, turning to smile and hold out his hand to Cornelius Christian.

"Cornelius you've sure had us worried. Where have you been. My lawyers wanted to brief you."

"Mr Vine I'm sorry. You know me."

"I know you Christian."

"What do you want me to say."

"Best thing is to tell the truth. After Mrs Silver you might be the first on the witness stand."

"Holy cow."

"And this woman Cornelius has got her whole bridge club behind her. Frankly I don't think we have a chance."

"I'm really terribly sorry."

"Forget it. Thing to do is fight."

The courtroom filling. Two teams of lawyers exchanging papers across the benches tables and chairs. Mrs Silver along with the rest of her bridge partners, glaring at me. A shuffling of feet on the floor boards. Be up standing in court. Judge entering from his panelled door. Climbing up to sit on his oak throne, yawning into his cupped hand and peering out over the assembled faces through his glasses. Vine with his lips compressed. As the sallow faced clerk says will Mrs Silver please take the stand.

Mrs Silver in her black tight dress she wore at the funeral. A corsage of pink orchids pinned at her neck. From which came her head and hair upswept in whorls of glistening blue rinse. Each heel click she makes across the floor. Is a thousand dollars she's going to put me in debt.

"Do you swear to tell the whole truth and nothing but the truth so help you God."

"Boy you bet I do."

"State your name and address."

"Harriet Silver, Hotel Apthorpe, Central Park West."

A gent approaching the witness stand. In his blue shiny suit. His eyes sunken in his grey jowled face.

"Will you tell the court Mrs Silver what happened on the day of March twenty eighth."

"Herbie was dead a day and I was in deep mourning."

"You were bereaved."

"Of course, it was no joke, he died before I knew what happened. Only two days after his physical for life insurance. I was knocked out. My girl friends said, don't, why should you stress yourself with the funeral. They said stay at home and have a rest in bed. So I was sentimental. I wanted a treasured last look to remember. It was dark in there. My eyes had to get used to the light."

"You refer to the Vine funeral parlor Mrs Silver."

"Of course. But when finally I could see, I hardly could see straight. That's not my Herbie, I said. Lipstick and rouge, his cheeks puffed out where they used to be caved in. I thought what's this, his business enemies, they can't leave him in peace, pulling a body switch. I said to the attendant, excuse me. Who is that. He said it was my husband. I said no, I am in the wrong room. Give me the right room. He said lady that's what we collected out of your apartment. Imagine, collected, he said."

"Is that same attendant present in this courtroom."

"Yes there he is, sitting over there."

Her fat falling in folds as Mrs Silver raises her arm to point a finger. Not nice when everyone turns to look at you. And the judge moves his glasses down his nose to peer over the rims.

"Now Mrs Silver, will you continue for the court."

"Could I have a drink of water."

"Of course, take your time Mrs Silver."

"It's my heart."

"Continue only when you're ready."

"I'm ready."

"What did you think you were seeing reposed there in that room that day in the Vine funeral parlor, Mrs Silver."

"I thought I was seeing some broadway side show. The attendant told me to shut up."

"And did you."

"I certainly did not. I demanded where's my Herbie. Then I see the nose. I'd know Herbie's nose anywhere, I go to take a closer look. And then I see that."

"You of course refer to that, as being Mr Silver the deceased."

"That's right. My legs were wobbling. I went dizzy. It was Herbie. A complete and total stranger like somebody on the subway. Already I could feel warts coming. I was so shocked."

201

"And then Mrs Silver, what happened."

"I said what did you do to him. The attendant said it was deluxe. I said deluxe. You think you did deluxe. You whorerized him I said. It was then he offered me a refund."

"And what did you reply."

"I said no to such an insult."

"Did the attendant apologise."

"No."

"What did he say."

"He said I'll pump you till you bust full of formaldehyde and sell me as a monster, and to shut my ass you god damn fucking bitch."

"Did Mr Christian do anything then."

"Do. It was what he already did."

"Did he make any menace."

"He could have been making doughnuts never mind menace. All I know is I fainted. And woke up in hospital covered in warts. Under sedation."

"And how have you been feeling since."

"If you call feeling torture. That's what I've been feeling. I fell over eight times. Once right into the refrigerator. My head aches. I have nervous trembling condition the warts left. My heart is involved. Herbie's face haunts me so I can't sleep at night. My new kidney condition I got as a result makes me go to the bathroom twenty times a day. When before I got this shock I went only twice, or three times if I was extra nervous."

Christian looking up. Grey sky out the window. Man sits court center playing his hands over the keys of a machine. Taking down all the words. On file forever. What did you do to my Herbie. I botched him. Pray for some monstrous holocaust to come erase this recent nightmare. Like a time on one of his binges, my father said he loved eating eels. Even when they wiggled on the plate. Said he'd show my mother that he could provide. And came back in the middle of the night. With eels. Boxes of them squirming and slithering all over the place. Woke me out of my sleep to show me. As I stood with my little brother screaming at the horror. And my mother beating my father's face with her fists.

"Will Cornelius Christian take the stand."

Christian mounting these worn steps, brushing back his delicate strands of hair. Feel itchy. Must be fleas jumping in this legal chamber. Counsel is scratching too. Fart's the only thing that scares them away. Be further accused of launching a lethal gas attack. On the dignity of the court.

"Do you swear to tell the truth the whole truth and nothing but the truth so help you God."

"I guess so."

"Yes or no."

"Well do I have to be specific."

"Yes."

"Well isn't there something about my democratic rights here. I just heard a whole slew of lies."

A gavel slamming the desk of the judge. As he turns and pushes his glasses down on the end of his nose. To peer at this witness. And ask.

"Do you swear, or not, please answer yes or no to the clerk's question. And do not make another remark like that in my court. Who are you in this case."

"I don't know, I guess the embalmer, your honor."

"Then answer the question, do you swear to tell the truth."

"Yes your honor. I swear to tell the truth."

"State your name and address."

"Cornelius Christian. I'm not sure about my address at the moment. You see the landlady got shot and there's a hunchback coming round collecting the rent and the landlady's nephew was charged with the crime."

"Answer the question, what is your address."

"Gee judge, that's what I mean I don't want to lie. I'm not living where I was because they're harassing me."

"I'll harass you into prison if I don't get some straight answers out of you soon. Counsel please don't scratch and you better get your witness here to behave, I'm not going to tolerate this kind of nonsensical conduct in my court, do you understand."

"Yes your honor. But please may I point out, that Mr Christian is a very unusual young man. He suffers from being over

203

courteous as a matter of fact. And not wanting to give any offense.''

"Counsel do you want me to have you both up for contempt.''

"No your honor.''

"Then have a word with your client. He is your client.''

"Well I think so, I just met him only a minute ago.''

"And yet you're able to say he suffers from being over courteous.''

"My client Mr Vine supplied that information your honor.''

"I can see we're getting no where. Now Mr Christian. Is that your name.''

"Yes your honor. Cornelius Treacle Christian. Born in Brooklyn raised in the Bronx.''

"You needn't supply your pedigree. Where do you live now.''

"Could that be confidential your honor. You see there's this steam ship company, they packed up my wife's body.''

"Good god, will you please stop this. What on earth is the matter with you. What steam ship company. Whose body. How does your wife's body come into this.''

"Your honor she died aboard ship. That's how I guess I got Mr. Vine into this whole mess. I had to pay off her bill at the funeral parlor.''

"I object your honor, I object. My opponent's client is using up this court's time blathering irrelevantly like this. I ask your honor to elicit this witness's address.''

"Take it easy counsel. Don't tell me what to do in my court. The court will get to that. And will you too please stop scratching.''

"I'm sorry your honor.''

"All right Mr Christian, calm yourself. We understand that you may have personal reasons why you do not want to divulge your address but the court demands that you do.''

"Yes your honor. I live near the Museum of Natural History. You just go down Central Park West, you know where they've got the City of New York Museum. They've got a lot of pictures of Hudson River steamers on a wall downstairs. Well if you head down that way.''

"Mr Christian, don't continue to waste the court's time. It's my last warning.''

"I was only saying how you can pleasantly get to my place."

"Tell us the street and number."

"Can't I just tell you how to get there."

"No you cannot. And let me say before we go any further here that you are not doing your employer's case or your own any good."

"That's prejudice, your honor."

"Will you shut up please, I'll say what it is. And also, I'll hold this entire court in contempt if you don't stop scratching out there. What's the matter with you people. Now Mr Christian give me your address this second."

"It's Forty Six West I think Seventy Sixth Street, only on the sign the end of the block it says Seventy Seventh where some kids changed it for a laugh I guess."

"Which is it."

"That's what I was trying to say before your honor, that I might say something that could be a lie when I was telling the truth."

"I'm going to allow you one last chance. We are going to give your address as Forty Six West Seventy Sixth."

"That's not it."

"Shut up, it is. Now counsel will you get on and examine your witness."

"Mr Christian were you employed by Mr Vine."

"Well I came round there one day and."

"It's only necessary to answer yes or no to the question, please."

"I guess I was. I was broke. I just got off the boat."

"And what did you do for Mr Vine."

"I checked the thermometers, ushered the bereaved to the various suites, and even ran out for cigarettes for the mourners who needed them."

"Did you prepare the body of a deceased known to you as Mr Silver."

"Yes. He was in the back room. He looked really awful."

"Had you prepared other bodies."

"Yes, I did. With George. He was showing me the tricks."

"You mean methods and procedures."

"Yes."

"Now you say Mr Silver looked awful."

"Yes. Although I knew that there was a youthfulness under his skin."

"How did you know this."

"Well I could just tell that he was a man of spirit. That maybe life hadn't been too good to him. Paying income taxes, maybe people shouting at him over his shirt counter and not being nice. All that kind of thing. But I knew that this was only the external manifestation of the man. That he might have liked classical music while he lived."

Mrs Silver's counsel slapping down papers on his table as he stands waving his left arm in the air and scratching under it with his right.

"Your honor I object to this insane line of inquiry. That anyone could tell from looking at a cadaver that he liked classical music."

"Overruled. It is quite conceivable that Mr Christian could see in this man something more than the flesh and bone he was faced with. Continue counsel."

"Well if you will please tell us Mr Christian what were you trying to do when preparing the body of Mr Silver."

"I was attempting great art in the manner of Mr Vine. Mr Vine told me that he was able to read the whole history of a man in his face. And that when you did you could embellish it with his past. His happy moments. You know, by bringing the eye sockets back to normal. Like the times he patted his dog's head in the kitchen at night when he was having a glass of milk and cinnamon bun after watching television. A moment like that can be a man's happiest. I've always been a student of human nature."

Mrs Silver's counsel again leaping to his feet, scratching a left hand in his crotch. The fleas like the shady spots.

"I object your honor. This is the most incredible nonsense. Unbelievable."

"Sustained. Counsel what relevance does a man patting his dog's head in his kitchen have to the matter complained of. Mrs Silver charges that she was spiritually disfigured when confronted with her husband tarted up beyond recognition."

206

"Your honor I am only trying to show that the Mr Silver with which Mrs Silver was confronted was indeed only a younger or truer version of her husband. Like a soiled painting found battered in an attic covered in dust and then immaculately restored."

Mrs Silver's attorney slapping his palm against his brow. His shoulders suddenly turning white with a cascade of dandruff.

"Objection. For heaven's sake is counsel suggesting that Mrs Silver had a dirty husband, that he was kept in a scruffy condition and in a manner of speaking was thrown out like so much garbage."

"Yes that's what I'm suggesting. And that Mr Christian attempted to restore this cast off body to a state in which any one who loved him would have liked to have seen him in death."

Mrs Silver's counsel falling backwards into his seat, giving his brow three more slaps in a row. More snowfalls of dandruff. As he sits scratching cross armed under the armpits. The judge leaning forward to peer at this ringside frenzy.

"Are you all right Mr Blitz."

"I am just temporarily stupified by counsel's most recent remark."

"Well perhaps if Mr Christian's counsel is finished, you'd like to cross examine Mr Christian."

A lifelike glow returning to Blitz's eyes. Perspiration across Christian's brow. Wipe it away with the back of a hand. The windows look out to a brooding grey. Sound of rumbling distant thunder. One nearly could make a run for it. Beat it just up the street into Chinatown.

"Now Mr Christian. You seem like a nice young man."

"Thank you."

"Did you ever embalm a body before Mr Silver's."

"Yes. I assisted with some."

"And before that did you take training."

"No. But I knew a lot of kids interested in wild animals and we read this book on taxidermy. I also learned to skin a chipmunk and prepare muskrat skins. Do you want me to continue."

"Yes do continue Mr Christian."

Christian looking out at the courtroom faces. Pausing in the flow as the head of Mr Vine's counsel bows slowly forward into his hands. Making him look as if he was pretty upset. And there standing right in the rear. My friend fat cheeks from the institution. Flashing open his coat. With a message.

FLEAS

"Well I mean that was in my youth. It was after I was orphaned."

"And you regarded this as some kind of apprenticeship to later becoming a qualified mortician, Mr Christian."

"Well skinning animals and stuffing them is skilled work."

"O I'm not suggesting for a moment Mr Christian that the work isn't skilled. I am merely pointing out that this perhaps was your total experience prior to embalming and preparing a human subject for burial."

"I stuffed a snapping turtle. It was the biggest one ever caught in the Bronx. Its jaws could break a steel bar in half."

"O. Do go on. Don't mind me Mr Christian. This amazed look on my face is just one of admiration."

"Well I thought it was itchiness the way you're scratching yourself. And it's distracting me."

"I'm sorry. Is that better. My hands in my pockets. Now what about this snapping turtle."

"You really want to hear this."

"I only want to hear what you feel will help us know something about your early work in undertaking."

"Well I don't want to mislead the court. I just knew about stuffing animals and making them look like they were alive. We did it with a big copperhead snake. We put it through the window into the front hallway of this house one Saturday night when they were having a party, and everybody in the house went mighty pronto out the windows. Except the invalid father in law in a wheel chair and they just slammed him unmercifully right through the screen door without opening it."

The judge leaning forward on one black robed arm. Hammering his gavel down with the other.

"If there's any more laughter I'll clear the court. It's bad enough the whole bunch of you out there scratching. You'd think the place was crawling with bugs."

"It is your honor."

"Well be thankful then they're only bugs and not copperheads. Continue Mr Christian."

"Well I was only showing I could do a realistic and lifelike stuffing."

On a side bench in his own judicial black robes, a gentleman seated. Behaving just like the judge, using his fist in the palm of his hand as a silent gavel. As he considers the pleadings. Someone else sneaking open a lunch box and taking a bite out of a sandwich. As Mr Blitz rocks back and forth on his heels. Sporting rather over large chrome buckles on the side of his shoes. And raising his chin and bad breath in my direction.

"You're a bit of a practical joker Mr Christian. Frightening people out of their wits and houses."

"That's not true."

"O what then is true Mr Christian."

"Well these people weren't very nice. They were stingy and mean and sat around drinking highballs and playing bridge every Friday night. I was underprivileged at the time. Besides I was only about twelve."

"And you stopped doing these things at thirteen Mr Christian."

"No. I did a few more things after that."

"O do please tell us. And what were these. This is a nice sultry day for stories."

"Well I don't think they have anything to do with this case."

"On the contrary they have a lot to do with it. Indeed it may show you're just a high spirited young man who likes to have a laugh once in a while."

"Well I used to collect dog droppings. And I used to put them on people's front porches and cover them in fallen leaves."

"Ah this was an autumn escapade Mr Christian."

"Yes it was. And then I'd light the leaves and ring the doorbell and folk would come running out of their houses to find a fire lit on their porch and they would start to trample it out."

"To put it, if I may, in a more vulgar way, these innocent people were stamping hysterically in dog shit."

"Objection your honor, objection. Mr Blitz cannot continue with this totally irrelevant skirmishing. Mr Christian was like any young man growing up in his community, and giving neighborhood oldsters a tough time. As a kid I used to put live snakes down people's heating pipes and they'd drop down on them from the ceilings."

A massive thunderclap and flash of lightning. Folk in the courtroom ducking. Rain pelting against the windows. Darkness. Courtroom lights switched on. My friend fat cheeks grinning and shaking his head up and down in yeses. As the gathering scratched and cowered and Mr Blitz raised his finger to point at Christian.

"And is it not true Mr Christian that you thought you would have one hell of a joke making Mr Silver look like some carnival doll. Just because you get a kick out of seeing people outraged. And have an innocent woman walk into this most traumatic experience of her life. To whom you issued the threat that you would embalm her."

"I thought it would calm her down."

"Calm her down. So to calm people down, you suggest embalming."

"For some it gives lasting peace."

"O this courtroom may laugh Mr Christian but I don't think that's at all funny. Pump full of formaldehyde. Sell as a bloody monster. Shut your ass hole you god damn fucking bitch. You said these words Mr Christian to calm Mrs Silver."

"I thought some strong language might console her."

"Console."

"Well that word just slipped in there."

"Lots of words Mr Christian seemed to have slipped in there. Including fill you full of formaldehyde. And sell you as a monster. Is that what you thought would console Mrs Silver."

"I thought it might improve her manners."

"Her manners."

"Yes they were appalling."

"This seems cavalier coming from you Mr Christian. Spreading a dog's doings on the front porches of community citizens."

"How dare you refer back to that. I told the court that in confidence."

"Dare, of course I dare Mr Christian. Just as you dared to make a laughing stock of the remains of Mr Silver and scar Mrs Silver's memory of her husband for life. How dare I. You bet I dare. And I further dare to hope that your shitty pranks get banner headlines coast to coast."

"Counsel that's enough now of that."

"But your honor it was Mr Christian who acquainted us with his daredevil community antics."

"Confine yourself to cross examination."

"Very well. Mr Christian. Who are you."

"I beg your pardon."

"I asked who you are. You said earlier you'd been orphaned."

"I am Cornelius Treacle Christian, of the Brooklyn Treacles and the Bronx Christians who got unloaded from a boat from Europe."

"I see. Not a very edifying background if I may say so."

"They were impoverished well meaning people proud of the chance this country gave them. And they would have viewed your vulgar insult as beneath contempt."

"I see we're getting a little bit of your strong tongue now."

"And I'll belt you out the window of this courtroom in a second, you sneaky little god damn fart."

"Ah that's more like it, a full flowering. No please, your honor, let Mr Christian continue."

"Counsel you've insulted Mr Christian. If he socks you I may treat it as an occasion of instant justice. And hold you in contempt for getting in the way of his fist."

"Your honor that's no way to run a court."

"Are you telling me how to run my court, a god damn store front lawyer like you."

"No your honor. Gee whizz suddenly I'm the guy who did everything wrong. Excuse me I need to take one of my heart pills. I feel real lousy. I mean my client isn't getting a fair hearing. Here's a kid up there tells us he's stuffing turtles.

211

Spreading dog shit on people's porches. When they're in the middle of their chicken dinners. Flinging poisonous snakes into the middle of bridge parties. When someone might be trying a grand slam. And I get held in contempt for getting in the way of his fist when he feels like throwing it. I mean is this the new liberty. That's come to swamp our way of life. Is this what our city has come to. When a weed isn't safe in a window box anymore. That even dead bodies have to take their chances. What's the life long struggle for, if you die and then get the biggest insult of your life. From someone whose been cleaning out rest rooms. One half million dollars damages will never compensate Mrs Silver for the horror of that day haunting her every waking and sleeping minute. And what a thought. That when she dies this could happen to her. A widow made overweight with nervous worry. She too could be flung into her coffin like a cut rate side street whorer. At a time of her life when she should enjoy. With her other widowed girl friends the bliss of a calm happiness without a husband coming home with his head in his hands with business worries. Her still youthful flesh could be getting golden at the best beach front hotels on the Florida coast. And where with the many swamps being reclaimed she could lie wrapped in the dreams of her retirement home. Her only heartbreak being the trouble she might meet finding the right antiques to grace her castle in paradise. Instead of here. In this bug infested dusty courtroom. During a thunderstorm. Is this what she stuck by her husband for through all his years of merchandising. With collar styles changing so fast her husband was sickened by the inventory dumped on his hands by a gimmick fickle, junior executive population seeking only a brief sartorial thrill. Yes, I dare to say it. There's what today's modern world has come to. Sitting in that witness box. Schooled in all the low foul dirty tricks that mature citizens of this country are now harried and hurried to their graves with. With the final ridicule lying in wait for them. Right in their very coffins. Where when they should rest in peace. They rest in horror. And in these days when our daily lives are being threatened whenever we go outside our homes and even inside. The one place left was the funeral parlor. Is that now too, to become an area of fear. I'm sweating. That's

all I've got to say. Except I say to you, who was known as
Herbert Silver. Wherever you now may be. Goodnight sweet
prince.''

> Don't
> Get your feet
> Wet
> In heaven

21

On that witness day, as the bugs were jumping over everybody, the court adjourned with a slew of suings for bodily injury bites. Cornelius Christian stepped down from the stand, walked four steps and swooned. And falling, dreamt of Fanny. That she was a girl with a black bow in her blond hair and I was a boy in my only best suit. And I took her to my first dance. Gliding over the floor. She in a wispy gown. Her smiles all glowing and glad. And she whispered in my ear. Cornelius what kind of toothpaste do you use.

Vine patting Christian on the back. His team of lawyers brushing me off. I was led under an umbrella down the court house steps and climbed into a Vine limozine. A sad look on the face of fat cheeks. But he smiled as he flashed open his coat with a new sign.

SLANDER NOT SLIME

Charlie sped me up town. To Thirty Third and Fifth. Rain flooding the streets. Folk rushing from doorway to doorway. Beneath those endless windows each with a name and product. How does all the commerce get done. A whole phone book full of lawyers. To take their clients by the hand and lead them through all the chiseling. A relief to see Charlie's grave face again.

"You did good up there Cornelius. You stumped that smart ass lawyer trying to put the big bite on Mr Vine. You know, there must be happiness somewhere, when a lawyer dies. In that courtroom, boy could you get a bird's eye view of the world."

Charlie leading Christian from limozine to one of the sixty seven elevators. In this vast rose marble hall. An upwards ear deafening express to the swaying eighty fifth floor. Step out and leave all these other folk heading for the top of this skyscraper. Walk down a hall over rubbery floors past frosted glass doors. Numbers and names. And this one Doctor Pedro.

A white coated and elegant legged woman gets up to lead Christian through a door. A tiny white haired twinkling eyed doctor sitting behind his desk. A rainy city below. See the Hudson River and the stony steep ridge of the palisades. And north past a peek of Central Park and over all the Harlem crazy streets. To the sad unsung gothic splendours of the Bronx.

"Come in, now what's wrong with you young man, take a seat. You're a good friend of Clarance. Clarance, he's a good smart man. Has the best job of all. Everyone comes to him he puts them in a box. They don't need a cure. A little candle light, music, flowers and a ride. You know why I have my office up here so high. I'll tell you. So I can look down and see all the jackasses. Whole place is full of them. You want to live long. Don't pray to god. You annoy him and he kill you faster. Now what's the matter with you. Nothing's the matter with me. I'm eighty six. You know why nothing's the matter with me. I'll tell you. I don't talk bullshit. That's why I am eighty six. Now what's wrong with you."

"I fainted in court."

"That was smart. How many fingers have I got held up."

"Three."

"Ever get headaches."

"No."

"Good. Now open your fly and milk down your prick. Good. Now touch your toes. Good. You crap all right."

"Yes."

"Good. If you eat good, crap good, work good, nothing can kill you except a long life. I send Vine my bill and you live happily ever after. How's that."

"O k."

"You look like you got brains. Are you smart."

"I hope so."

"Well it's good to be smart in this town. Where everything is

215

selling or stealing. Sure everybody's worried about crime. But I'll tell you. Without crime this city would collapse. Everybody come to me. They all want needles in their backside. Pricks up their ass hole would do them more good. They don't feel good in this town till you stick a needle in their rear end. So I take this out. Fat as a cigar. They see me coming at them with the dresses up and their pants down and they start running. I say why are you running. They say holy cow doc you're not going to stick that big thing in my ass. I say I'm too old for flattery. That sure, I'm going to stick this big needle in your ass. That's what you want don't you. I'm a good doctor I use a big needle. Well then they don't want this needle. So you know what I give them. Penance. I send them home to use their eyebrows. God gave you eyebrows to catch the sweat. So go scrub your kitchen floor. Down on your knees. I tell them. The whole god damn floor. Till it shines. That's the cure. For you too. God damn people think they can sit around on their god damn fat flat asses and get a needle in it and be healthy. That's bull shit. So you get out of here, you're fine. Don't get syph or the clap. Watch out for the crabs too. Clean your ass with soap and water after you crap. Walk three miles a day. And don't listen to jackasses. And wait. Before you go. You know how to test the real beauty of a woman.''

"No.''

"It's easy. You really know she's beautiful when you want to kiss the toilet seat she sits on. Goodbye. And watch out for jackasses. Hey wait a minute. You know what god is.''

"No.''

"God is what your desires are. What are your desires. They should be plenty ass and plenty money. So that's what god is, plenty ass and plenty money. Goodbye. Watch out for clap. It comes in the throat too. Hey wait a minute. You know I'm a bachelor. I bury three girlfriends. I should have been dead three times. You know why I don't die. Because I tell women what to do. Goodbye. Hey wait a minute. Don't forget. Watch out for jackasses. You know why. Because you just met one.''

Charlie delivering me that day back to my shady side street. Up Fifth Avenue. Through the flood of yellow cabs. Folk waiting. Doormen's whistles blowing. People stepping in under the canopies. In thunder wind and lightning. Flashing up the underside of the leaves in the park. The whole city washed clean. Dust and grime down the sewers. All ready for a brand new layer. Just as I crawled into my own little hole. And switched on a television set I bought. To watch the jackasses.

Took Doctor Pedro's advice. For a few minutes. Lifting up the carpet on the floor. To scrub. Until I nearly got smothered in dust. And next day Howard How called me into his office.

"What's bugging you Cornelius. I have complaint after complaint about you."

"I'm sorry Mr How somehow the struggle upwards seems too steep."

"Let us be confidential Cornelius. We're a team here. Just ask yourself. Are you giving of your best. Maybe word formation isn't the activity for you right now. How about selling. I know you're poised and articulate."

"I guess those are my strong points."

"But Cornelius can you be hard driving. Enough to be able to season yourself to sell in the furore of changeability. With the continual creation of new marketing concepts."

"Mr How right now I honestly don't think I could sell a nozzle, pump or valve to institutionalized patients who were building an asylum energy machine that goes on fire and they want to build another to put it out. I got my last employer into half a million dollar damage action."

"Hey gee Cornelius, hey gee. You're not going to do that to us."

"No no. It's just that I'm no damn good."

"Don't say that. Sure you are. Why don't you take a day or two off. I'll give you a shot at sales when you come back. But Cornelius, level with me. Could I really trust you in sales. Is there any chance at all that you could be an aggressive cut throat deal closer who can go out there and dig up the opportunities. All you have to do is keep your foot in the door. But can a guy like you take a few slams on the ankle once in a while. In the wide business spectrum that exists today you really got to maximise your opportunities. Don't insult the faith I put into you. They tell me from the department that everytime they look around they catch you watching them tear down that building across the street. Sure we all like to watch that. Like I mean, did you see yesterday that guy out there swinging on the girder, gee I couldn't watch, there he was up fifty stories, working while he's eating a god damn sandwich. I had to look through my fingers over my face. They say they got Mohawk Indians doing that.''

For four days away from the office I went out at noon looking for women. At last seeing one suitable coming with big tits out of the park. Just as I was going to ask her to come for a soda, she asked me where the Staten Island ferry was. I opened up my mouth to say I was glad she asked me that question and not a word came out. Because just behind her on the newspaper kiosk was a headline.

MONSTER EMBALMING
CHRISTIAN CLEARS VINE OF JUICY
GRAPES OF WRATH DRIPPING WITH DAMAGES

The girl stood looking as I stared dumbfounded. Until my tongue finally worked and I pointed at the stack of papers. Said that's me. She stepped back. As I pleaded.

''Really it is. Right in the headline. No kidding, don't go away. I'll take you right to the ferry.''

''Are you all right.''

''Yes I apologise for the coincidence. That I'm in a headline. You won't mind waiting while I read it.''

''No, sure.''

The testimony of a handsome blond Cornelius Treacle Christian was thought to have clinched dismissal of a suit brought by a Mrs Harriet Silver for half million buckeroos damages in the civil court in a judgement handed down by Justice Torn. Expert medical testimony had said Mrs Silver's fear of death had now become impossible to live with after her funereal experience in the Vine Funeral Parlor with the remains of her late husband Herbert who had been ''tarted up beyond recognition.'' However the judge in handing down his decision said that attention had to be paid to the fact that Mr Christian who prepared the remains had improved upon the condition of the body, and that it was in no less good condition than it had been in after he performed his tasks upon it, therefore it was now left to decide that if upon confrontation with such a body whose preparation was not to the liking of the mourner Mrs Silver, whether Mrs Silver had been damaged by suffering a "monstrous mortification." The Justice said that in spite of a most impassioned plea by counsel for the plaintiff, the position was akin to having a room decorated. And that one person might come in and say it looks swell and another might come in and say hey what the hell happened. The question then was a matter of taste. And if damages were awarded concerning a matter of taste the courts would be so jammed there wouldn't be room for a bug. This latter remark by the Justice is thought to refer to the spate of actions filed against the city for bug bites during the hearing.

Christian folding the newspaper. Taking a nice easy shallow lungful of mild auto exhaust. Look out now again around the earth. Only three thousand phone calls away from success. Till I can tuck myself into a green tapestried room. Somewhere up there in that mountain range of towering buildings. And meanwhile tell this waiting girl.

"I'm sorry about that. But it's the first time I've ever seen my name in the newspapers. It makes you think you're right there. Right on the page and that it's you."

She wore a pink thin jacket flying open over a tight purple sweater all under a big head of curly blond hair. Close up she looks worse and different than she did far away. When she looked swell. But when you looked close again she looked better. We walked around the corner of the park and by the big memorial to those who lost their lives on a battleship. As she sneaked looks at me. I convinced her what a waste of time and danger it was riding the ferry. And half way down Central Park South, just as I was going to reverse our tracks back to bed. A long grey chauffeured limozine with the porthole back windows squealed stopped.

Fanny Sourpuss stepping out. Breasts bouncing in a white

summery flowered dress, sandals flapping on her feet. Her long tan arms jangling a mob of bracelets. Walking right up to me on these hexagonal asphalt blocks. To raise her eyebrows at this girl.

"How dare you be seen like this with my husband you little tramp."

Girl looking at Christian for advice as she steps back a little to enquire.

"Hey who's kidding, who are you."

"I'm his wife and I'll give you a god damn sock in the eye if you don't get the hell out of here. And I'll god damn well bite your ear lobes off too."

"Gee do you really mean it."

"You're god damn right I mean it. Beat it."

As I stand watching her go wide eyed with one look back over her shoulder. And Fanny heaving, eyes blazing. Color in her cheeks.

"And as for you, you god damn son of a bitch. Who was that little blond dyed cunt, you just picked up, who was she."

"I was giving her directions."

"Directions my ass. You were going to fuck her."

"How do you know, you just got out of your car."

"I know when a guy's trying to fuck somebody. Besides I've been watching you since you came out of your house."

Glen sitting chewing gum, staring ahead through his windscreen. Double parked. In the humid afternoon. Taxis squeal by as doormen's whistles blow. A haze covering the sky. To make more thunder clouds collect in the west. Folk slow down to stare. At Fanny swaying with one fist pressed on her hip. And to see her nose, her eyes and lips and her whole lazy eyed face again. And smell her perfume.

"Look, that girl was a nice person."

"Nice person my ass, no girl's a nice person. I know what every one of these god damn girls are after. Don't tell me. Nice girl. The fuck she was."

"You're invading my privacy."

"That's right. I'm invading your privacy. You think you're so god damn beautiful walking around this town like a prize peacock."

"As a matter of fact I've been wracked by humility this morning."

Fanny dropping her arms. A long silent staring. The little light coming slowly bright in her eyes. Getting bigger like the small smile on her lips.

"O god Cornelius, you're such a dream, I can't get over you. My own my most cherished mortician and I kicked you out. It's just that I can't stand seeing you eating and drinking all my good food and booze and taking baths in my luxurious bathroom. That's all it is."

"What do you want me to do."

"Get a job as a house wrecker. With dust falling all over you and sweat pouring down your face, your veins and muscles bulging, your arms getting sunburned."

"Holy cow what kind of perversion is that."

"Come on. Cornelius. Let's go back to my place and screw."

Climbing into the limozine. Glen turning to give Christian a little salute from the peak of his black cap. Scared I might break his fingers for fooling with Fanny's long languorous legs. Those nice ones you wrap around to go to sleep. Summer makes me want to eat her. The peace and quiet inside this auto. Not to mention the lack of cockroaches. All the familiar little knobs sticking out of the upholstery. Blue and white little bags and boxes. And bigger bags and boxes. With names that say that's my prize I'm bringing back to my palace.

Driving across Fifty Seventh and Fifth. The tints of color in the passing throngs. Fanning themselves with the cool riches on sale. This morning's sunshine came down the street bright and fresh. Lapping the leaves outside my window where a pair of pigeons were flapping and screwing. And right in the middle of my little moment of beauty some crass fucker stops his car to honk his horn. Till the garbage men came waltzing along. Clanging, clattering and strewing the sidewalk and gutters with a new debris.

Upwards on the elevator. Fanny trembling and licking her lips. A flush creeping up her throat and into her cheeks. Kelly the operator calling after us as we headed out into Fanny's lobby.

"Have a good afternoon."

Inside palms and bamboo panelling. Wicker tables and chairs. Bowls of floating orchids and orange lanterns.

"Like it Cornelius. I cleaned out all that white shit. What the hell why not go tropical awhile. Makes a nice contrast in the chilly air conditioning."

On a glass covered bamboo cane table. Stacks of crisp white certificates. In their grey upper corners it says twenty five thousand dollars. On one after another. A sole parchment could change my life. Floated down to me in the struggle. Instead of putting the dimes together in a broken cigar box for an extra dollar. I could get on a train and go somewhere. Swivelling round in my chair in a parlor car. Ordering as many cans of beer as I wanted from the attendant.

"What are you thinking about Cornelius."

"Trains."

"You're looking at my bonds."

"Yes."

"Swell aren't they. Fifty in each stack."

Fanny taking a few steps. Stopping. Turning. To look at me. Potted palms in the corners. A pigeon strolling on a window sill. She falls backwards into the bamboo chair and throws her legs up over the arms. Big dark bruises above her knees.

"Caught you with another cunt. Claw her eyes out I would. And sock her all over the street. Then I'd knee her. Drag her by the hair in the gutter. She'd have plenty to remember me by."

Christian crossing the room. On the crackling woven palm leaf carpet. To stand above her as she looks up. Out of her tenderest eyes.

"Anyway, there's some chicken Cornelius. And whiskey. And me. What'll you have."

"I'll have the bonds."

"Then you better excuse me a second I'm going to put them back in my safe. But if you pour me a snort of booze and take down your pants. To hell with the bonds. I want to see it quiver. Bloop it di bloop. That's sound effects for your pants dropping. Am I glad to have you back here. You made me lonely. You made me blue."

"You kicked me out."

"I've got to tell you something sometime, Cornelius, do you know that. Strange you should think of trains."

This shadowy sultry afternoon. The heat rises shimmering over the city. Fanny's windows shut, awnings down. Wrap arms around another in our own little loneliness. In this tropical interior. Tearing and tugging at clothes. The whole world was out there just as it is today, last year. Feeling the merchandise on the counters. Shoplifting and pilfering. What hope for an agonised voice screaming fair play. Even as I stood getting weighed I was abused by the insolent tone of the speak your weight machine. Round about this time doormen's whistles begin to blow. Ladies go out to lunch. My shirt on the floor collected clean this morning from the Chinaman. Sweating in his hot laundry and cooking smells. Goes tapping each brown package with the little pink slip I gave him. His radio blaring, his wife sitting with her chop sticks over a bowl of rice. My wet dream came last night while I was standing at the corner of Eighty First Street and Park. Miss Musk prancing by in a satiny yellow drum majorette's uniform. Leading a Vine funeral. Her muscles quivering as she stamped each step. Saw me at the side of the road. When I asked her whose funeral, she tapped my prick with her baton. Said, didn't you know. It's yours, lover boy. And Fanny pleads with her eyes. A little girl. Lift her by the hips. Hands under the cheeks of her arse. Kneel with her back again on the floor. She wags her hair. Roll and scream against her throat. To hide awhile. In her limbs. In any cool of hot summer. When you hear shouts of families angry in their kitchens. Someone puts their shoes down hard at night over my head when I try to sleep. Terrible lonely sound. Fanny's taken me back. My city again. Whenever she holds my prick in her oils. Mr How don't be mad at me. I only want to slow the Mott empire down as it goes throbbing ahead. So the collision won't be so big in case it hits a recession. Gives the more lackadaisical of us a chance to swim. Always had this trouble of pulling my weight with the rest of the guys. Loosening my tie, rolling up my sleeves. And pitching in. Sadness struck me early in the midsection. And later in the balls. Makes you stagger confused from one lost opportunity to another. Those bonds. What chance have you got. When the whole damn world is written on paper already. And stacked up somewhere in a safe. With Fanny whispering. And she says Cornelius, sometimes I feel covered all over in the white milky sap of poisonous sumac. With all my good girlish looks, what a prolonged god damn disaster my life has been. I'm going to go west on a train. Did you know that. Right through Altoona. Through the Appalachians and all that spooky Pennsylvania. Where they got the hex signs up on the barns. They make you do things in the world because your name might start with a B. And because I was the biggest kid in the class they made me play the cello. I tried to sail in the god damn thing right across a pool in the creek. You never heard such belly aching everybody did when the veneer started to peel off and it all warped into a pretzel. People today sprawled everywhere all over the park. Don't know how damn lucky they are with their lives to live. Even hot as it is. Remember that morning, Cornelius. I brought you breakfast in my tight blue jeans. You said my tits gave you an appetite. And I said I had to go to a board meeting. And I came back and together we went to Brooklyn. Right out across Queens to Rockaway. You were listening to vespers. And where I was, was at the doctors. I don't know if I'll ever know what kind of courage I've got. When you get my hydraulics all horny, I guess I could even pull god by the prick. And I think if I wake up each day punching and fighting. The kind of way you do. When you seem to be able to be somebody when you're nobody at all. I won't let them tell me I'm dying. I didn't let them when they told me they'd have to cut my tits off all those months ago. Spend a fortune on operations. To hell with that shit. But they've scared me to a clinic. West on the train. And out there. I want to go slow. Please will you come. Don't say no. Never let it be the end of us. Marry me. All the colors get dark when the light goes away. And you wonder.

> How grey
> Is black
> When black
> Is grey

22

Cornelius Christian spent the heat wave in Fanny's cool apartment. The city's murders mounting to an all time record. Stabbing the most popular method of killing. A few rapes on rooftops. Kelly the doorman delivering a load of delicatessen goodies said it made you wonder what this century was coming to.

The word marry closed doors all over my brain. Staring down into Fanny's face. Asking me to join her in riches and walk with her to her grave. As a little girl she had braces on her teeth and scabs on **her** knees. She never swam in a lake and loved to swim in the ocean.

One more afternoon missing work and exhausted screwing Fanny, a tropical storm broke. Winds smashing down the street. A restaurant awning floated right by in the air outside the window like a flying machine. Lot of menus say these days your eggs can be styled to choice. Fried on the sidewalk. And sprinkled with rain.

The sheets of water fell. Flooding down the street. Fire department pumping out cellars. Sewers gurgling, washing away all the butts, dog shit and cigarette packs. A voice begging in this city. Out of eyes full of tears. Went downtown in the lull of the storm and bought a grey seersucker suit. Took the subway to Wall Street to look at the stock exchange. My, it was shirt sleeved and busy. Watched a broker oversee a stalemated minor collision between two taxis. He called upon the drivers to assert mannish instincts. To get out of their cars and fight. And he would be glad to referee.

Christian went north again on the Interborough Rapid Transit. The subway air fuming. A man sitting with a smile staring at a girl. Then someone vomited on the floor of the train. At the next station, as the doors opened a black gentleman stood shaking a monstrous prick, said who wants to suck my cock. Chap with glasses and a briefcase gasped, and announced, is there a health hazard here. And the old man next to him looked up and said don't ask me a question I don't know nothing.

Ran as another wave of the storm struck. Some poor blue suited son of a bitch, must have been from Michigan, trying to reach dry land, crossing the street, took a leap and landed up to his watery knees in an excavation hole in the gutter. A taxi driver who saw it threw his head back and laughed and crashed into the back of a bus.

Doorways crammed with folk. A woman saying to another, there wasn't one thrill in the whole evening. And I thrilled Fanny and she put away all her bonds. Said another checkup she had done on Vine found out he hires ex drum majorettes. And she suggested that maybe when they stagger out of his apartment house they can hardly walk to one of his limozines. And at that remark. My hand stiffened to slap her face.

Cross this thronged lobby. Everybody in galoshes. In out of the rain. Foot prints and drips and drops and umbrellas turned inside out by the wind. Up on the elevator. Off with my seersucker. On with my ring regalia. Walk in where all is fair and square on the white mat within the crimson ropes. Busting each other in the jaw. As O'Rourke sits, in his tattered robe, feet crossed up on his desk, the afternoon paper open across his knee.

"Hey what do you know, Cornelius."

"Hello."

"Haven't seen you for a week or two, champ. What've you been doing."

"Making word formations."

"That's good. For money."

"For money."

"That's good."

Christian putting on a pair of black leather mits. Strolling up to the punching bag hanging on a little hook from a ball bearing. Giving it a slam and lightly dancing away around the room. As O'Rourke turns his tousled head back over his shoulder.

"Hey Cornelius, you think this is a free country."

"Sure."

"I was talking to my wife last night. You know how you get into these discussions when you can't sleep. This is pretty personal, this question. You don't mind if I ask you a pretty personal question. Now promise you won't laugh if it seems funny to you."

"I won't laugh."

"Do you think a girl can get pregnant sitting in a bathtub. You know. By someone taking a bath in the same tub before them. Now take your time. I don't need an answer right away, but I told my wife it can't be done. I said it was impossible. That question needs some thought, think it over. Tell me in a few days. I'll live in ignorance awhile. Hey tell me, Cornelius, you got a girl friend now. You know I sort of feel you might be lonely."

"Yes."

"You mean you got one."

"Yes."

"That's good. Sort of serious question these days, all kidding aside, you need companionship in this city. You take her out and go places."

"Once in a while."

"Good. You met her around town."

"Used to know her as a kid before I went to Europe."

"That so. Childhood sweetheart. My wife was my childhood sweetheart. I never got a chance to know anything else. How's the shape."

"Not bad."

"You look good. Hey you know you've created some thinking in this place since you've been back. Been interesting. Everytime you go out of here and the Admiral comes in, he says what's with that guy Christian, he wants to know if you got some grudge. He says you should have stayed in Europe. I sort of told him what happened to you. But he says you're a threat to the United States. You think that's true, Cornelius."

227

"Yes."

"What. You mean I'm in the presence of a criminal. Hey get out of here. But seriously Cornelius. Now you tell me. What do you think about a thing like American girls."

Christian stopping, gloves down, flat footed in his tracks as he aims a blow.

"Whores."

"Hey you can't say a thing like that."

"Why not."

"Because it ain't true. My wife's American. You mean she's a whore. That's what you said to the Admiral, he had a fit. But you know what he says. He says you're right. But he says if he ever gets you in the ring he'll kill you for some of the other things you said. He thinks people like you are an encouragement for the Jews and the Niggers to take over."

"Good."

"Hey what do you mean good. And push the Irish out. Who do you think keeps this city honest. Wait till I tell the Admiral. He'll be in in a few minutes. Going to have his nails manicured. You know, the Admiral's a pretty important guy. Controls the whole harbour of New York. Could be useful. This is some harbour. Nice friendly waterfront where they're putting holes in each other's heads. And what's the Admiral doing. He's in here getting his nails manicured. You think men should have their nails manicured, Cornelius. Maybe since you've been away you think we've become all homosexuals in this country. Hey come on Cornelius, you think we're all homosexuals in this country."

"Yes."

"Hey you can't say a thing like that."

"Why not."

"Well it ain't right. That's why. Now I'll tell you right away if I was homosexual how could I have the ten kids I got, now you figure that out. I don't have time to be a homosexual. You see what I mean. I go home, before I have a chance to sit down, the kids are on top of me driving me crazy. I don't even have time to be sexually normal. That's why I was wondering about this thing in the bath, getting pregnant. Now you're an intelligent guy, Cornelius, you answer me that."

228

"By the laws of physics, it's possible."

"By the laws of what. Hey, don't hand me that laws of physics stuff, can she get pregnant or not. You got to tell me because I'm arguing all night with my wife and I can't get any sleep. She even wakes me up to tell me she knows someone who got pregnant sitting in the bath. I say for christ's sake shut up, it isn't the iceman or the milkman, o k so she got pregnant sitting in the bath, kid's already got a christening."

"It's possible, that's all I can say."

"I'm disappointed in you Cornelius. I told my wife if anybody could settle this matter you could. That you knew all about these little bugs and germs. Hey but I hear these English women have no morals at all, what about that. You don't have to marry them. They do it because they like it. Anyway Cornelius you're looking great, still got that nice left hook and right cross. Hey, I got a great idea. You know, the Admiral sees himself as one of the fighting greats. He says with his corkscrew punch he's invincible with one of the most powerful punches around. Now listen. You know how you get his goat. You answer him back. He doesn't like it. He's never heard anybody answer him back for years. Now you know what'd be good. We'll fix it up so you have a round or two. What do you say. I'll even tell him you're Jewish but you're called Christian as a disguise. How about it."

"I'm masquerading enough as it is."

"It'll really be funny. You fake it. Let him knock you out. Make the Admiral feel good. Come on, now, what about it. You'll be riding around with the Admiral on his yacht."

"I've taken so many beatings recently in various walks of life, I don't think I'm up to an artificial one."

"Look at it for the laughs."

"I am. It's soul destroying."

O'Rourke up on his feet. Head cocked, fists displayed. Throwing punches in all directions.

"You go in there Cornelius like as if you're going to kill him. I'll be referee. A few straight lefts in the mouth, not too hard because you might put him down. Get him around the belly.

Make him feel he's taking punishment and has got to pull the fight out of the bag.''

"Supposing he quits."

"He won't quit. Not in front of the manicurist."

"I don't know, I'm against harmful acts."

"What's harmful. You call it harmful rejuvenating the Admiral. He keeps the foreigners out of New York and the blacks up in Harlem. What do you want Cornelius, a blood bath in this city. Why is it there's so much honesty on the waterfront these days, it's the Admiral. You owe it to the country Cornelius."

"Thanks. You just said they were shooting each other in the head on the waterfront."

"But it's honest killing, can't you see the difference, the Admiral keeps it like that. Now watch me. See. A straight left to the Admiral's jaw. Then a right on the belly. Leave yourself open. He throws a counterpunch and you go down. Let him hit you at the end of the round."

"I think it's against my principles to make anyone a victim like that."

"Hey what do you mean, we're all victims. Hey you used to be one of the toughest little fighters I ever saw around here before you went to Europe. What happened. Even today, you come in here looking sad. Has something got you Cornelius."

"O k. I'll spar with the Admiral."

"Great."

O'Rourke with his laughing eyes, hands on his hips. As he stares out at Christian. This rocky tongue of land. Stuck out at the world with its big tall taste buds bulging with bullion. It might give you a second to stand up on the stage. Take a bow or jump off a building. An audience one minute who knows you. And boos. And the next minute comes another audience fresh from somewhere who say who the hell is that jumping. And claps if you get killed.

"Hey Cornelius, you know, you've changed. You used to be a wild guy here. Guts enough for an army. Was it those moral values in Europe. That you had to struggle against. You know them English friends you make, always trying to serve you last week's roast beef and the Irish who make believe you're a friend, then try to sell you last year's. All you hear from people coming back is how they got cheated, robbed and gyped. I try to tell them everybody is gyping you, only here they do it right in front of your face."

Door opening. Admiral entering. In a bundle of white bathrobe. A towel wrapped round his neck. His squeaking new boxing shoes. A frown of black eyebrows. As O'Rourke throws open his arms in greeting.

"Hey it's the Admiral. Champion of white man's rights. What this country needs is to make everybody Irish, isn't that right Admiral. Look, Cornelius Christian's here."

"So I see."

"What's a matter Admiral, Christian's not a bad guy. He's just gone a little liberal. It was that free thinking Europe did it to him."

"Don't talk to me about Europe. I'm a tax payer."

"We're all tax payers Admiral."

"I don't want my tax money supporting people like him, coming in here. Criticising this country."

"Hey Admiral he only said American women are whores."

"And it makes me very sad to agree with him."

"Hear that Cornelius. What the Admiral says. You agree on something. Both of you must be right. Coast to coast the country is crawling with whores. Hey wait a minute. What about my wife. You calling my wife a whore. Hey you can't say that. She's a mother of children."

"I'm not talking about wives. I'm talking about welfare keeping a bunch of whores on relief in this city, that I pay taxes for."

Admiral presenting his glove to be laced up by O'Rourke. As Christian spins round from the big creaking body bag into which he sinks punches.

"You deserve to pay taxes."

"Why god damn it, do you pay taxes."

"I live in limbo."

"That's the kind of smart talk they learn these days. I wouldn't mind having you on one of my ships. God damn free thinking, free fornication."

231

"Hey Admiral I'm in command of this sport arena here. Bad language is forbidden."

"If I had him just one day on one of my ships."

"Hey Cornelius has been in the navy Admiral. Can't you see the cut of his jib. Aweigh all anchors. Secure all bulkheads. Off to the beach fighting amphibians, we sail at break of day. To kick the shit out of the god damn ginzos. Forward with the Irish."

"God damn trash."

"What do you mean, Admiral, trash. Christian here says the Jews and the Niggers are taking all the seats on the subways. He says we should burn them in oil. Make room for the Irish."

"That's the kind of thing I'd expect him to say."

"Fight him Admiral, fight him. Use this place the way it's supposed to be used. For the manly sport. The art of self defence."

"I'm expecting my manicurist."

"Christian thinks you're a homosexual Admiral. That you got to have your nails beautiful. Why don't you hit him. Besides you should stop using this place like a beauty parlor."

"When you stop using it as a place of business I'll start using it for the manly sport."

"How am I going to sell my antiques if I don't keep in touch with my store. Got a great thing, I got them drilling holes in the picture frames to make it look like real worms been in the wood. Want to buy an old master, Admiral. Cheap. For the dining room on your yacht."

"Forgeries from some back room in the Bronx."

"Genuine, out of real European castles."

"O'Rourke have you ever even been in an art gallery."

"What for. I do all right. I got two recent college graduates. I always say if they got degrees, they get nervous when they steal. Makes them easier to catch."

A knock. O'Rourke shouting to come into the den of vipers. At the door a white uniformed girl hesitating. Pushing a trolley with a silver tea pot and tray of manicuring instruments.

"I'm looking for Admiral Brown."

"There he is. That powerful brute there."

"Shut up O'Rourke. Come in young lady. What's your name."

"Gertrude. Gertrude Gentle."

"Just come over here. I'll have some of that tea. You don't mind my calling you Gertrude."

"No sir."

"I'm sick of being called sir, call me anything but sir. Makes me feel I'm some sort of freak."

"Hey gee Admiral you're no freak."

"Shut up O'Rourke."

"Now Admiral none of that, I know what you've got in that teapot."

"I'm having a lump of sugar in it."

"Put milk in it."

"Miss Gentle, tell that man in the tattered robe there, didn't you ask for the Admiral's tea and isn't this what they gave you."

"Yes sir."

"See I told you O'Rourke, tea."

"Whiskey. Put milk in it. What about that Cornelius. Isn't this a disgrace. In a temple of athletic achievement. Hey, now Admiral, now why don't you, before you have your nails done, have a little spar around the ring with Cornelius."

O'Rourke switching on lights. Thunder rattling windows down the canyon street. Horns honking in the rain. See out there, folk without hats, sodden newspapers over their heads. For a moment in here. Safe and privileged. Washed my arse like Doctor Pedro said. Left Fanny biting her lip. After she blurted, you want to get away from me don't you. And I phoned Charlotte for a date. When you see so many people in the backs of buses in this town, wreathed in mystified smiles. Faces of the dead. All their flavour gone.

"Did you hear what I said Admiral. You scared."

"Ha ha, thanks for the stimulating suggestion O'Rourke. If you want to invite Mr Christian into the ring with me. All he has to do is accept."

Christian bashfully bowing his head. Demonstrate cowardice. With a straight gentlemanly refusal.

"I think I'd rather not."

"Come on now Cornelius, the Admiral promises not to use anything lethal. Remember Admiral, the corkscrew punch is illegal, you understand that. I don't want anybody hurt while I'm running this gym. Got that Admiral."

"It behooves me."

"Behoove behoove behoove, what do you mean behoove. Big words are banned here. All I want is your solemn promise not to use the corkscrew punch, never mind the behoove business. There now Cornelius, got the Admiral's solemn promise."

"I still think I'd rather not."

"Hey come on Cornelius. What more can you ask for than the Admiral's solemn promise not to touch you with the corkscrew. On your boy scout's honor now Admiral, you're not going to use the corkscrew."

"Don't be preposterous, when have I ever struck a man who couldn't defend himself."

"There you are Cornelius. Go in there with the Admiral. You'll get some pointers. Come on, before he gets manicured. The Admiral can make believe you're a Jew, and make believe he's black. And may the best race win."

"O k, all right."

"Attaboy Cornelius. Admiral, watch it now. No full weight behind punches."

"To me O'Rourke sport is give and take. I don't want to mix it with someone who can't defend himself."

"Cornelius is no cripple Admiral. But if you hold the corkscrew in check, nobody is going to get hurt."

"I can never promise to keep the corkscrew in check."

"But you just promised."

"It's an instinctive punch with me. And comes out of nowhere. I don't even know how I do it myself."

"It's pretty obvious Admiral where it comes from, look at the way you're set up, like a kid of twenty."

"Well I keep myself in shape. Every ship that goes to sea under my command is in a rigorous state of health and fitness."

"Now Miss Gentle, would you know by looking at the Admiral that he has one of the most lethal punches ever seen in the ring.

Naturally he doesn't like it talked about. But you can't deny it Admiral.''

"God damn it I don't deny it. I prefer it to be known. But anyone entering the ring with me knows the risk he runs by doing so.''

"Everytime you walk out of here, I can hear the muggers running Admiral. But I just finished, you heard me twice, telling Cornelius you weren't going to use it. You wouldn't be that kind of sportsman.''

"Why don't you buy a new robe O'Rourke.''

"Hey what's wrong with my robe.''

"This young lady here, I don't want her to think we boxers have no sartorial elegance.''

"Where do you get off with that word sartorial. Speak English. Cornelius there, he's got no elegance neither. He told me it was a cultured European touch to wear rags. Come on, you going to box with Cornelius or aren't you.''

"If he's prepared I'm prepared.''

O'Rourke leaping over a bench. Grabbing a pair of boxing gloves. Pushing them on Cornelius.

"Miss Gertrude, you tie up the Admiral will you. I mean his gloves. Make sure no flying laces.''

Two contestants center ring. O'Rourke hovering between them, a hand on Christian's back and another on the Admiral's elbow.

"Now remember, no hitting on the break. No rabbit punches. I'm going to watch for any foul blows in this. I want a clean racist fight.''

Bong the gong. Christian jumping back. Instantly employing the reverse shuffle dance. As the Admiral with a rotating straight left does the bull charge. Crashing into the ropes. Muttering, you son of a bitch, as Christian spidered away. And O'Rourke sits himself down to the tea pot.

"Well Admiral I'll just help myself to a little tea.''

"Get away from that tea pot.''

"Just a sip. Well what do you know, it is tea.''

"You scoundrel.''

"So this is what you train on Admiral. Now we know where

235

you got that corkscrew punch. Cornelius you duck when it comes.''

Christian doing his flubbididub step. Neatly avoiding the additional bull charge perpetrated by the growling Admiral. Who looses a right hook over Christian's ducking head.

''That's the way Cornelius. Show him the footwork. Dazzle him so he can't explode the corkscrew at you.''

Gertrude Gentle turning to O'Rourke with her eyebrows raised on a smooth powdered face.

''They're not going to hurt each other.''

''Shussh. Just humouring the Admiral along, he couldn't break a spider's web.''

''O this is just a joke.''

''Just a joke. That's it Cornelius, keep well away from that right. Circle. Watch it, the Admiral's getting set. Now Admiral remember what I told you. Make sure the corkscrew is at half power.''

''Shut up.''

''Hey I got to tell my fighter what to do. Watch it Cornelius he's sizing up your style. Hey, you're running Cornelius. Take your beating like a man. Don't go yellow. Personal bravery is what made this country great. As well as the big bombs we got. What's a matter Admiral, go after him.''

''He's backing away. I can't hit him.''

''Not surprising. Miracle Cornelius isn't making for the ferry. That was the corkscrew you just sent whistling past his ear. Are you all right Cornelius.''

''Fine. Just warming up.''

''I'm watching you Admiral. I don't want any unconscious bodies in this boxing room. I'm responsible for all lives in here. This is just like a ship.''

''Christian's doing all right. He doesn't need your shipboard advice. He's got a nice little punch. Just caught me. Nice punch. Only don't forget to tell me if I'm hurting you.''

''You're not hurting me.''

''Hey the two of you in there are starting to become friends. Hit him Cornelius. There you are Miss Gentle. Two fine men. Real sportsmen. Truly the manly art. Look at the Admiral's clean crisp punching. Note the way he flexes his knee and puts his shoulder into it."

O'Rourke pouring tea. Miss Gentle putting a cup to her lips. And splutters it out.

"O my goodness. I really thought it was tea."

O'Rourke on his feet raising a shaking fist. A general slowing down of action. Feinting and pushing. Huffing and puffing.

"Jew fight. Let's see some action. Get that Arab, he's wide open, Cornelius, for a belt to the nose. That's it, get him before he tries the corkscrew. Punish him around the belly. Now a left, hook him, hook him. Watch it Cornelius, that stance the Admiral's using is deadly."

Christian lowering gloves. Moving in with his chin. Ducking as a right cross from the Admiral flies overhead. O'Rourke jumping off the floorboards.

"I saw it, I saw it, that was it. The corkscrew Admiral. The dreaded deadly punch. At full power. You know it's fatal at close quarters."

"You just stop drinking my whiskey."

"You admit it. Well I saw you. If Christian hadn't ducked we'd be picking up his head from over there on Wall Street. Good mind to stop the fight."

A thump. Admiral's glove connecting with Christian's chin. Slowly turning him round as he plummets to the canvas, landing spread eagled on his back. Gertrude Gentle jumping to her feet. Hands to her lips. As O'Rourke winks and pushes her seated again.

"Hey you hit him with the corkscrew. Now don't say you didn't Admiral. I saw you do it. Look at him, you've knocked him right out. Told you not to use it, you don't know your own strength."

Cool moist wind coming in the window. Flashes of distant lightning. Admiral mountainously standing over the slain Christian. Lifting his chin. Raising a gloved hand of triumph. And with a slow swagger crossing the ring and slipping through the crimson ropes.

"What's the idea, Admiral, hey we've got to pick him up, just don't leave him like that. He needs artificial respiration."

"It was merely a tap. Leave him there. He's had that coming for a long time. Knock some sense into him. Won't be coming in here again talking a lot of nonsense."

"Well Admiral let me shake your hand. Now don't give me the dynamite shake. Just a shake. Didn't want to tell you, but you know that's the first time Cornelius Christian's ever hit deck, to use a sea faring phrase. Didn't want to say anything but he was middle Atlantic champ before he went to Europe. Seventeen straight knockouts."

"Well he had me guessing. Just for a few seconds. I've often refrained from using the corkscrew even when I've seen an inviting opening. But that kid's too smart for his own good. Not enough red blood these days."

"You bet Admiral."

"When I took my first ship to sea I used to skip rope around the quarter deck for two hours before breakfast. This country wasn't a whole lot of scruffy creampuffs then. That's how I got this stomach you call a beer barrel. Barrel of nails. You, young girl. Give it a punch. Try it. Go on. Don't be shy. That's it. There."

"O gosh sir, it is hard."

"You show her Admiral, armour plating. That's where, Gertrude, they got the idea, from the Admiral's belly. Bet Christian knew he was hitting something when he tried a few on that."

"That's what a clean life does O'Rourke."

"Cleaned out your teapot for you, Admiral."

"Miss Gentle take no notice of him."

"O I'm not Admiral. But is Mr Christian, is he all right."

"Good, my dear, to see someone like you so concerned. Gives your eyes a nice look. But I assure you he'll come around in a few days. Won't be able to chew for a couple of months, but he'll be all right. Well that was a good afternoon's workout."

"I just thought I saw him twitch."

"Gertrude don't worry. My corkscrew never does anybody any permanent harm. Just puts them to sleep. It's scientific. The glove rotates as the punch leaves and when it lands, quicker than the eye can see, it has an extra penetrating force. Developed it after years of experiment, based on the rifling in a gun barrel. Throw some water on him."

238

"Gee Admiral, look at him, felled like a tree. But Cornelius took it like a man. But you shouldn't have done it, Admiral."

"Do him good. Today's mollycoddling youth needs a shaft up the ass, excuse me Miss Gentle, my girl, but that's what youth needs. Stiffen their spines. But no hard feelings. In the ring I may be a killer but outside I believe in behaving like a normal human being. Any born boxer would have done what I did when he saw his opening."

"Your conscience is clear, Admiral. I think maybe Cornelius did have it coming to him. Like a lot of guys who feel this country could do with changing. And that our wives are out to get us for alimony and sell themselves."

"O'Rourke I think that kind of talk is out of place with Gertrude present here."

"But I like men who hate women."

"Hey get that Admiral. If Cornelius was only conscious he would have liked that remark."

"Goodbye O'Rourke."

"So long Admiral. And watch the corkscrew, it's banned from now on."

O'Rourke chuckling as the big brown door closes and clicks shut. Turning to the ring. The prostrate Christian. Open eyed face staring at the ceiling. A siren screaming. A bell clanging, down the street. A friendly fire somewhere.

"That was great Cornelius. Why the Admiral will be inviting you down to his boat, get free rides all round the harbour. I have to laugh, that was really good acting, for a second I really thought it looked like he knocked you cold."

Christian with arms stretched facing east and west crosstown. Blond head pointing uptown and dark heels downtown.

"Hey Cornelius, come on get up, what's the matter. The Admiral's gone."

O'Rourke bending over Christian. Touching his head.

"Christ, Cornelius, he really hit you. Wake up. Hey gee I'm going to have to get the smelling salts."

On this padded canvas floor. In the New World of pavements asphalt and cement. Stranded and needy in the arms of Fanny Sourpuss. Fearful souls creeping. Great silent weeping stream of people in the canyon streets. A broken cardboard box. To take

239

their dreams away somewhere under their arms. As I did on a bus north through Harlem. When I was a little boy. A sign, night crawlers and worms for sale. Cars roaring the highways. Night, noon, morning and afternoon. Nowhere to live. On a junk strewn continent. Rip up the soil, melt me back into the barren ground. Grow me once more wild to race fleet foot across this land. Beyond the salt flats. Piss down passing Pittsburgh. Walk again that bowery of scrawny necked men, with their condor heads, sitting arms flapped over their knees. Offering to sell their shirts and trousers, bargaining out of reddened lips. Polite and beaten. And one figure reared up begging. Into my high school friend's sneers. And I saw the eyes of a man. Who saw mine. When all the years I thought he was dead. And his hand dropped and his head hung.

> As he said
> Sorry
> Son

23

Wake this morning. Fanny pushing a breast in my face to soothe my jaw she said was all swollen up. And might be broken. Just when I was looking good in my new seersucker suit. Planning as I was a blistering series of creative utterances to make Mr Quell and his asskissers wide eyed with envy in the Think Room of the Mott Empire. And I get knocked out. For the count.

Cornelius Christian heading downtown for medical advice. As long cigar shaped clouds sneak over from Hoboken. The storm heading north east across Patchogue, the Hamptons and Sag Harbour. Shadows of buildings poking into the park. This bus with a great engine roaring, swaying from stop to stop. A hot sun shining in slits along the crosstown streets. See a dark complexioned kid pissing down from a window six stories up. The drops haven't reached yet, an old man sitting on the stoop.

A new day dawns living. Even in these gloomy ravines of sweaty armpits pushing trolleys of pink and blue dresses through this dingy garment district. Trucks jammed along the gutters. Cigars in big overseeing fat faces. Throngs charging through the doors of that department store. As I get off the bus at Herald Square. Where no one is waiting to give me a prize for my spiritual beauty.

Christian nipping once more into this cavernous entrance. Ascending again to the eighty fifth floor. With a chattering group of summery school children, their shepherding teacher giving me oblong looks. As I give her my child molester leer.

Last week wrote helplessly homesick to Europe. Begged them to have me back. After the debt collector leaped out from behind a hallway door. To pay up for excess baggage contracted while en route to this shore. No mention of the meals she missed, the towels she didn't use. Said I've got you at last Mr Christian. I peppered him with straight light lefts. A nice one on the throat drove him backwards into a girl carrying out a bag of moist garbage and she screamed. And the debt collector screamed as he turned around to apologise, taking from her as he did, a robust kick in the balls. Nearly waited to watch him writhe awhile. Over the strewn watermelon pips.

Doctor Pedro's ripe bosomed nurse, a fresh pink rose pinned on her white uniform, pushing open his door. He sits singing in his shirt sleeves, grey haired wiry little arms, his ruddy cheek pressed on a violin as he plucks its strings.

"Hey what happened to you. The cat got your tongue. Can't speak. What did you get, a sock on the jaw. You should make love not war. Who you fight with, some crumbum in the street. Grow up. Or sock him first. What's the matter I send you out of here cured and you come back busted. I have a good mind to charge you. You know how much I cost as a doctor. Don't ask. You couldn't afford it. Ask me why they change Eleventh Avenue to West End at Fifty Ninth Street, and Tenth Avenue to Amsterdam and Ninth to Columbus, and Eighth to Central Park West. Because people thought they were big hot shit up there. That's why. And up here I'm looking down into every jackass's chimney stack. Did you scrub your floor like I told you. You see, I know you didn't. Now look at you, can't talk. What the hell's the matter with you, you don't do what I tell you. You think I live for this long and talk bull shit. You got a swollen jaw, slight dislocation, it's going to be all right, nothing broken. Only thing you got going for you now is no one can call you a cocksucker."

Christian nodding thanks. Rivulets of moisture flow down between the cleavage of the arse. Out the window over the head of my wry little doctor the shadow of this building cast over a mile of rooftops. Over which, if I see the Admiral again, I'll bounce him belly first, black and blue.

"Hey wait a minute. You want to know how to be happy. I tell you. Every day you should walk sixty blocks. To keep the muggers away, make like you're a little crazy. Thirty downtown, thirty uptown. Then go to the Sixth Avenue Delicatessen. Order a hot pastrami on rye, use plenty of mustard, a dish of coleslaw, a bottle of beer. Watch the fucked up expressions on the faces of your fellow man. And be glad you're not like that."

Nurse putting my file away. Genital glow of her smile. The little doctor singing and plucking his violin again as I go out the door. Strange pains in my chest. A few up the arse as well. Thousand directions to head when I go out of here. Instead of back to Mott.

Elevator packed with a batch of Atlanta Georgia straw hatted, whale bone corsetted Colonial Dames of America. As we plunge down perfumed smothered to the street again. Except that, good lord someone on this elevator has stepped in dog shit. Use my ventriloquist's technique to sneak some words out from my beleaguered jaws. Choose a roundabout way to civilly suggest.

"Forgive me madam, I happen to be standing rather close to you and I wonder might I ask if you and your friends are Daughters of the American Revolution."

"O my, how did you ever know."

"I knew madam."

"Well isn't that something, Jean, this young man knew we were daughters."

"My jaw's broken, and I really regret having to mutter to you in this way, but one of your party has, I am sure, stepped into canine excrement."

Lady's face flushing pink and patches of red appearing on her throat. As all elevator chat ceases with another fifty two floors to go. In agonizing silence. Almost impossible for me to utter anything right these days. But I can't stand anymore stink. Whole bloody lot staring at me. During this eternal ear popping descent. And noses twitching as they sniff. The whole god damn bunch are deliberately smelling me.

Elevator loading and unloading. Christian threading his way through the noisy chattering lobby. And out on the street past a man selling rosary beads and polka dot bow ties. Go west in one's

243

misery towards the docks. Where the big ships can take you away. Sail out just as I sailed in. On a monstrous boatload of sorrow.

Christian stopping where it says Tavern. Go in here and have a glass of beer. Pulling open this swing door into darkness. Move down this long mahogany bar. Cooler than the heat of the street. Fans whirring. Blow away the smell of that elevator. White aproned avocado bellied bartender wiping up the slops of beer. Pass a little group of four in earnest conversation.

"Now why don't you get wise."

"Why don't you get wise."

"I am wise."

"A wise guy."

"Hey both you wise guys dry up. And let's have four more beers. Give that guy one who just came in. He looks unhappy."

Raise my glass in a silent salute of thanks. Because if I felt like speaking I'd say no thanks. Come in here to a whole new world. Take refuge at random. Sit on a bar stool and think. Feel alive working in a funeral parlor and now see death groping in every corner of my brain. Whole city staring awake at night. By day another black gentleman sticking his prick in the subway train. To a bunch of mother fucking white cocksuckers. And a greasy faced lady of riper years jumping up with her knitting in one hand, tried to grab it. He retreated along the platform pushing and shoving his prick back into his trousers. As she followed shouting, wait a minute I want to talk to you. For light relief I went up to street level to take a walk in the park. On top of a boulder in the sunshine, eight guys wearing lipstick sitting in a circle jerking off. Waved and invited me to join. As one marked time with a tambourine. And coming along the path in nice linen suit and white spats, an elderly man passing me said welcome to the asylum.

Raised voices at the other end of the bar. Tall crew cut beefy guy in a thin green sweat shirt, screwing up one side of his face to tell a shorter grey suited man.

"If your kind of speaking is so hot what are you doing in a dump like this."

"What are you."

244

"I'm here because I'm wise, that's why."

"Wise."

"Yeah wise."

"Well I carry twenty thousand dollars worth of insurance."

"Tell me another."

"I have a brother who lives out in Manhasset and he's insured for forty five thousand dollars."

"You know what. I think you're full of shit."

"What are you jealous because my brother's insured for forty five thousand dollars."

"Jealous of you. Why you're full of shit."

"Just say that again."

"You're full of shit."

"Say that without smiling."

"You're full of shit."

"Well just don't say that again, that's all."

"You're full of shit."

"I'm warning you, say that once more and you'll be sorry."

"You're full of shit."

"I'm just waiting that's all, you'll see."

"I see you full of shit."

"Is that all you can say."

"I like saying you're full of shit."

"Some guys don't know when they've said enough."

"That's right. Because you're full of too much shit."

"I don't think I like this company. I'm going."

The tall beefy gorm reaching out to grab and raise this smaller man on his toes. Pulling him upwards by the scruff of his shiny nylon shirt and tugging his tie crossed with the latest in stripes. As the other two companions step back. And the bartender gets hurriedly busy spacing out whiskey bottles on his shelf.

"Not so fast dude, I said you're full of shit. Are you going to make a liar out of me in front of four other people."

"I'm going."

"Am I right or wrong."

"Let me go."

"See this, this is my fist. Am I right or wrong. Are you full of shit."

"For the sake that we can all live in peace maybe you're right."

"Then what are you."

"I don't know if I am."

"Look dude I'm not kidding. Making me out I'm a liar. You just made a liar out of me. Say you're full of shit."

"I'm full of shit."

"Now dude don't that make you feel better. And your brother, he's full of shit. Go on, say it."

"And my brother's full of shit."

"And your brother ain't insured for no forty five thousand dollars because no guy related to you is worth that much because you, dude are full of shit, just like your brother and your father and your mother."

"Leave my mother out of it."

"I said your mother."

"Don't you say that about my mother, you leave her out of it. What's she done to you. My mother's a fine woman."

"Not after she had you dudie boy."

Little grey suited man raising his arms, palms held up to hold back the avalanche of horror. His glasses flashing tears on his eyes.

"You big dirty rat you. Sure, you could knock me down. Sure, you could pummel and sock me. Sure, you big bully. I'm depressed. What you've said to me is so awful. If I was bigger you wouldn't say it.

"Sure I would dude."

"Making me say that about my brother, one of the kindest guys I've ever known. And a mean guy like you, pushing little people around. Picking on me when I've done nothing to you. Makes you feel brave because I'm scared of fighting. Sure, you can poke me right now in the face and break my jaw. I'm not tough. I'm not strong. But I told you not to say what you did about my mother. I told you. And you went right on and said it. Boy that's lousy. Now you won't let me walk out. You just rode me into the ground. You rat. I'm heartbroken."

"Who you suddenly calling a rat, dude."

"You. You are. To say that my mother was full of what you said. I'm crying. I loved that woman. I loved my mother."

"Hey dude, wait."

"No I won't."

"Stop crying for christ's sake, dude."

No. I'm going to make you pay. You'll pay. Because my mother she was the most wonderful person who ever lived. I kneel and would kiss the ground she walked on."

"Hey dude, come on. I take back what I said. Gee will you stop crying for christ's sake. Listen to me. I'm a rat. A lousy lousy rat. You could flood your lungs the way you're crying. Come on, straighten up and fly right. I was kidding everything I said."

"You said she was full of shit. She slaved her whole life raising four kids. She ironed and did without for us. My father kicked her around. She's dead. O god my mother, the most blessed creature whoever lived in god's kingdom is dead. And I heard words, rotten dirty filthy words said about her, the dearest and best person in the world."

"Dude punch me. I shouldn't have said it. Come on. I know kiddo. Don't I have a mother myself. Your brother in Manhasset, it's a classy district, his insurance could be eighty five thousand dollars and I wouldn't think it was too much. Only stop the crying, Harry."

"My name's not Harry."

"O k tell me your name."

"Sylvester."

"Sylvester. I'm called Ed. O boy Sylvester. You're a great guy. A real good guy. I'm apologising. What do you want me to do, go down on my knees."

"Yes I do."

"Hey come on. Sylvester."

"You better. Because you better start praying."

Bartender turns around from his bottles to take a rag and wipe back and forth over the bar, and slowly begins to crouch. As Sylvester steps back. The other two guys trying to stand behind each other. A smile on Ed's face fading. A tiny pistol emerged from the little man's jacket pocket. Slowly raising it in his hand as folk shrink. Big Ed putting his hands up in front of his face. To block the lead. His mouth making words that don't come out. And then opening wide to scream as bullets go into him. Red little holes on his chest. Find yourself counting. Three four five. Big Ed, hands behind him clutching the bar rail. Six. And he falls to the floor. One leg bent under. One eye open, the other closed. Blood seeping from the corner of his mouth. Hear Clarance Vine's voice. Tell me all over again. It's the discourtesy which causes the murder in this town. And Doctor Pedro. Says every day walk sixty blocks. Over coleslaw watch the fucked up expressions on the faces of your fellow man. And here's one now. On the bar room floor. Be glad you're not like that.

Grinning
Dead

24

On this murderous steamy hot afternoon. Christian entering the bright cool air of the pure white Think Room of the Mott empire. Mr Quell, head of Thinking, stopping mid aisle in his shirt sleeves. Hips wider than his shoulders. Ears big as hands. Tiny red mustache hiding his upper lip. Long fading pink hair combed in a marcel wave over his bald head.

Where the hell have you been. You heard me. What's the matter. Have you got laryngitis.''

JUST SLACK VOCAL CORDS.

''What are you trying once more, to be funny Christian. Well this really is something, isn't it. Now you can't speak. Writing on pieces of paper. When we couldn't get you to write on paper when you could speak. Go on. Go and see Mr How. I don't think I'm all that whole heck of a lot in need of your services at the moment.''

Tighten the teeth a little. Awful how one wants to take him and flick his tie up in his face. Or dump on it a whole heck of a lot of shit. An overall brown would help with his vulgar choice of colors. Wants me to enter his own little power struggle. To improve his department. And fill Mott's orbit with another triumph of thought.

How has a nice new secretary. I've not seen before. My deep serious silence might make her think I'm an acting deputy assistant department head. Howdy chickadee. Why don't you accompany this big spender to a nightclub. Watch me feel absolutely at home among the celebrities. Baby, me no cog. Come roll with me. Me big wheel.

"Mr Christian, Mr How will see you now."

THANK YOU.

"You're welcome but gee I'm sorry I didn't know you were deaf and dumb."

JUST DUMB NOT DEAF.

"O gee."

Christian moving along through these typing sounds and ringing telephones. The massive ass flattening continues. Everyone looking so god damn composed. Or else up at the clock. Stand stagestaggered now in front of Howard How's door. Down the street I walked into a big building. Right at the bottom of Broadway. Stood at the counter in the massive shady room. Said in my most nervous muttering whisper. How much is it out of here and back across the Atlantic on the cheapest boat.

"Mr Christian please go in, Mr How will see you now."

Howard How, his hands flat out on his desk. Same sandy face. Parts his hair one third and two thirds. Lot of son of a bitches try to be smart aleck with two fifths and three fifths.

"Sit down Cornelius. Boy what a busy day. First free second I've had. And it has to be another problem with you. Your file here, Cornelius. Doesn't need more than a look. All I got to say, gee it really is too bad. Late. Miss work. Can't get in touch with you. Today you come to work in the middle of the afternoon. Mr Quell says you're writing notes on pieces of paper. What the hell's happened that you can't speak."

I THINK I MAY BE HAVING A NERVOUS BREAK-DOWN.

"You know, Cornelius, I'm going to be candid, you were really one guy, out of the hundreds and hundreds I see, that I would have sworn would go places. Somehow it just breaks my heart. Isn't the renumeration enough. That's o k you don't have to write an answer. But look, this report. When you weren't looking at them tearing the building down, or were they building it. Gee, you're even getting me confused. Anyway if it wasn't sending dirty remarks by semaphore to the guys on the building over there, you were sneaking looks at Mr Quell's Wall Street

Journal. Are you having a shot at the market or something Cornelius. If you're here at all, you're heading for the water cooler or just coming back. And if it's not that you're hanging over the desk of someone who's working, and making undermining remarks. What's the matter, Cornelius don't you like us here at Mott. O k, if the answer's not too long, write it down.''

IT SEEMS THAT WHAT I DO JUST ISN'T MAKING ANY IMPRESSION ON THE WORLD. I HAVE A FEELING OF WORTHLESSNESS.

''Hey now Cornelius. That's no way to feel. Sure you're worth something. You know, I've told my wife about you. Even said she wanted to meet you. Meet our kids. But please just from our side look at it. I mean if it's any consolation, your fourteen visits to the rest room in one day, may not have made an impression on the world but it sure made one on us. O k, if you have an answer write it down.''

I HAVE A NERVOUS KIDNEY CONDITION.

''Sorry to read this Cornelius. We have a whole range of company medical services. Why not get your self a check up.''

I'VE BEEN TO THE DOCTOR.

''Did he tell you it was something serious.''

HE TOLD ME THE ONLY THING I HAD GOING FOR ME WAS NO ONE COULD CALL ME A COCKSUCKER. I APOLOGISE FOR THE LANGUAGE.

''O k, I'm adult Cornelius. But let's not try to be too comical, what the hell kind of doctor you going to. Gee it's only that some day you could be up there with the celebrities.''

MY DOCTOR SAYS EVERY CELEBRITY IN THIS TOWN IS A JACKASS.

''I won't dispute your doctor's medical advice, Cornelius, but some of those celebrities are important people. But who knows, maybe being a celebrity is a medical problem. Anyway my problem is, Cornelius, I got to use a disheartening word. By the rule book I'm supposed to fire you. You've given me a moral and ethical nightmare. You might say these have been heart rending days. I know there isn't anything evil and filthy in your background, Christian. But we don't even have one reference, outside the funeral parlor we can fall back on. Maybe you're just having

251

a bad month. If you need it, why don't you reach out for help. It could rid you of your feeling of worthlessness. I mean, what the hell, we're all worthless. Come down to it. I mean couldn't some guy walk right into my job and where would I be.''

MR MOTT ISN'T WORTHLESS.

''No he's not. I'll grant you that. He could be worth a hundred million.''

THAT'S WHY HE CAN WALK INTO A ROOM AND SAY WHAT'S ON HIS MIND.

''Yeah, I'm reading you, it's a good point. I guess for guys like me it's what I'm carrying in life insurance that counts.''

DON'T MENTION INSURANCE.

''Why not.''

JUST LEFT A PLACE WHERE A GUY GOT SHOT FOR IT.

''Is that right. Well maybe it's amazing the subjects that can get you into hot water these days. But now just let me ask you just one question Cornelius, I don't want you to take it in the wrong way, just write yes or no. Didn't you have a father to look up to and to respect.''

NO.

''Sorry to hear that.''

HE WAS A GOD DAMN BUM.

''Holy gee Cornelius, you can't say that about your own father.''

HE WAS A SHAM, PHONY AND BRAGGART.

''Hey come on. It really hurts me to hear, I mean read you on this. Can a son really grow up and say that about his own father.''

YES.

''Those are strong words Cornelius, I don't mind telling you. But that shouldn't hold you back from your goal in life. You know I even thought I'd like for my little boy Billie to grow up like you, Cornelius. Maybe that's what you need, wife and kids, to make a go of it. Make you feel you had something to win for. A son. That you've got to make it. For him. When your boy and girl's future means more to you than anything else in the world. But why do you do it. Hang over the other guy's desks making

252

these cranky, crippling statements. There are pages of them written down here in the complaints. I don't know, I've got the whole personnel of this company to worry about and I find myself getting up in the morning enraged at some of the things you've been doing. And I got to level with you, Cornelius. Your kind of attitude is just not going to help us knock hell out of the competition in this industry. I mean to put it frankly you are sabotaging us. Same thing as a bomb or something blowing the hell out of us. I mean if you came out there to Forest Hills and saw what I've got. Wife, three swell kids. Moving along with a few little improvements all the time. Built a little cantilevered back porch out on the back of the house with my own two bare hands. Rigged up an extra shower down in the basement. Put up new storm windows. Cut down my fuel bill a whole fourteen percent. These are the real things Cornelius. Like the four new snow tires I got stacked up in my garage, ready for winter. You know, I look forward to using those tires. Look at them there in the garage, thinking how I'm going to cruise right over the snow and ice after Thanksgiving. A swell thought on a hot summer's day. I've got growing my own herb garden. Did you know that. Back there on the good earth after a hard day at the office, a great feeling. Sorry keep forgetting you can't talk.''

IS IT ALL LOVE AND BEAUTY OUT THERE.

''Why no Cornelius it's not. I'll be frank. I got this guy next door complaining I'm screwing up the air, sending wop smells from my garlic patch over into his back play area. You got to expect this kind of little ethnic trouble from time to time. I mean, believe it or not, the guy's a real wop himself.''

THEN NOT EVERYTHING IS SWELL OUT THERE.

''No Cornelius, not everything is swell, I would be less than candid to say it was. But there are good guy neighbors too. The fellow across the street. Everything is going swell with him. He just made vice president in charge of sales for a big east coast pharmaceutical operation. Got himself a three car garage. His wife is a kind of sex beauty queen. She's got some shape. He's got a lot going for him. And one thing, we're absolutely agreed on. He's never going to sell out to an undesirable. And I'm not. We shook hands on it.''

WHAT ABOUT THE GUY COMPLAINS ABOUT YOUR GARLIC.

"That's a valid question Cornelius. I'm glad you asked it. Well, I don't know. He might do that kind of thing, maybe, and sell to an undesirable. I don't know he must have something. He's been burglarized four times in three months. My wife's seen these guys pulling out of their garage with a big truck. We've only been burglarized once. But you know, there's something funny about him. Hardly ever see the wife and he keeps to himself. Never see any friends coming or going. Plenty of times I struck up a conversation. But he doesn't want to talk. I mean even in your own garden, some people will hold garlic against you. That's o k by me. The guy's maybe worried about his taxes or something."

HE MIGHT HAVE AN ILLICIT STILL IN HIS HOUSE.

"Ha ha, hey that's really a good one Cornelius. You see, that imagination of yours. If we could harness it. Don't you love your country. Want to do something for it."

I THINK THE NIGGERS SHOULD TAKE IT OVER.

"Now what kind of a controversial remark is that Cornelius."

THEY'VE GOT BETTER MANNERS.

"Holy cow, ethnically Cornelius you're way off. What the hell kind of opinion is that."

THEY'RE A PASTORAL PEOPLE.

"O k, maybe I'll grant you that. I mean that's interesting. But supposing the bloodbath comes. When the pendulum of property values is going to sock some of us for a loop. You know the god damn riots that go on already. I mean Forest Hills could go black overnight. I mean pardon me Cornelius, but what the hell are god damn manners in the middle of the bloodbath. I mean I can't go out on my back cantilevered porch after dark without wondering if some black son of a bitch is going to jump me. Right up out of my own god damn herb garden. I mean there's a guy now, about once a month shoots some resident dead. I mean he could just take your wallet, but no, he kills you right afterwards. You call that manners."

CROOKS HAVE TO BE CAREFUL TOO.

"Well it's four o'clock. And my dander's up. I mean what the hell do you know about property values Cornelius. Although we got the tennis club out there, you still lie awake in the bed at night, next to your loved one, wondering if the guy across the street's going to sell to an undesirable. And you wake up the next morning, grabbing the binoculars to see if some dark faces have moved in and your life's investment is shot to hell. Boy I'll tell you, a man's life is only worth what his next door neighbor might suddenly make it. I mean if you forget a minute about the god damn vandalism. With kids breaking the windows, stealing your car, or what's worse the battery. And your trying to start it for two hours. Hey come on, come out and see me, what do you say. You'll love my wife, Jean. I mean she's dying to meet you."

AM I FIRED.

"Now why do you have to bring up that painful subject Cornelius. I'm using my own judgement about that. Mr Mott always wants a full reservoir of brains to give a constant supply of clear thinking. Just like that reservoir you talked about when you first came in here."

I GUESS WHEN MOTT WANTS A DEEP THOUGHT HE TURNS ON THE TAP.

"Right."

I POLLUTE THE THOUGHT SUPPLY.

"Right. No. Not right. No. You just get leaves and debris in it. But come on, don't you know you're among a scrupulously selected collection of the best young minds in the country. And you know, you inherited those brains. That's why Cornelius I find it hard to take what you said about your father. I don't want my kid to be mystified by his father. I would die, Cornelius, rather than do anything to embarrass my boy. They could put me on the rack and torture me, I wouldn't care. I'm that kid's hero. I want him to look me straight in the eye. And not think his dad is making a cheap buck somewhere in a dirty deal. When I say something I want my little Billie to feel it's the god's honest truth being spoken. If I say it's pouring rain in Death Valley every day of the week, I want Billie to say, my dad said that, and my dad speaks the truth. Will you come out, and see me Cornelius, I mean I don't live in a palace but I just know

255

it would make you see that this country isn't just a whole great lot of runaway fear and terror. That the rewards are there.''

I'LL COME.

''Gee that's swell. And you know, maybe I'd like to ask you just one question. I mean gee, what's it like to be standing over a bunch of dead bodies all the time, like you used to do. Did it teach you anything. I mean jesus christ that's what's going to happen to us.''

IT TAUGHT ME DEATH IS BETTER THAN DYING.

> Better than
> Hapless
> Better than
> Glee
> The cat's
> Meow
> In this midnight
> Sea

25

Fanny Sourpuss in the middle of the night. Rolling over in bed as I came in. Opening one eye and then the other. Squinting in the light. Let myself in with the key she gave me. The night duty doorman kept me half an hour showing me the latest judo tricks he learned at class and said let's see you try and throw me now Mr Peabody.

I got him on the floor in the grapevine. Nearly woke the building up with his Pakistani screams. We both stood up to bow to two residents returning from a ball. They were tipsy. Just as I finally got, standing at five bars in Greenwich village. Having two beers in each. Heard a lot of jackasses that Doctor Pedro spoke about. Hopelessly remote celebrities. Then took a walk all the way uptown on Fifth to cut over to the delicatessen. From which I nearly never got delivered. As I step through this brown hot darkness towards the voice of Fanny.

"It's you. What time is it."

"Two."

"Where you been."

"Standing at a bar."

"Are you still muttering like that. They must have thought you were nuts. Throw me my cigarettes. You weren't trying to screw any cunts."

"No."

"Just had a big dream you were. And some god damn pussy was putting her leg over your prick and it was about a foot wide.

She could have raced it at Hialeah. Well at least you came back. God it's hot. Son of a bitch Kelly the doorman was screwing around with the air conditioning this afternoon. Said it was an immorality. That if god wanted us hot we should be hot. Then that stupid Arab or something, who keeps making eyes at me, busted the whole thing for good. And everybody in the building is telling me to get it fixed as if it's all my fault. Come to bed. You hungry.''

"No."

"Hey tell me something. Did you love your wife. I sometimes think you're such a cold hearted fish. And you just threw her in the grave. That you don't have feelings for anything."

"I've got feelings."

"Come to bed."

Lie stony and stiff next to Fanny Sourpuss. Wait till she goes to sleep so that I can ponder more. Because tonight I went to the Sixth Avenue Delicatessen. For a taste of Doctor Pedro's happiness. After my walk. Tall blond lady came in and sat across from me. In a loose green dress with greener buttons down the front. She put ketchup on her french fries. And held her pinky way out when digging with her fork. Smiled when I pushed the sugar her way for her coffee. She said it's a hot night. I said yes. And saw her putting her hands below the table edge where she pulled back and forth on a wedding ring. She bit her lip before she spoke.

"Do you come here often."

"Well my doctor told me to come."

"Your doctor."

"Yes he said it was a good place to come and look at the people."

"Well it sure is a place you can see people, but what kind of people."

Her hair swept up on top of her head and her cheeks a little puffy and her lower lip hung down. Her teeth looked newer than the rest of her. Said she was single and lived just a few buildings away. She lifted one eyebrow extremely high above the other when she asked a question.

"What do you do if you don't mind me enquiring."

Everytime she leans forward. See the dark moist line of cleavage between her two big breasts. Borrow, if he's not using it this late at night, Mr Quell's title for a while.

"I'm department head of publicity for an industrial corporation."

"Is that right."

"Well yes it is. I mean I'm considering other proposals at the moment. At my age it's all right to be department head but I wouldn't want that to get chronic."

"Ha ha, no, you wouldn't want that. You could be a magazine model or an actor or something like that."

"Well I am considering seriously other proposals and job opportunities."

"You got a kind of funny way of speaking."

"It's my jaw, hurt playing polo."

"Gee do you play polo that game on horses."

"Down in Virginia. On the weekends."

"That's some game. Expensive."

"O it costs a little. Like the best things in life. What do you do."

"I'm I guess a kind of person you might think got caught in a rut. If you wanted to be really funny you could call it a career. I'm a legal secretary. I always lived with my mother till she died last year. I just take what comes. Is that cheese cake good."

"Yes delicious."

"Well I guess I'll have some. You sound a little like you were English or something."

"Some of us down in Virginia, round where the better estates are, speak like this."

Sipping a last cup of coffee. I had another. And she had another. And told me about her mother, a night nurse with a lot of rich families along Park Avenue. And said as her face got a little flushed. You want to come up and see some pictures of her, my grandfather was a horse trainer, before we got poor. And I've got lots of pictures.

Up in the elevator. She kept bending her door key between her thumbs. Walked down a narrow public green corridor. Through her brown apartment door, and past a tiny kitchen. Her little living room. Glass cocktail table. A white cat in the corner taking a shit in kitty litter. Stack of books. She said please sit down, Mr Peabody or do you mind if I call you Jason. I belong to a book club, Jason. That's all I really do. Is read. Can I get you something to drink.

Sound of a container of milk plopping twice to the floor in the kitchen. Christian sitting with a glass of milk. Looking across at this woman standing at a bookcase lined with books of knowledge. Down in the delicatessen got a hard on under the table watching her take bites out of her cheese cake. Doctor Pedro must have meant for me to chase my opportunity. Given by this by no means beautiful creature. I said no thanks to viewing her mother's pictures. When suddenly she said please, would you do me a big favour. And take me home. Just so that I have some company. Just to my door. Because only three days ago a girl was murdered in the next building. And you look honest. And this late and hot at night I don't like going back to my apartment alone.

"Thank you madam. I am very grateful you don't think I'm a sexual maniac."

"Ha ha, gee you can be funny."

And then she got her pictures. Of her mother. As a little girl on the stone porch of an ivied entrance. And an older one, smiling in white by a straw hatted patient in a wheel chair. Said Kennebunkport, Maine. How does one stand up with all these photographs laid out on your lap. Said her name was Marigold, of the Aster family, of flowers. Two little pottery lamps glowing near the window. Four rectal lonely looking oil paintings on the walls. We sat there till right near midnight and cats meowing and screaming down in the alleys and long after I knew I would get my ass broken by Fanny. Who would be shouting where the hell were you.

"I think I better be going."

"O no, please, don't go."

"I must, my mother is waiting for me."

"I thought you said you were from Virginia."

"Well my mother is up here for a week's shopping."

"Please stay. Jason, you're the first person I've had here visiting me in about three months. It's kind of a wonderful thing for me. I used to belong to a bowling club. Till it ended up being all women. Do you bowl.''

"No, not yet. But my bloody mother might sock me one with a bowling ball.''

"Ha ha, but at your age, being so attached to your mother like this. My mother I think ruined my life.''

"Well christ sometimes I want to break away, but she's the sweetest dearest most wonderful woman I've ever known.''

"Well I guess she didn't have to struggle. Guess you've been sheltered all your life. I'd like to meet your mother sometime.''

"Well I better now be going.''

Marigold leaning over close to Christian, pushing him backwards on the couch, her mouth opening. Darting her tongue in between my tightening lips. Feel her heart pounding and she's landing kisses all over my face. When I hardly know the woman. Sweat pouring off her. Breasts sumptuously large and smothering. As one struggles to get the unusually strong arms from around one. Without giving offense to this entwining vine. As she squeezes one belch after another of pastrami out of me.

"Please don't go. I've got a few things going for me, I really have. I don't know how it will make any difference but I hold a speed typing championship. The scroll's right there up on the wall. Don't laugh at me. I'm desperate. And I'm so lonely. And I don't want you to go. Please. I'll give you fifty dollars.''

"I'm sorry.''

"Please, one hundred.''

"Madam, you mustn't say these things.''

"Isn't it enough, you want more, Jason. I'll give you some more. Anything you want. I can give you a good time. I'm good at screwing. I really am. And if you get up and go I'll die. I'll throw myself out the window.''

"Don't do that.''

"I will. Jason, I will.''

"I could be the murderer killed the girl.''

"Jesus I don't care. Just don't leave me. I'd rather to anyway get killed if you're going.''

"Can't we talk about this sensibly. The streets full of men looking for women.''

261

"But I want you. I don't want another one of them hairy old grease balls. Why can't I have something handsome for a change. You've got such beautiful hands. I watched them while you were eating. And you're young. I'll undress you. I'll do it all."

"I've got to go."

"I've got more money."

"Madam I'd never dream of taking your money, unless, ha ha, it was really a lot."

"Marigold's my name. And I'm not kidding."

"Look I have a doctor, he says there's a cure, just scrub your floor and you'll be all right."

"I want a fuck. I can't stand the loneliness. It's been a whole year. Since last summer in Paris. Please. Please. I'm telling you. He was just a porter on the train. I had him for three nights. He was good looking even though he stunk of garlic and stole all my luggage and money and everything. But I'd give it to him all again. Can't you understand how desperate a girl can get. What's wrong, here, let me show you. I'm not that bad. My tits are good. I'll undress. I'll show you."

"Please don't, no please."

"Yes yes, then you'll see."

"Madam I'm going to leave no matter what you do."

"It'll change your mind, I know it will. Now. There. Here, look. Look at them."

"Yes I am. They're very fine."

"Feel one, go ahead, they're firm. I never had any children and they're really firm. Give me your hand. Now doesn't that feel firm."

"Yes. It's very fine and firm and madam I'm a compassionate person. But somehow I think we're getting into an awful misunderstanding here."

"Don't I even give you an erection, don't you have one."

"Well I'm so concerned at this moment that I don't know."

"I'll feel for you."

"No please, it's o k."

"Just let me show you my thighs then. I got really good thighs. No fat or anything. All solid."

"I wish you wouldn't madam, I can see that you're wonderfully built."

262

"You don't know how damned miserable it can be. All right. All right."

"Madam please, don't cry, everything's going to be all right. My mother gave me this problem."

"O I don't care, don't say anything. I don't want a whole bunch of excuses. I can really make love. And I don't know maybe you're just a pervert."

"Yes, I am a little bit of one. But it's really that I don't want my head broken when I go home."

"You're a fairy."

"Well not completely."

"I've made a god damn fool of myself. You knew damn well what I was after when I asked you to come up here."

"I did not. I accompanied you because you asked me. As any southern gentleman would do, when asked by a lady for protection. I have codes. I would never take money."

"Don't be so high hat about money. You're just a nobody exactly like me. Department head, my ass. I don't care if someone kills me. Just so long as I can kiss him while he does it. That's just the way I feel. When that murderer comes, black, hairy or greasy. I'll be kissing him while he's killing me. Because he'll be doing me a god damn favour. So get out you, get out. And cut out calling me that crazy old madam stuff. And leave me alone."

Marigold seated on her pea green couch. Little white lace covers on the arms. A large fold of her belly bulging over the waist band of her tight stretched panty. Clumps of her hair studded with bobby pins hanging over her neck. Tears down her face. Clutching her hands under her breasts. Two lamps ridged with soot stain. Sad altar of light either side of the window at the end of this tiny room. Air conditioner humming. Avoid leaving a pickle and coleslaw fart to foul up her life further. Least I can do. While the naked shoulders of this citizen of this city tremble. With her two unhandled sacks of flesh hanging forward over her wrists. Strange bereft beauty. Now the tears running down to her nipples. Pause and drop off. Little suicides. She waits for the sacred sacrifice of murder. Makes the city live. Takes the conceit of life away. Dogs lick up your blood. Go back and touch and comfort her. Say, please don't worry. In July in a window in the

Bronx they write every year Merry Christmas. Bewilder the elevated train travellers a little more. And if you're travelling that way, it says Dead End above the hospital ambulance entrance at Bellevue. Be a gentleman your whole life. To all women. When prick hungry, feed them. When out of style, dress them. When they say why don't you give me a surprise. Sock her cold for a change. Wake her up on the lawn where she can see her picket fence. While you clip the grass around her pedestal. Getting it ready for when she's a statue. Worshipped as she waits no longer in tears.

> After
> Her murderer
> Has
> Come

26

September sun tanners in the park. Gang of marauding kids swinging chains and carrying pipes stuffed with gun powder and nails. They like to pop them off at the older pedestrians. And Fanny said I want you to stop work. You go out each day and how the hell do I know where you are if I can't call you at that stupid Think Room.

Kept handing around my notes at the office. Nice little answers to some big questions. Especially when Mr Quell asked how long is this silent business of yours going to go on.

DOC SAYS COULD EASILY BE CURED IN SIX MONTHS.

Quell said meantime I could learn to make coffee for the rest of the Think Room. And serve his cup extra hot. Which I did sweetened with a chocolate purgative. Guaranteed to cause copious evacuation from the most concrete of bowels.

Fanny when we woke in the morning after my cheese cake and milk evening with Marigold, socked me because she said I had lipstick under my eye. I explained it was the Pakistani elevator operator who wore the color as part of his religion. Got it on me when I stretched him out in agony in the grapevine. Some people will accept nothing but a lie when you're struggling to tell the gospel truth.

And one morning the police came. To say that the Pakistani gentleman had his nose broken and his jaw in four places. Willie came in drunk at dawn and beat the hell out of him. Wrecked the lobby and smashed the front door. Not a sound reached us up in bed. Except the other residents shouting they were getting a committee together to throw her out. And my thoughts thumping in my brain. To get out. Get out.

Took Fanny one night for dinner. To a fancy place with a canopy on the street. Followed now by her detective in another car. She wore a black sequined dress. And turned every head in the dining room. Had rich red wine and porterhouse under the ancient looking ceiling put up last month. The waiter splattered mayonnaise on me. And did other demeaning things. I was amazed how calm I was. Till Fanny said to him, why don't you just fuck off sonny boy and get me the headwaiter. And for the rest of the night he stood staring, wiping forks in a corner. When I know the bastard wanted to go beg the chef to let him spit in our custard. And wipe his feet in our steak.

Each Friday with my cashed paycheck I counted out another ten dollars for my ticket back across the sea. Took some pills for the relief of occasional simple nervous tension. And vomited. Finally saw a composed face on the subway train. And looked down at the lady's luggage. To get an address from where she came or where she was going. And it said Devon, England. And I nearly sobbed.

The guys in the Think Room talking about dolls and dates, all sporting shoes with the broad toe while mine were still medium and narrow. A particular smooth smarty ass from Spuyten Duyvil and Yale said what's a matter Christian, you trying to be out of step. And I scribbled my little note on a yellow Mott memo pad.

YES AND SHUT UP BEFORE I BREAK YOUR PARROT HEAD.

Kept cleaning out my desk. Mr Quell came stood over me and said just before he had to rush back again to the crapper.

"You do all those little things, don't you Christian, that will get you absolutely nowhere."

And one cheery moment one late afternoon looking for mail, caught a glimpse of Fat Cheeks turning the corner of my block. Miss seeing him all the time I'm away. He was getting competition on the east side of the park. A bald bearded man, dancing with a sign in front of the Fifth Avenue steps down to the zoo.

I AM THE WORLD'S LEADING EXPERT ON THE NURSING MADONNA

When I saw Fat Cheeks again. I was strolling down Columbus Avenue. Wasting more of the Mott Empire's time. By sizing up the crazy architecture of this town. And lo and behold there he was in front of a mattress store, with a sign of big pink letters on white.

DON'T BE A MEANIE ANY MORE

Sneaked looks at Fanny as she lay awake all through the night. Asked her what she was thinking. Said she was thinking about once when she worked in a dry cleaners. Stacks of the filthiest clothes shoved at you all day over a counter. The dirtiest dirtiest job in the world. Jesus it was dirty. My hands were black. At dawn she'd pass off to sleep. Never lets me out of her sight. And when my prick wouldn't go up. She made her two hard little white fists and shook them at the sides of her head.

"You don't love me, you don't love me."

Tried to get out of the bed. Slipping from under the sheet. As we both slept way past noon. One wondered what the fuck was wrong with the women of this country. Reached to comfort her with a friendly little pat on her tit.

"Get your god damn hands off me if you're spending the god damn day out in Brooklyn."

"Forest Hills."

"It's all the same. One ass hole of the world is the same as another. Brooklyn, Canarsie, Elmhurst, a whole bunch of rubes with their little nicy nice wives patting their little baby's asses with talcum powder out in the sticks."

"Queens has some very favoured residential districts."

"It has shit."

"I thought you liked it the day I took you to Rockaway."

"Cornelius, I did, I did. But then god damn it. What do you want me to say when you start calling out Marigold in your sleep."

"That's a flower."

"That's a god damn girl's name too. Let Glen drive you."

"I can go on the subway."

"How do I know that's where you're going."

"Because that's where I'm going. Howard How invited me."

"Why don't you quit that god damn two bit job."

"I want to keep my dignity. And Mr How has faith in me."

"Dignity my ass. I saw your notes and sheets of paper you write all over. Making believe you can't talk anymore."

"I've got to. Because every day they're trying to figure out a way to fire me."

"Christ Cornelius, don't fool with me. I can make you rich. With just a signature. Give you everything you want. Don't be stupid."

"What about all those guys you've fooled around with."

"They were one night stands. Those guys are a dime a dozen."

"Did you pay them."

"That's a dirty low remark. I can have any man I want. Paying me. Anything I ask. Lined up they'd go right round the equator. What the hell ever made me think I could do you a favour. You can be such a snotty kid. Throw me my cigarettes. Last night you couldn't even get it up. I know you're screwing someone else. And if I ever catch you I'll kill you both."

And these times on her face, she'd lick her lips, as a smile would come.

"Gee I like talking about what I would do to the cunt I catch you with. Twist her tits. Crush in the toes of her shoes. Pull her hair out in such big nice marvelous lumpfuls. Scratch her all over face like a gorilla was drying it with barbed wire. But o jesus, is the boogey man going to get me. Is he going to, Cornelius."

Fanny lay stiff and silent. In her semi tropical interior. Showed me the stack of letters Sourpuss's first wife wrote. To all her relatives, mother and father. To Bergdorf Goodman, Tiffany's and Santa Claus.

Dear Neighbor or Store Owner,

I just feel so sorry for you that Fanny Jackson that hooker and cheap whore was raised on your street or shops in your store. Now running around with my husband whose money she is trying to get to run up more of her bills. And staying with him in hotels. You have my sympathy for that kind of neighbor or customer you got.

Just believe a friend.

I wore my Vine Funeral Parlor suit. With the cool light weight drape. In last night's paper they said that was the look that was in. And a dark green knit tie. Thrown to me by Fanny out of Mr Sourpuss's collection. With the uncustomary stiff white collar and non matching blue and green striped shirt. Sitting back in the limozine's air conditioning. Patting the brand new cow hide. With the chauffeur's window closed. And Glen grinding his usual gum. Cruising out towards Flatbush in the late cooler afternoon. Over the bridge. Down through the grimy factories. Along Queens Boulevard. The stacks and stacks of apartment houses. Boxes and boxes of little homes down all the crosshatched streets. Never went back to the delicatessen. Took blueberry pie and cold milk instead in the window of the automat on my favourite hill on Fifty Seventh Street. Met the man again who played chess in the park. Listened as I chewed my crust.

"You know sir, the big lies that go floating around this country, and the people, they know those big lies and they keep getting all added together and they hang over the whole place in a big poisonous cloud. And one day that cloud's going to get so heavy it's going to sink right down and smother everybody right all over this land."

Out there New Calvary Cemetery. Where one went in happier days burying the dead. Stones stick up over their souls. While those alive are still shoving and pushing. And wearing that look, don't touch me or you'll get an electric shock. Last week went out and thought what the hell why don't I go a little nuts for awhile. Sidled up to various overweight ladies. Stopped them with my best accent in their predatory tracks. And with a whisper. Madam, be assured that I am not inclined to either rob or rape you, but would like merely to ask, are you by any chance surrounded by an erogenous zone. One smiled and said sure I am and a good looking young man like you can penetrate it any time. Encouraged, to the next lady I voiced a most unforgivable thing, and she promptly dropped her shopping and screamed for a cop. Whole place builds up in you. Little towers of discontent. Topple over in a rubble of broken dignities. Carry it all full of pain. Like how all these folk stand and stare as we drive by. Through their most crummy neighborhood. Goodbye Woodside. Hello Forest Hills. If only I could be a son. Just as there are daughters. Of the American Revolution. Instead of being coughed up here on the shore. From a pair of simple immigrants. Who never knew what the hell hit them. I tried to make pennies from the neighbors down on the stoop in the street as soon as I could speak. White skin of my mother seemed blue underneath when she died. As her blood was brown on the sheets when it dried. Never spanked or hit me. Always said I was a quiet little boy. And when my second foster mother caught me. Pulling my prick into her dictionary. Trying to land sperm on the dirty words. She said I'll slap you I'll slap you, you dirty little thug. Wasn't long before I was putting earthworms in her spaghetti, and had a hole in her bathroom wall, watching her take a bath. Shoved my little brother naked out into the hall. To give her a fright with his hard on. She got sweaty faced and started screaming, they're doing it deliberately to me. And boy I'll say I was. All you have to be is a little kid and you soon find out how lousy big people are. Then when you start growing up good looking in the neighborhood, the neighbors make believe their rotten dirty looks and shouts they gave you all your life, never happened. Good to start getting fantastically handsome and to watch them grow old and deserve all that they're getting. And on Independence Day, toll that big bell. When it rings, each red blooded citizen will step out of his door. Walk up to his neighbor. Howdy do, how you doing pardner. And punch him one in the kisser. In honor of all neighborhood loathings. That upon this day no undesirables are running over their lawn. Or bog trotters wiping asses with shamrocks. Or polacks goosing his dogs. Or bohunks the other side of the tracks pissing on their dishes in their sink. Just a lot a swell kids standing howling in tears as their big bellied daddies beat the shit out of each other.

"This is the address Mr Christian. Number's on that sign on the lawn."

"O k. Pull over and wait. If I'm long I'll tell you."

"You bet Mr Christian, take all the time you want, there's a good ball game on the radio. Even got a book on judo, thought I'd learn some of your tricks. Couldn't be happier. Have a nice afternoon.''

Christian stepping up these moss green steps. A crescent path of crazy paving across the lawn. Tall oaks and elms. Blue spruce trees on either side of the rustic door and the stone porch. Dark inside the screened windows. Must be the wop's house over there with, good lord, a policeman at the front door.

Chimes ringing as Christian presses the little white button. Cross section of varnished log, says Jean and Howard live here. Little freckled faced kid charging round the side of this gabled slate roofed cozy house. Pulling a red wagon. Beneath the great shady trees. Wop's three car garage with a big driveway under the side of his house. Hear light steps. The floor squeaks. Red dress through the dulled copper screen door. Which opens. Slender fingered hands wiping an apron. Two big bright dark eyes. In the heart of a face. On a delicate little body.

''You must be Cornelius Christian.''

''Yes I am.''

''Well please, you sure are welcome, do come in. Howard is just out back hammering, making a climbing ladder for the kids. I've heard so much about you.''

Umbrella stand. Two pairs of galoshes waiting for winter. On the red tiled floor. Cool and dark. Into a big blue carpeted living room. Under an archway a table set to dine. Mrs How's legs delicate shapely stems. All tanned. Hues of white either side of her achilles tendon. Small neat ass like a pair of ball bearings under her thin red dress. That makes me gulp.

''Please take a seat. I apologise for those stupid comic books all over the place. I'll tell Howard. Like some iced tea.''

''Yes I would, please ma'am.''

''You're so polite, just like Howard said, with ma'am and all. You just sit yourself down now.''

Howard beaming in. Hand outstretched. Pair of kaki trousers, open necked white shirt, sleeves rolled up. And a pair of blue sneakers. Just like Fanny's who calls them yatching boots.

''Hi Cornelius I thought you were going to call me from the station for me to come down and meet you. Did you walk.''

''I came in a car.''

"Didn't know you could drive. Hey good, why that's great you're talking again."

"Yes. I can't drive. I was driven."

"Have they gone."

"No."

"Why don't you ask your friend to come in."

"It's a chauffeur."

"A what."

"A chauffeur."

"Come on, you're kidding me Cornelius."

"No."

"Well I'll be damned. Let me take a look. That big grey job."

"Yes."

"That's custom made. That's not yours."

"Well let's say I just have certain things available to me."

"I was never deceived by you, Cornelius. Always thought you were one of these ivy league kids from a rich background. The neighbors are going to think you're somebody big. Gives me a kick to see that parked out there. With these sons of bitches around here getting a load of it. Ah, Jean, you've met the genius."

"Yes I have. Howard push the table over a little for Mr Christian. Few crackers here too, but don't want you to spoil any appetites."

Mrs How, sinews of her arm flexing as she puts down the tray. Came with a sheaf of paper to write my notes. Blew the gaff right off the bat soon as I saw her strange beauty at the opening screen door. Sent a flush of blood between my legs. Pronto made me say yes I am.

"Cornelius let me tell you. Chrissakes."

"Don't keep using that word Howard."

"I'm excited. Hey, feel at home, take your jacket off Cornelius."

"No. That's all right, thanks."

"Well anyway I think you are some kind of genius Cornelius. The whole front page of this morning's paper. Happened just yesterday afternoon. Twenty squad cars came roaring down the street. Wowie. The whole block surrounded. Isn't that right

Jean. They went up that guy's crazy paving with guns drawn. You know what was going on in there, you'll never believe it, I mean you will believe it. A god damn twenty thousand gallon still, just what you said. Damn thing's copper, two stories high, took out the floor, pipes and vats going all over the place. Remember once saying, didn't I Jean, that the guy must be lush by the smell sometimes came from his house. Cornelius, how did you know.''

''Just said the first thing that came into my mind.''

''Well I'm going to leave you two boys while I feed my two boys and girl and fix dinner.''

Mrs How wiping her hands on her apron. A big blue leafed flower with a yellow center. Got to stop the thoughts I'm thinking. Avert my eyes from the tanned silky smoothness of her face. And lips big and soft. Thought I saw her lick them as she came into the room. In fact I know damn tootin she did. And her ball bearing ass swivel as she went out.

''Well you know Cornelius, I tell you, I don't mind Italians but I'm sure glad to get rid of that wop. He's the kind of guy who gets over emotional and kills rather than discusses. I was becoming a candidate for depression like the guy across the street. I mean he's still smiling, but he doesn't know that I know he's getting electroconvulsive therapy. This wop next door wouldn't mow his lawn or stop his god damn killer mutt from coming over and manuring ours. Would you believe it, last month he made one of the biggest contributions to our church building fund. Maybe when the grass on a guys lawn gets long you should get suspicious right away. Hey how about a little shot of vodka in your iced tea. I really feel that way today.''

Howard pouring into Christian's held up glass. Sprigs of mint roll over, sink and rise again between the cubes of ice. Oily whorls eddy in the tan liquid.

''Well Cornelius. So here you are. Driving around in a chauffeured car. Is that address of yours over in the west side a blind or something.''

''Kind of.''

''You're just full of surprises. Belong to the Game Club Quell tells me. And I hear the tennis and squash courts they got are really something. Like to take up that game of squash. Jean says, I got a bit of a spare tire. By the way, I like what you're wearing."

"Thank you."

"You know Cornelius I'd like to brush up my personal defence. Time was when I came home in the evening I used to put my eyes down and imagine there were all kinds of wooded acres around me and no other houses. Now with this guy with a gat sneaking out of your shrubbery to take your god damn valuables off you and shoot you dead on your own front lawn, all I do is tremble around from the garage. I'd like to know how to stomp that son of a bitch."

Howard How socking a fist into the palm of his hand. When I said I liked brandy he said let's go out and get the best. Backed out of his garage in his station wagon to the street. Where I said let me do the honors. And we piled into the limo and Glen cruised us along the winding streets. Howard squirming around in his seat.

"God dang Cornelius if this don't beat all and tickle me pink."

Parked across the street from a local store. Where a real old timer was stocking good brandy and still slicing ham with a knife. And back again past these houses where it looks as if nobody lives. To Howard's den panelled in pine. A collection of pipes he never smokes. Said his street didn't curve as much as the others. But it had its share of big shots.

"Come on Cornelius, let me play you some stuff. I got some real good recordings of real top notch composers. While Jean's putting the kids to bed."

How blaring out the music. Wants me to really get a load of the fine acoustics. And bruise my ear drums. Took a pee in the powder room inside the front door. Green fluffy rug on the black and white tiled floor. Big H on all the towels, light blue and pink flowered. A basin with two soaps to use. I freshened up as evening came with a cooling darkness. Little kids in off the streets. Lights on. And I guess machine guns ready. People moving in the kitchens of other houses. And Howard stirring his special drink. Kept mixed and waiting in the refrigerator all afternoon. Pours me a glass and sits down feeling his way with a hand behind him, all changed to a clean white shirt and loafers with a mahogany gleam. A shelf of books on business management. Three on fishing.

"Cornelius, it's kind of good to have you come out here like this. Meet my wife and kids. Hear the katydids out there. Couple of years ago we even had a bull frog croaking. That's what a man sweats in the rat race for, so his kids can have it a little better than he did. But you wonder sometimes. Two days ago there was a praying mantis out there on the front lawn. A car full of passing roughnecks over from Woodhaven see it and they stop. And what do you think they did. They dropped a god damn rock on it. That's what they did. Right on top of one of the most beneficial of mankind's insects. I went in the house and cried. I mean what do you do these days faced with the dilemma of what's right and wrong. What do you tell your own kids. I mean how are they to come to grips with the uncertainties. As a young guy in today's world do you have an answer Cornelius."

"Yes. Everybody should get down and scrub their floors. And their stoops. Right out to the sidewalks. Also keep their ass holes clean. And carry a machine gun."

"Gee I'm a little nonplussed by your candour Cornelius. You're not a kind of subversive are you. You know the other day, what you said about your own father. That hit me hard. But I've been thinking too. About what you said about Mr Mott. It's true, he comes into a room and says what the hell he wants to say. With no regard for somebody's feelings. I bought a pair of golf shoes once in a lunchtime sale. Was trying them on when he walked into my office. Didn't even wait for me to explain. Says where did you get those crazy pointy two tone shoes. As if I was wearing them all the time. It wasn't the way he said crazy, it was the way he said those words pointy two tone. I was disparaged. Well let's drink to that one."

Howard in fluffy red socks. The mahogany lustre of his loafers. Putting his hand to his straight sided glass and tossing back the hootch. A lady working in the kitchen with a dark complexion. Standing over the stove. Gave me a little nod and smile as I peeked in the serving hatch. Gave her the hi sign of one undesirable to another.

"Guess Cornelius, it's come to the fact that you can take a

shower, shave, comb your hair, put on a clean shirt, get in a new car. And not one thing makes you look like a bum. But you stop to watch a red winged black bird in a vacant lot, and suddenly a squad car sails up to question you. Police tell you to drive on, you're loitering. I'm not knocking our way of life. It's got to be like that I guess with some of the best homes these days being shot up and their inmates murdered. Maybe something has gone wrong with our values. You soul search and ask yourself what kind of an assessment can I make as a dad to tell my kids. That they're going to grow up into a holocaust of dirty deals. I can't tell them that. It's not that I'm asking my kids Cornelius to get on their knees at night and chant god bless America. But holy shit, pardon my french, when are we going to emerge into a calm sunny peace of the kind that this sort of neighborhood should have. Chrissakes you wake up one morning and you're living next to a distillery. You know don't you, there isn't another living soul I could talk to like this. Hey let me kind of freshen up your drink there kiddo. Libate a bit.''

How pouring out his pineapple flavoured mixture, stretching back in his chair with his glass raised towards a corner of the room. End of his cigarette lights up as he sucks in a lungful of smoke.

''See that fishing rod, Cornelius. Well strictly between us. You know what my ambition is. To one day tell them to shove the whole god damn Mott empire. And buy myself a little old general store somewhere way out in the sticks and just go fishing. And not be troubled by all these conflicting emotional pulls. There, there, did you hear that. That's that bullfrog. Croaking. He's come back. Isn't that sound wonderful.''

Two little sandy haired boys and a tiny dark big eyed little girl. In a procession. For a hand shake. And wave goodnight in their matching blue kimonos and yellow slippers from the top of the stairs. And with candles lit on the dining table, Mrs How in a long clinging mauve gown.

''There she is Cornelius, isn't my wife something.''

Asparagus and shrimp salad. Howard smilingly pouring out a bottle of white wine. And smashing back his own concoction between sips. Tipsily saying, Cornelius, you got to stay the night.

Send that chauffeur away. Be my revered guest. We got a whole god damn rambling guest and bathroom right in there next to my den. And I went out. Looking left and right in the dark for any guy toting a gat. Told Glen who was snoring fast asleep behind locked doors in the limo's air conditioning, to head back to Manhattan. And he said Mrs Sourpuss's instructions were to wait, to take you home.

"And my instructions are, and I won't god damn well tell you twice, is to beat it."

"You bet Mr Christian. You bet."

Nice to wipe your hands of a chauffeur. And watch the shadowy limo blazing red rear lights glide softly away down the street. Come back up on this hilly little lawn. See the domestic warmth glowing in the windows. Hear a door close across through the trees. And a nervous shout. Is that you Hector.

A decanter of milk on the white table cloth. Howard said it put the fire out when the hootch in his belly got hot. Mrs How handing round the salads and choice of two home made dressings. Heaped bowl of steaming corn cobs. Plate of sliced red and yellow tomatoes. Sprinkled with herbs and wiped with garlic. All out of Howard's garden. As the bugs bang against the screens to get to the candle light.

"Cornelius, Jean's my own real pal. Aren't you Jean."

"Howard you're drinking too much."

"No I'm not, this is a celebration. Like hot dickety dick, it's Saturday and I'm going to tie one on tonight. Right Cornelius. And we're going to scrub down our front stoop. Just like you say. And I'm going to ask that policeman over there if we can try some of that wop's moonshine. What about that Cornelius."

"Yes fine, Mr How."

"Ah Cornelius I hope you've still got the old umph pa pa. And none of this Mr How business. Now you just chew off them there golden kernels from that cob. Use your fingers. I know when I hear the old umph pa pa from somebody. And Europe, Cornelius, has taken away your old umph pa pa."

"Howard what have you been drinking."

"Umph pa pa, that's what. Good old pal, Jean. And Cornelius. My boy Cornelius. Boy do you get old Quell hot under the collar.

I love the way he comes fuming in to me sometimes shaking and quivering, get that damn Christian out of my department, he says. I keep telling him I can't do a thing, that you're one of Mr Mott's proteges and very close, really close and an old, old friend of the family.''

"Howard stop, that's not fair to talk like this about the office that way to Mr Christian. You've had too much to drink.''

"Now Jean, what are we scared of. Good old pal, Jean. From a good old Virginia family Cornelius, on her mother's side that is. Married beneath herself. Just like her mother did.''

"Have some of your milk Howard.''

"No Jean I will not have some of my milk. I will have some of my brew. How's the boy Cornelius. How's the boy. Imagine a whole distillery. I called John my broker. Told him. Said John what about the property value. He said Howard, don't worry that could be an invitation to serious industry right on your doorstep.''

"And you stole that ladder, Howard.''

"I did like hell, I just carried it over to us, that's all. Make something for the kids to climb on. They won't be needing it again.''

"That was stealing.''

"What. From a bunch of crooks. Besides the cop on duty said I could take it. Sure, I slipped him a couple of bucks. It was being used illicitly to climb among the wop's god damn pipes.''

"And don't say wop. That's not nice.''

"Wop wop, wilyo, ginney. I mean that damn guy has slandered the neighborhood. But boy I'll give him one thing, he minded his own god damn business. In fact he was the best neighbor we've ever had. Had kind of fine characteristics in his face. Like Cornelius there. Not like some of the places we've lived with the next door guys behaving like tarzans out in their backyards trying to mow their lawns in two seconds to make an impression on Jean.''

"You've got such an imagination Howard.''

"What about that son of a bitch who swung off on the end of his god damn clothes line from his bedroom window in leopard skin tights.''

278

"He was sick Howard."

"He was a god damn peeping tom that's what he was. And we had to move away. And that other bastard standing naked at his window every morning so you could see him."

"He was a child, a mere boy."

"O boy, some boy. I mean I won't go into it. Yes, I will. I'll go into it. And boy that boy. I'll be frank. That son of a bitch had a whopper."

"Well Mr Christian, I hope you're not going to think that this is the way we live and behave all the time. Howard's just putting on a show of manliness. As a kind of contrast. Because he thinks you're so. Well I don't know how to say it."

"Say it, Jean, say it. Cultivated. Isn't that the word you want."

"Well if you like. That's why there's wine. We never drink wine. But I guess we put on airs just like everybody else tries to."

"Cornelius, honey, is just the product of immigrants, I've told you. But what he's got, nobody in this city's got. Not Mott. Not anybody. I don't know, we live in trying times. Where there used to be wilderness and god's natural wonders, now we enjoy hamburger joints, gas stations, utility poles and used car lots. Everywhere they're tearing down the old elegance. Maybe the only remnants left now and isn't this true Cornelius, you find in the funeral business."

"Well I guess that's right."

"And Mr Christian what do you know about the funeral business."

"Cut that out now, that's taboo, Jean. That's Cornelius's own little personal private history. We've been through all that. Ask him about his mom and dad."

"Can I ask you about your mom and dad Mr Christian."

"Yes, by all means. Do."

"Well who were they."

"They were nobody. And they both died when I was quite young. Or at least I thought my father did. And I guess he's dead now. He thought he was some kind of actor. He wore spats. White ones. Carried a cane. And checkered caps and knickerbockers. He could tap dance. My uncle, a simple man, loved my mother and had a building business, he lived in Rockaway and I guess gave my little brother and I some of the advantages.''

"How romantic Mr Christian. I mean, somehow I don't want to sound patronizing, but that's beautiful.''

"My mother took in washing, did sewing, I guess scrubbed her fingers to the bone. When my uncle took my brother and I away from the tenement district to a better neighborhood I was ostracised. And as I grew up, with my beauty unseen in my heart, rich socially superior girls ignored me.''

"There you are Jean, let him tell it. That's the kind of country it is. Boy it's time for some of us who question to stand up and be counted.''

"Sit down Howard. Mr Christian is just kidding.''

"Hell I'm going to stand up. No one's kidding me. And toast one. To Cornelius. Whoops.''

"You've spilt that sticky stupid drink of yours all over the table Howard.''

"O we'll mop it up, mop it up. Fill up another. Need any more. Just slip over there to the distillery. Home home on the range. Where the antelope play. Where the god damn coyotes howl. And the suburban sprawl flows free. I'm a poet. Could have been a moose too. My father belonged to the loyal order of moose. Now, a toast. To Cornelius. Who rose triumphant out of Brooklyn and the Bronx with that ritzy accent. Welcome to my home. Now that time you said. Or you wrote on your little pad. That not everything was swell out here. That's what you wrote Cornelius. Now let me tell you. What more in life does a guy want. With his little kiddies safely tucked up there in bed.''

"You hope they are Howard.''

"Don't interrupt Jean. And those kids growing up a hell of a lot smarter than I am. Going to go to the best colleges. I got a beautiful wife. Jean there could have swirled across the silver screen. Now Hector across the street. O k, let's face it, his wife has got some shape. But nothing like Jean's. Jean stand up.''

"You sit down.''

"I said stand up Jean. Let Cornelius see. The most beautiful wife in this purlieus. Sure, right in the god damn purlieus, and I know it. Guys' tongues are hanging out at every barbecue.''

"I'm sitting right where I am Howard and you better take it easy. I hate to tell you what you're going to be like in the morning. In this purlieus. Moaning and blaming me that I didn't stop you. So I'm telling you to stop now."

"Jean's right, I'm real shook up next morning, but boy I'm sure real happy tonight. And there you sit, your parents come off the boat like cattle. And you grow up privileged. As if you were really somebody. And I ask, why are you letting your country down. Why. After your mother and father got their start here. You beat it to Europe. To lotus eat. So all right, they took a few knocks. And got knocked out. But this country for all its faults is where the story is. This is where the big pimple is going to bust. Mankind is working things out for himself right here in the capital of the world. And yes, go ahead smile, Christian. And part of the problem solving in that capital goes on in the Think Room of the Mott empire. You're a traitor to the capital. A god damn traitor. That's what you are Cornelius. With that phony accent and aloofness. Why don't you behave like an American, like the rest of us. You think you're too good for us. You didn't even graduate from college. And did you even serve your country buddy. Were you there when the salvos were slamming the yellow foe."

"Stop it Howard, stop it. You're being hostile and unfair to Mr Christian."

"Keep out of this Jean. Let me ask him, right here and now. Did you serve your country."

"Well yes I did."

"And did they give you benefits when the war was over."

"Yes they did."

"And what did you do. You took those benefits to Europe. To the scallywags and French. Well anyway I'd like to be your friend. Only you ought to wise up. Whose chauffeur is that you've got. What kind of monkey shines are you up to. Don't think you çan pull anything over on me. Don't you ever think that. Hey the table is swaying."

"You're swaying Howard."

"Holy mackerel. Subversion. Under the table. While I'm speaking out on the issues and uncovering the facts. Some bastard is always shaking your guidelines. And you know, I

281

don't think you've ever known Mr Mott from a hole in the wall. I just think you by accident ended up at one of his son's foolish parties, that's what I think.''

''Howard, leave Mr Christian alone. You're just saying that because you've never been invited.''

Howard How, perspiration on his brow, pointing with an unsteady finger. Which he pulls back from the candle flame with a smell of burning finger nail. Mrs How with her lips compressed, small fists placed either side of her plate. Want to ask for another helping of salad. Because it doesn't look as if we're ever going to get to the raspberry sherbet.

''Hail to victory. Go team go. Umph pa pa. Second string quarter back. That was me. When I was in high school. I was too light when I got to college. Who's that sitting over there. That you, Jean. Scrub the stoop. I'm going right over now to that distillery.''

''No you're not Howard.''

''Who's going to stop me. You think because you've got that punk Christian with the fistic reputation. The Think Room boys might be scared but you don't frighten me. Try to stop me. You just dare.''

Howard How stumbling towards a pair of doors behind drapes leading out somewhere. Bumping his knee on a radiator. Holding it with his hands as his jaw twists with agony. And wipes it away with a new smile.

''Ha tricked you, tricked both of you. You didn't think I was going to leave you alone, the two of you did you. And while my back was turned, how do I know lover boy wouldn't try something funny with my little old wife.''

''Howard why don't you shut the hell up. You invite Mr Christian out here. And insult him. And I'm finding it an awful bore. Do you understand. Two can play this game. Here you are Cornelius, let's both have a good stiff brandy.''

''Well then goodbye. Goodbye to both of you. It's off to the distillery we go, hi ho.''

''Well go ahead and god damn well go hi ho to the distillery then.''

''I'm going, don't you think I'm not.''

A voice singing out under the trees. A window slamming shut. Mrs How in her mauve raiment. Over the merest of mounds. Cock back her arm and her muscle might go pop. Never thought wide assed How behind his pair of glasses had a stunning wife. A gem unearthed in the dead center of Queens. Smelling fresh of soap and faint gardenias.

"Mr Christian I'm really sorry. Please don't take Howard too seriously. What can I get you."

"O I'm fine thanks really."

"Come on, let's both admit it. You're not enjoying this. Sad thing is Howard means what he's saying. He really resents you. I can't understand it. Because he talks about you so much."

"I understand Mrs How."

"Your continued politeness is very nice. But the evening did get just that little bit ugly."

"Is he safe out there."

"O yes, to cover thirty yards. So long as he doesn't break a leg in the children's sandpit. And the policeman on duty doesn't shoot him. I've got fresh coffee ready. Would you like it with your brandy."

"That would be fine."

"You didn't know it, did you, Howard has a small drinking problem. He was very bright in college. In fact he was brilliant. And in spite of our having all the good things, he feels sometimes he's not made anything out of his life."

"Do you like it here, Mrs How."

"It's nice for the children. But I'd rather live, and I guess it sounds crazy, in a ghetto. About ten o'clock some mornings this can be like the frozen wastes of Antarctica. But you don't tell your husband that. When he's finished complaining about taxes. That you're going nuts out of your mind in this sylvan setting."

Her hair shining in the candle light. And glinting in her big black eyes. Dip a nose into this brandy. To the sweet mellowness, pale, gold and old. From another land they call France. Dog barks. See Mrs How's silver slipper. Her pale nailed toes wiggle. On antelope ankles.

"Can I ask you a really personal question, Cornelius."

"Yes."

"O I better not, you'll think I'm being risque."

"O no."

"Well then I'll ask you. Because I've always wondered. Can a dead female if she were good looking and young. O god I shouldn't ask."

"Ask."

"Well if she were there, lying on a slab, could she arouse you."

"Well Mrs How, I don't know, it's not that it's a trade secret or anything but there are those who might think it unethical to remark upon."

"O come on, tell me, it's one of the few things I ever really wanted to know."

"Well, the answer is I guess, that you do rather size people up and of course, the supply of beautiful dead young women is not too plentiful, but even in death a woman can have a certain attraction."

"So for a female who's still alive there must be lots of chances left."

"Well Mrs How I don't want to disillusion you, but there are those who prefer deceased females."

"O I know all about real necroes. I was thinking of nice young clean cut morticians."

"You mean the sort who plays lacrosse and ambles into the preparation room to embalm smelling of bay rum."

"Exactly, exactly. That's exactly what I mean. What was that."

"Sounded like a shot, thirty eight calibre."

"O god."

Christian trotting after Mrs How through the curtained doors. Across a little patio. Down steps, brushing by shrubbery. A light switched on. A shadow running along the side of the wop's house. Towards a white form stretched on the lawn. A voice shouting over the darkness. As I step and crack a loud twig.

"O k everybody. Don't move. Let's see."

"That's my husband."

"He's o k lady, he might have a hernia but he's not hit. I shot into the ground. He was trying to break in there."

Howard flat on his face out like a light. Tree leaves rustle. Crickets chirp. Mosquitoes buzz around the ears. And one's just drilled for blood in the side of my neck. Lights go off everywhere. **And** nobody pours out in this purlieus to see what's the matter with one of its prostrate citizens.

Howard How lugged feet first. Mumbling something about buying land from the Indians for three lousy white pots. Christian gripping him under the armpits, the policeman holding by the ankles. Loafers fallen off. Taking him backwards across the patio. Through the french doors of the dining room. All the good eats and brandy left under the candle light. Balding policeman in his short blue sleeves. Smell of gun powder. As we hoist Howard How up the creaking stairs. Folk are always heavier than you think. Flake him out on a big double bed. Under a painting of Niagara Falls. With a crimson, fluffy counterpane, just like Howard's socks. And he has a handful of grass clutched in his first. And a patch of sweat on his crotch.

Policeman as he goes down, looking back up the stairs. At the colored engravings of vintage cars on the wall. All the things in other people's houses. Seem better than what you have in your own. Protocol now to get the hell out of here. And brave the terror of a walk down this suburban street. If the policeman doesn't shoot you, the guy committing hold ups with the gat will.

"Sorry about that Mrs, guess it's natural someone wants to know what went on in the house next to them. In a nice neighborhood like this. But he wants to watch himself. I got my orders."

"Thank you officer."

"Any time lady you need any help, just give me a shout, I'm right over there."

"Thank you officer."

"Got nothing else to do."

"Well thank you very much officer."

"Thank you lady."

Policeman backing out on the patio as he pushes closed the dining room doors. Mrs How standing staring. Tiniest bit of moisture in her eyes. Looking right at me. When I don't know where else to look. Except right back. And say something before she hears the pounding in my chest.

"I guess Mrs How I better really be going too."

"No please don't."

"Well this is an imposition with Mr How not so well."

"He's just plastered. Doesn't mean the end of hospitality. Come on, I'll show you to your cell."

Through Howard's den to a pine panelled room. An old foot pedal sewing machine. College pennants on the wall. One says Bucknell high up between the twin pink spreaded beds. Crunch of summer seaside sand on the floor. Childhood smell and taste of breezes salty. The wooden jetties out on Far Rockaway. And the fear of shark. When you wade out toward the tumbling grey waves.

"Please if there's anything I can get you, just shout. I'm going to clean up a little before I go to bed."

"Thank you."

"And you know, I am sorry. You're nothing like I thought you were. And Howard will be so chastised in the morning."

Christian sitting on the bed. Lamp glowing under a white glass. Two green shades pulled down on the windows. The softness of her voice. The tending of her hands. That you could marry. Take her away, out into the wilds of some underdeveloped country. Like Ireland. Plop over the turf and sow a spud. Sit each night deep into darkness by a fire. To the sound of ocean waves.

Christian stepping back into How's den. Push the black button for white light. Peal up a stack of magazines. Country Gentlemen. Glossy pages of hope. Anything lavish always helps me to sleep. Nice to see these faces the last thing at night, the cream of St. Louis society. Photographed in their rose gardens, next to wives and both with their backs up against mellowed stone walls. Just peek out between the curtains on Howard's windows. Not a breath of air. To fan my hopes. That I would explode in the sky over America. A big shot. And all I got was a bang which came rectally out of Quell in the next cubicle as I was happily reading his Wall Street Journal. All I brought with me here. Was Helen. She lies down like veils do. In her growing old grave. Left lying, left lonely. And before her covers die in their dust. Let them lift up purple. The color she wore. To see her a living wife again. When I was so young and terrified to be wed. Just sit now. Turn off the light. The dark in someone else's room. A highway's roar not far away. In Grand Central Station nearly took a train on track twenty eight for Boston because it was called the Puritan. Needed to go where there's that kind of beauty. And a bunch of little kids shouting at people as they went by, hey mister you dropped your wallet. And when I smiled they said gee he's smart. All those hours and days ago. And all those months and years. When Vine in one of his quiet evening bull sessions told me how he looked up at the memorial tower on the seaman's institute at the Battery. To think of all the lives lost out on the water. To whom he could have given a warm burial.

Slant of light coming in the door. As it opens. And a foot tip toes in. As I sit frozen. In an indelicate fear. Of someone with a gat. Or an impure desire. To make more moral mincemeat of me than I am already. And the light comes further across the floor and covers the tips of my stockinged feet.

"Who's that."

"Who's that."

"O god it's you Cornelius. Those are your feet. God it gave me a scare."

"It's me."

"Whew."

"I'm sorry Mrs How I was just looking to find something to read. And just turned the light out to think."

"I do that."

"Yes, you can think then."

"Yes, you really can think."

"Well that's what I was doing, thinking."

"What were you thinking if I can be so bold as to ask."

"I was thinking about marriage."

"What a thought."

"Yes, it was."

"And what were you thinking about marriage."

"Mrs How I was thinking that two people could live together and face the world."

"Were you thinking that."

"Yes I was thinking that."

"I've thought that too. And you know I'm sorry, it was tasteless of me to ask my question."

"O no."

"Well I know that your wife died. I guess you were two young people alone."

"Yes, we were."

"Well two together can face the whole world."

"Yes. They can. And winds can blow around them. Rain, storms and things like that can beat on their bodies. And together in a stone little safe house, they can brave any night through till morning. Wrapped in each other's arms."

"Cornelius that's a beautiful thought you speak."

"Mrs How."

"Yes."

"I'm awfully attracted towards you."

"Are you."

"Yes. I am. It's unfair to say to you so suddenly. I can only tell you because we're in the dark. And you seem so happily married. And I hope you'll forgive me for saying it."

"Why."

"I don't know why. I guess it's just because I feel I don't belong in this country. I feel such an interloper."

"What a foolish thing to say. That you don't belong. Of course you belong."

"I know I'm sounding awfully conceited but I mean, all I'm saying is my song is sweet. And everybody everywhere looks at me and says, well fella you may be beautiful but can you sell it. And if I've got to say no I can't, if I've got to say that much longer, I'm going to die."

"God I know what you're saying. Cornelius I really do."

"Do you."

"Yes."

"I'm glad Mrs How. Tell you the honest truth I'd come out here to pull an awful low down trick on you and your husband, making believe I couldn't speak."

"But I was looking forward to reading your little notes. After what Howard told me some of them said."

"When I saw you at the door. A whole flood of honesty swept through me. I couldn't lie. Not to you."

"Gee."

"Mrs How. Can I ask you. Please, just to come a little closer. I really like your smell."

"Do you."

"Yes."

"I'll come closer. Sit on the arm of your chair."

"I won't touch you."

"I know you won't."

"And Mrs How, the thing that makes me saddest of all, is how, since I got off the boat, so many people have helped me. Did nice things. Were good hearted. Your husband helped me. And Mr Vine the funeral director, you must have seen his ads recently, he just about saved my life."

"He must be a nice man."

"Yes. And the crazy thing was all through my childhood. I felt nobody liked me. A woman stared at me all the way down the aisle with hatred when I was making my first holy communion. Kept looking down at my white shoes that were a little grey at the time. I know I poured sugar in her husband's gas tank and that she could never prove it. But any kid does that. Really put his engine on the blink. And she begrudged me for it. I don't want to sound self pitying."

"O no you don't sound self pitying, not at all. Kids around here are always doing that kind of thing to Howard."

"I guess your husband takes that distillery next door really hard."

"O I think he knew it was there all the time. Howard's a foxy one."

"Mrs How, you do really smell nice. Your lids. They drop incredibly half way down your eyes."

"You see pretty well in the dark."

"Thank you."

"And I think you smell kind of nice too."

"Thank you."

"And you know, Cornelius, you mustn't feel like that about yourself. On a little scrap you wrote to Howard. You said you felt worthless. If the song you sing is beautiful, someone will hear it and think so too. I mean you might not even like this but Howard in his way must have heard it. I certainly have. And something in me. Guess like sinews or a vocal cord, vibrates. And Cornelius, don't you have someone.''

''No.''

''Everybody must have. Just someone.''

''Mrs How if it wasn't now. And say it was years ago. Like in high school. Would you have liked me.''

''Of course I would. But why do you say that.''

''Because no one really did. Not if they were beautiful like you. And could have what they thought was better than me.''

''Someone must have thought you were good. Otherwise you could never be like you are.''

''My uncle bought me a green bicycle. And there was an aunt who baked me apple pies, juicy, sweet and with cinnamon. I used to go and eat them on Saturday mornings.''

''The whole pie.''

''Yes.''

''I think you want a lot. Out of people Cornelius. That's real work peeling a whole bunch of apples. But anytime you want, you can come out here and I'll bake you an apple pie.''

''Would you.''

''Yes. Of course I would.''

''And you wouldn't mind if I ate the whole thing.''

''No I wouldn't mind.''

''I'd like to come and eat an apple pie baked by you. Mrs How.''

''Would you.''

''Yes I really would. I can taste it already.''

''Can you.''

''Yes I can. Makes my mouth water. And you wouldn't mind would you, if I had a great dollop of ice cream on it.''

''No I wouldn't mind. What I mind I guess is what I'm doing here sitting on the arm of your chair. Because I can't stand this much longer. Because from me you can have whatever you want. Any kind of pie. I'll give it to you. But please, please, don't make me sit here any longer waiting. Because I'll run. I'll run. O god I'm a bad bad girl. To fall like this down into your lap. Kiss me kiss me. O god. Kiss me. I'm going to break my marriage vows. With you.''

Mrs How's lithe limbs locking around Christian's neck. Lips on his eyes. Unstrange tempo. Of times with other bodies. Tapping on one's own. Wakes you rearing up. Tasting flesh with its sound and smell and softness. Under a mauve silken sheath. Crushings of elderberries. Peaches on trees. Sappy peeling bark. Tall grass where there might be snakes. Walk through the danger to touch the ripe sweet fuzz. Swimming in the juice. With a sprinkle of salt, eat the sin. Committed on How. Moaning round up there, unconscious I hope, on the bed. Not wondering as Quell does twenty times a day. Where the hell is that Christian. Mr Quell, that Christian you so ardently seek, is in the crapper. Because he doesn't want some really lousy tedious clerical thing to do. Wants to do what he's doing with this wife. Called Jean. Howard's own real pal. Best god damn piece in the purlieus. Whom I sneaked looks at all evening long. Small, dark irised, fancy assed licking her lips. Jigging her leg up and down. A smile for me lurking in the back of her eyes. Just as you, Howard were warming up to Cornelius Christian with a bunch of brand new unfriendlinesses. Now your wife's shedding her dress. She mustn't think you'll wake up by falling off the bed. Get reminded you had a guest. And holy cow, now the phone's ringing. Right in the middle of Mrs How talking a mile a minute in the dark.

''Let it ring Cornelius, let it ring. God almighty I'm going to break my marriage vows. I'm going to break them. God almighty is this what it's like. My mother never told me. She never told me. Or mentioned a thing. About how to be a bad girl after eight years of married life. Every inch of you Cornelius. Let me touch every inch of you. The damn phone ringing. Maybe I shouldn't, shouldn't, shouldn't after all these years. Of my nice little married life. Break my wedding vows. But yiminey yiminey. I'm all wet and streaming between my legs. I can't help myself. Mother. I can't. Quick. Let me lock the door. At least let me do that. And get this phone off the hook.''

Little noise her feet make. Two leaps and maybe one bound. And a click. And another leap and bound and she's back. And absolutely out of all her clothes. Smelling nearer and better than ever. In places where I put my hand. Nobs of her spine down her back. Lifts her right tit with her hand and pushes it in my face. Talking a mile and a half a minute. Her mouth biting in my hair.

"I can't help myself Cornelius because I want you. So terribly much. Just on this ordinary day the way it's been. No one could ever have told me I'd be wrecking my life. Right in the middle of the night in the middle of my marriage. From the best family in Charleston and I might just as well have been from Damascus. Heard tell all about Daniel Boone and nobody ever told me about falling from grace. Simple West Virginian girl. With no dirty thoughts. Liked the legs of the tennis stars. The way their hair bounces when they serve the ball. Your hair's like silk. Crowns the face of a saint. With I hope the desires of a devil. Never even opened a man's fly before. And you've not got buttons. Like I expected you to have. Got to keep talking. Please don't mind. Should I sit on it. Like this."

"Yes."

"Yes to you. Yeses and yeses. Make believe I'm dead. Helpless on a slab. And that I don't know what you're doing to me. And I do. Because I'm all alive. Talk dirty to me."

"I can't."

"Go on. Like say anything you can think of."

"Can anyone hear us in here."

"On my sports night that's what you say. To such an innocent girl as me. I used to think if I ever took it up the ass the neighbors would find out. Shake a finger and say I wasn't devout. I'm just ordinary Episcopalian and you're a fraidy cat. Talk dirty. Or am I too big of a surprise."

Mrs How's teeth and lips and mouth. Sucking on Cornelius Christian's neck. All the room filled with breathing. And ears god damn alert for any other sound. Like a shoulder against a door. And a shout. Hey what the hell do you think you're doing locked in there with my wife. Enraptured on the American flag. With the latest stars it has, one for black, one for brown, one for yellow and ten for white. The rest for all the miserable. Fly it to show the neighbors what god damn country we're all living in. Over in that bastard's garden with the patriotic statuary it's

292

America. While that son of a bitch with his shades pulled down thinks he's in Minsk. Because nobody's sure with all the micks, wilyos and Rumanians. And Miss Musk whose folk are from Hungary. Got it up her. For the greater glory of my country. In Vine's best coffin. We could have been pulled by bicycles with spokes woven red white and blue in crepe bunting. Accompanied by the community band. Shaking the casket to hell. Out in the torrential July fourth rain. Keeping us cool in our heated entwinement. Soften the cardboard all over town. Dream often of Miss Musk. Parading, twirling, knees pumping to the drums. Does plenty to a baton and boy what the hell can't she do to a wang. And George one day called us both to the preparation room. Said just see the size of this guy's prick. And Miss Musk flushed all over pink. So did Vine. And Charlie. And Fritz. I just thought wow. And wrote it down in my record book. With grey headed George nearly beside himself, having seen such a whopper. And wherever you are. Dead or alive. Eyes spy. Collecting little facts. Keep them lurking, skeletons in the closet. Clanking. To fuck up all the harmony coast to coast across this land. Sail down a highway and nobody gives a shit where you've come from, so long as they think you're hot shit for going where you're going. Foot on the accelerator. Slamming the miles dead. Streaking away from all your troubles. On the Salt Flats with your low numbered license plate. Mine says zero as I go coo coo on two feet down the street. Ears lighting up red about once a block with a big spark of whimsy. Asking more questions of unaccompanied ladies. When was your last adultery. It was while hungrily licking his face. Taking advantage of his beauty and youth. Setting an awful example for your kiddies upstairs in bed. Your exquisite dark fragility. And things could be swell if I only knew the answer to this country. Who is the big shot who sits secret somewhere at the very end of all the graft. Smoking a cigar in his big leather chair. Listening neither sad nor glad to the Mormon Tabernacle Choir raising their voices in a great celebration of candour. The janitor across my street said, hot day today, and that's the truth. That nobody else is telling. About anything. Sat mornings at my west side window watching the garbage snoopers. Envied their search for pots to piss in. And even for pianos to play. As one son of a bitch with flowing red hair sat down and sparkled his fingers for two hours over the ivories of an out of tune baby grand blocking the sidewalk. That someone musical was throwing out. Know I must go. Goodbye. Goodbye. To the tinkle of my fountain hidden up inside you. Mrs How. My watch says by the ray of light coming in. It's time to ask for welfare. Save my soul. Lost in Queens. Frightened by all the heart chilling terror. Mrs How. Never untwine your arms. Never let me go. To sail an ocean. Die away from here. But if I don't I'm doomed. Because they don't want my song. And all that's left is death, waiting down all the streets. Carried living in all the cars. And a knife grinder once walked from stoop to stoop. Ringing his little bell. Handing you a sharpened blade. Collecting his money. That grew into a mountain. Where my Fanny Sourpuss lies crucified growing cold in her skiing snow. One of her breasts as big as your buttock. Could make me rich with her signature. Said she was bought and now she can buy. Keep me grievously pained in this paradise. I was twelve and thin and ugly. And there, just one row over, at her desk, Charlotte Graves, the only girl who loved me. When they said I was nearly the dumbest boy in the class. Next to Twitches. Who was branded monumentally stupid. Put sitting in the last seat in the last row. His neck dirty and he had scaly ears. And I went to see what made him dumber than me. His house sitting on a hill. Wondered why they had all the broken ice boxes on their lawn. I whistled him out and asked him. He said because they might need them sometime. I thought that was smart as hell. And knew neither of us was so dumb after all. The sun is going to come now on the brown bright oak leaves. Of autumn. And before disaster gets me. For the adultery on this shady street. A seed planted in the glimmers of love and anguish. All over even before it's begun. O god Cornelius I can't stop it I've come. Never felt so good and bad at once. When am I ever going to see you again. Bake you apple pies.

Tell
Me

27

A still time of night. When you can hear a car travelling blocks away. And when Mrs How put the receiver back, the phone rang again. Could hear Fanny Sourpuss's voice. Clear across the room. Asking in her charming way. Who the hell are you, you cunt. Where's my husband.

And I've been everywhere. Ever since. Once sightseeing on a boat around Manhattan. And twice dumbfounded around the block of the House of Detention for Women. Listening to them scream down from their barred windows. Come up and fuck me some time, hey blondie, you muff diving cocksucker. Tried an excursion to the Bronx Zoo. To see what the other animals were like. And a cobra was spitting poison at the eyes of onlookers the other side of the glass. Just trying to make them blind.

Because on that Forest Hills night Mrs How held the phone right away from her ear. As the shouting you could hear all over Queens, came through. I want Cornelius you bitch, who are you, who are you. And then the phone gave a large click silent. And Mrs How slipped a record on Howard's hi fi. Creeped over to me. I said it sounded like a former landlady of mine who was a nutty crank. And Mrs How said her nerve was coming back, even though Howard and she would never be the same again. And when she said maybe that's horribly sad don't you think. I tweaked her nipple. And she tweaked my cock. And we listened to a symphony. With her juicy grape fruity ass pumping all over me. And the heel of her shoe sticking in my spine. And when all the groaning was over and my trousers still down. She said, it's none of my business and I may have said talk dirty but whoever that landlady was after you on the phone, my goodness, I've never heard such filthy language before. And something told me she might hear more. As I lay wondering and still. Too frightened to move. And when I did, I did like a streak. Standing up to the pounding on the front door. And screams of open up you bunch of fucking rubes.

Fanny was dressed in her gladiator's outfit. Sandals tied with thongs all the way up to her knees. Beige covert cloth skirt she wears for action, the fabric showing the long muscles in her thighs. Big nipple tips of her tits under a thin grey sweater. Never seen anything so strong all at once. Hammering at anybody's front rustic door. Knew all the neighbors would be wakened and looking out. Comes kind of hard for them hearing they are rubes living in such a privileged district. Where Fanny Sourpuss shouts at Jean How who wouldn't open up the door.

"All right you cunt, I'll just go to your neighbors and borrow an axe. And chop the fucking thing down."

It was not credible while it lasted. And utterly incredible as it continued. And began without any hoo ha at all. Standing the three of us. There in the hall. Mrs How saying lower your voice I've got children please, don't wake them up.

"And you little black eyed cunt, you've been sucking the skin on my husband's neck."

"He's not your husband."

"He's my god damn husband."

"Stop shouting in my house, I'll call the police."

"Sister I'm not only going to shout I'm going to slaughter you."

"Don't come another inch near me. You're in my home, get out."

Amazing how fast women accept each other as enemies. And Fanny's right hook looped overhead and right into Mrs How's eye. A cry of anguish as she put her two hands up pressing her face. I waited for her globe to bounce out of her socket on the floor. As another one had done once before. And her mauve sheath she'd hurriedly pulled over her head to answer the quaking door, was now torn clean from round her shoulders. As one does in troubled times. I looked at the architecture down the hall. The kitchen all half tiled. With a green and black motif. Any second I was waiting for a bleary eyed Howard to come stumbling mumbling down. All ready to sell to a black. Or a blue. Or even the recent kind of whites he had carrying on in his hall. Everytime my brain made words to say, my voice refused to come out of my throat. Holding my arms tight around Fanny. Her hands held up with her pointed talons ready to claw.

"You little college alley slut."

"I'll have you know I went to Bryn Mawr."

"You went to shit, you cheap cunt. I have more brains in the end of my little prick in my pussy than you've got between your ears and those of all your relatives."

Just one last skirmish as I was steering Fanny through the hall. With Mrs How after me shouting why do you have to go. Send her away. You stay. I want you. And with a massive heave ho. Fanny was loose again. In what might have been the vestibule. Slamming Mrs How by both naked shoulders right through the powder room door. That didn't open soon enough. Now splintered brightly when before it was stained dark brown. She landed backwards in her own toilet bowl. The seat of which was lifted much earlier in the peaceful evening by this present scrupulous gentleman taking a pee. And now it takes neatly a small pair of cheeks. Lavatory rolls unraveling. While Fanny pulls and tugs with hands clutched in her hair. Mrs How kicking and screaming. I pressed the little flush button. The cascade of water brought about a surprised pause in the melee. Recommencing with Mrs How's raised up foot pounding Fanny one in the belly. I saw the distillery policeman's face at the broken window, shaking his head back and forth. And he just raised his hand to brush the whole scene away. And something clicked right in the middle of my brain. That Fanny Sourpuss was not going to die. Not till a lot more of the rest of us did. Including me. Who at that magic moment in shoes but sockless was crushing under my heel the shattered remains of a glass bowl of powder puffs. Towels pulled from racks as Mrs How was pulling to get out of the toilet bowl. A big H getting trampled underfoot. Fanny, who knows exactly how to ruin a person's house, turning on both faucets in the wash basin. Which previously was just holding its own. Used to hide my dirty pictures in the hollow hole of its pedestal in my blond foster mother's bathroom. Where I knew she would find them. And throw a fake heart attack. Her eyes getting wide in her greasy skinned face. And just as I felt the basin water splashing on my ankles, behind me now I felt a shadow. As if Howard was standing there. With all the faith he's put in me crumbling in an avalanche. Right into this powder room. Of scratching, pushing and contusions. And when I turned it was Glen. In his grey chauffeur's uniform. A smile across his face. His hat quite properly held over his left wrist by the visor in his right hand.

"Can I be of any assistance, ladies and gentleman."

Back all the way to Park Avenue. I sat in my corner of the limo. And Fanny in hers on the left. Watching the buildings go by. In the faintest rays of early morning. Pale faces in other cars, asleep by day. A sprinkle of lights still on. As other citizens worry and pray. And across the tip top gravestones of New Calvary Cemetery, the slender ashen towers of Manhattan stand. On the seat between us, Fanny's hand slowly reaching. Until it touched mine. To make a whole body quake. Gathered in her arms. I sobbed.

"O honey baby, my honey baby, never knew you could be so human, it makes me feel so good to have you cry."

Sunday afternoon after that night of Jean and a morning of Fanny. My balls swollen. Strains and pains all round the leverages to my perpendicular. And my voice fading fast. Heavy hearted I went to Doctor Pedro. Where he lived palms on a terrace eight stories up overlooking the zoo in Central Park. A white coated butler leading me to him seated in a monstrous chair, wearing fluffy slippers with Sunday fat newspapers strewn over a silken rug. When I said it was my testicles he said open up your mouth. When I said it was my voice, he said open up your fly.

"I can tell by your throat it's your prick that's getting you into trouble. You went to the delicatessen and picked up a piece of ass. Instead of a piece of cheese cake, maybe."

"No. I went to Queens."

"They got twenty three cemeteries out there. What are you doing in Queens. I can see you are really sad. Young man, you should fight. You know what this place is. A god damn run away horse. You go down, if you don't get up on it."

"I feel I'm dying, doctor."

"Sure you're dying. What do you want me to do, tell you you're not dying. Dying is good for you. Take some every day. Because you're going to get it anyway. Sure it's tough. Such mountains of money around. So what if a few little people get crushed. It don't matter a damn. Go down the street and there are swarms. Ninety nine percent jackasses. But you, you're no jackass, you understand me."

"Yes doctor."

"You want me to send you a bill and scare the shit out of you."

"No."

"Then don't tell me any more dumb things. I hear enough already. But you know, I'm going to give you some good advice. You should get on the boat and go back where you came from."

"I came from here."

"No you didn't. I did. Because I came from over there. You, you go back. You came here with sadness. Clarance told me. Sure, I shout a lot. I scare people. Sometimes I like to hear myself talk. But I tell you for your own good. Don't stay. You waste yourself here. You want some crazy jerk for no reason at all shoot you in the head and then where are you. Out in Queens under the ground. Come back when you can afford bodyguards. Ha, ha, you think I kid you. Sure it's funny. It's fatal too."

"But how do you survive doctor."

"Me, it's easy. I hum, I sing, I play violin. I don't have any dreams. I don't have any hopes. I get up at six o'clock every morning. Say hello to every animal in the zoo. Instead of eating lunch I have a little snooze and give myself a hard on. The rest of the time I'm too busy to die. The secret is, you give a little. Take a little. And if you're plenty strong, sure, you take a little bit more."

Christian turning out that door. And the bronze plaque engraved Doctor Pedro. Who cures each time the world is crushing you. Smile back over a shoulder at his twinkling eyes. Closing my file. And the tears seep out on my face as I go along this hall. Outside a breezy autumn day. Wind flapping canopies along the avenue. Brought my sorrow to this shore. Carried it over the snow. And for four hundred and eighty six dollars and forty two cents they put it in the ground. And that was the end of me.

And Fanny and I. For ten days we lived. Hand in hand walking the city. Crossed between rivers. Up Madison, down Park. And one dawn I sat high up at the window. Two black women cutting and stabbing below in the street. Rushing each other with broken bottles and umbrellas. A dance of death back and forth. With murderous screams and shouts. Till one lay dead or dying. And Fanny still had her body and I had mine. Which she said laid the worst farts of this century. That she'd like to bottle to send a few lawyers to smell. Whom she went to see nearly every afternoon. Two discarded dolls of her dead husband's, suing with paternity claims. And his first wife wanted back the part of ear Fanny bit off. Or one hundred thousand dollars for every gram that was gone.

And Fanny, through all her tribulations, hummed me a lullaby. Her spine bending like a great white pipe in her tanned back. As she sat in bed. Rubbing cream in her hands. Watching the jackasses on the television box. After a day in vegetable markets along Ninth Avenue. Buying egg plant, grapes and avocadoes. She built sandwiches floor by floor. Big castles on a plate. Put them in front of me with her smile. And that was our marriage. Made of love, salami and cans of beer.

"Cornelius you're the only thing I've got. The only one I'd ever really trust. You sneaky bastard. If there were no other women in the world. You'll be here when I get back, won't you. Don't tell me any lies. God you've got to be. Don't ever let me buy you. As guys bought me. Lying in the dark. All you ever feel is the size of their pricks and you say you've had your's buster, that's all you're going to get, get off."

The days when she waited for me in the evenings. I was glad to see her face. Shouting her name. Wondering which room her head would come from. To reach out and touch her smile. Kiss her big toe she stubbed all black and blue. And I saw that evening as if it would never end. Or the train ever go. Watching her pack her clothes. A whole acre of apartment to bring her back. And the thought that made me think it wouldn't, closed my mouth so I could hardly speak. To say stay. Don't go. And you do. You let life move on. Wherever it's wandering. And once when I read a sign out loud. Transients Accommodated. Fanny said I hate those words.

Glen pulled up outside the canopy. The Pakistani loading on the luggage. Nudging me once in the chest. Come on Mr Peabody try and throw me. And the night cool with a slender nearly fragrant breeze. Always feel at my most ridiculous getting in this car. While that bitch out of the embassy, watches with her peeing poodle and her bouffant hairdo. And Fanny presses in my fist a set of keys.

Pigeons cooing high in the cornices. And flying across this grey indoor sky. Fanny Sourpuss clutching Cornelius Christian under this mountainous arch as they walk down the marble steps. Into the vast shadowy vault of Penn Station. To the feet and heels passing, hands clutching luggage, little lines buying tickets. And souls sailing away. Towards Altoona. Pulled by the trains out across the Lehigh Valley.

This hour before midnight. Deep under steel and stone. Near each other. While all these wheels wait on their tracks. Stand next to the steel stanchion bubbling with rivets. Under all the vasts of girders, pillars and glass.

"Cornelius this is how I first came into this town. Shouting to everybody, get your dirty hands off my life. And got everything I tried to get. Sold my blood, my ass and everything except my tonsils. Only because they took them out when I was nine years old. Wake up each morning and think I'll never smile again. Not once did you ever say you'd come with me. You dirty rat. Your god damn cold heart. Never once did you say you loved me. Guess it's all just as well. And you know. Old Sourpuss used to walk into his club, look at the bulletin board and see what members had died the night before. He kept waiting for the day he'd walk in and see his own name up there. And it was. And if this clinic isn't any good, mine's maybe going to be.''

Throwing her hair back. Follow Fanny along the narrow corridor to her suite. On those legs you hate to think will ever disappear from this world. The blue cover of her bed turned back for sleep. The black smiling face that says good evening madam, anything I can do, anything at all. You just push my signal there.

Time to leave. Conductor passing down the platform, swinging a green lantern. Cries of all aboard. In the long dim cars a silence of people waiting in their seats. The freckles look so dark on Fanny's face. Crushing my arms up against her breasts. And anytime I ever saw anything floating in the sky, even a scrap of paper, I stopped to watch till it was gone. Like a dream that Vine's hands were green, and slowly they vanished till he had none and I woke up. Went past his new edifice tonight. Hammers hitting and the floors rising in the sky.

Car attendant sticks out his head. Time to get aboard my lady. Kiss touching her lips. They move and eat when she cooks. And a last time press mine on her cheeks. Can't make them smile even with my sunniest face. Said once when I was trying to get in her that she was like the rock of Gibraltar. And wished I had whispered she was of the softest silk. For she was. And you know the winter's come in the tall city when the elevator shafts are howling. And the strange chill you feel driving by the rows of faces standing along Forty Second Street. A shore line of sharks to bite into the stream of passing people. Fanny said there are hookers in this town who peddle their ass for a couple of bucks to play a horse. Both lose. Standing in the center of the whole world.

''Cornelius you're going to beat it when I'm gone.''

''No.''

''You are.''

''No.''

''Don't shit me.''

Saw her face. Turning aside so close in through the window. Lips still. Eyes aglisten with tears. Car K beginning so slowly to move. While it's there. You can hold it all back. Grab her shoulders. Keep her. Till she's gone in your dream. And then she stays. As the train's last red lights go rattling. Away in the dark.

Flushing
Toilets
Along
The track

28

At midnight. Christian walking along this blinking canyon of
daylight. Past a window selling cupid undies. Hotel doorways
reeking of loneliness and death. Glowing signs say come in and
let us take the money out of your wallet.

Christian wandering away from the lighted avenues. Further
and further downtown. Crossing through bereft empty side
streets. One eye on the shadows. Another out west and which
way will she go. Through Scranton or Altoona. Or click clack by
Ashtabula and Sandusky on the Erie Lake. Misery comes with
you wherever you head. On this paper strewn street. Passing
these doorways. Hear a voice. Says pardon me would you give me
a light.

Her black skin was like she lived in another country. And I
came over there on my scooter and knocked on her door. Said
when she was bored she posed naked for the art student's league.
Puffed on her cigarette and said if you're not doing anything I
live that way.

We went up narrow stairs. Down a hallway that looked like a
coffin. She had three little interconnecting rooms. Just space
enough beside her bed to climb in. And sitting on her toilet bowl
one's ass could be caught between the walls. On top of a table she
took off her clothes. Said photograph me please, because I'm an
esthete. I stood behind her camera pressing the button as Hephzibah told me to. She shook and shimmied. Said it started her
engine. Shifted her into top gear. Kept feeling for my wallet as

we screwed each other all over her unwashed dishes. And in the tight squeezes on the bare rickety boards of her floor. And she said when we finished, with your accent you must like tea. I said yes and tinted toast too. Told her I was an actor out of work and she said you sure are in tune. Man. And I'd like us to play again sometime. Gave her the phone number in my west side hall. And thought going back down the stairs. That Fanny's gone. By now nearly all the way to Buffalo. And I need her so.

Stood desolate on the street corner. Varick and Broome. Looked up to read a sign. Said Entrance to the Holland Tunnel. Remember a little guide book I read as a child. That round here was The Long Distance Building. With telephone wires out to all the world. Let things go away. Just so you can start chasing them again. Paper said this morning there was a new move against crime. And even while I sat having tea, I thought the black girl would put out her white palm and say. Twenty bucks please. And instead she read me my horoscope.

Christian entering a bar. Up two steps. The only one in all these streets. Of closed and shuttered buildings. They say go in and drown your sorrow. Drink it as a friend. When lonely it gets. For all her blond limbs and pale eyes. Ratted on her already. Couldn't stand the pain. Of her missing. Fight to live. And don't die. Of my whole life ahead, can only see the veins of my hands stand out blue, resting on this bar.

Christian lowering whiskey after whiskey. And lurching to the phone booth back in the dark. Dial the number of Charlotte Graves. Can I come out to see you. Why not tonight. I'm sorry you were asleep. Can it be sooner. No Saturday is the earliest. And now I wait. Till the end of the week. A voice telling another down the bar, boy what a murder that was, an Italian pineapple in her mouth blew her head and you couldn't tell her hair from her teeth. And when I lay with that dark skinned heart pumping against mine. Wondering what to say into all the frizzy black curls. With my little sorrow. Still lurking from a childhood of pain. Why don't we go back to love again. Spit over trees and piss in picnic brooks. Freeze up our lips on a hard cold ground. Bellywopping down the hills. Fumble through our coats. Tasting snow in our teeth. Gloves tied to sleeves. Perhaps it wasn't

305

always a dump, this place. Playing marbles along the gutter. Boxball on the sidewalk slates. Autumn so gold. The springs squealed on her metal bed. She had my marbles out to play. Nice big shiny cockroach crossing the ceiling. Must seem like to him the Sahara. No where to stop for water. And then with her black Frizz like an electrocution out from the sides of her head, she said I'm going to have your baby. Because you just fucked me mister good and sound. I'll call you on the phone. Tell you how many pounds it weighs. And don't think I'm kidding.

Hear another voice on the back of my neck. Christian turning to a man nodding his head.

"Hey can I buy you a drink."

"No that's all right thank you."

"O sure. Just being friendly. I want everybody to be happy. Like anybody should be. This is the only country in the world I'd want to live in."

"Have you ever lived anywhere else."

"No."

"How do you know."

"Hey now fella don't start getting wise."

Christian turning back to his glass. Away from this pasty face. Which leadeth itself by the still waters and he can't swim a stroke. While he drowns singing his litany. My wife is wonderful. My kids are wonderful. And my name's Mr Contentment.

"Hey buddy, just let me say it again. I don't need to go no other place."

Christian moving away down the bar. Everywhere. Some guy scattering sunshine. And all you can hope to do. Is burst into tears and wash the fucker off his feet. Can't you see you son of a bitch the last thing I want to be is happy like you. Or the god damn part you played in your mother's life. Much prefer to tint you up for burial. As a deceased personality. Memorable in your coffin.

"And buddy, if you don't like this country why don't you get out of it."

Amazing. As one stands here. That I was just thinking that. And leave a wife behind. Without a headstone for her grave. Because they said it needs money for a six foot foundation. And the deed they gave me. This indenture made the eighth day of February. For the use of one lot of land as a place of burial for the human dead. Now never go back to see you before I go. Or lay my head on your grave. So many whispered words to so many others ever since. You were just a few shivers. A sadness settled on all the pillows and sheets. Like my last entwinement with Fanny. When she whispered against my ear. I come to you in the night. You're like a lake in a forest where nobody was and nobody ever knew it was there. And when I slip in for a swim, so scared of drowning because nobody is around to save you. Just maybe a bird flies over and chirps a sound. And in this shadowy bar one more of those little dipping birds. Woman customer says it's kind of cute. The bartender moving down, quietly wiping around and under my drink.

"Don't mind that guy buddy. Few months ago his whole family was killed. A train wreck crossing Snake River, Montana. They drowned in the rapids. Don't know why they were out there but I know how he feels. He's so lonely he thinks they're all still alive. He don't mean harm. Had two brothers myself crushed by a bulldozer. Here this one's on the house."

Another beer. And a shot of rye whiskey. Slapped down and pushed right at me with all this understanding. Just when one was nearly ready to play ping pong with that oaf's bicuspids. Or if his head was a tennis ball, Mrs How could clap for me as I served ace after ace in the ivied cathedral of tennis near her nice little home. Summer's over. Collect the dirty looks of all the faces in this town. Make enough humus to grow crops to feed all the starving foreign hoards. Black girl's filthy exhibition was mixed with smiles. And wide eyed demeanours. Held up squeezing her tits and said as I was trying to figure the crazy camera out. With these man, I can get anything I want, so that I'm rolling with dough, that's how you get to be a wheel, man, by rolling with dough. And I jumped like an invention back down her stairs. Only four blocks away from the Mott empire. Where I went in and said can you use me. If I'm of any use. Mr Christian what exactly can we use you for. Butter me as a slice of life. Eat me as laxative. Those who gobble the most will shit the more. Sail your ship of industry under the Brooklyn Bridge. Where recently folk ride across naked on bicycles. Dismounting in the middle to make courtesies to the Queen of Nutdom. You wonderful people here tonight in this bar. Thank you for allowing me to stand in your company. Because the whole world would clap for joy if they could have me washing dishes. The friendly brain I have in my head. Has got me nowhere. The rest of you run a few yards away to keep looking back to see if I'll get up again as I'm going down. And if I do, you bastards. I'll take the whole imagination of the world with me. Shut it off with a switch like they use on railway tracks. For the train. That took her away. I let her go. Her life got in my way. Blocking my hopes. Sitting forever surrounded by her money. Up to my teeth in her. And couldn't believe my lips. Crossing back in the gigantic gloom of the station. That even if I helped her go. I loved her I loved her. And one night in the automat a friendly black face looked down at my plate. Said, beans boy, it seems, them things you got am beans. Told Fanny and she laughed. Said say it again. And I said it. And she rolled on the floor clutching her sides. And I sit here. On a stool. No bands no nothing. Thought I would become. And now. It's time to be. And I'm not. Bent drunkard foolish at a bar. Every one of my best recent foots forward, someone stepped on the toes shined in my favourite store. Crawl now. On my hands and knees. Up a gangplank of that ship. Only days now to go. And hear the bartender telling a guy.

"Don't mister get hot under the collar. Just telling you we don't want fights in the bar. Beatings outside. We let everybody come in here to knock around their girl friends and wives and the rush would block the street with traffic."

Christian swirling the heel of his glass in a big circle in the wet. Make all your shapes round. My Rockaway uncle. Might be feeble voiced in some boarding house room. Find him hair all grey. Sinewy strings strung under his throat. Ebb myself. And can help no one.

Door opens. Man comes in. Christian turns stares. That face. One of the first I saw on this shore. Sits at the end of the bar. The dark hair. As he takes off his hat. The wide brow. The quiet sympathetic eyes. And the voice, I'm sorry sir, about this. Steve Kelly, customs will get me. Puts a shot of whiskey to his lips, downs it and takes a gulp of water and is gone. Three o'clock in

February. When all sky was blue and high. Over this city. Where I still hear words. Put them all together. They hurt so much. When Fanny said please don't use my towel. O god what a thing to say to me. As if I was unworthy. And she said, hey wait a minute, you're hurt, just because I said don't use my towel doesn't mean that my fondness is any less. Did all those lousy things I did in the neighborhood because with my name they called me a hebe to my face. The guy's heads I had to put up against walls and say take that back or I'll ram your brains through these bricks. And one girl I yearned for from a distance. She wore big fat plaits of dark hair down her back. And years later and older I walked with her to school. Through icy woods. The frosted bracken breaking. The wind freezing our shins. She laughed when I couldn't pronounce a word. As I spouted poems I made up in my head. That she said were beautiful. Until I said, a big dose of castor oil was better than college. And that's what I would say to any audience of shitting graduates. Toilet paper for parchment, when seeking employment, folks. Mr Quell went to college. Princeton as a matter of past fact and future face. Where they shout fire when a girl goes by so beautiful. Bet he wished he was back there with his bowels. And where tonight. Is my little brother. When I went east over the ocean. He went west. As a ghost. To Denver. Became a piano tuner. Play an anthem or two for the inhabitants of this bar. Let them know they're in patriotic company. Give them a red white and blue night to remember. The biggest jamboree of loyalty in their whole lives. Right in the center of everything. Where this is tonight. Folks. Before the boogey man comes. And the sand man too. To put you to sleep. Like seaweed waving up from the seabed against your toes.

"Knaves and thieves."

Cornelius Christian shouting the words up at the ceiling. As the faces turn around. All the way back into the dark interior.

"Knaves and thieves."

"Hey buddy what's bothering you."

"Knaves and thieves."

"Hey fella you ain't by any chance a medievalist out on a spree."

"You knaves and thieves, give that man a prize."

"Buddy you better quieten down or I'm going to throw you out."

"To the joust. Knaves and thieves. To the joust."

"That's it buddy I warned you."

Bartender with his rolled up sleeves, running down to come out from behind the bar. Just like one before. Trying to step on my feelings. Just tattoo a few on his jaw. Give him a solemn memory. In honor of the freedom of speech. When you want to shout. That you can't stand anymore. Of shit and concupiscence. Wait for the first hand to touch me. Before I start swinging. Always like to be fair. Before breaking a jaw. Whoosh. Wham. Bam. Bunch of beans boy. Them things you got am beans. And hello. What's this darkness. That's come. To invite me in. After a few fist swings. Just to celebrate goodbye. And leave you. And wake up a jackass.

"That's what the hell you are. Mr Christian. You wake up a jackass. Now you know what. I have exactly the job for you. Where you can get your ass broken ten times a day. Join the fire department, that's what you need."

Cornelius stretched on his back. Surrounded by screens. A bottle dripping moisture into an arm. Trays of instruments. The light over my head. See the face of Doctor Pedro. The tiniest of smiles behind his consternation. And the walls everywhere are tiled.

"Sure. Someone hammer you on your head. That's right. You got cut."

"Doctor where am I."

"You're in the hospital."

"O."

"You had delirium. You call for me. Instead of your mother. I come. Like a good doctor should. Dreaming I am fucking somebody, a nice big fat woman with an ass like a cathedral and a face like a transmission of a truck. But who am I to be choosy at my age. And how do I know I could do what I was doing in my dream if I was awake. How many favours are you going to do for me."

"I'm very sorry doctor."

"Next time wear your football helmet when you go out. Rah

rah, ciss boom bang. You want to splash your blood around this town who's to stop you. You'll wake up one of these days looking at Clarance instead of me. You know what he makes you do if you couldn't pay the bill. He makes you do like a restaurant. Instead you don't wash the dishes, you polish up his customers in his caskets."

"Yes doctor."

"How do you feel."

"I feel awful."

"Now there, look at her she's a pretty nun. She going to take good care of you. But I stay and watch how they sew up your arm and head so it looks good. If they don't do a good job, I break their ass, how about that."

"That's fine doctor."

Cornelius Christian looking down his shirt. Arching up his head to see his chest covered in blood. All so calm, all the red. Turns light brown. Death is a visitant. Comes with shrewd glee. Watching for hours laughing as you warm up. To kill yourself. And cool off to die. Before the darkness came there were all the churning faces. So many, you couldn't be fair to everyone with a sock on the jaw. And this tender nun's face. Looks down in my eyes.

"Mr Christian, O Mr Christian. The things you've been saying in your sleep."

The moments come back. Keep wanting to close my eyes. Close them. Goodnight. And Clarence sits there. Glittering in the green darkness. His voice so soft and calm. Hear him now. Across his desk drawling his careful words. Cornelius, it's good to have you here. Back with me again. There they all are. Waiting. And I have thought more than once that as they lay there just fresh collected by Fritz, that when you give a little color to their cheeks that they have smiled at me. Makes you nearly switch on the infra red and start resuscitations. But Cornelius, I learned more than once that efforts to bring the dead back to life can meet with hostility from the relatives. That's why now the drama of cremation interests me. The hall of flame. The hearth of heaven. Lot of folk don't want to be enveloped by heat planned thoughtfully in advance. They feel it's going to

311

hurt. But when they are clinker cinder and ash, what could be cleaner or drier. A devouring conflagration. Pine trees, plenty of them. Lining the path in their marble plant pots to the edifice of sacred fire. It is an ancient method. Persons of distinction have been burned. Maybe too, they might have shouted, dang if that ain't real hot. And Cornelius. My new subterranean situation. Come. This way. See. The couches are hydraulic. Just like the barber's chair I told you about. And green. My morticians in pink. Isn't this beautiful. Makes you feel at home. Miss Musk died you know. She lived in Norwood in the Bronx. Reservoir Oval East. Isn't that a nice address. I embalmed her body and all. You remember the physique she had. It was really something living. But beyond all earthly beauty dead. And Cornelius I want you to come clean with me now. Did you dishonor her in one of my deluxe caskets. Well, believe me, I'm relieved to hear that. What deceased could rest in peace on the satin where that happened. And Clarance I lie. To you about Miss Musk. Because the night I prepared Herbert Silver and all the other deceased were tucked up safely asleep. Peaches and I creeped hand in hand to the laying out room. Planting kisses along each other's neck. She kept saying lordy sakes I shouldn't be doing this as she ripped off her clothes. Threw them over the trestle of the crimson coffin. The sight of her body made me pale with anger. That we hadn't done this sooner. Hands flying all over her. Couldn't believe the feel. Of her luscious limbs. Tugged her by the hair. Down into the folds of satin. She bit. She blew. I pinned her squirming under me, nipples brushing back and forth across our chests. Her groans were loud and my screams nearly woke the dead. But please, Clarance, don't let me interrupt you, you were saying. Yes I was saying, Cornelius, that there, standing by the door in his tailcoat. Is my floor manager. You remember Mr. Hardwicke. From my west side branch. He's wearing a slightly lighter shade of tint in his hair. And that door there is the pedestrian entrance for those who want to walk to death. And up there. Behind that glass enclosed balcony. Is the restaurant. For the living to dine. In the time they have left. While watching down on the holiest of rites. Witnessing this scene and the quiet industry of these great artists at work. This gathering of future

312

customers can enjoy a tranquil assurance when they think ahead. And eat their asparagus. Appetized by the pine scented breeze you smell blowing across the plaza. So convenient for those who want to remain near. That purple fire hydrant was installed specially for me by the commissioner. And I certainly do not think that a bar or two of contemporary music is out of the picture. The gentleman with the red flowing mane of hair and handsome roman face. That's Jack. I've hired him to play his own compositions. Even some rather high stepping ones. And sometimes the clapping and bravoes would burst your god damn ears. He was a prodigy. And now he is a genius. I know that everyman who works for me never wants to leave that room. Cornelius can't you see now why I'm so sorry you left. That standing here you can inhale the awe and reverie that pervades this sanctum. Enthroned by its requiem. A king among those remains collected from every corner of every borough. Although the influx recently is heaviest from the South Bronx. Over there is Tina, the Two Ton, her volume is a real challenge. And her surface a whole landscape. And we have our special annex for the darker complexioned, stab wounds being a distinctive feature of that department. Cornelius I'm glad you're here. Good to see you dead. And that I can put color back in your cheeks. And these others, the tenderest deaths of all. See them. The little children. Forgive me Cornelius, I still find that hard to take. The prostrate simple serenity of a child. And over there is your uncle. A kind large handed man. Altogether now in one big happy family. Passions cooled. Making room for others in the heavily crowded shopping districts. And there are those too, who in life might have been a burden to their dear ones, such as an alcoholic or an addict. And through here, my special room. Round like my east side chapel was. Those arms sculpted on the walls embrace you. This is my masterpiece. And I am shamed sometimes to admit it. But I like it best here with these hundred thousand dollar people. As you know the big boys all come to me now. Some feet first. Himie The Horse, Zeke The Zero, John The Big Sneeze. Reuben The Gonad. You remember our meeting we had that day. All of them good family men. Although there are times when they find it necessary to eliminate others. But want such elimination to be

313

carried out with a suitable send off. This Cornelius is the arch dynasty of death. Where the power and glory of the high and mighty receives its ultimate enshrinement. The monument to my life. Multiple bullet holes, semi decapitation, these are no problem. A rubout by a close discharging shotgun. Bam. At the head area. That certainly is not nice. When it sends the ears flying. But given a few photographs of the subject in life, even that challenge we turn into a triumph in wax. And where possible we use the original eyes. Ah Cornelius you are a good listener. Alive or dead. Never met anyone in my life before to whom I could say so much. And who understands so well. And that way there is the roof. Ascension by express elevator. To the solarium. Where a cherished one can get a tan for real. That alone is everything I have ever dreamed of. There on the skyline. Silhouetted against the heavens. Corpse Castle. No no, Cornelius, rather the Palace of Peace. And people passing in their own lives, just might nudge a travelling companion and say, and these words Cornelius are what I live for. They say. Do you see that. Over there, scraping the sky. Those golden pinnacles. That's Vine.

Christian's eyes opening. To see there, calmly staring down. Clarance Vine. Any second I'll feel the puncture of trocar. Those same quietly impassioned cheeks. Always freshly shaved. The stiff white collar. Neat little knot of the Game Club tie he wears tonight. At my funeral. Or assessing my moisture content. At my embalming. Hope he's come to close the casket. Extra special care taken of a former employee. Time to usher me softly to rest. Or god am I dead. Or holy shit am I still alive.

"Cornelius, Cornelius, can you hear me."

"I think so."

"You've got friends Cornelius. Why haven't you come back to see me. Doctor Pedro and I want to help you. I mean it Cornelius. This is no way. You'll get yourself killed."

"I'm going back home across the ocean, Mr Vine."

"Home is where your hat is. All you have to do is hang it in my new branch. Charlie, Miss Musk, they all ask after you."

"I got you sued."

"That's just the name of the game Cornelius."

"I'm not dying am I."

"That's what you thought wasn't it, that you were dead, when you saw my face. Come on, admit."

"It was for a second."

"Well boy this hospital hasn't ever heard some of the things you've been shouting. A famous man just died upstairs. But they tell me all the histrionics have been down here. You got in dutch all over again Cornelius. The police were waiting to get a statement. Just damn lucky I knew another precinct captain. Broke two jaws, two people's noses, one man's testicle crushed. I don't know how his other escaped. A guy had to hit you with a champagne bottle to stop the carnage. Ordinary whiskey bottles made no impression. Patrolmen say the place looked like a slaughter house. Cornelius you've got to be careful, there are people who try to get even in this town."

Eyes cloud over. Clarance your voice is fading. Going to sleep. I'm tired. Of everything in this native land. Man stopped me yesterday on the street. Said he was in awful pain with something in his eye. He was looking for an apartment and had gone along to see it and couldn't find the janitor and someone said the janitor was upstairs and when he went up to look, there was the janitor sucking this sailor's cock and the janitor said he was busy, come back in ten minutes and bring a friend and I'd like to ask do you want to come. And down in the subway again. On an empty train. Another guy comes in. Opening his fly. Takes out his prick and as he pulls, turns to politely ask do you want to eat this. I was weary. With no appetite left. Said sorry. That I was looking to see what else was on the menu. Next station he got off pulling as he went. Dividing a path through the people along the platform. With your prick out the whole city knows you mean what you're pulling and stand back. And the screams in that bar. As I was rolling over and over again on the floor. Fighting backwards into a room filled with packing cases. Sending out left fists. Hooking a right hook two feet deep into someone's belly, knuckles hitting the inside bumps of this total stranger's backbone. Voices. What's the matter, you got no respect for America. Bar room floor where I could see the milling shoes. Thought in all the melee to give Quell a hot foot as soon as possible. Darkness. Then the sirens. Warehouses, dark stoops.

And the night air is crisp and chill and the stars are out straight above me. A doctor's hairy hand and wrist watch. Taking my pulse to see if I'm still alive. Pass over iron clanking sewer covers in the street. And the drums are beating. Throbbing from river to river. Corridor to corridor. Where the dead are being wheeled away with their sheets bunched and thrown on top. Signs up on the walls. Don't stick things in your ears. And another time in another empty subway station. Sit on a bench. See a man. Far far away at the end of the platform. Walking slowly closer and closer. Passing bench after empty bench. And sits right next to me. And I swear to christ I couldn't believe it myself. Big slow rumbling growls began to come from between my curled up lips, showing a slightly vampire tooth on the left side. Then the gentleman rose, bowed and apologised. Said he was a pastor of a Baptist church. And he would be glad to have me there. Blond as I was among his dusky congregation. Would have got down on my knees to ask his forgiveness but he might think I was trying to blow him. And no one wants to know you. Unless you're jackass grinning in the latest best of latest places. Shut off their ears, turn away eyes at your loneliness and despair. Rush to gladness, the shiny and the new. Like the mealy mouthed cunts back at the office. The guys. The shitheads. O yes, Christian, I think he went that way again, to the rest room, with the Wall Street Journal, o about two hours ago. And I went surging through this city. Looking like no one else would to find the owner of a dollar lying in the street. Hello. Can you hear me. All the faces in that bar. One doll thought it would be fun to scratch my eyes out. And my fists were singing. And her lips became bruised tomatoes nailed on her teeth. Women first. As I hit her. With the whole bar trying to hit me. Someone said I could talk myself out of anything. Meager told me I would never admit I was wrong. Two foster mothers in a row said I was a born little liar. When I was only diplomatic. And Meager told me I made a social mistake. When I drank my soda first before others were served. Told me you can't get out of it, you violated the rudiments of good manners. You drank your soda first. I was just tasting it to see if I got the wrong one. See, there you go, trying to get out of it. But you're not going to get out of this

316

one. Even aboard an ocean liner. With an east bound contract ticket says Deck R Cabin 34. Adults one, servants none, total one. Mutually agreed between carrier and passenger that if the ship goes down. That's just tough titty. Each hour now, one hour less. Getting out. Running along the shore waving to the ship, shouting wait for me. Open my eyes. Let the light in. Feel pain in my arm. All the promises told. Your mother is somewhere sonny. Your father is gone away but he'll be back. Lie here. Hands care. A dark complexioned policeman once put his arm around my shoulders. To comfort me when I was little and lost. He had the saddest and kindest face. To tell you as a child. Don't worry son. And I did. Listening so hard to what they told me. Show honesty in the squeeze of your handshake. Grow tall strong and bronze like the buildings. Tear them down before they get ghosts. All over this city.

> Too rich
> To laugh at
> Too lonely
> To love

29

Clarance Vine brought me from the hospital back to my west side room in a brand new blue limozine. The city waking. As the night time citizens go to sleep. Stacks of newspapers slapped down on the sidewalks from delivery trucks. Folk at the bus stops. Blond girl carrying her laundry to drop off on her way to work. And one morning when I was an early riser buying a bun, a guy standing inside a door of the confectionary shop opened it as customers approached and they all say thank you. And he says after they've gone, sure I opened it for them, because I didn't want to get hit in the head when they push it open themselves.

Go purring four wheeled down my one way street. To leave the quiet peace of the limo's black interior. Romeo, the chauffeur dark and swarthy. With Vine, he helped me up the steps. Wobbling as I went. Shook hands with Clarance. How short he is. And stands so high, a stately gentleman. As folk come out the door heading for work. Their hair wet with water. Parts gleaming along their skulls. Giving me side glances. With that look, who do you know that I could meet to get to know so that everybody would like to know me.

Lay two days in bed. Throwing my shoes at the scouting cockroaches. And listening to symphonies on the radio. Bathing my eyes and head in lemon scented water. Drinking apple juice, eating pears and slabs of Swiss cheese. Whole basket of fruit sent by Clarance. One arm under bandages. Felt someone watching me from across the street and pulled down my shade. Opened up

318

a letter. The only mail I get. Another invitation to have your rupture fixed. With an agent taking truss measurements just downtown.

And Friday when I had the strength to walk and even skip and hop, I answered the phone. A motherly voice saying, you Christian. And before I could say Peabody. She said you blond fucking white bastard I'm gonna cut your balls off. You mother fucker. We got pictures of you doing it. Putting your white prick in my daughter Hephzibah's mouth.

Made a very slow replacement of the receiver. And lay playing with myself another day. Looking behind me now as I move hastily along the street. Trying to curl my right hand into a lily white fist again. Little bumps of bloody scab on my skull. Get a wigwam. Put in on the subway. A nomad. Platform to platform smoking my peace pipe till it's time to go. Or some god damn bastard crowds me trying to eat some of my thanksgiving corn. In monkey city where everyone's making faces.

This Saturday. First falling leaves. The sun in clear blue skies. Parade of dogs and owners crossing to the park. Stillness of air. Warmed by this Indian summer. And up there in their glistening palisades of buildings those dirty rich sons of bitches. Chewing pills and patting lotions on their faces and ass and staying the hell away from the likes of me.

As I go now north by the roaring rapid transit up into the Bronx. Everyone staring. At my pair of peach colored shoes. Hand lasted all the way from Bulgaria. Found in the back of old man Sourpuss's closet as I was nosily looking a last time through Fanny's apartment. In front of the building. Saw Willie waiting, great bare haunches of his shoulders in his underwear, sitting on the curb by the pee stained fire hydrant. And just as I was leaving and putting the set of keys Fanny gave me on the table, the phone rang and kept on ringing. Picked it up. Heard far away. My name. Cornelius. Cornelius. And I listened and listened and said hello, hello. And the voice wouldn't speak. Could only hear the echo of my name. All the way from Minnesota. Till my own voice couldn't speak. A night bleak and black out to the end of the wires. Beyond the golden plume waving fields of maize. The beginning of nowhere. Nothing to be said to anyone anymore. And say something. Are you there. Then heard goodbye. Then I waited and waited. And hung up quietly as I could so that she would never know. Like she told me her husband old Sourpuss used to say. That if ever he lost his money. He would just go away. Far far at the end of a telephone line. Away from wherever anybody ever knew him. And keep his mouth shut. His phone dead. Silent and disconnected. That's how you finally go.

Christian standing splay footed in the first car of the rocking subway train. Chains swaying, wind blasting in around the door. The sunshine as we come up out of the earth. The tracks ahead, two gleaming silver rails. The stations with their plank floors and gabled awning roofs. The last stop. Go down these iron shadowy stairs I've descended so many times before. Quiet shirt sleeved afternoon drinkers in the tavern. Wait for the bus across the street. By the cemetery's gates. Climb aboard. Along an aisle of faces. With tiny recognitions locked behind the eyes.

Christian walking again along this curving Parkway. All the way to the monument. A bronze eagle with its talons on a pink marble ball. And the names of the patriotic dead. The cannon where I used to play. An Indian battle field across the street. A water fountain. A thumb over the spout to squirt other kids' faces. The fence where we all sat watching the green zooming fireflies and jerking off. Summer simple pleasures. The walks home from school. Hoping the knowledge in the books I carried would go up my wrist and into my brain. Wondering where everybody was. What's doing. Sucking sodas in the sweet shop. Sitting empty mouthed because I hardly ever had a dime. And over there now, parked on the highway, policeman sitting drinking beer in their car. Wearing nice blue uniforms waiting for speeders. Look at me from behind their sunglasses. Never seen such bellies in blue. They saw my shoes. And hooked a thumb in my direction. I just looked back at them with that air, that I know somebody who knows somebody who's something and you better watch out. And passed by putting an extra inch on my chest. Made no impression but they're not arresting me.

Charlotte in her long lacy white dress, a straw wide hat on her haystack hair. As we go down the red steps of her house. Her jaw dropped when she saw me. From the top of my blond head to the tip of my peach shoes. And I raise my bandaged arm. A last little wad of dollars for spending in my pocket. A breeze after this late high sunned still afternoon. She said her mother said we could borrow her car.

"Charlotte, where should we go."

"Let's go anywhere."

And we drive north. By the back childhood streets. Where so much of my life began. The last hours of which I thought I was living only days ago. The nun in the hospital said when I said I was dying, that o Mr Christian, you're not ready yet to meet your maker. Who I said lived on a hill with lawns around and buttercups sprinkled in the green.

Cornelius steering this dark grey eight cylinder coupe of a car. Stopping at a roadhouse by a great block of apartments in the woods. Drinking scotch and soda in the blue dim lights. And drive further north past the brick sprawling building with the blue slate roof where I went to school. And outside the sunny class rooms spruce trees grew in their blue tips to touch the windows and there were little hills and mountains for miles around and lakes clear and magic. And better than all the algebra, the sound a twig makes on an endless aimless afternoon. To touch her skin is better than all the history or civics. You lived when you didn't know you were living. And dying you know. Because you'll do anything to make it stop. When it's too late and it won't. Like Fanny Sourpuss gone forever on the train. Way beyond all those young yesterdays. Everything a dream on our lips. Better than today. When I drive Charlotte's mother's car without a license. On a last night to remember. Of all the other nights on these roads. Carrying my hopes. Of richness. To look down from a height on everybody. Lumped together so that it's easy to see that you're better than the whole god damn bunch.

Turning left up a cobble stone road. Along trolley tracks. To the wooded top of this hill. And left between these straight narrow high elm trees. Where I know there used to be a place. Down a cinder drive to a parking lot. Of this old but lavish eatery. With its factory windows. In the balmy air. Where

Charlotte and I can go hand in hand to a white covered table I can see through the leaves out on a terrace of sunken garden.

Cornelius Christian standing on the top green step inside this entrance. Palm leaves wag as waiters head to and fro, high nosed and sniffing and brow lifting. Follow this pointing disdaining major domo. To a table remote and lonely. Sit on these chairs iron, white and filigree. All so cold and silent. Son of a bitch waiter staring at my shoes. Touch the silver salt and pepper things. Show him I'm totally at ease. And Charlotte's so sad. At my affront to fashion.

"But didn't you know that peach is really the snazz."

"No I didn't know."

"I'm starting a fashion."

"But they looked at us."

"I thought you were so tickled pink to go out with me."

"I was. I am."

"I feel smooth in these shoes. I'm proud of these shoes."

"We're just sitting here. And nothing is happening. They're just ignoring us. And listen, hear them laughing, all those other people in really expensive clothes in the other room. The men had black shoes and dark ties and white shirts. They're all so formal. And the waiters are hurrying around them."

Charlotte Graves' wavy worried lines across her brow. Waiter lurks near a pillar. Brushes back the hair on his balding head. Sneaking a look. As Christian raises a hand. To give a delicate snap of thumb and index finger. And see the sneering bastard's nostrils dilate. As he turns to hot foot it away. And leave my god damn arm stuck up in the empty air.

"I see. Ignored. My own toes are inside these shoes. Which I'm wiggling at the moment. This place was just a factory once. Way out in the woods. They had police dogs to nibble at the unruly. Also a policeman patrolling with a night stick up and down between the tables."

"Cornelius, this is our first big night out together. Can't we go somewhere else. I'm dressed in the best I have. This belonged to my grandmother. She was married in it. I cut the hem short. It's an heirloom. Don't think please that I mind, it's only that we're here. And I don't want everyone just to notice us."

"You're a kid Charlotte."

"I'm not a kid. I feel awful. And I can't help it."

"You shouldn't let these waiters scare you."

"We could have been taken into that other room where they have the music and dancing. And there's nothing in here."

Christian turning swiftly round towards the lurking waiter at the kitchen entrance, who just as swiftly turns to disappear through the squeaking swinging pantry door.

"Son of a bitch."

"You see what they're doing to us. We don't even have menus."

"Doubts about my taste are evident. Do you want me to hide my shoes."

"It's too late now. They won't come to us."

"We'll wait. Smile."

"I can't."

"Charlotte you have such a real mouth. And such large teeth. And such a worried frown. Face my shoes. Remember the summer when we were kids. The labor day picnic and parade. I saw you coming out of your house, in a white silk blouse, and the same haystack hair. You gave me the biggest hello I've ever had in my life. I can still hear it. It made me even march in the parade, no I'm lying. I skulked behind the trees, stealing ice cream for my little brother, while the citizens of my country marched. You're such a kid. My shoes are in bad taste. My shoes are in bad taste."

"Please, o my god, don't shout. I don't mind your pink shoes."

"Peach."

"Peach. But should we go."

"No."

"Can't we ask for something."

"For them to forgive us. And me for my shoes that might have cost eighteen dollars."

"Just, Cornelius, so that they come and go from the table."

"Alas. I reckon I do lower the tone."

"Cornelius."

"I've got such a beautiful name."

"We come from the same background. Our backgrounds are medium and middle. We can't be sure we're right, that's all I'm saying. The better people are right."

"We're not the better people."

"We may be better than some people. But we're not the best people, that's all I'm saying."

"Charlotte you were so tan and lovely at the labor day parade."

"Please Cornelius, I just don't want all the best people thinking we can't be just like them."

"I took you on your first date. Bought you a soda after the movies. I remember distinctly my aplomb. As I said to the candy store man, two pineapple please. I was his customer. He welcomed me."

"Because you were nice."

"What am I now."

"You're different. You're not the same Cornelius Christian I used to know."

"Who am I."

"You're just not the same as you were before you went to Europe. And before you—"

"Got married."

Charlotte Graves. Her profile. The worriment on the long apple splendour of her face. As she turns to look round her. Two lonely people bobbing way out here in this sea of empty space.

"Please Cornelius. They'll start to listen to us."

"Good."

"You said I was so tan and lovely at the labor day parade. You don't think that now."

"You're still an apple I'd love to eat."

"I didn't go swimming this summer. Working in the city I don't get a chance. But the last few days I got a tan. That's why tonight to come out to the country and all."

Christian picking up the salt cellar. Silver and weighty. Hammering it on the table. Shouting.

"Service. Service."

"O gosh Cornelius that's the last thing I want you to do."

"I am merely asking for service. Service."

The peeking heads of waiters. Starched wing collared shirts. Airplane bow ties ready to take them off. Down their little runways. Flying the lavish people their suppers. As Christian's voice echoes back down a long corridor. And Charlotte Graves stoops her head.

"Now you have ruined the whole evening. No one has ever behaved in my presence like this before."

"Do you want me to leave."

"You know I don't want you to leave."

"Well that's just fine."

"No it isn't fine. You're being conceited."

"You do want me to leave. Do you. Tell me. Do you want me to leave."

"Yes. Leave."

Charlotte Graves, her sigh weary voice. Anguished and sad. Smell her perfumed cleanliness. Back in the funeral parlor I could take free sniffs off the roses. Cold sweet fumes out of an ice box. The dead warm up a little when they ferment. Kept the framed coffin photograph of myself close by my bed. And the worst thing that could happen to me didn't seem too bad. Alive now I stand. And as a matter of courtesy, wait. Give her a chance of reprieve. She wants none. Push my chair gently back beneath the table. Walk right in front of this headwaiter. Straightened his back to get a better look down his arched nose at my peach tootsies. As he rocks back and forth on his.

Christian climbing the steps of pale green carpet. Waiters stationed in their dark regalia. One here, one there. Towels over arms. Reach this top landing. If ever I needed to break wind. Now's the time. And it only goes bleep. When you want it to go boom. To feebly jet me out of another spiritual insult. It matters what people think of you. And they'll think a lot. If they think. That if you don't hire a finger to shoot them. Then you'll sue.

Cornelius Christian standing under the starriest sky. Up there on the hill. A roaring trolley goes by all lit up on its tracks. A frost and chill in the air. Summer all over. The backyard games. Put a penny in her slot up under her dress. That you can't play now that she's all grown up and beautiful. Made myself peanut butter and jam sandwiches to bring to school. While a foster mother watched to see if I sliced the bread too thick. And nobody ever brought me to a restaurant. Always thought they were special places for the rich to attend. And can't get myself to go. And leave her. It's a long walk anywhere without her mother's car.

Christian crossing on the pebbles. Strewn over the cinder and ash. And by a shrub. With ballooning pink and purple flowers, kneel at this tiny open window. See all this great room. Held by pale yellow fluted pillars. Where they visited hoot, hiss and who are you, upon me.

Charlotte Graves head bent at the table. All its whiteness meek and round. Waiters pass by with laden kitchen trays. Two wait and whisper. She turns looking up the empty stairs. Where I'm gone. Bites her lips. And her pinkly tinted nails. She was the first one who ever showed me I had moons on mine. She scratches a finger at the table things one by one. Looks up again. At the waiters. Who turn away. Taking their platters held high over shoulders towards the room beyond. Where the gay and better people live and tinkle laughter in their crowded lavishment. And where I should have demanded to go. Me the sultan. Of fistic swat. Only for my arm. I'd slam this place into respect, submission and christendom.

Charlotte Graves lifting her straw wide hat. Placing it gently back on her straw blond hair. A mouse alone. Out in an open shorn field. The head waiter comes. Stands. Shifting down his cuffs. A hovering hawk. As her head rises. From the black shoes and trousers. To the glistening white shirt front and face.

"Would madam like some service for herself."

Charlotte Graves shaking her genuflected head. The gentle bird wings of her shoulders. In the eighth grade in school. She folded her little note into a tight tiny wedge of paper. Gave it to Meager to give to me. It said I love you. And after that I never needed a mother and father. Or anybody else's love.

"Isn't there anything I can get madam. Like water."

Charlotte's hair shining. Washed in beer. A basin full. Smiled when she told me. Of all those cans I could drink. Foaming cold and delicious. She's seated there so silent and still.

"An omelette for madam. Crepe suzette. Steak. Would madam then, like some explanation."

Charlotte shaking her head up and down. I was cavalier with her love. And taunted her. Heartless I said I don't like you. She blushed pink. And the way girls run, she ran away up the street. Arms clutching her books. You have to do this to someone who is better looking. And I did it to her and she cried.

"Well madam, we have certain unwritten rules. Which it is understood people understand before they come here. We do not mind when persons come where this is not their natural habitat. We try to make them feel at home and not as if they don't belong. Maybe madam would like to be seated in the other room."

Charlotte turning her head back and forth. That son of a bitch. Who does he think he is. Pick on someone his own glandular size. Down there with a shy innocent girl he thinks he can push around.

"I don't want to hurt madam's feelings, but should madam be interested in my advice, I would say he is not your kind. We expected him to leave. But we have a lot of experience in telling who is who. No gentleman would treat a lady the way he has treated you. He shouted for service."

"Because you wouldn't give us any."

"O no nothing like that."

"It was like that."

"If madam will permit me, we get lots like him. We know his kind well. Distinctly from the other side of the tracks."

"He's from my side."

"Look, we know you feel you owe him some kind of loyalty, but boy I wouldn't like to have to count the trains on the tracks between you and him. Girl like you could meet people of top quality. And really frequent places like this."

"I wouldn't want to."

"You're a hard kid to please, you know that. You don't mind if I say one or two very personal things. You know, I can tell you're a girl who comes from real nice people. Only don't take what I'm going to tell you wrong. But that dress you're wearing looks like it belonged to your grandmother."

Charlotte Graves folding her fragile wings. Honeysuckle flowers close up at night. When the chill and dark comes. The humming in my ears. All the shy souls going up to heaven.

327

Lifted out of evil. Away from this son of a bitch who has hurt her bad.

"Hey kid I'm just trying to help you out. You don't want to misunderstand me. I'm just joking about the dress. O k I think it suits you. But a kid with your looks wants to show them off. Guy with a lot of dough would like to be seen with you. I'm not saying you looked like you stepped out of an antique shop."

"You are."

"No no. You got real good looks. And tone. Excuse me for saying it, but that guy was a greaseball."

Charlotte Graves, easing her head down. Shoulders slowly heave. Ocean waves when a glowering sky makes them pound. All the looming ogres. They come upon the meek and weak.

"Hey I said something. Look, you're going to cry. Don't cry. I said something. I did, didn't I. Just tell me what I said."

This major domo straightening, looking around. Raising his arm to the balding waiter standing at the pantry door.

"Hey Harry, what am I going to do."

Harry ambling over. Waddling flat footed, toes pointing out. Looks down at Charlotte Graves. Her hair in glossy tresses curled down her back. Slender arms. Sweet skinned. Her crocheted alabaster dress.

"Leave the kid alone. For crying out loud. Here kid. A towel. Help you mop up. Don't worry kid, it's all right. Nobody's going to hurt you. What did you do this to the kid for. She's crying."

"It was that guy."

"So what. No need to make the kid cry."

"I was trying to steer her straight."

"I suppose big head waiter, you know how to straighten everybody out. What the hell it's none of your business."

"She came in here with a guy who was a phony. I could tell a mile off."

"So what. Everybody in this place is phony."

"Look Harry boy, you call Mr Van Hearse and his party in there phony."

"Yeah Fritzy boy, I call them phony. What the hell is he but some guy who makes rubber goods."

"Don't say that in front of women. Mr Van Hearse is a public benefactor."

"Don't start giving him titles. He makes rubber goods."

"You said that once Harry boy, you don't have to say it again."

"I like the sound. Fritzy boy."

"I'm busy. I'm head waiter here. We better clear this table."

"Why don't you leave the kid."

"We got to clear this table."

"Who's coming. We don't need this table."

"Look Harry boy, who gives the orders around here."

"And you look Fritzy boy, I'm just telling you to give the kid a break."

"And I'm giving you an order to clear the table."

"Thought you were trying to help this kid."

Fritz cocking his head and waving an upturned palm towards the quivering Charlotte Graves.

"She still thinks the guy who walked out on her is something. When he's a phony. A phony cheapskate."

"Now look Fritz, cut it out. You're really hurting the kid's feelings."

"Any kid go out with a guy like that deserves to have her feelings hurt."

Harry pushing forward, his face rearing up against the tip of Fritz's nose.

"And I'm telling you, look Fritzy boy. I don't care if I've got to take orders from you. But you're not going to upset this kid any more. Because I'll slug you. That's English. Understand it."

"You touch me and you're fired."

Harry holding his shaking knotted fist under Fritz's eyeball. Just like brotherly love anywhere, it starts best with a good bust in the face.

"And you say one more thing to this kid and I'll slug you right out the window up there. That's definite."

"Tough."

"About this. Yeah."

"We'll see. Harry boy."

"You'll see."

"I'll see. Don't worry."

"Go ahead. Fritzy boy. I'm worried."

"You just clear that table like I said, that's all."

"And you just leave this kid alone, that's all."

"Clear the table that's all."

Fritz heading for the pantry with a backwards look over his shoulder. Might have seen me up at the window when Harry said he'd knock him out of it. Makes a punch seem harder if you can sock a guy through a miniscule aperture. If I hadn't just recovered from one brain softening melee I'd go back down there and heap upon the both of them a singsong of fisticuffs most various. But I'd like to have one's knuckles rehardened before conducting any more classes on discourtesy. Open to the public. Many of whom these days, are savage.

Harry leaning over Charlotte Graves. Picking up her knife, spoon and fork. Putting them on his tray.

"Sorry kid I got to do this. Don't worry. This happens to everybody, if not every day at least once in their life. Don't mind that guy, this joint's a dump, believe me. Cockroaches crawl over the kitchen like anywhere else. We just had to give your boyfriend the cold shoulder. Because the owner thinks he's going to make this dive into a classy establishment if he makes a few people think they're not wanted. Some hope he's got. Just clear away these few things. Make more room for your elbows. I know it's kind of late to say these things. But look, I didn't have anything personal against your boyfriend. Here, here's a rose."

"Thank you."

"Look, I tell you what. Why don't me and you go somewhere. I'm quitting this job right now. I know of a swell place just a couple of miles over on the main highway. Nice floor show, take your mind off this. What about it, huh."

"Thanks but."

"Look, believe me, he's gone. Your boyfriend's not coming back. He's run out on you and left you here. All alone. Come on. We could go to a nice quiet place if you want. With soft lights. Then I'll take you back where you live. Take you right home."

"I can't."

"So o k. I've got to go and do my job. I've got to clear this table then. I'm going to even have to take the table cloth, even the chairs even the table. So no use waiting. That kind of guy just never comes back. What do you want to waste time waiting for. Come on. You going to go out with me. O k sister that was your last chance. It's your life. But I tell you, you're wasting your time waiting. Look kid. Say let me get you an apple. I don't want to see you just sitting there."

"I'm all right."

"Have an apple. Free. No. Well have a piece of chewing gum then."

Harry taking the small green package from his breast pocket. Slides off the wrapper. Unfolds the silver paper. Holds the thin grey stick out to Charlotte Graves. She shakes her head. And the pantry swing door opening. Fritz. Surveying with his uplifted chin and dark glittering eyes. As Harry turns and points his finger.

"See, see what you done. She won't budge."

"The table's got to be cleared that's all."

"Yeah, that's all, that's all."

Harry muttering. Carrying away his tray. Laden with the little vase and all the feasting instruments. The red rose clutched in Charlotte's hand. As Fritz rears by her auburn elbow.

"Look Miss, I've got my orders and I got to keep my job. Don't listen to this waiter. All he's looking for is some innocent kid who don't know what she's doing to go out with him. He's got three kids. I counted them myself. And his wife's so fat she can't walk. Can't even get near enough to kiss her. Just what he deserves. You see you can't trust anybody. Got to take this table cloth. Like I'm saying I've got to do my job. Just like that waiter, give you a rose that don't belong to him."

The table cloth drawn from the table. Grey now under Charlotte's lifted arms. Fritz folding the glistening linen as he takes it away. Dancing it from his fingertips at Harry as they pass.

"Baby snatcher."

"What's a matter, jealous. Fritzy boy."

"Some Romeo."

Harry's hands closing on the back of Christian's chair. White

331

and iron and curved in lacy weave. Where I sat all that nearly a lifetime ago. Wishing a future. Through days that go by trampling all my dreams. Fanny Sourpuss had a steady boyfriend when she was a girl. He was rich from the other side of the tracks. And when his senior prom came he took someone else. And broke her heart.

"The chair. Sorry I've got to take this. Honey you're making this the saddest day of my life. I feel it."

Harry lifting the blue pillowed seat away. As Fritz comes. Hawk wings spreading shadows. Descending upon this huddling fragile person. Whose small hand printed the first sign of love in my life. Make her safe, please. From anyone stepping on her soul.

Footfalls of Fritz and Harry. Across the maple floor. Emptying the pots of waving grass. Even the flowers out of their holders high on the wall. And on the edge of her chair. She sits in all her plaintive grace. They come now. A signal. To take each a side and lift the table away. Her elbows up. Clenched fists pressed on her tears. A rose against her cheek.

In the dimming light. Two dark emperors return. In their kingdom of loneliness. Under this ceiling. The thuds of feet. Stop behind her. And the hands reach. Touch and wait.

"Sorry miss, we can't help it, we've got to take your chair."

"Sorry kid."

Stillness of this autumn night. A sapling woman. Cut down. Kneeling on the floor. Her white dress aflood. Head deeply bent. Silently she weeps.

Fritz and Harry at the pantry door. Slowly turning to look back. The chair pulled between their fists. And they glare at each other in the face.

"You lousy rat."

"You lousy rat."

Charlotte Graves. Pale stem of a flower. Broken to make grief. Tip toed through woods with me by a frozen brook. One sleigh riding snowy winter. Long before a city chilled a heart. When I was first in grown up love. She turned to me. Tan hopes glistening in all the gay blue green beauty of her eyes. She said. Do you think when it's all so cold and ice like this. That summer will ever come again. Down over the hard trees. While we were gabbing on the grass. Backs against the bark. Tasting life. And feeling swell.

> When the maple leaves
> Were falling
> And the polly noses
> Fell

30

An Admiral on my bridge. I stand. At the top of these gentle green steps. Grey topper, tails, white tie and ivory handled ebony cane. To wait now. And look down. Into the bright light of pillars, palms and canopies. As Harry peers out his pantry door. To take a gander at this scene. And the whole bunch of gems sparkling across my toes.

"Holy mackerel."

And Fritz rushing up. Mouth opening. His arm pushing out at Harry. As all lids rise a little higher than usual over their eyes.

"What's this, somebody arrived. Wow. A personage."

Harry slapping his own face. And I do believe even buckling his knees.

"I should live so long."

"Shut up, maybe you won't. Get out the table."

Fritz striding forward, arms aplomb. Lips asmile. To receive this glistening guest. Who drove furiously sweating right down the hills into Yonkers town. Through back ancient streets by the river's industrial shore. To get a habeas corpus haberdasher out of bed. And slapped down the last of my little wad of dollars into his fist. To hire my raiment. And this hosierhatter said. As I was dressed for leaving. What are you. Some kind of nut mister. And I said no. I'm a miracle.

Cornelius Christian's hair gleaming in the light. A pale yellow rose in his buttonhole. Where the hell did he get that. Don't ask. Just watch Fritz taking his silken hat. And shiny cane. Waves an arm and bends a bow of welcome.

"Sir."

As Christian stands pausing to give a general perusement to his toggery. Flex a muscle under my silken shirt. Wiggle the large tricksy jewels on the present barefooted footsies. Say o fudge to the frills and furbelows. Forget the awful athlete's foot I had in high school. Use my slow majestic funeral step. Good as any frisky hoofing anytime. Put the frozen smile of the potentate across my appearance. Move down the stairs. Into the flooding lights of lime. Blazing in the midst of this preposterous eatery. And hi there you, Charlotte Graves out on the bobbing waves. I'm a ship come to safely take you back to shore.

She sees me. Her head lifting. Eyes alight with tears. Who sweetened my heart so many years ago. As I stood skinny in the big terrible eyes of the world. She rises. So still she glides. Across the knots of maple grain. To lay her head against my breast.

The table lifted back. Harry unfurling its white cloth. Smoothing out the wrinkles to place a vase and rose. Fritz, chin high, surveys. And turns urgently whispering.

"Harry, the condiments and cutlery, you fool, fast."

"O yeah."

The laying out of the eating instruments. Plates flashing in the light, with a final polish of Harry's sleeve. Fritz marching forward, heels tapping on the floor, large menus pinched under an arm. To silently seat these two guests. And hand each the palate tinkling parchments of delight.

"Good evening madam, good evening sir."

"Good evening."

Christian dancing an eye down the gilded nourishing words. Fritz with his pad held high and pencil poised. To await this greaseless gentleman's desire. Whose cheeks twinkle as he enquires.

"What's choice."

"Sir, may I be so bold as to suggest the consomme en gelee."

"Ah. Charlotte, for you."

Charlotte Graves. Her smile a dawn rising. A radiance of teeth between lips. The tender back of her hand brushing aside a lock of her hair. And finger tips touch away the moisture under her eyes. As Fritz leans deeply to suggest.

"Might madam like some kind of fish to follow."

"Shrimps. Please."

"Crustaceans for madam. And for sir."

"Smoked salmon."

"Saumon fume for sir. And to follow, sir. For madam."

A shy faced Charlotte. She looks up and across at me. As her lips ask.

"Steak."

And Fritz inclines the head.

"Mignon."

And Charlotte raises her brows.

"I guess so."

Fritz flourishing his yellow pencil and pauses on his pad.

"Rare, madam."

"Yes."

"Garlic, madam."

Graves looking out across this dazzling expanse. Over all the white. Over all the silver. All the way to Christian's champion face.

"Should I."

"Feel free."

"O k garlic then."

"Very good madam. Vegetables. For madam."

"Asparagus."

"Excellent. Asperges for two. Potatoes. For madam."

"Boiled please."

"And for sir."

"Fried."

Christian reaching his pale white delicate fingers in under his shimmering black lapel. To take a thin platinum case from his pocket. Snapping it open to offer Charlotte Graves a cigarette. She lifts one out and puts it between her lips. Fritz strikes a match. A flame to light love.

"Allow me madam."

And madam blows out her smoke. A billowy white. Fritz retreating backwards from the presence. His head nodding towards Christian this present potentate. As Harry hurries with a crystal pitcher of water, pincers and lemon peel. And stoops smiling.

"Good evening madam, sir."

336

"Hello."

Harry pouring his aqua into two tall glasses. As he leans deeper to ask.

"Will madam have some peel."

"Please."

"And for sir."

"Ah. I think so."

Harry steps back a step, sweeping low.

"I hope the water will be to your satisfaction."

Fritz standing at Harry's elbow. A footstool in his hands. As he bends forward to Cornelius Christian.

"Sir. May I. For your feet, sir."

"Ah."

"Make sir more comfortable."

Cornelius raising and crossing his heels on the crimson satin cushion of this ebony stool. A flashing glint of rainbow light across his toes.

"Thank you."

"A pleasure, sir. And now perhaps sir would like something to drink. A white wine to start perhaps. With the poisson and madam's crustaceans. I can recommend this one."

"Cordial."

"Very good sir."

Fritz withdrawing. A rearward step and a genuflected head. All the humming voices. And her eyes look at me. To see her sweet skinned hand reach across the table. Placed over mine. Her smile and hushed melodious voice.

"I'm sorry."

Cornelius Christian. Forgiver of all minor sins. That sea traveller. Who tells the world. That's all right. And raises his foot. Held table high. Gems gleaming. On all my toes.

> You see
> The color
> Of this too
> Is peach

31

Ten o'clock this chill October. Look down the morning street. Bags packed. Ready to go. See if the way is clear. Of all the ghosts still trying to get me.

Out the front door. A last letter waiting. Offering life insurance with disability provisions. Protect against permanent amputations. And a post card from Minnesota. Picture of a long shady street. And where it says correspondence. It says nothing but goodbye.

Cornelius Christian lugging his portmanteaux along the pavement. Step over the dog shit. Look in each doorway as I pass. Behind each parked car someone might be crouched like Hephzibah's jet black mother with a razor to cut off my balls. And me with only a pair of tender fists left against all the knives and guns.

Taxi pulls stopped at the corner. The end of the block. My breath steamy in the air. Heave two lonely bags in the back. Hear a voice say up front.

"Where to bud."

"Pier Fifty Seven."

Flood of traffic comes down the avenue. Just as we go across. Saw fat cheeks huddled in an overcoat slumped on the stoop of a building. Might have said so long on his sign. Sky red, raw and autumn. Read the Almanac this morning inside the newspaper's front page. The time of high water at Hell Gate, the temperature in Elkins, Roanoke and Detroit. Fifty degrees in Denver. Gentle to moderate southeast to south winds becoming northerly. To-morrow fair with seasonable temperatures. Under the shadows of black trestles and girders. Pass whirring by the windows. See the red stacks of the ships. And the green cap on this driver's head.

"Hey pardon me bud. But haven't I seen your face somewhere before. I mean excuse me, are you a celebrity I should know."

"No."

"Gee but I swear I know your face."

Christian slumping in his seat. Change my expression to one of total disfigurement that not even Hephzibah's mother would recognise. With all the photographs she's got. Of me in the alto-gether. As we go up this ramp and head downtown. And when I returned with my evening wear to Yonkers by the river. The haberdasher said I'd ruined the clothes and wouldn't give me my money back. Said white faced it was the best outfit in his selec-tion and it was rags already.

"Hey wait. I know. I knew it. Sure, all I had to do was slap myself in the head. You was a fare nearly a year ago. I'm useful to the police. Never forget a face. I let you off at momma Grotz's before she got shot. You didn't have nowhere to go. Well what do you know. Isn't this a coincidence."

"Yes."

"Hey where are you going. On a cruise or something. You must have made it big. Sure, I thought to myself, when I first picked you up, there goes a guy ought to get a nice respectable job making good money. None of my business. But I mean it could be history."

In this flood of cars. Passing by the ships waiting on this shore. Out there across the Hudson, the palisades. I saw from Doctor Pedro's office window. Which is up there on the skyline to the left. Where he's playing his violin, and maybe scrubbing his floor. Looking down on this morning's jackasses. Of whom there is just one less left.

"Sure I know you. Told you all about the pet shop I had. Because I didn't want to hurt people. Is that bad I don't want to hurt people. I say phooey to anybody who wants to destroy people. Three months ago I nearly died. I had an exploded intes-tine. Because I get so worried. Sure I'm human. I don't want everyone never to hear of me again. When all the other thoughts they got push me out. I mean I'll tell you, you meet guys in this town pretending to be high society. Guys who'll stand around being nobody for an hour so they can be somebody for a minute and maybe bore ten years' patience out of a big shot's life who don't want to listen. But then you get the other kind. The acquaintances. Who really want to let you know they're close friends by drinking all your drink and eating all your food. So I ask sincerely, who needs them.''

Slam the door shut of this yellow black checkered cab. Outside this big grey stone arched entrance. Hardly anyone here. Under the glass and steel. My footfalls down this wooden pier. Push my passport into a man sitting in a chilly kiosk. Climb the gangway. With an ink stamp on a green page. Date and month of departure. And after those waiters crowded around me. Gasping at my palate. While I was basking in Charlotte's smiles. Smashing back the vintages, the brandies and crepe suzettes. Until in all my raiment. And smoking a Mott manufactured cigar. I gladly raised my arms. Stretched out and satisfied. Said shoot me. I can't pay the bill.

> And ask
> God please
> Why do I get
> Grief on a platter
> And pleasure on
> A spoon

Ship pulling out mid stream. Seagulls perched high in the rigging. Pennants wagging and the waves goodbye from the shore. Taxi driver said who knows we might meet again. And said no when I offered him a tip. Walk now along the deck under the lifeboats. Greased and ready for lowering. Ship's whistle. Blast quivers my spine. As tugs cast off. You're leaving nowhere when the whole place belongs to someone else. And there sitting in the second class lounge. As I jumped out of my skin through this two class ship. Marigold I met in the Sixth Avenue Delicatessan. A mirror held up, looking at herself and powdering her nose. Travelling east with me out of this city of gloomy coincidence.

340

The ship gathering speed. The sun a red round globe. Hangs staring. Behind the city's veils. A day darkening like the dying. A hundred thousand windows stacked up. Canyons pass. Of crosstown streets. Avenues sinking between the blazing buildings. Go downtown on the tide. Fingers touching these scrubbed wood rails. On the stern of this ship. Breeze on my face. First scent of an ocean. That lies out there. Ebbing through the Narrows and past Sandy Hook. That flash of light. A rooftop glints a gold goodbye.

His head leaning down to rest on his hands. Harbour's waters tumbling up grey. Washing white like thighs along the steep black side of the ship. A bell rings. And why are you standing. With your hope and sorrows old. Silent and still. Listening. A shout. They'll never hear me. Across the lowlands of Brooklyn. And up through the catacomb hills of the Bronx. When I was a little boy. Left in a brand new foster home. I went out playing the afternoon around the block. Got lost, so busy telling all the other kids a fairy tale of New York. That my real father was a tycoon and my mother a princess. And it was just like a pale light of autumn. Where Fanny walked holding my hand that day. Not far from Mount Kisco. She tugged me close. Near a stone grey wall. Cows were crushing old apples. Under the lowly hanging leaves. And the sweet juice was running out their jaws.

> Her spit
> Was white
> And
> Beautiful